THE
SAVAGE
KINGDOM

THE
SAVAGE
KINGDOM

AN ANIMALIAN NOVEL

SIMON DAVID EDEN

SIMON AND SCHUSTER

First published in Great Britain in 2014 by Simon and Schuster UK Ltd
A CBS COMPANY

1 3 5 7 9 10 8 6 4 2

Simon & Schuster UK Ltd
1st Floor, 222 Gray's Inn Road
London
WC1X 8HB

Simon & Schuster Australia, Sydney
Simon & Schuster India, New Delhi

A CIP catalogue record for this book is available
from the British Library.

PB ISBN: 978-1-4711-1874-6
EBook ISBN: 978-1-4711-1875-3

Typeset by Hewer Text UK Ltd, Edinburgh
Printed and bound by CPI Group (UK) Ltd, Croydon, CR0 4YY

www.simonandschuster.co.uk
www.simonandschuster.com.au

for Millie

This book is dedicated to my beloved daughter as her presence in my life inspired its creation. That said, it might never have found its way on to the page without the faith, unfailing encouragement and positive injunctions of my wise and beautiful soulmate Helena – love, light and gratitude always.

Don't walk in front of me, I may not follow.
Don't walk behind me, I may not lead.
Just walk beside me and be my friend.

Albert Camus

PROLOGUE

Drue Beltane sat alone in the dark, cocooned in a threadbare goose-down quilt. Her heart raced. She drew a gulp of musty air and held her breath for a silent count of five, before softly, silently, exhaling – a trick she'd been taught to calm her nerves when taking tests at school.

The trick failed. And, as thoughts even darker than the ancient priest-hole in which she was hiding began once again to take shape in her mind, the fearful twelve-year-old sought touchstones, familiar points of reference, to help suppress her welling sense of foreboding. She picked at the frayed hole in the left pocket of her flannel pyjamas; worked the hinged, clam-like case of her mobile phone; pressed her toes into the pitted contours of the smooth limestone floor beneath her bare feet.

Just like the walls that surrounded her, and the ceiling that she could reach if she were to stand and stretch, the floor was cold, vaguely damp – though not actually wet – to the touch, the moisture held inside the fabric of the stone, somewhere deep beneath the surface, like a memory.

A secret chamber little bigger than a double wardrobe, the priest-hole was concealed behind a false panel adjacent to the soot-blackened fireplace in the Beltanes' sixteenth-century flint-faced cottage.

Drue had lived in the cottage in Kingley Burh – a semi-rural scattering of farms and houses that lay between the industrial outskirts of Portsmouth and the cathedral city of Chichester – her entire life, and never before had the hideaway unsettled her. On the contrary, it had been the focus of many a dare and game throughout Drue's early childhood, a doorway to the world of unbridled imagination. But now, forced to confront its true purpose, she finally understood what it must have been like back in the days of old, when deadly feuds and religious persecution had swept through the country like a plague.

Drue's fingertips crept to the inscription that had long ago been gouged into the heavy ashlar block above the entrance hatch, like initials notched in a tree trunk, or a prison sentence scratched into mortar:

Ex umbra in solem

Drue had asked her history teacher to help with the translation of the text, and the result was just as cryptic in English as the original Latin:

From the shadows into the light.

Why she was hiding was also something of a mystery to Drue, but the gravity in her father's voice when he ordered her to remain hidden, completely still and completely silent, until his return was something Drue had never heard before, and it frightened her to the core of her being.

There was only one way in or out of the priest-hole, and the panel that served as the door was secured from inside by a tapered wooden peg, slotted through the rusty eye of a wrought-iron latch. Drue had checked and double-checked that the peg was firmly in place a dozen times since climbing inside, but still she ran her fingers over it once more.

Don't open the hatch for anyone but me, her father had commanded. *Promise me that whatever happens, whatever you hear, you'll stay hidden until I return.*

Darkness. Silence. And then . . .

A crash!

Drue reacted with a start. She listened for her father's voice. The call of her name. Instead, she heard . . . grunts. Snuffling. Scratching.

The sound of breaking glass.

Something heavy – a chair perhaps – being knocked over and dragged across the quarry tiles of the kitchen floor.

The creak of the stairs.

Muffled footfalls on the floorboards above her.

The slam of a door (her bedroom door!) being thrown open and crashing into the desk where she sat most days to do homework.

Whoever, or whatever, it was, was now in her room.

Drue thought about springing out of the priest-hole and bolting for the front door. Then she remembered her promise to her father, and she forced herself to sit tight and listen.

The house was alive with movement now. Whatever was out there, it wasn't alone, and the disturbing, audible destruction of the property and the family's belongings was accompanied by a raucous cacophony of grunts, yaps, squeals and hissing. The invasion seemed to go on forever. And then, as abruptly as it had started, it stopped.

Drue could feel her heart pounding, was afraid it beat so fast and so hard it might be heard. The wood-ash dust of the adjacent chimney caught in her throat and she had to summon every ounce of willpower to stifle a cough.

She waited.

Listened.

Silence.

It didn't seem possible, but somehow the darkness grew darker. The cell began to feel more like a tomb than a sanctuary. Drue wanted to cry out. To throw open the door. To run! But she clung to her promise, to the hope and security bound up in it, her father's words a silent mantra echoing in her mind like a silent mantra: *Stay hidden until I return.*

Still, the claustrophobic gloom and uncertainty gnawed away at her resolve. Every second spent in that dank, dark chamber now seemed like an eternity. She placed a trembling hand on the iron latch, was almost ready to remove the wooden peg and abandon her hiding place when she heard . . . a log tumble from the basket beside the fire, no more than an arm's length from where she sat cowering in the shadows. But what had disturbed it?

A hiss. More snuffling. A guttural grunt. Scratching. Something was clawing at the hatch itself.

A fleeting ray of hope: perhaps her cat Will-C had come home to find her. But no. Drue knew his every touch, every gesture, every sound – his meowing, purring, even his funny, wheezy little snore. This was different. These were the sounds of a hunter. A predator tracking a scent. The stuff of nightmares and scary films.

Drue slowly moved her hand away from the latch and buried her face in the quilt. She prayed that whatever hellish creature lay on the other side of the false oak panel that separated them, it wouldn't find a way through.

Movement on the stairs again.

More scuttling on the quarry tiles in the kitchen.

Dogs barking somewhere outside.

Then . . . silence.

Drue bit on a corner of her quilt and prayed her father would call out her name. But the longer she waited without hearing his voice, the deeper the seeds of doubt took root: what if he never came back? What then? What if he'd returned already, only to come face to face with the intruders? What if he lay injured, in desperate need of her help?

Another breath. And then, with the lightest touch and the greatest care, Drue eased the peg from the locking plate, swung open the hatch and climbed out into the moonlit living room.

For a moment she kept quite still and listened to the distant clamour: cries, screams, hollered commands, the unmistakable unsettling *crack* of a twelve-bore shotgun. Had their neighbour, old Farmer Callow, seen off the danger? Whatever had happened, the house itself was quiet now, and it seemed to Drue that whoever, whatever, had been there had gone. The coast, if messy, seemed clear.

Drue picked her way across the room. She wanted to switch on a light, but didn't dare. The tall barley-twist lamp by the window had been toppled and was speared through the shattered screen of the TV. The sofa and chairs had been slashed and spewed stuffing. Her dad's prized collection of *National Geographic* magazines was scattered across the floor.

Drue made her way to the kitchen. The door was ajar and she peeked round it.

Almost every pane of glass in both windows had been smashed. The curtains that Drue had helped her mother sew hung in shredded rags.

Compost spilled from toppled potted herbs, one of which, a variegated thyme, now appeared to be sprouting from the toaster. Cutlery and shattered crockery – including her maternal great-grandmother's fine bone china – littered the floor, along with the entire contents of the walk-in larder: brown rice, buckwheat flour, pasta, cereal, broken eggs, biscuits. Cranberry juice bled from a crushed, upturned carton in the open fridge; splintered jars of tahini, preserves and organic honey formed sticky islands in a lake of spilled rice milk.

Drue stared in amazement. It was so awful, so radical, it was almost funny.

Then a bag of blue tortilla chips beneath the kitchen table suddenly began to shuffle as if possessed.

It startled Drue. She took a step backwards and instantly felt the jagged edge of a shard of glass beneath her bare feet.

Though the cut wasn't deep, as the glass nicked the high arch of her instep, Drue gave a faint yelp.

This brought the tortilla bag to an abrupt halt.

Then, slowly, a slim, whiskered, twitching snout appeared over the edge of the crumpled foil. It belonged to the dormouse that had been concealed inside the bag, greedily munching on the looted contents.

Indignant, Drue clapped her hands to frighten it away.

But, instead of darting for cover, the dormouse stayed right where it was. It fixed Drue with a defiant, beady-eyed stare and, cheeks still bulging with corn chips, continued to nibble on its late-night snack.

Drue clapped her hands again and made a gesture to shoo the dormouse away. Still the tiny creature paid her no mind. Drue picked up a broom and wielded it as if she were about to strike (though she didn't actually want to hurt the dormouse; she just wanted to remind it who was in charge), but still it continued to chew its mouthful of food. And then, when it was finished, it squealed.

A single, shrill, plaintive *squeeeeeeeal*, which stopped Drue in her tracks.

In an instant, there were ten ... twenty ... thirty mice spilling into the kitchen from all directions. Then came the rats, both black and brown, bristling with menace. Finally, a mink appeared, long and lean, cold eyes narrowed to slits.

Drue lowered the broom.

For a moment she thought that she must be dreaming. That the whole thing – the promise to her father, hiding in the priest-hole, the ransacked house, everything – must be a nightmare, a terrifying figment of her vivid imagination, and she actually said out loud: 'OK, you can wake up now!'

But, as the rodents closed ranks and began to advance, and the mink rose up on its hind legs, hissed and bared its needle-sharp teeth, Drue realized, to her horror, that what was happening was all too real.

PART I
THE SIXTH WAVE

CHAPTER ONE

The beginning of the end of the world as we knew it began with the disappearance of a three-legged, short-haired, house-trained cat named Will-C. At least, in retrospect, that's how it would seem to Drue Beltane.

In truth, the cataclysmic events that would change the course of life on Earth in the early part of the twenty-first century could be traced back to a much earlier time: the dawn of industrialization. An evolutionary leap that struck fear into the hearts of all the creatures who shared the planet with humans, the untamed birds, beasts, fish and reptiles of the wild: the *Animalians*.

Not that the Animalians themselves, at least not the vast majority, knew just what fate had in store for them. Their lives for many generations had revolved around their primal instincts, the survival of the fittest: food, water, shelter and procreation. These were their key considerations. Their only considerations.

Few had ever questioned the order of things, the nature of their individual journeys and how they might relate to the whole. Such matters were far too abstract; as remote and inconsequential as raindrops falling on a distant sea. Until the day the winds gathered up those same raindrops to create a swell, which grew into a wave that would crash on to the shores of every country in the world; a devastating tidal wave of vengeance.

The first Will-C knew of the brewing conflict was a summons from the local Feline Proxy (each species in each shire had one such elected representative) to attend a midnight summit in the ancient yew forest of Kingley Burh, deep in the heart of the rolling chalklands of the South Downs.

The fact that the order had been issued by the District Proconsul of the West Sussex Chapter of the Council of Elders, and even Truckles like himself who lived with humans were to attend, only added to the intrigue, and Will-C wasn't quite sure what to make of it.

One thing was clear, however: it had to be a matter of grave importance, as gatherings on such a large scale, which brought together such a vast array of species – foxes, weasels, wild boar, badgers, ravens, deer, dogs, cats and so on, many of whom were avowed enemies – carried considerable risk.

Not that even the bravest of them would dare to breach the established code of conduct under which the Great Summit operated; breaking the temporary truce that applied on such occasions was an offence punishable by death. But if a human were to happen upon them, to witness the session in progress ... well, the consequences would be unthinkable, disastrous.

For as long as human beings had walked the Earth, they had sought to conquer or destroy what they didn't control or understand. Because of this – despite their origins, their evolution, their technological prowess – the fundamental laws and traditions of the animal kingdom had remained a closely guarded secret that had been kept from humans at all costs. As a result, the Summit meetings were always conducted in the strictest secrecy, and were also extremely rare.

In fact, Will-C had only attended one such assembly in his lifetime: crisis talks held in the wake of the Borneo slash and burn forest fires of 2006. This had devastated massive swathes of the natural habitat of South-East Asia, wiped out one-third of the orang-utan population of that area and, according to eyewitness accounts, caused a feathered blizzard to rain down from the smoke-filled heavens, as flocks of exotic birds were overcome by the intense heat and choking fumes rising from the raging inferno.

As Will-C had only been a kitten back then, he had lacked both the concentration and the vocabulary to fully understand the wider implications of the impassioned high-level debate at the Great Summit. But the memory of his late father (a barrel-chested granite-grey tomcat, considered by many to be one of the finest Feline Proxies ever to hold the post) gravely recounting the details of the man-made disaster, and placing it into context with some that had preceded it, had left a lasting, extremely vivid impression.

Despite his gene pool and signs of early promise, Will-C had never risen to high office, but his prodigious memory for detail – which had made him a natural Clerk of the Feline Council – enabled him to recall by rote the names, dates and places that had peppered his father's address to the assembly that night.

The Bhopal disaster in India in 1984, for example, in which forty tonnes of deadly pesticide was accidentally released into the environment, causing widespread devastation.

The Sandoz factory chemical spill in Switzerland two years later, which had turned the River Rhine blood-red and slaughtered over half a million fish by the time it reached the North Sea.

And the deliberate, indiscriminate flooding of 600 square miles of pristine, densely populated tropical rainforest. This consigned entire generations of hundreds of thousands of different species to a grim and watery grave and some disappeared from the face of the Earth forever. All in the name of progress, and all to transform the once wild and noble Suriname River in northern South America into a vast stagnant lake of dead water the humans called a reservoir.

The thought still made Will-C shudder. He hated water at the best of times, but an unforeseen, inescapable flood was truly the stuff of nightmares.

And so it was that in the days leading up to the Great Summit Will-C had been filled with a growing sense of dread. What was it that Man had done this time to threaten the natural order of things? And what action would the Council of Elders deem necessary to right these wrongs?

Will-C knew better than to waste too much time on speculation. *Worry gives a small thing a big shadow*, his father used to say; but it hadn't made the wait any easier.

Will-C had lived with the Beltane family for more than

twenty-one feline years – over half his lifetime in fact – and the bond they had formed in that time, particularly the friendship that had developed between him and the human child Drue, had a special quality, a depth to it, that was unlike any inter-species relationship he'd ever heard of. And that was what really troubled him.

Deep down inside, Will-C sensed that whatever was to follow would be history in the making, and he only hoped that it wouldn't place his beloved adopted human family in mortal danger, or force him to make a choice between their kind and his own.

CHAPTER TWO

On the night of the Great Summit, Will-C was to be found curled up as usual at the foot of Drue's bed. He opened half an eye to check that his companion was sound asleep, gauged her shallow breathing for a moment and then, as she shifted position beneath her quilt, nimbly lowered himself down on to the woollen rug below.

He paused for a moment to ensure that Drue really had settled again, then padded swiftly across the white-painted floorboards, through the door which was always propped ajar for him and out of the room.

Descending the single flight of stairs, Will-C made his way at a trot to the kitchen. The room was cool and dark. He headed directly for the door at the rear, nudged his cat flap open with his muzzle and slipped stealthily through into the garden.

Ears pricked, senses alert, Will-C drew in the chill night air and began to process the wealth of information carried on the breeze. With the moon obscured by heavy cloud, his nose would tell him as much, if not more, than his eyes about the activity that had taken place on his own patch since sunset.

The hedgehogs had been busy. The bats too. A Eurasian badger had clearly dug her sett nearby, as her powerful musky scent was unmistakable. On any other night, Will-C would have taken that as a cue to complete a full tour of the perimeter of his territory, but this was a night like no other.

He shook his coat – which jiggled the penny-sized ID disc on his collar – and studied the vast dark sky.

The Full Worm Moon – so called because it heralded warmer ground temperatures and therefore increased the activity of earthworms – was still a few days away. That meant that the garden path would be cold under-paw, and for a moment Will-C considered turning around and slipping back into Drue's warm and cosy bed. In truth, it wasn't an option. As Clerk of the Feline Council, Will-C's attendance at the Great Summit was not only expected, it was demanded.

He negotiated the broad, weathered flagstones at a lope, and consoled himself with the thought that at least it wasn't raining. Cutting through a small hole at the base of the tall green beech hedge that flanked the Beltanes' cottage, he moved deftly through nettles and bracken until he reached Oakwood Lane.

The long, narrow stretch of compressed broken stone snaked through the landscape like a dried riverbed, its grey, pitted tributaries forging a dusty link between the settlements that Humans had long ago built in the surrounding forest: Callow's Farm, the sawmill on the grand Oakwood Park Estate and the village of Kingley Burh itself.

A lumbering 4 x 4 thundered into view, taking the curves in the road so fast that its enormous body rocked with the motion. Its fat tyres chewed through the bluebells and the wild garlic bordering the soft verge.

Will-C averted his gaze as the dazzling full-beam headlights washed over him. The vehicle hurtled on, boring a broad gilt tunnel through the dark night. In its wake, a hundred pairs of eyes flashed and then vanished in the hedgerows.

Will-C paused to let the night fold back around him, then sprinted across the lane. Safely across, he leapt the rubbish-strewn drainage ditch that ran alongside it and headed north towards the ancient yew forest.

'Hey, Will-C. Wait.' The voice came from a tangle of brambles. Will-C slowed his stride, but didn't stop.

'Wait, Will-C, it's me.'

Will-C recognized the raspy voice. It was Yoshi, a gangly cat from the village: an untidy parcel of skin and bones who had no fur, just a few wispy guard hairs that sprouted from his spine and tail.

'Hey, Yow,' said Will-C in greeting as Yoshi scrambled up alongside. All around, the woods were alive with movement.

'There's going to be quite a turnout,' whispered Yoshi excitedly.

'Looks that way,' answered Will-C.

'Have you heard . . . you know . . . anything about what it's about?'

'I don't know any more than you at this point, Yow,' said Will-C, picking up the pace again.

'It's got to be something important though?'

'I imagine so.'

'Something really important?'

'Could be.'

'What does the Proxy say?'

'Haven't seen him yet.'

'So what do you think it might be?'

'Like I said, I really don't know any more than you just now. Best wait until we hear what Hobbes and the Council of Elders have to say.'

'Could be the flu,' panted Yoshi. 'A genetic mutation that jumps species. I heard that birds can catch it from humans now.'

The trail narrowed as it passed through a stand of holly bushes, forcing Will-C to slow down again.

'Or maybe it's that immigration business. Did you hear that they've reintroduced wolves in the Highlands of Scotland? Wolves. I mean, really . . . Why not throw in some sabretoothed tigers while they're at it? They used to live there too. I mean, don't humans know anything about evolution?'

'Actually, evolution wasn't the problem. Hunting . . .' began Will-C.

'Scientific research! I bet that's it,' said Yoshi. 'I had a cousin who knew someone who had a friend whose whole family were sent to one of those laboratory places with the big walls and the barbed-wire fences. He never saw hide nor hair of them again. Maybe they're planning to build something like that around here. You think? Maybe?'

Numerous animals cut across the path, forging trails through the dark woodland, and, whenever a feline did so, he or she would exchange a nod or a greeting with Will-C.

All were slightly on edge – a mix of anticipation and trepi-dation – and the natural inclination was to huddle with their own kind.

Though the lowest of the low in terms of officialdom (his role at the Great Summit would consist of nothing more taxing than taking mental minutes when the Feline Proxy was speaking), Will-C had an easy nature which encour-aged others, especially those like Yoshi – an immigrant from the Far East who lived on the margins of local Animalian society – to confide in him.

Will-C didn't judge, and he didn't discriminate, and, as he bore his own physical shortcoming – his missing hind leg – seemingly without complaint, he'd become a sounding board for any feline who found the elected representatives distant or intimidating. Will-C was, in a word, approach-able, and that of course had its pros and cons.

'You wouldn't want to be a beagle, that's for sure,' said Yoshi, with a little burst of speed that brought him up along-side Will-C again.

'No,' said Will-C.

'Or a guinea pig,' said Yoshi. 'Can you imagine? It's a good thing that they're stupid. Did you know that in South America, where guinea pigs come from, there are tribes with medicine men who actually rub the poor things on sick people? I mean, really. How disgusting is that! No wonder they squeal when humans pick them up.'

Will-C smiled and nodded in agreement. He'd heard all Yoshi's stories and crazy theories a hundred times before, but he liked him well enough, and didn't want to offend him, so, as ever, he just let him chatter away.

Despite having Yoshi for company, Will-C was making good progress until a heavyset tortoiseshell tomcat, with a chewed-off ear and a broken nose, emerged from a thicket of tall yarrow to block the path. A motley crew of feral cats closed ranks behind him.

Having little appetite for either fight or flight, and fearing for his safety, Yoshi finally fell silent and dropped back behind Will-C.

'Ey, Freak,' growled the torbie.

'Hello, Lennox,' replied Will-C, doing his best to seem pleased to see him.

'Y'sin Obz?'

'I'm sorry?'

'Obz.'

'Obz?'

'Obz.'

'Oh, Hobbes, the Proxy. No. Not yet.'

'Hey, Pond-Life,' said one of Lennox's crew to Yoshi.

'Hi, Yucky,' teased another.

'Um . . . it's . . . YOWshe,' replied Yoshi timidly.

'Love the hair,' another of the gang cut in.

'No, wait. There's more than one . . . love the hair*s*!'

Will-C sighed; it pained him to see Yoshi being bullied, but he really couldn't afford to delay matters further by trying to intervene.

'Mange mites and chiggers,' said Yoshi, peering up at the moon, 'is that the time? We really must be getting along.'

As Yoshi attempted to sidestep him, Lennox blocked his path and squared up to Will-C, his bulky frame casting a moon-shadow as deep and dark as his voice.

'I 'eard there's sumfink major brewin' . . .'

'Something major, yes, yes, indeed,' said Yoshi, trying to escape the nips and swipes being dished out by the gang.

'Sumfink really major—'

'Quite so; that's just what I was saying when . . .'

'Clam it, maggot! I'm talkin' to the Freak,' growled Lennox. 'I 'eard tell there's sumfink major brewin' an' I ain't so sure that Obz is the kitty cat to 'ave in charge.'

'Hobbes is the elected Feline Proxy,' replied Will-C timidly.

Lennox's crew immediately chipped in with a chorus of disparaging remarks about rigged ballots and sympathy votes and how Will-C was not the feline his father was. All the while Lennox studied Will-C closely.

Finally, Will-C raised his voice to be heard above the cackling dissent.

'Look . . . look . . . why don't we just . . . just wait and see . . . see what the Proxy and the Council of Elders have to say, OK? Let's not jump to any conclusions, and let's remember we're all in this together. We have a responsibility to stick together . . . and to present . . . a . . . a . . . united front. Solidarity, that's the thing. And whatever differences we may have we should respect them, but set them aside until after the Great Summit.'

All eyes turned to Lennox. But the big cat's glare never left Will-C.

'It's . . . in the statute after all,' added Will-C nervously. 'And don't worry . . . because worry . . . well, worry gives a small thing . . .'

'A big shadow,' said Lennox, completing Will-C's sentence. 'An' your old man left you a giant one to crawl out of, Freak.'

Will-C wilted. Lennox was right: he could never truly live up to his father's legacy.

Lennox sniffed, puffed out his chest, lifted a leg to spray the adjacent yarrow and ambled off into the undergrowth.

'You tell Obz I'm watchin' 'im,' he grumbled as he tramped away. 'An' come the full moon, make sure that pond slime stays 'ome; 'e's an embarrassment to cats.'

And with that parting shot, and his entourage cackling in tow, Lennox disappeared into the woods.

Crestfallen, Yoshi began to slink away. Will-C halted his retreat.

'C'mon, Yoshi. Pick up the pace, we don't want to be late. And you were telling me something about guinea pigs. Is that true about the medicine men?'

Yoshi's ears pricked up and he lifted his head. As Will-C took off along the trail at a canter, the untidy parcel of skin and bones fell in beside him once more.

★   ★   ★

As the midnight hour approached, the cloud cover above Kingley Burh melted away to unveil a broad, star-filled sky. Moonlight bathed the Bronze Age burial mounds of Bow Hill, swept down the steep, grass-covered valley slopes that surrounded it and lanced through the canopy of the largest ancient yew forest in Europe, throwing shafts of light on to the hive of activity below.

Thousands of creatures of all descriptions – some, like Night-Nifts and Skerrets, that were not even known to Man – covered every branch, rock and blade of grass. But despite the numbers there was order amid the apparent chaos. In accordance with official protocol, the animals formed a series of wide concentric circles – like the growth rings inside a tree trunk – that stretched out, layer after layer, through the woodland.

The older members of each genus were given priority, forming the circles closest to the centre, with the Proxies, like points on a compass, completing the innermost ring. Inside this, occupying what was for the duration of the proceedings hallowed ground, were gathered the senior members of the Council of Elders: a red stag, a Skerret, a long-eared owl, a wild boar, a fox and the District Proconsul himself, a very large, rotund, dark olive toad named Natterjack.

As the booming hoot of a barn owl announced that the historic Great Summit was about to be called to order, Will-C and Yoshi barged their way through the dense crowd, apologizing left and right. Yoshi fell back as Will-C took his rightful place behind the Deputy Feline Proxy – a Siamese named Rani – who in turn flanked Hobbes, a Blue Burmese with hooded yellow eyes who was the Senior Feline Proxy.

'You're late,' spat Rani.

'I'm sorry,' replied Will-C weakly.

'Yes, you are,' agreed Rani.

Hobbes, whiskers bristling, gave them both a sidelong glance of disapproval. Then, as the hoot of the barn owl died away, all eyes turned to the imposing Council of Elders. They were lined up in front of a massive 2000-year-old yew, its trunk so broad it rose like a fortress wall behind them.

Natterjack disappeared into a hollow in the root structure, worked his way up through a cavity in the trunk to a better vantage point and emerged with a theatrical flourish, high in the snake-like limbs.

The air was filled with expectation as Natterjack surveyed the crowd: a squat, warty general inspecting his troops. He waited patiently for the animated chatter from a thousand beaks and snouts to die away, then puffed out his fleshy chest for dramatic effect and began his speech.

'Comrades, Proxies, fellow Animalians, *Truckles*,' – the latter laced with disdain – 'I, your District Proconsul, with the power vested in me by the honourable Earth Assembly, have summoned you to this emergency meeting, one of tens of thousands taking place in every forest, on every mountain, in every ocean circling our great and sacred planet, to alert you to the gravest danger we have ever faced.'

If the forest were silent before, it was now possible to hear the worms burrowing through the earth beneath the trees. Natterjack stroked his wide throat before continuing.

'The name given to this deadly and sinister scourge is the Sixth Wave. Mass extinction on an unprecedented scale. Mother Nature herself, in her infinite wisdom, has been responsible for the five previous mass extinctions that our world has suffered; these were painful but necessary measures to ensure the balance of the natural order of things. But the sixth – potentially as devastating as all the other five combined – is being caused by the activities of just one species of primate . . .'

He jabbed a webbed finger into the air to accentuate his point. 'MAN!'

The word set off a chain reaction of grunts, squeals and chirping throughout the forest.

Faelken, a ghostly silver-grey gyrfalcon, drifted silently down from the night sky and settled on a high branch of the ancient yew adjacent to Natterjack. The Proconsul acknowledged the fearsome bird of prey with a conspiratorial look, then rose up on his hind feet and stretched out his front legs to appeal for order. The Proxies in turn appealed to their clans to fall silent once more. But it took the roar of Rauthaz, the regal red stag Elder, to gain everyone's attention.

'Animalians,' he boomed, 'hear this now: your Proconsul speaks the truth. Why, just a half-day as the gull flies from this very wood another giant sea vessel has capsized in rough waters releasing over 25,000 tonnes of black death into the ocean.

'Two hundred and fifty miles of coastline have already been scarred with the toxic pollution that humans draw from the depths of the Earth, and a 100,000 seabirds have lost their lives or been maimed.'

'Rauthaz the Elder says right,' volunteered a jittery whiskered tern. 'I flew over the wreck on the way here. The black poison was still spilling from its insides.'

The crowd acknowledged the first-hand testimony with weary nods and sighs. A debate ensued as to how long it would take Mother Nature to heal the damage done by the stricken oil tanker, with the Elders agreeing its impact would be felt for generations. But although the report was grim and disheartening, it was nothing that the crowd hadn't heard before.

A flurry of protests and inter-species discussions were watched with eager anticipation by Natterjack, and he weighed the mood and tone carefully before interjecting once more.

'The honourable members ...' he began over the cacophony. 'The honourable members of the Earth Assembly,' he continued, quietening the ranks again, 'the highest and most powerful authority in all of Animalia, have completed, through their agents, a long and thorough investigation of this latest human outrage, just one of a number of terrible events collated from around the world in the last full cycle of seasons.

'Their findings do not bode well, comrades, and it seems the hour of change is upon us. Until now, our esteemed elected leaders have always advocated tolerance. But all the evidence now suggests that humankind's reckless exploitation of the natural world will continue unabated until there's nothing left to destroy.

'Any hope we had that humans as a species might evolve and recognize the error of their ways has evaporated like morning dew on a meadow. Far from trying to live in harmony with nature, it's clear that humans feel they're apart from it, above it, and that the world and everything in it is theirs to use and abuse as they see fit!

'No other creature on Earth takes the raw materials of the forests and the great plains and the oceans of the world and turns them into mountains of poisonous waste that cannot be fed back into the land. Only humans! Though they can't escape the great cycle of life that eventually claims all living creatures, the damage they do generation after generation must in time bring that cycle, the very life force that binds us all, one to another . . . to an end.'

The majority of the crowd – even many of the Truckles – nodded in agreement as the damning appraisal rang true.

Natterjack sprang from one limb of the ancient yew tree to another, working his way closer to the crowd, bridging the distance between his words and their awestruck targets.

'Every fifty breaths another species of animal becomes extinct. And, as the ranks of humankind continue to expand, they now number almost seven billion! So half of all the bird and mammal species alive today will disappear within two generations.'

The crowd was rattled as Natterjack pointed this way and that, selecting would-be victims at random.

'Ferret, starling, vole, cat! Any one of us could be next!'

Suddenly Will-C found himself eyeball to eyeball with the warty amphibian, who tightened his clammy webbed digits round the black cat's neck. Will-C struggled for breath, and was greatly relieved when a cry from somewhere deep in the woods distracted the Proconsul.

'So what are we to do?'

Natterjack's eyes narrowed. These were the words he'd been waiting for. He released Will-C, puffed out his chest and pulled himself up to look as commanding as possible.

'What are we to do? Why . . . we're to unite!'

'Unite?' said a dozen or so animals in unison.

'Exactly so,' said Natterjack. 'A strategy to regain control of the Earth has been debated at the highest level. A unanimous agreement has been reached. Direct action has to be taken to end humankind's dominance and irresponsible stewardship of the planet.'

'But how?' came another worried voice.

'Simple,' replied Natterjack. 'Together, we repel the Sixth Wave.'

'And how exactly are we supposed to do that?' squealed a field mouse.

Natterjack's tongue flicked the air. This was to be the defining moment of his tenure as District Proconsul and he relished every single second of it.

'*By the complete and total eradication of the human race.*'

A collective gasp rose from the crowd and washed back through their number like a tidal wave. On it travelled, deep into the heart of the woods, to the outermost ring of onlookers: Natterjack's words repeated over and over in whispered disbelief.

The toad could see the fear, the shock, the uncertainty in the faces below him, particularly those of the Truckles. Each group turned to their respective Proxies for some hint of assurance – surely even the Earth Assembly wouldn't take such drastic action?

Natterjack was a master of manipulation and he saw in those frightened faces his destiny unfolding.

'It's true we have before us an ordeal of the most grievous kind. For those of you who have lived with humans, you Truckles who've shared their food and slept in their strange, flat-walled caves, this action will involve the greatest, most painful personal sacrifice. Your bravery will not go unnoticed or unrewarded in the battle against the monstrous tyranny we now face.'

Mind racing, heart pounding, Will-C struggled to comprehend the situation. Yoshi and the other cats looked to Rani and Hobbes to voice their doubts, to challenge the Proconsul and the Elders, but they did nothing. Said nothing.

Then a familiar stocky figure caught Will-C's eye. From his expression alone, it was clear that Lennox – along with his entire crew – now believed that he had been right all along: elected by popular demand or not, Hobbes was not fit to hold the post of Proxy and, in Lennox's opinion, Will-C, by association, was no better. It was only the respect that Lennox had had for Will-C's father that had kept him in the fold, that had kept him from removing Hobbes and Rani from office by tooth and claw, a decision he now bitterly regretted.

Lennox turned and shouldered a path through the heaving crowd. His motley crew followed as Will-C, shamefaced, looked on. Whatever else the future would bring, it was clear to Will-C that Lennox's fragile loyalty had melted away in that brief, silent exchange.

A milk-white dove named Livia – Proxy to the rock and collared doves – took to the air and spoke eloquently about nature's love of diversity; how humans were an intrinsic part of the balance of life on Earth. The long-eared owl from the Council of Elders was quick to remind Livia that the planet had done very well for millions of years before humankind came along.

A noble Rhodesian ridgeback named Jacob argued the case for clemency for those humans who were known to live in harmony with nature and the animal kingdom.

'And what of our debt to the sons and daughters of Japheth?' he said. 'Were it not for his father's Ark, we wouldn't be here today.'

'Myths and legends,' muttered the Skerret Elder dismissively.

Jacob was undeterred.

'Myths and legends? Does my honourable friend suggest that we're to reshape the past as well as the future?'

'We,' replied the shrew Elder as the Council exchanged worried glances, 'are merely messengers. The Earth Assembly has spoken. The verdict is final.'

Still Hobbes said nothing. And finally, exasperated, Will-C found his voice.

'Suppose . . .' he began falteringly, '. . . suppose there are Truckles who won't . . . who won't take part? Suppose there were some who . . . might . . . some who . . . that might even . . . defend their adopted human families against attack?'

All eyes turned to Will-C. The Elders frowned. Hobbes offered a thin, apologetic smile. Rani swallowed hard. Natterjack glared.

'You would dare to defy the office of the Council of Elders?' said the toad, incredulous.

'No!' spluttered Hobbes. 'No he wouldn't.'

'Does he speak for all felines?' snapped the Skerret.

'No!' said Rani and Hobbes in unison. 'He doesn't!'

'Our aim is victory,' bellowed Natterjack, reining in his fury, turning his attention to the crowd once more. 'Victory at all costs. Victory despite sacrifice and terror. War has been declared, and anyone who stands against the revolution will be cut down along with the humans.'

Another wave of anxious whispers rippled through the assembly.

Livia beat her wings and turned small circles above the crowd. Concealing her anxiety and darkest fears, she appealed to the vanity of the Elders in a measured tone.

'But surely the wise and honourable Council of Elders has the power to lodge an appeal on our behalf? If sufficient names were gathered from the ranks to support the Council in such a bold and brave decision, perhaps war could still be averted. An appeal would at least allow time for further debate. We all know that the humans are reckless and foolish, but we've always found a way to live alongside them. Live and let live. It has always been our way.'

Livia's words gave a glimmer of hope to the Truckles. 'Even the honourable Earth Assembly would surely not countenance bloodshed without a majority vote.'

Natterjack realized that Livia had struck a chord with many, and they were now adding their own voices to the call for an appeal. 'The time for talk is over,' he bellowed. 'It has been decreed that we'll wage a war to the death by land and sea and air!'

In a breach of protocol, Livia swooped over the heads of the startled Elders and flew at Natterjack.

'No. I implore you, Proconsul. This war is unjust. If we meet the humans' violence with violence, then we're no better than them.'

Natterjack gestured to Faelken, who pinned back his wings and plummeted towards the dove.

In a flurry of movement, Livia spotted the danger and took evasive action, but she was too old and too slow.

Faelken struck, plunging his talons into her body as he continued his rapid descent. The speed of the attack was frightening, and Livia was driven into the hard ground of the forest floor before she could struggle free. At the point of impact, Faelken released his grip and soared skyward.

The show of lethal force and Livia's crumpled, lifeless form silenced the crowd. Seizing upon the fact that the dove had broken with protocol, and secure in the knowledge that few among those gathered had heard her final plea, Natterjack rallied the troops once more.

'Listen well, fellow Animalians. If the humans learn of our mission, they won't hesitate to slaughter each and every one of us, and our babies too. There'd be no negotiation, only certain death for all Animalians.'

His gaze fell on the lifeless dove.

'We cannot tolerate a single traitor in our midst. If we fail to measure up to the task we've been set by the Earth Assembly, then the future is lost. There'll be no more natural history . . . only human history. And that cannot be tolerated!'

Finally, Natterjack began to elicit cheers and cries of support from the wider circles.

'The reign of Man will end swiftly and without warning, by tooth and claw and talon. Spread the word to all those who weren't able to attend and report back with the names of any that stand against us. Pay heed that there are few canines present here tonight. As a species, they enjoy less freedom than most, and many may not have been able to slip away unnoticed. There are some, however, who've been corrupted, brainwashed by their human hosts, and from them we can expect treachery and fierce resistance.'

Jacob felt the weight of Natterjack's gaze upon him.

'That cannot deter us from our aim. We must be victorious to ensure a future for the animal kingdom. We must fight together or we'll all die together. Are you with me, Animalians?'

'I'm ready,' came a spirited voice from the crowd.

'Victory!' shouted another. Then another. And another.

'Very well,' croaked Natterjack. 'The mighty sun will rise and fall twice more before battle is joined beneath the Full Worm Moon. Until then take only water. We must fast to sharpen our instincts. Once the enemy has fallen, there'll be flesh aplenty to fill our bellies. And let that be our finest hour!'

The Animalians erupted and sent a unified cry through the forest; Natterjack relished every whoop and caw and howl.

Not everyone shared in the excitement, however. For Will-C, Yoshi, Jacob and all the other Truckles, the ease with which Natterjack had whipped the crowd up into a frenzied mob, hungry for blood, could not have been more terrifying. And even one or two of the Council of Elders exchanged worried looks as the District Proconsul – with Faelken at his side – drank in the moment like a tyrannical, power-crazed dictator, eyes blazing with a chilling, almost human intensity.

CHAPTER THREE

Drue had sensed that something was wrong before she had even opened her eyes the fateful spring morning that Will-C vanished. True, she had slept fitfully throughout the night, her duvet offering scant refuge from a gale that had threatened to rattle her bedroom window right out of its sash cords, but it wasn't just that; and it wasn't the fact that she had remained in her own bed, in her own room.

Ever since she could walk, at the first sign of an approaching storm, Drue, an only child, would scamper barefoot down the hall to snuggle up in her parents' bed to escape the twin terrors of thunder and lightning.

Her father had tried to dispel her fears by teaching her to read the garden for early signs that bad weather was on its way: the appearance of seagulls riding the thermals above the woodland beyond their cottage; low-flying swallows; spiders shortening and tightening their webs. But Drue had simply used this knowledge to present a case for heading straight to her parents' room at bedtime, to save everyone time and trouble later on.

But this was different. Drue couldn't say why exactly, but it was. And when she awoke and discovered that Will-C was not curled up in his favourite spot at the foot of her bed she felt that her worst fears were confirmed. If her father's homespun country lore had taught her anything, it was to trust in her instincts. If some new chapter were about to begin in their lives, she only hoped that it was one that she could still share with Will-C – that he hadn't been run over crossing the road or got caught in a snare that Farmer Callow's son laid for rabbits.

Drue simply couldn't imagine her life without her feline companion as a part of it.

Described as black on his official chart at the Downs Homeopathic Veterinary Surgery (though if you looked closely in the right light you could see that the coat sagging from his underbelly was really chocolate-brown), Will-C was so named because Drue's father Quinn didn't approve of animals being kept as domesticated pets. *Captives* he called them, *Prisoners of Paw*.

So, whenever Drue had raised the subject of really wanting a captive herself – which she had done all too frequently ever since she could speak – her mother had intervened, smiled a sympathetic smile, tucked a stray wisp of hair behind Drue's ear and said: '*We'll see*,' before moving swiftly on to another topic.

Even back then, Drue knew that this was merely a subtle way for adults to say no. But she never let on that she knew, never kicked up a fuss or threw a hissy fit, and she never let it quell her desire that one day she would love and be loved by a furry companion of her own.

★　　★　　★

That day came later the same year that Drue's mother Serah had died. A year, it seemed to Drue, devoid of seasons, where spring had segued directly into winter; the longest, coldest and darkest on record.

It was the year that would usher in Drue's ninth birthday. But, as she was still frightened, angry and hurting from the loss of her mother, she had no interest at all in marking the occasion with a celebration. She wouldn't even discuss it. In fact, she couldn't imagine a time when she would ever want to celebrate anything ever again.

Without the light of her mother in her life, it seemed to Drue that the beginning of each new day was just another burden she had to endure, and birthdays were no exception. Why mark the passing of time when all it did was carry her further away from where she belonged, and where she longed to be?

Cutting off her friends, even the closest of them, Drue withdrew into herself and took to seeking out shadows whenever she could. It was as if punishing herself, being deprived of sunlight, laughter and companionship, would somehow, in turn, punish the cruel world itself.

To begin with, Drue disengaged from school completely, but, realizing that this only drew extra attention, she began to make an effort in class. Nothing like her old self of course, just enough to disappear below the teachers' radar. Just enough to ensure that all those who would put an arm round her, or fuss over her joined-up writing, or compliment her on her hair – *I only washed it, for heaven's sake* – or even praise her for simply sitting at her desk, when that was where she was meant to be, would stop keeping an eye on her.

And so the routine was established, with the days turning into weeks and the weeks into months, and Drue spending more and more time in her bedroom alone.

Her father knew better than to intervene, though he too was still bereft at the loss of his wife and soulmate, and would have given anything to spare his daughter such torment. But Quinn Beltane was no stranger to bereavement; his parents and even his two brothers, one younger, one older, had long since departed this life, and he knew that everyone needed time and space to deal with the mourning process in their own individual way.

When Drue's ninth birthday finally arrived – it was on a Sunday in early spring – the whole county of West Sussex, the whole of the south coast of England in fact, was shrouded in a thin, pale mist, through which fell a light but incessant drizzle.

Perfect, Drue had thought as she'd opened her curtains. Rising late, she had pulled on the same clothes she'd worn the day before – faded jeans and an old sweatshirt – and, tying her hair back with a tatty green scrunchy, she ambled down to the kitchen.

Despite the weather, her father had been out in the garden top-working one of the established fruit trees. Drue had watched him through the window above the sink. She knew from experience that he was rind-grafting.

In previous seasons, she had helped him with the task, her job being to prepare the tiny, tapering scions, three buds long, that would be bound with twine and grafting wax to the cuts in the thicker branches. Quinn had explained that it was a means to introduce a new pollinator for the adjacent trees, or to create a new variety from stock that was getting a little old and tired, but to Drue it just seemed like magic, plain and simple, a way to grow pears on an apple tree.

As usual, Quinn had seemed to sense his daughter watching him. He'd waved and smiled, and when Drue withdrew from the window, he'd quietly downed tools and headed back to the house.

Once Quinn had pulled off his mud-caked boots and waxed field coat, and washed his hands, he'd planted a kiss on Drue's forehead, and silently helped her to prepare a non-celebratory birthday breakfast: freshly squeezed orange juice with pomegranate, loose scrambled eggs, grilled home-grown tomatoes and buttery toast. The one non-negotiable stipulation in the domestic arrangement was that Drue still had to join her father for meals.

As Quinn brewed tea in a pint-sized mug with a chipped rim, Drue had helped clear the table and clean the dishes before retreating to her room.

Lying on her nineteenth-century cast-iron campaign bed – which had originally belonged to her maternal great-grandfather (and which she and her mother had painted white and adorned with fairy lights to expunge any lasting trace of battles in foreign fields) – Drue had gazed up at the glow-in-the-dark stars she had long ago stuck to her ceiling, and realized that they had completely lost their magical allure.

They still shone, but no longer glowed with the promise of intergalactic adventures and the secrets of the universe; they were just silly, ugly, pastel-coloured bits of plastic that she would ask her dad to get rid of the next time he was doing some decorating. The toys on the top of her wardrobe could go too. Even Babycakes, the threadbare zebra who had shared Drue's pillow since she was three, would not escape the cull. As far as Drue was concerned, it was time to put aside childish things.

Drue had heard the back door close as her father returned to work in the garden, but thereafter, with her iPod earphones in place, and the player set to random, she had shut out everything but the compilation of songs that hadn't been added to for almost a year: the soundtrack of a brighter time, a different world.

Drue really had become quite adept at building a mental barrier between herself and her life in the present, and it had worked on this occasion too . . . for a while.

Then, in her mind's eye, Serah had appeared.

Drue could see her mother's smiling eyes, grey-green and vivid; she could detect the soft fragrance of the lavender water Serah had used to iron her clothes; she could feel her mother's tender touch, those slender fingers (with the bitten thumbnails that Drue used to chastise her about) that had once stroked her cheek, and tied her shoelaces, and probed her hair like a mummy-monkey, every time there was a fresh outbreak of nits at school.

Head lice! Drue remembered how they'd made her mother's skin crawl. The shock and horror of the time they'd discovered them while on the way to stay with Auntie Mary for the weekend; how they had had to break the train journey to buy some fruit shampoo to soak Drue's scalp before they got there. They'd often laughed about that. They had often laughed.

Not that Drue had never seen her mother cross; she had,

and she had been on the wrong end of her temper on more than one occasion. But whatever the cause, however terrible it seemed at the time, it always soon blew over.

Kind-hearted; a wise soul; a loyal friend. These were the ways in which the people who'd known Serah well spoke of her at the funeral. But whatever it was that had defined her character – a soft touch, Drue's father used to say teasingly – there was no doubt that Serah had been blessed with a miraculous ability to make people see the best of things.

Even when it came to death and dying.

Drue understood that, because of her mother's faith, because of her belief in a life beyond this one, she wasn't afraid to die; she was just very sad that they wouldn't have more time together in this world.

They had talked about it many times – though Drue preferred not to do so just before bedtime – and they had discussed in depth the reason that her mother had to pass over, as she put it.

Drue had listened intently to the big words like chemotherapy, immunotherapy and lymph nodes, in the hope that one of them contained a secret incantation that would make her mother well again. But none of them did.

Drue took to whispering special prayers every morning and every night, but it seemed that none was heard.

When her father finally broke the news that Drue had been dreading, his dark eyes welled with tears. Drue felt numb with shock.

At first, to her surprise, she couldn't cry.

Then slowly, over time, her shock turned to anger. Her anger turned to fear. And soon her fear metamorphosed into guilt. Drue became convinced that somehow she must have been responsible; that the loss of her mother was a divine punishment for some bad thought or naughty behaviour.

Inconsolable, her tears finally began to flow, and she cried until eventually there were no more tears to shed. And then she cried without them. With the outside crying done, she cried inside. And, for all her father's love and understanding, it seemed to Drue that crying on the inside was all she would ever do for the rest of her life.

Until, that is, the night of that ninth birthday, when Serah's presence seemed to fill Drue's entire bedroom. Drue had been lost in her melancholy thoughts when she suddenly caught the smell of lavender, as heady as a field in summer.

Drue sat up in bed and, as she did so, she saw the heavy calico curtains at her window move. She knew it couldn't be the wind as she had closed the sash before going to bed, so she assumed it must be a draught coming under the door on the other side of the room . . . But then came the tap-tapping . . . like a finger drumming on the glass, louder and more persistent than the rain that had been falling since morning.

Without thinking, Drue had whispered, 'Mum. Mummy?'
Still the tapping continued from behind the curtain.

Drue swung her legs from the bed and padded across the moonlit room. A moment of hesitation, and then she tugged open the curtains and gazed out at the night. At first she saw nothing more than the drizzle and the blinking light of a distant passenger jet crossing the vast black sky.

But then she saw him: a cat . . . a bedraggled little creature with big, shiny, almond eyes, perched precariously on a high branch of the apple tree outside her bedroom window. Thin as a stick of Brighton rock – and surprisingly agile despite missing a hind leg – his dark coat was as coarse, matted and sodden as the scrawny, wild mountain goat that she and her dad had rescued from the swimming pool on their last family holiday in Mallorca. But, ragged or not, as he mouthed faint, plaintive meows, he melted Drue's young heart.

Though utterly convinced that her mother had sent the cat as a sign that her spirit was still as close as ever – and Drue was bursting to tell her father just that – she decided that, for the first few weeks at least, it might actually be best to keep her new-found friend a secret, just in case those first few weeks were all that they had.

And so their relationship began. Using a school fleece for a blanket, Drue made up a bed in the back of her wardrobe. Every day she cleaned and groomed the cat's coat with one of her old hairbrushes until it gleamed just like those of the panthers she'd seen in her father's magazines. Every morning and every night she fed him scraps she had liberated from her own plate.

* * *

And so it went on. For a time. Until one evening Drue and her father were clearing away the dirty dishes after supper. The kitchen window was the perfect spot from which to observe the bats skittering between the garage and the ramshackle old hay barn adjacent to the house, and Quinn Beltane seemed lost in reverie as he washed the cutlery and followed the nocturnal display.

As had become the pattern, Drue seized the moment to

surreptitiously palm some leftovers – in this instance a wedge of root-vegetable pie with parsnip pastry – from her dinner plate and tuck it up the sleeve of her cardigan. Her eyes darted back to her father, and it appeared that he hadn't noticed. But, as he retrieved a clean tea towel from a drawer beside the sink and handed it to his daughter, he said: 'Carnivora.'

'Sorry?' replied Drue.

'Carnivora,' repeated her father as if the word alone said all that needed to be said.

Drue lowered her eyes. She sensed a lecture coming, and she could guess what this one was going to be about. Her father proffered a baking tray for drying.

'Carnivora,' Quinn said again, 'a large order of flesh-eating Mammalia, including the canine, ursine and *feline.*'

Drue gave the baking tray all of her attention, considerably more than was required for the task in hand. Her father took it from her, stacked it on the worktop and handed her another wet dish. With a sigh, he continued.

'Angel, a cat cannot live on carrots and peas and parsnip pie.'

'We do,' countered Drue immediately; drying that baking tray had bought her precious time to formulate a hasty defence, 'and people are meat-eaters too.'

'That's different.'

'Why is it different?' asked Drue. 'You're the one who's always saying that we ought to treat all living things with equal respect. So why can't cats like peas and carrots and broccoli and . . . and beans on toast for that matter, just as equally . . . as equally much as we do?'

44

'Because it's just not in their nature.'

Drue could feel Will-C slipping away from her.

'Well, maybe that's because of nurture, not nature, like Mum used to say; why some kids will only eat junk food and not things that are good for them.'

Quinn could see that his daughter was going to fight her corner to the bitter end and he suppressed a smile.

'That's a point well made, but you see, Angel, cats aren't just carnivores, they're obligate carnivores; they have to eat meat because their digestive systems can't get the necessary amino acids from vegetable matter. Human beings can.'

'Oh,' said Drue, truly deflated. She opened her mouth as if a brilliant new defence strategy had just occurred to her, and she was about to launch into it, but all she actually said was 'Oh' again.

Quinn watched his daughter for a moment and then lifted her chin.

'But then again, there's always an exception to every rule. So come on then, let's see what a four-legged vegetarian obligate carnivore looks like.'

Drue could tell from his tone that Quinn was going to let Will-C stay, and she threw her arms round him, stretched up full height to kiss his stubbly cheek and then scrambled off up the stairs to fetch her feline stowaway, words tumbling in her wake.

'Actually, he's only got three legs, but he doesn't seem to mind.'

Her father called after her, 'Sounds resourceful; no wonder you two get along so well. And what's the name of our esteemed guest?'

'Will-C.'

'What's that?' said Quinn.

'You know, like Mum always said . . . *We'll see. We'll see.*'

Quinn smiled to himself. He felt a tremendous weight had been lifted, and he said a silent prayer of thanks to Serah. He knew that deep down there would always be a place of hurt and longing in Drue's heart, just as there would be in his own, but at least his daughter had found her spark again. Her smile.

And so it was that Will-C took up permanent residence in the Beltanes' detached flint-faced cottage on the outskirts of the village of Kingley Burh. In the three years that had followed, he and Drue had become inseparable. Best friends. And nothing, it had seemed to Drue, could ever come between them.

CHAPTER FOUR

Following the District Proconsul's key address, the Elders had been tasked with drawing up a battle plan and allocating specialist assignments to the species best suited to the task. Cutting off human communications and power generation was given top priority.

Though they didn't fully understand the principles by which such things worked, the Earth Assembly knew that Man's dead trees with black snakes of fire (pylons carrying telephone lines and electricity cables) were key, because they could see the energy auras, the luminescent radiation, that emanated from them, and other structures such as satellite receiving dishes, mobile phones, generators and power stations.

Burrowing creatures such as voles, moles and rabbits were to weaken the foundations below ground, while shire horses, deer and the larger mammals (elephants, bears, bison and so on depending on geographical location) would use their brute strength to topple whatever structures they could. Their winged comrades – in flocks so vast and dense that day would appear to turn to night – would disrupt any remaining radio signals.

Another two hours passed before the Animalian Elders in Kingley Burh felt satisfied that each member of the community knew what his or her role was to be, and which targets they were to focus on. No Truckle was expected to attack their own adopted human family, so they were each allocated alternatives. Many, in fact, would not even see frontline action; they were to form part of the support network. As it was spring, there were newborns and young to take care of, and medicinal roots and herbs to be gathered for the treatment of warriors wounded in battle.

Finally, the ancient forest was alive with movement once more, as all the creatures melted away into the night. The prevailing mood was now one of sombre resignation, even for those in favour of revolution and reform, for in the wake of Natterjack's rousing oratory, and the Elders' strategizing, came the realization that a dangerous, bloody, unprecedented mission lay ahead.

Though all agreed that their coordinated efforts and the element of surprise would give a united animal kingdom the edge at the outset, the talk soon turned to Man's weapons of fire: vast lakes of chemicals more deadly than cobra venom; rolling iron shelters with skin thicker than rhino hide that carried humans above the clouds, and as deep into the ocean as a mighty blue whale could dive.

There was no question that modern human beings made formidable foes. And ones who also had a powerful psychological advantage: for thousands of years they had waged war, and hunted and killed for pleasure – the latter being something almost unthinkable in the realm of Animalians, where, with very few exceptions, a life would only be taken as a source of food, for survival.

Not that these were issues that Will-C had had time to contemplate. For though Lennox and his gang had long since departed, the remainder of the feline population of Kingley Burh gathered round Hobbes and Rani seeking guidance. These were Truckles, just like him. They loved their human companions and wanted no part in waging war.

There was talk of mutiny, of organized resistance, of somehow bridging the linguistic barrier to alert their adopted families to the impending danger. But what of the Proconsul's warning that humans would not discriminate between them when it came to a question of survival? Would they be willing to risk condemning their own Animalian kith and kin, their children and unborn babies, to certain death by aiding the enemy?

Will-C's mind swam, his thoughts as knotted as the exposed roots of the yew trees. He had to save Drue – but how? What would his father have done in the circumstances?

Instinct.

He had to trust his instinct. But what was his instinct telling him? Space. Breathing space. Thinking space. He had to formulate a plan and it was clear he couldn't do so there and then, not with all the distractions.

'Am I not your elected Proxy?' said Hobbes suddenly, to quieten down the agitated cats, his authoritarian timbre an echo of Natterjack's own. 'Very well, then you must trust me. For now, we must heed the words of the Council of Elders . . .'

'And become savages,' came a cry.

'No. Not savages. Soldiers. We are at war now and we must follow orders. Go back to your homes and prepare for the battle that lies ahead.'

These were not the reassuring words that the Truckles had been hoping for. As the Proxy and his Deputy departed, Will-C confided in the small band of stragglers who were left behind.

'They say we're all soldiers, and it's true, in that we have no choice but to fight, but who you choose to fight for is up to you. Maybe there's hope yet.'

'And who will lead us? You? It's hopeless,' said a Devon Rex.

'The forces of the Earth Assembly are too strong. We'll all be killed along with the humans,' said a Persian Blue.

One by one, they turned and padded away, ears back, heads down, tails slung low between their legs. They were beaten before the fight had begun. But, after a few paces, Yoshi turned back.

'It's true, isn't it, Will-C? There's nothing we can do.'

'Then go. Go with them,' said Will-C.

An ominous shadow crept across the ground and engulfed them. As they turned their gaze skyward, Faelken swooped down as if from the moon itself and settled on a jagged aerial root of a fallen tree. His piercing gaze locked on Will-C.

'The Elders have called for a gathering of all Council officials,' rasped the bird of prey.

'But the summit meeting is over,' replied Will-C.

'It's a private session. They're expecting you now.'

'Where?'

'The Weoh Oak by the river,' replied Faelken as he turned his attention to Yoshi. 'Elected officials only.'

'I'll be there,' said Will-C.

The Gryfalcon picked at his talons. Those same lethal barbs that had cut short Livia's life.

'Tell them I'll be there,' repeated Will-C, summoning more authority as his hackles rose. The gyrfalcon eyed the two cats a moment longer and then took to the air, turning a broad, lazy circle before drifting over the treetops and out of sight.

Yoshi shivered. The temperature beneath the forest canopy had dipped in the last hour and a chill breeze now snaked through the trees. Without a coat of any kind to maintain his body heat, Yoshi felt the cold more than most.

Will-C lifted his nose to read the swirling downdraught; a damp, briny gust infused with a distant ocean neither feline had ever seen.

'There's a storm coming. Go home, Yoshi. Be with your family. I'll find you when the time is right.'

'But what will you do?' asked Yoshi.

'I don't know yet,' replied Will-C honestly.

'I couldn't hurt a human.'

'You won't have to. I promise. Now go. I need to find out what the Elders are planning. Maybe there's a way out of this yet.'

'I don't trust them. Look what happened to poor Livia,' whispered Yoshi.

'Livia made a mistake. She broke with protocol,' replied Will-C, a little more sternly than he'd intended.

'But it was murder, plain and simple.'

'Yes,' agreed Will-C.

'Well then. We should report Natterjack to the authorities,' said Yoshi, frightened and frustrated.

'The toad has a hundred witnesses who would testify before the Earth Assembly that Livia was advocating treason.'

'All the more reason not to trust him,' said Yoshi, trembling.

'Anyway, it would take days just to get word to the Assembly, by then the war will have begun.'

'So what do we do?'

'I'll attend this meeting. Listen to what else they have to say. Then decide.'

'And if it's a trap?'

'Don't worry. Not even the District Proconsul can defy the summit truce or break the Code of Conduct without provocation. Now go, before you make me late again.'

A light rain began to fall as Will-C bounded deftly on to the moss-covered trunk of the fallen tree, and without a backward glance sprinted off into the shadows of the forest.

CHAPTER FIVE

Drue dressed as quickly as she could in the clothes that were closest to hand. She tugged her mobile from the charger on her dressing table, slipped the phone into the pocket of her jeans and hurried out of her room.

An hour later, having searched in every room, every cupboard, every nook and cranny in the entire cottage with no sign of Will-C – let alone her father – Drue bounded out of the kitchen door into the back garden.

It was still early; the sun had just risen above the stand of beech trees to the east, but was barely visible behind a veil of clouds. Cumulonimbus – *Thunderheads*, Quinn called them – and they meant just one thing: there was more bad weather on its way.

Drue zipped up the neck of her fleece and moved across the lawn. Here and there the gale that had rattled her bedroom window had left its mark – toppled plant pots, a rambling rose torn from its ties, twigs, even branches as thick as broom handles, snapped from the fruit trees.

'Will-C!' cried Drue. 'Fish, fish, fiiiiiish!' she added,

knowing that day or night he was unable to resist the promise of a freshly boiled coley fillet.

Drue checked the vegetable patch, the potting shed, behind the screen of the compost heap and the old hay barn. Finally, she made for the double garage where she expected to find her father at his workbench. As soon as she opened the side door and saw that their old Defender pickup was not parked inside, she guessed that Quinn was out on a call. An original Series II workhorse built in the early 1960s, the Land Rover was equipped with a winch that had saved many a red-faced motorist from the surrounding drainage ditches and muddy fields, and, for a good many locals, Quinn Beltane's was the first number to call in a crisis.

Sure enough, when Drue finally reached her dad on her mobile, she discovered that he was on the other side of the village helping to shore up a rivulet that had broken its banks and flooded the lane that led to St Nicholas's Church.

Quinn wasn't one for long phone conversations, so Drue got straight to the point and asked if he had seen Will-C before he'd left the house. He hadn't. She explained about her search, and he told her not to worry, before reminding her to wear her hooded waterproof jacket over her school uniform as there was more heavy weather on the way.

The phone call did nothing to alleviate Drue's concerns. She completed a wider search of the garden and the surrounding hedgerows, and then returned to the garage to fetch her mountain bike.

By the time Drue arrived at Church Lane, Quinn had the

situation well under control and several volunteers armed with broad yard brushes were helping to sweep a lake of sludgy water from the cobbled bridleway back into the flow of the stream.

Clad in waist-high waders, Quinn hauled a sodden, mud-caked plastic shopping bag from the current, deftly scaled the slippery bank and dumped it on to the growing pile of rubbish he had retrieved from the riverbed – drinks cans, discarded bottles, even the rotted remains of a Christmas tree, its root ball still encased in a red plastic pot.

'What are people like?' said one of the volunteers, stopping for a moment to rest his scraggy ginger beard on the handle of his broom.

'It's a throwaway society is what it is,' said another.

'The problem is there is no "away",' added Quinn.

'You're not wrong there, Mr B,' said the man with the beard respectfully. 'You're not wrong there.'

'Dad!' hollered Drue, pulling her bicycle up short of the slimy debris. Then she almost fell off of it, as beside her, a pair of black Labradors corralled in the rear of a parked Volvo threw themselves at the back window, snarling and barking furiously.

'Morning, Drue,' said the bearded man.

'Hello, Mr Deacon,' said Drue politely, sidling away from the agitated dogs.

'No school today?'

Before Drue could answer, her father cut in.

'Angel, what are you doing down here? If this is about Will-C . . .'

'Will-C?' said Mr Deacon.

'My cat,' said Drue quickly.

'I thought we discussed . . .' began Quinn before Drue started up again, her words tumbling out.

'But Dad, he's missing. I've looked all over. I think something bad has happened.'

Drue could see from her father's expression that he wasn't too pleased. She lowered her eyes.

'It was probably the storm that spooked him,' said Mr Deacon. 'Look at my two,' he said, gesturing to the barking dogs. 'They've not stopped the whole morning; good as gold as a rule.'

Drue glanced back at the black Labs, their snouts pressed to the saliva-smeared, part-open window, teeth bared, menace in their eyes. 'Monty! Nelson!' barked Mr Deacon, even louder than the dogs, but his remonstration did nothing to curb their noisy protest.

'Reckon you can manage from here,' said Quinn to the others as he scooped up Drue's bicycle and swung it into the back of his pickup. He then wriggled out of his wet waders. Drue clambered into the cab.

Mr Deacon read the sorry look on her face.

'And don't you worry, young lady. Your cat'll turn up. Soon as he's hungry, mark my words. They know what's good for 'em,' he chuckled.

Drue didn't respond, her eyes still on her shoes, hands wrapped round the mobile in her lap. With a cursory wave to the others, Quinn climbed behind the wheel and fired up the Land Rover.

For a while father and daughter drove without exchanging a word; only the drone of the bio-diesel engine and heavy tyres ploughing through deep puddles punctuated the stiff silence.

As they turned through the five-bar gate and on to the little drive that led to their cottage, Quinn spelled out the deal: he had work; Drue had school. He thought Will-C would show up before too long and, as his forestry duties that day would involve a storm-damage survey of the surrounding woodland, he would be well placed to keep a lookout on his rounds.

If there were still no sign of Will-C come lunchtime, then he would spend his entire break conducting a thorough search of his own. But Drue had to promise not to skip school in order to look for her cat. He didn't want to have to be worrying about the whereabouts of both of them. Drue solemnly nodded her assent, then slipped from the cab and disappeared into the house to change into her uniform and collect her books and folders for school.

As Quinn sat in the Defender, waiting to drive Drue back into the village, he rolled down the window and peered at the sky. The clouds still held rain, but it wasn't yet falling. But the thing that really struck him was that there wasn't a single bird in sight.

None in flight. None to be seen or heard in the surrounding trees. None on the rooftops. None feeding on the seeds and scraps of bread that Drue regularly topped up on the bird table they had made together. On any other day the finches, blue tits, serins, sparrows, buntings, even a pair of great spotted woodpeckers and the odd pheasant would be squabbling over the feast of crumbs, or letting it be known

57

in very noisy terms that Drue had fallen behind with her duties and a fresh supply was required.

Quinn surveyed the landscape, a pensive look on his face. Then, as Drue re-emerged from the cottage, carrying her school bag, his features softened into what, he hoped, was a reassuring smile.

CHAPTER SIX

Lessons began with English and history, and, though the latter was a subject that Drue had always enjoyed and seemed to have a natural affinity for, time seemed to have slowed to a snail's pace.

It took every ounce of her willpower to feign an interest in the names and dates and places that were scratched in white chalk on the blackboard, and on several occasions when the teacher, Mr Tiller, had asked questions and scanned the room for answers, Drue had had to hide behind the girl sitting in front of her for fear of being called upon. Her mind was very definitely elsewhere.

The school administration had banned the use of mobile phones for Drue's year group as many of the children couldn't resist the urge to play games, send texts or photograph one another during lessons. As a result, it wasn't until the mid-morning break, while all her classmates spilled out into the playground, that Drue had lit out for the Second World War air-raid shelter – which now served as an extra storage shed for the groundskeeper's gardening equipment

– in the hope that she could make a quick call without being spotted.

The news from her father was less than encouraging – there was still no sign of Will-C – and Drue's heart sank, knowing that she would have to endure another agonizing series of lessons before the bell rang again for lunch, and she could make another call. Her one shred of comfort was that if her father said he would look for Will-C then he really would look; he always kept up his side of any bargain and delivered on a promise.

Still, Drue toyed with the idea of sloping off across the waterlogged sports field behind the shelter and resuming the search herself. And she might have too, if she hadn't run headlong into Mrs Gamph, the Deputy Headmistress, as she emerged from the shelter.

With her phone confiscated until the final bell, and the added threat of detention hanging over her, which would keep her from the search for even longer, Drue was forced to suffer in silence and return to classes.

And so the remainder of Drue's morning unfolded in much the same manner as the first half. It wasn't until lunchtime that she discovered that she was not suffering alone. Having planned to ask one of the girls in the year above if she could borrow a phone to call home, Drue fell in with a group in the canteen who had spent half the day secretly texting one another, and friends further afield, about their missing pets.

There were pupils from at least five different schools in the county who had a similar story to tell, and 'Lost' posters with photographs of some of the missing animals – cats mostly, but also a number of dogs and even a Burmese python – had already been posted on Facebook, Twitter and various online blogs, with contact details.

Though the news didn't bring her any closer to Will-C, and the conspiratorial gossip about unscrupulous gangs down from London stealing pets in order to claim reward money made her fearful that he might be suffering in captivity somewhere, for some reason Drue still felt sure that he was alive, and that somehow they would be reunited.

With a whole afternoon of science and maths stretching out ahead of her, Drue silently cursed the school and all its rules and regulations and wished that she were possessed of magic powers: the power to make time – the unbearable hours, minutes and seconds until the final bell at four o'clock – vanish.

Perhaps if she'd known it was to be the last time she would ever hear it, Drue might not have been in quite such a hurry to wish it away.

CHAPTER SEVEN

Since he'd parted from Will-C on the night of the Great
Summit, Yoshi had kept constant vigil at a window in
the home he shared with his adopted human companion, a
kind, elderly spinster named Mrs Haruki.

A full day, a night and half a morning had already passed
without further word from his trusted friend, and, though
weary from lack of sleep, Yoshi was keenly aware that the
sun that presently warmed his wrinkled skin through the
window was the last before the Full Worm Moon would fill
the sky – the signal for the war between humankind and
animalkind to begin.

It was therefore with a mixture of relief and trepidation
that he observed Will-C's human companion approach the
house. Even at a distance, he was sure it was her and, as she
wheeled her bicycle up the hydrangea-lined path to the
front door, Yoshi abandoned his post and scrambled into
the hall.

Having extended her search for Will-C without success,
Drue had spent her Saturday morning distributing A4-sized

'Lost' posters she had designed and printed on recycled paper during a late-night session at her computer. They featured a prominent photograph of Will-C, his name, home contact details and the words:

Missing:
Ever So Friendly Three-Legged Cat.
Reward.

The chalet bungalow was just one stop on a lengthy door-to-door tour that Drue had planned, and so it was with some haste that she rang the bell and tried to peer in through the adjacent living-room window.

On the other side of the door, Yoshi looked up at Drue through the mock stained glass of the glazed panels and waited for someone to respond. Again the bell chimed, and it took a moment for Yoshi to realize that Mrs Haruki was not at home.

Drue pushed the bell a third time, then reached into the rucksack which filled the wire-framed basket attached to the handlebars of her bike.

Inside the hall, Yoshi was seized with panic. He had no idea what had brought Drue to the house, but he sensed that it was something important relating to Will-C, and that maybe if he could get her attention he just might learn what it was. As Drue moved away from the front door, Yoshi bolted back down the hall, into the kitchen and out through his cat flap in the back door as fast as his paws would carry him.

By the time Yoshi rounded the house, Drue was already closing the front garden gate behind her. As she climbed astride her bicycle, he dashed the length of the lawn, cut across a flower bed and leapt a privet hedge to reach the drystone wall that bordered the property.

Yoshi did not present the prettiest of pictures at the best of times, but, wheezing and gasping for breath, his wispy guard hairs erect, he was quite an apparition, which actually helped to catch Drue's attention. She paused to consider the odd little creature.

'My goodness,' she said, 'whatever happened to you?'

Yoshi, of course, like most animals understood very little human language, but he nonetheless tried to bridge the linguistic divide.

'You're Will-C's friend,' said Yoshi in a strangled whisper.

'Haven't seen you in a while. Is Mrs Haruki OK?' said Drue, oblivious to Yoshi's comment; all she had heard were meows.

'Where is he? Will-C. Why hasn't he been to see me?' replied Yoshi.

'What is it, you funny little thing?' said Drue, petting the hairless cat.

'Is that why you're here? Is it Will-C? Has something happened?' said Yoshi anxiously.

'I wish you could talk,' said Drue. 'Maybe you could tell me where he is.'

Even though he hadn't understood a word she'd uttered, Yoshi could sense something, a sadness, a regret, in Drue's voice.

Drue let the cat nuzzle her palm.

'Is that his scent you can smell? Is it? Do you know where I can find Will-C?'

'Will-C!' exclaimed Yoshi. The shape of the sounds was familiar. He had heard them before when they'd been out in the cornfields hunting mice and Will-C had been called in for supper.

'Will-C! Yes. Will-C. You're trying to tell me something,' jabbered Yoshi.

'Are you trying to tell me something?' said Drue softly.

'Will-C!' spat Yoshi again, desperately trying to make a connection; doing all he could to make his vocal sounds match Drue's, though of course they didn't.

'Well, little friend, I've got to go,' said Drue.

'Is he at home? Is he hurt? Why are you . . .?'

'Take care,' said Drue as she pushed off on her bicycle and pedalled through the parked cars on the narrow street.

'Wait!' cried Yoshi. 'Wait!' But he realized it was no use. Humans were the one species it was almost impossible to communicate with beyond the absolute basics: happy, sad, playful, hungry, angry. If Will-C's companion had some news about him, Yoshi was never going to get it by asking.

I'll find you when the time is right, Will-C had said. And though his nagging doubts persisted, and he felt that some action was required, Yoshi decided that the only thing to do in the circumstances was to follow orders. He would just have to sit it out a while longer and wait for his friend to make contact.

Retracing his steps – with a slight detour to the neighbouring garden for a call of nature – Yoshi returned home. As he made his way back down the hall en route to his lookout spot by the living-room window, he suddenly froze.

For there on the mat, propped up against the front door, was . . . Will-C!

Yoshi examined the 'Lost' flyer more closely. The words on the page meant nothing to him, but the image was unmistakable. Like a reflection frozen in a puddle or a lake. And the fact that Will-C's human companion had just visited meant that she must have slipped it through the door while he was circling the house.

He'd seen this kind of thing before, when the cairn terrier who'd lived across the street had disappeared several summers earlier. The cairn had never been seen in the neighbourhood again, and eventually two others moved in to take her place.

The message was as clear as day: Will-C was missing.

Natterjack, thought Yoshi, his anxiety giving way to sheer dread. It had to be something to do with the toad.

CHAPTER EIGHT

The ancient forest of Kingley Burh had a completely different character by day and, as Yoshi picked his way through the labyrinthine yews, moving through pools of sunlight and mottled shade, he tried to regulate his breathing to fall in with theirs.

It was Will-C who had first shown him how the trees' powerful living energy fields snaked from one to another like writhing, invisible serpents, and how, with practice, it was possible to tap into them to calm the nerves or clear the mind. Yoshi hoped they might also strengthen his resolve, as the deeper he delved into the wood, the more he saw of the preparations for war. Burrows, warrens, nests being camouflaged or reinforced. Talons, beaks and claws being sharpened. Combatants engaged in mock combat to quicken their reflexes and hone their fighting skills.

From time to time Yoshi also glimpsed a human moving through the dense woodland – generally accompanied by a noisy canine Truckle crashing clumsily through the undergrowth or straining on a leash.

Whenever this occurred, Yoshi, like the forest's wild Animalian inhabitants, stopped in his tracks and remained perfectly still until the danger had passed. Not that the humans were hunting; they seemed to be following their normal curious patterns of behaviour – foraging without gathering anything – and Yoshi surmised that, apart from their dogs being even more protective and territorial than usual, humans had no inkling of the fate that was to befall them before the day was through.

The Weoh Oak that Faelken had spoken of was a massive structure of bleached, bark-free limbs, radiating from a cavernous trunk. Robbed of its life by a lightning strike hundreds of years earlier, the dead tree had become a landmark – and a host for creeping ivy and mistletoe – that every creature born and raised in Kingley Burh knew of.

It stood beside a river in a clearing beyond the forest canopy, and, as more sunlight penetrated to ground level by the riverbank, so the gorse, bulrushes and cordgrass grew in lush abundance around it. Yoshi took advantage of the natural cover and cautiously traced a wide half-circle as he crept closer to the giant oak.

Ears pricked, senses alert to the slightest sound or movement, Yoshi edged forward one very careful paw-step at a time.

A movement in the undergrowth to the east saw him change course. And, as he made his way through the reeds and rushes towards the sound, the ground beneath him softened, each paw-print filling with a pool of dark water as he progressed. Another few metres and Yoshi caught a glimpse of his friend.

Will-C and a number of Truckles – all of whom had been

vocal in their opposition to the war at the Great Summit – were imprisoned in a network of upturned, half-submerged, rusty metal supermarket trolleys.

Sodden, hungry, fearful, most were still and silent, resigned to their fate. Others whined and whimpered as they clung to the sides of the trolleys, treading water to keep their snouts above the surface.

Will-C shared a cage with two other cats: CoCo, a chocolate tom from neighbouring West Stoke, and a grey female whom Yoshi didn't recognize. Alongside them was a floundering King Charles spaniel puppy. As the weary dog's eyes closed and she slipped beneath the waterline, CoCo – clinging on for dear life to the wire-mesh roof himself – reached down and hauled her out by the collar. The spaniel sputtered as she came back into contact with the air, her floppy ears and coat now slick with algae.

'Will-C,' whispered Yoshi, 'it's me.'

Will-C did not respond. In the grip of his water phobia, he had retreated into himself. He remained still and silent, paralysed with fear, staring off into the middle distance.

'Will-C,' hissed Yoshi again, creeping a little closer.

But his efforts were in vain. For the very thing that had helped to mask Yoshi's stealthy approach from potential enemies had also hidden them from him. And in a sudden, frightening blur of movement Yoshi found himself pinned to the ground, the flesh at the nape of his neck clamped in jaws set with razor-sharp teeth. He was surrounded by a sneak of gabbling weasels and rats.

An albino mink appeared and rose up on its hind legs, tilting its head this way and that, studying Yoshi with beady pink eyes, as if trying to decide exactly what it was he was looking at. Smoothing its whiskers with the back of a paw, the mink gestured to the weasel restraining Yoshi, and he dragged the cowering feline through the marshy shallows towards the trolley-cages.

The weight of the trolleys had embedded the frames deep into the silt of the riverbed, and submerged flat rocks had been used to seal the open panels by the handles, which were the only ways in or out of the grim cells.

The mink leapt deftly from cage to cage, snapping at any paws that poked out through the wire, forcing the captives to plunge back into the murky water. As he surveyed the makeshift prison, deciding where to incarcerate the new arrival, he absently spun a trolley wheel.

'Whatever it is, we don't want it in here,' sneered CoCo.

The mink's head whipped round and he hissed.

'There!' he snapped, indicating that Yoshi should be placed in with CoCo and the others.

'We're too many already,' protested CoCo, knowing full well that the mink's sadistic nature would ensure that Yoshi would be joining him.

The rats forced Yoshi kicking and squirming beneath the water, prised the stone gate free and bundled him through the gap. As he surfaced, choking and gasping for breath inside the cage, CoCo helped him to find a paw-hold.

The mink hissed and bared its teeth and then scurried back to dry land, leaving the weasels and rats to keep watch over the prisoners.

'Yoshi. Are you OK?' said CoCo, keeping his voice down so that the guards couldn't overhear.

'What's wrong with Will-C?' said Yoshi by way of reply.

'I was hoping you could tell me. He's been like that since they put us in here.'

'Who did this?'

'Natterjack.'

'And the other Council Elders, do they know?'

'Couldn't say. It happened right after the Great Summit meeting.'

'The private meeting?' said Yoshi.

'Right,' continued Coco, 'only it wasn't a meeting: it was a trap and we all walked straight into it. It was dark. We were outnumbered.'

Yoshi craned his neck to survey the adjacent cages.

'Natterjack's spies must have been spread throughout the wood during the summit. All those who openly opposed the war were instantly rounded up.'

'How come he didn't just . . .'

'Kill everyone? Like Livia, you mean? Too conspicuous. Even the Proconsul has to answer to the Earth Assembly eventually.'

'So we're safe.'

'Until tonight, when the full moon rises and the battle with humankind begins. Who's going to notice the disappearance of a few Truckles with the biggest war in the history of the planet going on?'

CoCo and Yoshi eyed one another for a moment. CoCo was right. There would be bloodshed. There would be loss of life on both sides of the conflict. With humans out of the way, perhaps even the Earth Assembly would become a victim of the war, overthrown by ruthless tribal leaders and corrupt officials like Natterjack, who were hungry for even more power.

'Then we have to escape,' said Yoshi.

'How?' replied Coco. 'When there are guards and spies all around.'

'There must be a way,' said Yoshi hopefully. 'Will-C would know what to do.'

But one glance at Will-C confirmed he was in no position to help anyone.

'He's been that way since they put us in here. Hasn't made a sound.'

Yoshi carefully worked his way round the cage to his friend. He lost his footing on several occasions, back legs thrashing furiously in the water as the wire mesh cut deeper into his pads with each slip, but eventually he reached Will-C, and was able to nudge up against his limp form.

Yoshi searched for a flicker of recognition in his friend's eyes, but Will-C stared back at him with a blank expression. Yoshi tried gentle persuasion. Pleading. Cajoling. He told Will-C about Drue's visit to his house. How Will-C's human companion was looking for him. None of Yoshi's words hit their mark, however. And whatever fate held in store for the captives, it seemed that CoCo was right. Will-C's sharp mind and experience were no longer assets they could rely on.

Having eventually drawn a sharp reprimand from a weasel guard, Yoshi fell silent. He did his best to lift Will-C a little further out of the water, but he too was now feeling the effects of the spiralling current. Anchoring himself in a corner with Will-C, Yoshi huddled close to share what little body heat they had left between them. All he could do now was wait and hope.

CHAPTER NINE

The computer screen blinked and beeped to indicate to Drue that another friend was online. Messages had been traded back and forth for hours and, as the growing network of children with missing pets continued to grow apace, it had become abundantly clear that the problem was not a local one. Nor even confined to the British Isles. There were postings and blogs from as far afield as Oslo, Adelaide, Santa Monica, Muleta, Allahabad, Beijing, Munich and Moscow. Yet still the link between them had not been established.

Drue logged off from the chat room and sat for a moment to ponder the implications. Then she googled the news pages. The headlines were awash with the usual mix of scandal, crime, politics, sport and celebrity gossip. But not one carried a mention of what was, in Drue's eyes, the key story breaking around the world. Frustrated, she switched her computer to sleep mode.

Outside her window, the sky was like a vast glowing bruise, every shade of red through purple bleeding through the bone-white stratus fingers that floated just above the tree tops in the distance. As ever when Drue surfed in cyberspace, time seemed displaced, but even so the setting sun still took her completely by surprise. Had she really spent the entire afternoon on her computer?

She stretched and yawned and moved closer to the window. The sash cords were worn smooth and brittle, and the pulleys had seen better days, so it always took a little effort to slide it open. When she finally did so, she poked her head out to taste the fresh air.

The apple tree was in bud, and sprigs of pale pink blossom brushed Drue's hair as she rested her forearms on the sill and squatted down to watch the dying light. For a moment she was transported back to that first encounter with Will-C. The tree had grown a fair bit since then and so had they. Drue's eyes soon welled with tears, but she fought the impulse to cry; that would feel like an admission of defeat, and she wasn't about to give up just yet.

An untidy plume of shimmering starlings drifted across Drue's eyeline and settled in the stand of tall birch trees in the field beyond the perimeter of the Beltanes' plot. She realized there were also blackbirds, thrushes and crows in among them, a mix of species that Drue had never before seen on the wing in a single flock.

She watched them for a moment, and had the unnerving sensation that they were watching her right back. Then the spell was broken by the familiar drone of Quinn's car turning in beside the garage. Drue slid the window shut and withdrew to join her father.

★   ★   ★

Supper that night was a solemn affair, Drue picking at the cheese crust of her favourite pasta bake as she relayed to her father all that she had learned that afternoon.

Quinn Beltane was no fan of the internet – or any electronic gadgetry, come to that; he only carried a mobile phone at the insistence of his headstrong daughter, and could do little more with it than answer an incoming call – but he listened intently to all she had to say. And for once he didn't raise any objection to the time she had spent in front of the screen. On the contrary, to Drue's amazement, he suggested that she keep a close eye on developments and keep him informed.

From Drue's perspective, this was both a comfort and a concern: it gave her a renewed sense of purpose, but it also suggested that her father had read more into the news than he was letting on.

The remainder of Drue's evening had passed uneventfully. After washing the dishes together, she had drawn a hot bath while her father busied himself in his study beside the kitchen. It was not until he knocked on her bedroom door some hours later and announced that he had some unfinished business to attend to in the village that her uneasy feeling returned.

He very rarely left her alone in the house, and never at night. Not that she had ever felt unsafe. There was always kind Mrs Dean across the street, and Drue had her trusty mobile for emergencies. But it was the second breach of an unspoken protocol in the space of a day, and it set her thinking.

Quinn promised to be as quick as he could and insisted she bolt the door after him. Drue did so and scurried back up to her room to keep vigil at the window. Clad in her pyjamas, she tugged the heavy goose-down quilt from her bed, draped it round her shoulders like a cloak and – checking that her phone had sufficient charge – settled into a comfortable position on the wide window sill to keep watch.

An external solar light with a motion sensor lit the path at the rear of the cottage and, as the broad beam had been activated by Quinn's departure, Drue noticed a large dog moving across the garden. She slapped her palm on the glass – hard enough to startle the animal; if Will-C were to arrive home suddenly, Drue didn't want him to be frightened off by a strange hound on his patch.

'Oi! Shoo! Go on. Clear off!' bellowed Drue.

The dog glanced up at the window.

Drue slapped the glass again and waved him away with a scowl. As if heeding her advice, he dropped his wrinkled head low and moved off around the house.

As the security light clicked off, Drue relaxed back into her quilted cocoon. Had she moved to a window on the other side of the cottage, however, Drue would have seen that the stray canine hadn't moved on at all; he had simply switched his attention to another patch of ground. For this was a bloodhound and he was at work. Sagging jowls close to the earth, he employed his long, droopy ears to help waft layer upon layer of chemical clues into his twitching, restless snout.

Will-C had been gone for two days, and rainfall had diluted his scent, but even if he'd been gone for two weeks this inveterate tracker would have had little trouble picking up his trail.

And the moment he found it – the faintest trace still haunting the small exit hole in the two-metre-high hedge of the perimeter – he took off across the path, cleared the garden gate in a single bound and loped away in the direction of Oakwood Lane.

On the face of it, the bloodhound's progress through the forest was seemingly effortless – but beneath the surface his innate olfactory skills worked at an incredible rate, with subtlety and precision. In a single intake of breath, the lumbering canine could capture, sift, sort, identify and log for future reference – or compare and contrast with those already stored in his mental filing system – hundreds, even thousands, of odours at once.

Like a prodigiously gifted composer-conductor faced with a full orchestra in mid-symphony, he could detect the faintest note, sharp or flat, the slightest variation in tone, rhythm or tempo, of any instrument in the entire ensemble, and then, despite the multitude of contrasting sounds, could home in on that particular passage and isolate it as if it were playing solo . . . and all this at a trot through unfamiliar territory. Which is why, by the time he approached the makeshift prisoner-of-war camp beyond the Weoh Oak, the hound was acutely aware of the number of Truckles present and how desperate their plight.

The presence of the guard detail was no surprise to him either. But rather than trying to conceal himself from them, he chose instead to amble quite brazenly into the thick of the hidden rats and weasels who were primed and ready, waiting to spring an ambush.

'Who's in charge here?' barked the bloodhound loudly.

For a moment the Animalian guards stayed hidden in the surrounding undergrowth.

'Well?' boomed the bloodhound impatiently. 'I don't have all night.'

Finally, a grey weasel emerged from the bulrushes a little way ahead of the hound, and several others poked their noses out of the bushes. The weasel said nothing, but eyed the big dog with great suspicion.

'Are you in charge?' repeated the bloodhound, returning the weasel's stare.

'And who might you be?' said a disconnected voice from the bushes.

Mink, thought the dog. *A nasty bite. And bolder than a weasel in a scrap.*

'I'm a Clerk of the Court of the Earth Assembly. I've come to question the prisoners,' replied the bloodhound.

And now the mink showed himself.

'Question them? Why?' said the mink, approaching the bloodhound with caution.

'And you are?'

'Mustela, Chief of the Guard,' replied the mink.

'May I commend you, Mustela, on matters of security. You have the prisoners well guarded. I'll be sure to mention that when I report back.'

'Well . . . just doing our . . . duty . . .'

'Good. Now, if you'll permit me, the prisoners may have information that can be of use. Things that were not revealed at the . . . Great Summit meeting.' The blood-hound was bluffing: his nose told him that a vast number of species had been gathered together in the forest and, though he hadn't been aware of it, that suggested an official summit.

'The Proconsul said nothing of your visit to me,' said Mustela suspiciously.

'Do you wish to question his methods? I'll be happy to let him know.'

The mink drew in a long breath. He noted that the bloodhound wasn't wearing a man-made neck-shackle as Truckles, particularly canines, were wont to do. And crossing Natterjack was not something he wished to chance.

'Let him pass,' said Mustela finally.

As a pair of weasels led the bloodhound on through the shallows towards the cages, the mink continued to watch him closely. Without taking his eyes off the canine, he hissed an order at the black rat beside him.

'Find Natterjack.'

The bloodhound spotted Will-C in an instant, but he gave each of the cages and the captives due attention before settling on the trolley containing Drue's three-legged companion. With a glowering look, he commanded the weasels to stay back.

'You there, what's your name?' growled the bloodhound at CoCo. Before the chocolate tom could summon the strength to reply, the bloodhound lowered his voice to a conspiratorial whisper. 'It's OK, I'm a friend . . . I'm going to get you out of here, but I need to know what's going on.' Then loudly, 'You're going to tell me what I need to know, one way or another.'

'Who are you?' replied CoCo, genuinely puzzled.

'That's not important now. What's wrong with Will-C?'

'He's in shock, I think,' said Yoshi.

'What happened at the summit? Why are you being held here?' whispered the bloodhound.

'Don't tell him anything,' said CoCo to Yoshi. 'It's got to be a trap to get us to say something Natterjack can use against us.'

'Who's Natterjack?'

'Hah, you see? How could anyone not know who the Proconsul is?' said CoCo.

'That's right,' growled the bloodhound loudly, 'the Proconsul! So it'll be better for you if you tell me what I want to know.' Then quietly, 'If I can get you out, do you have the strength to fight?'

'The weasels or the humans?' said Yoshi.

'Shut up, Yoshi. He knows we're not going to fight the humans; that's why we're in here.'

'Humans?' whispered the bloodhound, alarmed. 'What are you talking about?'

'Oh,' spat CoCo sarcastically, 'so you're the only Animalian on the planet who doesn't know there's a war on?'

The bloodhound was shocked.

'The battle to stop the Sixth Wave,' explained Yoshi, 'the war to wipe out the human race.'

The weasels had edged a little closer and were beginning to take an interest. For a moment the bloodhound lost his composure.

'It's been decreed by the Earth Assembly,' continued a puzzled Yoshi. 'How can you not—?'

'SEIZE HIM!'

The piercing cry surprised everyone, including the

guards. Natterjack had returned with the black rat, and his steely glare was accompanied by an accusatory webbed finger thrust in the bloodhound's direction.

In an instant, the quiet riverbank was transformed into a raging battlefield. The weasels and rats lunged at the hulking bloodhound, while he in turn threw his considerable weight against one trolley-cell after another, toppling them and freeing the startled captives. Finally, with the prisoners liberated, the canine began to lash out at his assailants. He worked his powerful jaws, sinking his teeth into the soft bellies of his adversaries, batting them away with a skull as hard as flint. Swathes of reeds and rushes were crushed by thrashing limbs and falling bodies. The air was thick with noise, spittle and spumes of muddy water. The River Ems ran red with blood.

CoCo and several of the other freed prisoners fought bravely alongside the bloodhound. Yoshi and Will-C, however, were engaged in a battle for survival of a different kind. While most of the captives had been thrown clear of the upended trolleys, they had been trapped inside theirs as it plunged into a deeper, colder, faster-moving stretch of water.

The shock of the impact had wrenched Will-C out of his comatose state, but, as he now found himself submerged, twisting and tumbling in a rushing stream, it was as if he'd woken from a terrible dream only to find himself trapped in an even more terrifying nightmare. Kicking and sputtering, without any notion of which way was up or which was down, he suddenly broke the surface and sucked in a deep breath.

Finally, fortune smiled and Will-C was able to claw at the soft clay of a high bank and haul himself clear of the drag of the current.

Sodden, panting, exhausted, it took him a moment to get his bearings. He pricked up his ears and caught a faint echo of the brouhaha upstream. The images came flooding back as fast as the river itself: Natterjack, the weasels, an ambush . . . Yoshi! There on the opposite bank, lying face down in the water, lay his hairless friend.

'Yoshi!' cried Will-C. Despite the fact he had survived his ordeal in the river, Will-C's lifelong water phobia still taunted him from deep within his subconscious.

'Yoshi!' he called again. Still, Yoshi made no reply. In desperation, unable to sit by and watch his friend drown, Will-C did the only thing he could do . . . he took a great gulp of air, and despite every fibre of his being screaming *NO!* he sprang back into the swirling water.

The powerful current caught him instantly, and he had to fight against it with every ounce of strength in his body. Down into the depths he tumbled, thrashing and wriggling, but the current carried him forward, and gave him just enough momentum to reach the reeds and rocks on the riverbed, which he used to haul himself across to the bank. When he finally emerged, thrashing and gasping, he realized he had been carried several hundred metres further downstream, but he had at least reached the other side.

As he dragged Yoshi on to dry land, water streaming from the feline's mouth and nostrils, Will-C was relieved to see the gentle rise and fall of his friend's bony ribcage: confirmation that he was still alive.

Will-C looked up at that moon again and his thoughts turned to Drue. Time was running out for both of them, and though he tried to banish the terrible notion that kept creeping into his mind, he couldn't shake it off entirely; with the battle due to commence in just a few short hours, it was entirely possible that he might never see her again.

CHAPTER TEN

Water. Cool. Clear. Deep as the Atlantic. Sunlight drilling down through the surface, shimmering stalactites of pure, bright energy, slicing through viscous aquamarine. Drue followed the beams, sinking slowly towards the point where the light began to fade; a tiny lone figure adrift in a liquid void. Below her lay darkness, black as charcoal, and something ... no, not some thing, a ... what was it? A feeling. A presence. Beckoning. Was this an ocean? Was she really breathing underwater?

A pinpoint of light appeared below her now, just as the darkness seemed to fold in above. Drue tried to see her hand in front of her face. She was unable to do so. Serenity gave way to self-doubt. Doubt carried her away from the point of light back to darkness, back to her bedroom ...

★　　★　　★

'Shh. It's OK, sweetheart,' said Quinn as Drue's eyelids flickered.

The words were intended to soothe, but the tension in Quinn's voice was apparent. Drue had been asleep, cocooned in her duvet on the window sill, but, as her father scooped her up, bedding and all, in his arms, her dream faded away and she opened her eyes. Quickly and quietly, he carried her across the darkened room, out on to the equally dark landing and down the stairs to the hall.

'Where are we going, Dad?' said Drue drowsily. It had been a long time since she had been carried in her father's arms and it triggered warm memories of summer holidays and long drives through the night, the sound of her parents' voices, a silky lullaby that rocked her to sleep in her car seat.

'Why are all the lights off?'

'I need you to promise me something, Angel,' said Quinn gravely as they reached the living room and he set Drue down gently on the sofa.

'Don't open the hatch for anyone but me. Promise me that whatever happens, whatever you hear, you'll stay hidden until I return.'

As he spoke, Quinn released the false panel that concealed the entrance to the priest-hole. Fear quickened Drue's pulse.

'What's the matter? What's wrong?'

'Trust me, my darling; there isn't time to explain it now.'

'But what . . .?'

'Quickly, child, we don't have much time.'

Drue gathered her duvet round her and padded barefoot over to her old play-cave. Before she climbed inside, her father hugged her, kissed her forehead and held her tight for a moment.

'Now I need you to promise me, sweet girl. You keep this door locked until I come back, OK?'

Drue nodded. 'I promise.'

'It's the most important promise ever. Don't open it for anyone but me.'

'I said I promise.'

'I love you, Angel.'

'Where are you going?'

'I'll be back as quick as I can.'

'Can't I come with you?'

'Not just yet. Later.'

'What if I get scared?'

'You? You're my brave girl.'

'I've got my phone if I need you,' Drue said brightly, trying to take the edge off her own anxiety.

'Don't use it unless you absolutely have to.'

'That's what you always say.'

'But tonight is different . . . Just . . . Only use it if, if . . .' Quinn thought twice about what he intended to say and decided not to say it.

'If what?' said Drue.

'Just not unless you really have to, OK? But you won't have to. I'll be back before you know it. I love you.'

'I love you too, Dad.'

And, with that, Quinn Beltane kissed Drue's cheek and handed her the peg that secured the latch from inside.

'Mind your fingers,' said Quinn as he swung the false panel back into place again. Then he tapped with a knuckle as a signal for Drue to bolt the latch. Drue rapped on the panel in reply. Quinn drew a deep breath. He checked the living-room windows were locked and secure, drew the heavy curtains to block out the moonlight and then moved off into the kitchen.

As he strode to the back door, Quinn noticed Will-C's food and water bowls on the flagstone floor. Drue had boiled up a fresh coley fillet – Will-C's favourite – earlier in the evening, and there it sat waiting for him, completely untouched.

Quinn opened the back door, lifted a large, heavy cardboard box from the worktop and carried it outside. Locking the door behind him, he moved as quickly as he could to the Land Rover Defender, hefted the box inside and slid in behind the wheel.

As he fired up the engine and pulled away, Quinn realized that he hadn't switched on his headlights. Though still a little short of its peak, the full worm moon bathed the landscape with a burnished flaxen aura that was almost bright enough to drive by. Nonetheless, Quinn flicked on the lights, pumped the accelerator, and swung the vehicle out on to the road.

In the trees, in the hedgerows, in the shadows cast by parked cars and wheelie bins and lamp-posts and cottages, bright Animalian eyes followed the red tail lights of the Defender as it ploughed on through the night.

CHAPTER ELEVEN

The Full Worm Moon had never in its history shone with such powerful significance. All around the world the citizens of Animalia had watched and waited patiently to bathe in the glow of the golden orb, before launching the Earth Assembly's deadly coup: a battle plan conducted with astonishing military precision.

The element of surprise played a key part, but also the might and resourcefulness of the animal coalition was so overwhelming that the human race capitulated, crumbled in its path, faster than even the Animalian War Council had anticipated. In just a few short hours, animalkind had broken the back of humankind's resistance.

The creatures began by targeting all communications, transport and energy-supply systems simultaneously; this initial strike was designed to stretch the enemy's resources to breaking point and create panic.

It worked perfectly. With the emergency services swamped and the world's armed forces hampered and diverted by gridlocked road systems, failing rail signals and blank screens in the control towers of the world's airports, the information vacuum caused chaos.

In the global blackout, the leaders of nations were unable to communicate with their military commanders, and the military high command unable to issue orders to their troops. Even the greatest of strategists, with deadly weapons of mass destruction at their disposal, were left chasing shadows. Shadows alive with dangers they were ill-equipped to combat.

Tanks became tombs as snakes and poison dart frogs attacked the crews from within; billion-dollar Stealth fighters were useless in skies choked with millions of birds; nuclear submarines helpless against giant cranch squid and blue whales. Without a clear target, nuclear warheads and chemical weapons provided little or no defence.

Forced to engage in direct physical combat, the humans met a foe more deadly, cunning and versatile than any they had ever faced before. A motivated fighting force of vastly superior numbers, prepared to battle to the death, day or night, on any terrain, in any conditions, in the air, on the land and at sea.

By the time a global state of emergency was declared and talk of a unilateral surrender spread by word of mouth, it was too late. Negotiations were impossible without any means to communicate with the enemy.

Nobody was spared.

For the first time in its brief history, humankind was truly united . . . and then teetering on the brink of extinction.

The fact that the humans would play a key role in their own rapid downfall was something the Animalian High

Command had anticipated. Though they didn't fully comprehend the workings of their technology, the animal Elders were aware that most of the human population had become slavishly reliant on these machines. And this reliance had replaced their natural instincts.

The moment their phones, computers, cars, planes, televisions and internet ceased to function, the humans' fear would begin to feed on itself. And so it proved to be. With nowhere to run, nowhere safe to hide, people soon turned on each other in a last desperate bid for escape, shelter, survival.

There were exceptions to the rule. Devoted mothers and fathers battled gallantly to save their loved ones; many brave souls sacrificed their own lives in an attempt to spare others, and thousands fell protecting their kith and kin. But it was only the indigenous tribes of the world's ancient deserts and rainforests – wise to the rhythms and body language of the creatures they lived alongside – who had anticipated the coming conflagration and reinforced their tribal defences. Only they, and those who were shielded by faithful Truckles, survived the initial attacks in any great numbers, and even their future was far from secure.

In the industrialized world, the outcome was never in doubt. At least when the end came, it was mercifully swift. It had to be. The Elders of the Earth Assembly's War Council surmised, in the early stages of planning strategy, that the moment the humans realized their species was doomed, they might in desperation use their rudimentary grasp of the elements – their dabbling with the fabric of the universe – and in so doing trigger a global nuclear holocaust. That had to be avoided at all costs.

Unlike their adversary, the majority of Animalians had only ever taken a life to sate their hunger and feed their offspring. They didn't kill for sport, or pleasure, and it gave few of them any satisfaction to do so; they were therefore keen to be done with the cull as quickly as possible.

Again there were notable exceptions. Those animals tasked with storming research laboratories and factory farms and slaughterhouses were confronted with scenes of humiliation and torture so terrible that the images would live with them forever, and they wasted no time in wreaking a terrible revenge on those responsible.

And so it was, with meticulous planning and after centuries of subjugation, of being hunted and butchered and enslaved, of observing their most feared adversary at close quarters, that the Animalians scored a critical, decisive victory.

Tooth, talon, claw and animal cunning had been instrumental in delivering it, but, in truth, as every Animalian knew, it was the human race's own arrogance and ignorance, its lack of true understanding about the rhythms of the Earth's fragile ecosystem, that had signed its death warrant.

Only two things had been underestimated in what was otherwise – from a cold, hard, military perspective – a faultless campaign. The first was the depth of loyalty of the Truckles, from whose ranks the Domesticated Animal Resistance would emerge. And the second, which would have an even more profound impact on the future of the planet, was the nature of Nature itself.

CHAPTER TWELVE

The distant clamour of battle from the surrounding hills and villages was carried on the wind through the broken windows of the Beltanes' cottage. The sound that really troubled Drue, however, was the one inside her own mind . . . the faint echo of her father's words: *Promise me that whatever happens, whatever you hear, you'll stay hidden until I return.*

Retreating step by anxious step in the kitchen of their ransacked cottage, armed with nothing more than a broom to stave off the terrifying advance of the mink and the rats, Drue would have given anything to be able to turn back the clock and retreat once more into the shadows of the priest-hole.

But there was no going back.

And it was clear from the look in their eyes that the creatures intended to tear her to pieces. Her foot still bled slightly from the cut in her instep, and with each and every footfall Drue left a deep crimson smudge on the quarry tiles.

The mink's eyes never left Drue as he stooped his head

to lap at her spilled blood. A sinister chitter of approval passed between the rats. They could sense Drue's fear and vulnerability; it was time to move in for the kill.

Mind racing, Drue hurled the broom at the advancing rats, snatched two handfuls of spilled flour from the worktop beside her and tossed it into the eyes of the creatures nearest to her. It gave her a few precious seconds to scramble to the stairs.

A rat leapt on to her back and plunged its teeth into her forearm. Drue screamed, but kept moving, racing up the stairs two at a time. She stumbled sideways and crushed the squealing rodent between her shoulder and the masonry. It fell away with a dull thud. Drue scrambled on up the stairs as the rats and the mink gave chase. Scratched and bleeding, she somehow managed to tear herself free of her attackers before falling through the open door of her bedroom. Rolling on to her back, she rammed the door shut with her feet just in time.

Tears streamed down her cheeks as she spun round and pressed her weight against the door to keep it shut. She could hear the rodents shrieking, claws tearing at the wood panels. Her heart pounded; she was breathing hard. For a moment she allowed herself to hope that she might be safe in the confines of her room. The respite was short-lived.

A stone hit the sash window. Then another, and another. Carrion crows had begun a relentless aerial bombardment.

The wardrobe. Block the window with the wardrobe ...

Just as the idea sprang into Drue's mind, a fist-sized hunk of flint burst through a glass pane, exploding into the room in a shower of jagged shards.

Drue screamed.

A crow swooped in and flapped wildly round the ceiling before diving at Drue with talons raised.

Drue dropped to the floor and scuttled beneath her bed.

The crow followed. Drue grabbed at whatever came to hand – a shoe, a CD case, a ring binder of school homework – and hurled them at the bird. Still it came, its beak jabbing her flesh as she tried to wriggle away.

Spilling out from under the other side of the bed, Drue came face to face with a second crow who was perched on the mattress above her. As it thrust its beak at her eyes, she ducked, lunged for the hockey stick by her bedside table and brought the staff down hard on the creature. It didn't move again.

The first crow took to the air once more, a frenzy of black feathers. As it traced wild loops round the confined space, it sent the central pendant light spinning. Drue waved the hockey stick above her head to keep the bird at bay.

Splinters fell from the door as the rats began to gnaw their way through.

Drue thrust her hand into her pyjama pocket. Her mobile!

Still thrashing blindly with the stick, she flipped open the phone and stabbed the buttons. No signal.

'No!' she screamed in alarm.

The crow tore at her again. Another bird flew into the room. And another.

Drue triggered the phone's camera flash to momentarily blind the birds. She dashed to the window. Outside, the wisteria-clad walls were thick with creatures scaling the tendrils: hundreds of bright, beady eyes glinting in the moonlight as they climbed up towards her.

Stashing her phone in a pocket, Drue used the hockey stick to bash out the remaining daggers of broken glass, clambered through the broken window and out on to the broad sill.

A rat sprang on to her. Drue managed to shake it off and saw it plunge to its death on the garden path far below.

A bat joined the fray, its fleshy wings beating against her face.

Drue swung at it with the hockey stick, which flew from her grasp and disappeared into the shadows.

With violence closing in on her from every direction, she leapt in desperation for the apple tree. The top branches snapped on impact as she tumbled through the leafy canopy. Down she fell, her body battered and bruised by the branches that thrashed past her.

Drue's rapid descent ended abruptly as she crashed into an enormous branch. The collision punched the air from her lungs and she felt a searing pain shoot through her side. *Had she broken a rib?* She couldn't tell. And there wasn't time to dwell on it. She was still some distance from the ground, four metres or so, and already the rats were surging up the trunk.

A brace of bats dropped from the sky. Drue anchored herself to the tree with one arm and tried to fend them off with the other. One of the creatures became entangled in her loose hair, and she shrieked and clawed it away with both hands.

She slipped and was suddenly dangling precariously

upside down, her right foot, snagged in the crook of a forked branch, the only thing preventing her from falling.

The bats were now joined by the carrion crows, who resumed their brutal assault. Drue fumbled for her mobile again, but it slipped from her grasp and tumbled to the grass below. Defenceless, Drue squirmed and twisted and screamed for help as the rats scurried ever closer.

Even if she had seen the bloodhound bound into the garden, Drue would not have read the terror in his eyes. Scattering everything in his path as he sprinted through the shadows towards the apple tree, he saw the child slip from the tree and plunge towards certain death.

Drue's shrill scream sliced through the night.

Then, just seconds before her body struck the ground . . . a giant white-tailed eagle plucked Drue from the air and carried her skyward. Muscular tendons flexed tight, talons broader than human hands, and strong enough to crush bone, locked firm round her upper arms. Higher and higher it soared, leaving the furious mink and snarling rats and bats in its wake.

First the apple tree shrank into the distance, then the cottage, then the neighbourhood, then the whole village, as the eagle carried Drue ever upward, spiralling on through the clouds. Soon all she could make out below was the patchwork of moonlit fields and forests, and unchecked fires blazing right across the county.

She felt her eyelids grow heavy. All the fight had been beaten out of her. She ached from bruised head to throbbing ribs, to limp, blood-streaked feet. It crossed her mind that the giant bird of prey might have plucked her from the jaws of death simply to carry her back to his nest for a brood of eaglets to feast on. Even if it had, gliding on the thermals eight thousand feet from the ground, there was nothing she could do about it, and, despite her best efforts to remain alert, she drifted into unconsciousness.

With Drue hanging limply beneath him, the white-tailed eagle wasn't hard to spot against the full moon, nor difficult – or dangerous – to follow. The crows realized this and, gathering reinforcements from the local flocks of jackdaws and ravens, they regrouped to hunt it down.

Unable to do battle without dropping his catch, the giant eagle had to rely on his stamina and experience to outmanoeuvre them. Pushing out over the English Channel, he stretched his massive wings and beat them for all he was worth. In the distance, a bank of dense cloud spread from sea level to almost thirty thousand feet. He knew it offered a good place to hide if he could reach it.

As if from nowhere, a lone snipe dropped out of the sky like an arrow, emitting a spine-chilling *kreeeeech!* The eagle spotted him and banked into the heavy crosswind to avoid being impaled on the snipe's long rapier bill. Momentum carried the overexcited wading bird into the path of the winged posse who were forced to break formation. Apologizing left and right, the snipe attempted to ingratiate himself with the disgruntled flock.

'Almost 'ad him. We can still catch him.'

The distraction was just enough to allow the eagle to pull away, and before the posse could close the distance he and Drue were enveloped in a thick, swirling mist.

By the time they broke once more into the open starlit

sky, the pursuing pack had been reduced to a squabbling rabble chasing their tails in the cloud bank far below.

The eagle breathed a little easier, but he still had a distance to travel, and he was beginning to feel the effects of checking Drue's fall. Every muscle, every sinew, every tendon had been stretched to its limit. And, although he continued to hold her fast with his powerful talons, he felt himself tiring. It was therefore with a sense of great relief that he spotted the English coastline once more.

Adjusting his bearings, he began a gentle descent. Tired as he was, he pushed all thoughts of rest to the back of his mind. There might yet be dangers ahead, and he needed to stay sharp, focused. Not that the approaching landmass was unfamiliar; he didn't need a map or a compass to recognize it – like all Animalians, he could read the biomagnetic energy rising from it like humans read a road sign – he just prayed that he had sufficient strength left to cover the remaining expanse of dark ocean before losing his grip on his precious cargo.

PART II
CLOUD-WATER FIRE

CHAPTER THIRTEEN

Petroleum. Drue had always disliked the acrid smell of it, having grown up with the baked-popcorn aroma of the homemade bio-diesel her father ran his Defender on, so the fumes that acted like a smelling salt to revive her were both unpleasant and unsettling.

Where am I?

Drue opened her eyes and took a moment to get her bearings.

Did I die? she thought. *Is this what life after death looks like?* She was in an unfamiliar sleeping bag, rocking gently from side to side in an unfamiliar hammock, which was strung across the inside of an unfamiliar furniture-removal van.

Drue cast her eyes over the cavernous rusting hulk of the vehicle. Enough light penetrated the interior to enable tall yellow grass to have grown up through a gaping hole in a wheel arch, so, as her pupils adjusted, Drue was able to glean a fair amount from where she lay.

An oil-spattered canvas tarpaulin was draped over a stack of crates and boxes between Drue and what would once have been the driver's cab. One of the rear doors was missing – the panel it had hung from was badly buckled and twisted – and another grubby tarp had been strung up with ties to replace it.

Beyond was daylight, a long, vertical strip of it visible between the tarp and the remaining door. *What had happened to the night? What happened during the night?*

The last that Drue could remember was falling from the apple tree in her garden. Somewhere in the fog of her mind she had a vague recollection, of sprouting wings and soaring like a bird. *But that wasn't possible, was it?* With all that had taken place, Drue was no longer sure that she had such a firm grip on what was real and what was not.

Maybe I did die. Maybe I'm an angel, she thought as she craned her neck and reached behind to feel her shoulder blades in search of wings. There were none.

Drue stretched, swept her dishevelled hair from her face and considered her surroundings again. A second hammock had been stowed and hung from a rack attached to the side of the vehicle.

Beneath it, a makeshift settee had been constructed from an old bench bus seat. Though well-worn and scarred with black patches of what had once been chewing gum, Drue recognized the green and yellow tartan fabric. It matched that of the South Downs bus that she had often used to get from the village into Chichester for shopping and the cinema, and the Monday-night meetings of the local youth theatre.

Maybe I'm still near home, she thought. The possibility seemed comforting.

Wherever she was, she ached all over.

Drue's arms and legs and face boasted a latticework of cuts and scratches and threads of dried blood. She unzipped the sleeping bag and discovered that her right leg was visible through a gash in her pyjamas. Her shin was badly grazed and sporting a huge yellow bruise, though someone had cleaned it and applied a dressing and sticking plaster over the wound. Drue dabbed at the gauze and raised her finger to her nose.

Tea tree oil. The pungent scent of the natural antiseptic was unmistakable. And it immediately brought to mind one person.

'Dad,' said Drue softly.

She wriggled out of the sleeping bag, swung her legs over the side of the hammock and put weight on her feet to see if she could stand. It hurt more than a little, but she was determined to investigate further.

Picking her way to the rear of the van with great caution, Drue peeked outside and surveyed her surroundings. The wide, clear blue sky was streaked with mares' tail clouds, but beneath it all Drue could see in every direction was the desolate landscape of a breaker's yard. A graveyard of car parts and mangled vehicle shells, many of which had been crushed flat and stacked like slices of a giant metal loaf. A tangle of soot-blackened exhaust pipes and piles of car batteries formed the foothills to an ugly, towering mountain range of bald used tyres.

Still barefoot, Drue picked her way between dirty puddles. She noticed that they shimmered with syrupy rainbow colours – a cocktail of gearbox oil, brake fluid and antifreeze swimming on the surface.

A painted pig, clad in a chequered waistcoat and cap, grinned at Drue with a frozen smile from the shell of a former butcher's van. She passed a milk float that still had rows of plastic crates filled with empty glass bottles in the rear, and the caterpillar tracks of an earth mover, its mechanical shovel slumped on the ground in front of it like a toothless, gaping jaw.

Drue turned a circle. Raised a hand to shield her eyes from the sun.

'Dad!' she hollered. 'Daaaaaad!'

Her voice echoed round the scrap-metal canyon.

'*Daaad . . . Daaad . . . Daaad . . .*'

Drue saw the shadow on the ground before she saw the bird. The dark outline of one of nature's most deadly raptors engulfed her. For a moment the peregrine falcon remained hovering, silhouetted against the sun, then it swept back its wings and plummeted down from the sky at phenomenal speed, aiming straight at Drue.

Drue tried to run for cover . . . tripped on a half-buried engine block, lost her footing and hit the ground, hard.

Gripped with panic, she rolled on to her back, dug in her heels and began to scoop up whatever she could reach – clumps of earth, stones, a windscreen-wiper blade – which she hurled at the onrushing bird. Her efforts were futile. In an instant, it was upon her. And then, in the blink of an eye, in one graceful, fluid motion, it transformed into . . . Quinn Beltane!

One second the falcon was diving towards Drue, deadly talons outstretched. The next her father was at her side, hand clamped over her mouth to silence her scream before it left her throat.

Quinn hauled Drue from the ground and ran with her to the nearest shelter – a cement mixer that lay on its side like a giant fossilized prehistoric egg. Father and daughter tumbled as one into the gaping mouth of the big mixing drum.

Quinn pressed a finger to his lips as a signal to Drue to stay quiet, but he kept his other hand clamped over her mouth nonetheless. He raised his head a little to peer up over the cement-caked rim of the rusty bowl.

A moment passed before Quinn motioned with his eyes for Drue to follow suit. She gazed up and saw a large flock of kittiwake seagulls passing overhead.

Several dropped out of the loose formation and, cawing, turned lazy circles over the tyre mountain range. They glided close enough for Drue to see the distinctive black wingtips and V-shape on the upper wings of the younger birds' grey-and-white plumage.

It was not until the kittiwakes had drifted away and out of sight over the mangled horizon that Quinn finally released his hand from Drue's mouth.

Instantly, she squirmed out of the drum and launched a verbal tirade.

'Get away from me!'

'Drue . . .'

'No. Get away. You're not my dad! Where is he? What have you done with him!'

'Quiet!' ordered Quinn, scanning the sky. 'You'll bring the gulls back.'

'I don't care!' cried Drue. 'Who are you? What are you?'

Quinn tried to close the gap between them.

'Drue, trust me . . .'

Drue kept her distance. 'No. I saw you. You . . . you came out of the sky . . .'

'Drue . . .'

'Where's my dad?'

'Listen to me!'

'Get away! Get away!'

'Look, I know it's scary . . .' Again Quinn stepped towards Drue with an outstretched hand.

Drue picked up a discarded length of exhaust pipe and swung it at him with menace.

'Stay away from me!'

'You're frightened . . .'

'Not of you!' yelled Drue.

'Angel, please . . .'

'Don't call me that. You don't know me! You don't know anything about me!'

Quinn's shoulders sagged. He was physically and mentally exhausted. He backed away, retreating into the shadow of a burnt-out transporter.

'OK, look. Just . . . just don't stay out in the open. Please. There are patrols . . .'

'Patrols? What patrols?'

'You saw the gulls. There are terns in the area. Even some razorbills. We're very close to the coast. How's your leg?'

'Who are you? Where am I?'

'I'll tell you. I'll tell you everything. But not out here. Inside.'

'No!' Drue swung at him with the metal pipe.

'Drue, put that down before you hurt yourself.'

'Stay away!'

Drue stood firm. She was petrified, more frightened than she had ever been in her entire life – compared to this even the battle with the mink and rats seemed tame. Still, her defiant streak shone through. And she really was good and ready for a fight. Quinn measured her with a glance and nodded his approval.

'You'll need to be strong if you're to survive this. We both will.'

And, with that, Quinn turned and, using the valleys of wrecked vehicles for cover, he began to work his way deeper into the heart of the scrapyard. He moved quickly, in short bursts, keeping low to the ground.

With his stubble, dark Latin eyes and unkempt, shoulder-length salt-and-pepper hair, the stooped figure in tan khakis and a corduroy work shirt certainly resembled her father; but, after what Drue had seen, it could be a body-snatching alien from outer space for all she knew. On the other hand, she had just won an argument with him and still felt like she'd lost, and that was just like her dad.

'Why should I trust you?' Drue called after him.

'Because the last time you didn't, it almost cost you your life. And without Will-C, Angel, I'm all you have left.'

And then he was off and running again, towards the hideout, and Drue knew in that instant that, however weird and disturbing the situation, whatever the explanation for the bizarre birdman transmutation, one thing was clear: the figure darting for cover in the shadows of the scrapyard was exactly who he said he was.

He was Quinn Beltane. He was her father.

CHAPTER FOURTEEN

Drue returned to the van to find her father busy at work inside. He had stripped the tarpaulin from the crates to reveal a supply of tinned foods and a stack of plastic twenty-five-litre jerrycans filled with water. When he had finished appraising the inventory, he tugged some equipment from a backpack and set about constructing a small flat-packed solar oven – a simple construction of foam sheets laminated with reflective foil, that slotted together to form a box that trapped sunlight.

Drue set down her pipe staff as she climbed back into the vehicle. Quinn appraised the makeshift oven. It would do in the circumstances.

'I thought you didn't agree with water in plastic bottles,' said Drue, waving a finger at the jerrycans. 'Not good for the planet.'

The comment was meant to break the ice in a light-hearted way, but, as Drue spoke, her lips began to tremble and the feisty, street-smart urchin dissolved into a frightened little girl.

Quinn cradled Drue in his arms as she sobbed.

'I want to go home. I just want to go home!'

'Shhhhh. Sweet girl.'

'What are you?! What's happened? I don't understand. I don't. The whole world can't just . . . change . . . like . . . like clicking channels on TV. It can't. It just can't! I want to go home. I want to be with Will-C.'

'I know, my angel.'

'Tell me! Dad! Tell me it's all going to be OK.'

Though the narrow escape had taken its toll on his daughter, for now at least she was safe. Quinn didn't need reminding of how close he had come to losing her, and as he held Drue his eyes welled up too.

'I love you, Angel. I . . . it's . . . It's just . . . I'm here, OK.'

Frightened, confused, aching, Drue clung tight to her father and gave way to her tears.

*   *   *

Later, as Drue kept an eye on a simmering pan of brown rice her father had brewed up on the solar cooker, and Quinn sat peeling carrots and dicing courgettes to add to the pot, he began the daunting task of preparing his daughter for a new life in a new world. Ever pragmatic, he started with the essentials.

He explained that the animal kingdom was waging war on humans. Drue had had a taste of that first-hand, of course, but she had hoped – prayed – that the events of the previous night were a freak of nature, a crazy, isolated incident that could be explained away as some kind of weird accident. But Quinn's words suggested otherwise.

'So is it like the elephants I read about in Africa,' asked

Drue, 'trampling villages because people were building on their breeding grounds and taking their food away?'

'Something like that,' answered Quinn. 'Only this is on a far bigger scale.'

'Maybe they'll stop if the hunters and the people who cut down forests and that would leave them alone?'

'It seems it's too late for that, Angel. It's not just one species: the entire animal kingdom is working together, right across the county, possibly the whole country.'

'Right around the whole world?' asked Drue, incredulous.

'Maybe so,' said Quinn cautiously, trying to protect his daughter from the stark truth as best he could.

'But not pets. Not . . . Will-C?'

'No, not the likes of Will-C. There'll be lots of animals who'll remain loyal to their adopted human families.'

'And what will happen to them?'

'They'll do as best they can, I suppose.' Then quickly, 'How's that rice coming along?'

Quinn scooped the diced vegetables into a steamer and fitted it over the pot of rice.

'Don't change the subject.'

'A couple of minutes and it'll be done. Hungry?'

'Dad . . . you can't just make out like everything is . . . is . . . You turned into a freakin' bird!'

'A falcon. And don't say *freakin'*!'

'Dad! How did you . . .? That's . . . that's mental. Are you, you know, like the X-Men or Spider-Man or something; like a mutant with magical superpowers?'

'No, my darling. No magic. No superpowers. I'm a Nsray Adept.'

'A what?'

'A Nsray. It's the name of a people, a tribe if you like; the word derives from an ancient language called Aramaic. *Nazuraya* means to be skilled in secret knowledge . . .'

'Boring!'

'OK, OK. We have this ability . . ."

"Yes."

"Locked in the DNA of our people is . . . the power to . . . adopt animal form."

"Then we're not from here?"

"Here? Sussex you mean? Well, our ancient ancestors came from Mesopotamia, a settlement by the Black Sea.'

'That's a sea like a lake.'

'That's right.'

'We did a thing on it at school.'

'Oh. Good. Then they did teach you something besides gossiping on the *interweb*.'

'The *interweb*? Dad, you are so *old*.'

'Old and hungry. And a hungry Beltane . . .'

'. . . is not something to mess with.'

'Exactly. So let's eat. Then I'll tell you. I'll tell you everything.'

Drue spooned the steaming rice and vegetables on to metal platters and handed one to her dad, who in turn poured her a large beaker of cool water from a jerrycan. Then, with a theatrical flourish, as if it were a priceless, magical elixir, Quinn produced a small bottle of soy sauce to garnish the meal.

As they ate, slowly, thoughtfully, Quinn outlined his reason for choosing the scrapyard as a temporary 'safe house': the toxins from the adjacent landfill site had contaminated the ground so badly that most animals, even the scavengers, avoided the place. And now that there were easy pickings to be had in every village, town and city in the county, it would be some time before even the rats would return.

Quinn listed their tinned food supplies (enough to last several months if they planned their meals carefully), which were to be supplemented with fresh fruit, roots and wild herbs, gathered during daily trips to the woodland beyond the perimeter fence.

In addition to the basic camping equipment they had to hand – cooking utensils, bedding, a Swiss army knife – Quinn had also constructed a makeshift rainwater shower and latrine – to be used sparingly under cover of darkness – a short distance from their main hideout.

Quinn explained that he was also scouting for a back-up safe house, in case the one they were using was ever discovered, and he emphasized that although they could make use of solar power for heating water and cooking, Drue was never to light a fire. Ever. Smoke would definitely draw attention to their position for miles around.

Finally, Drue could stand it no more and she returned to the burning question.

'Tell me again about the Nus ... Naz ... the freaky-becoming-a-falcon thing.'

'The *Nsray*.'

'Nsray. OK. Yeah. Sounds kinda cool. Like something from my manga comics.'

Quinn shook his head dismissively.

'*Doesn't matter what you're reading, as long as you're reading,*' said Drue, mimicking her father's voice.

Quinn chuckled, finished the last scraps on his plate and looked at his daughter's face, soft and innocent despite the cuts and bruises. Her clear blue-green eyes were pools of wonder.

'So,' said Drue, 'can you only change into one thing or all different kinds?'

'Any animal.'

'Cool! Go on then, turn into a . . . a . . . oh . . . I know . . . a velociraptor!'

'Any *living* animal.'

'A Bengal tiger then.'

'And it's not a party trick. Like I said, there's no magic. No superpowers. It's just . . . a skill. A gift . . . a, yes . . . a gift. One to be protected and respected.'

'Could we maybe be a bit more specific?'

'Hmmm?'

'Context . . . you know . . . how does it work? What's it feel like?'

'You were supposed . . .'

'To be *listening* not *talking* . . . and I am. But still . . .'

'Just like your . . .'

'Mum.'

'You are so like her in so many ways.'

Quinn studied his daughter's face.

'OK,' he continued. 'A long time ago . . . our people were driven out of their homeland by the Hittites. They had one of the most powerful empires in the world, even more powerful than the Ancient Egyptians, and they were constantly at war over territory.'

'But couldn't the Nus . . . Nsu . . .'

'Nsray. *Nass-ray.*'

'Couldn't they fight back?'

'In self-defence, yes. They were formidable warriors. But given a choice the Nsray must always follow the path of non-violence.'

'What about fighting to protect their homes?'

'You know what a nomad is?'

'Someone who doesn't live in one place. Like in the Sahara Desert, where they move in search of water.'

'Exactly. Well, the Nsray had been nomads in the past. They became nomads once more. It wasn't for nothing that they were known as the Cloud-Water People: they drifted like clouds, flowed like water.'

'So where did they go?'

'They were driven further and further west until they reached Jutland – what we now think of as Denmark and the northern part of Germany.'

'And they were allowed to stay?'

'The Jutes were certainly a more peaceable people, and in time the Nsray forged close bonds with them. There were even marriages between the clans. Didn't put paid to their wanderlust though. Many migrated further still, their long-boats carrying them to France, Spain, North Africa and eventually here to England.'

Drue pictured the Nsray nomads catching sight of the Sussex coast for the very first time. Excited children with bright eyes and wild, salt-licked hair swarming the prows of the longboats. Sails whipping in the wind. Oars crashing through rolling waves as they approached the great chalk cliffs. Even the young faces lean and tanned like leather from a life lived outdoors.

'But what about . . . what about the . . .' Drue struggled to find the appropriate word, '. . . the *changing*?'

'Becoming the falcon, you mean?'

Drue nodded.

'A useful form to adopt for reconnaissance work. Sharp eyes.'

That didn't answer Drue's question as Quinn knew very well.

'You remember the eagle that carried you here?'

'That was . . . you?'

'And the bloodhound.'

'The one in the garden!' exclaimed Drue.

'The one you chased away.'

Drue blushed at the thought.

'*Shape-shifting*,' said Quinn.

'But how? How do you do it?'

'Well, it's a . . . well, an ancient art. A state of mind.'

'Then are you . . . you know . . . normal?' said Drue timidly.

'I don't know about normal,' replied Quinn with a smile, 'but human. Yes, I'm flesh and blood all right. Look here . . .'

He rolled up a sleeve to reveal a series of bite marks and lacerations inflicted during his battle with the mink and the rats at the Weoh Oak.

'You see. Cut us and we bleed, but, well, the Nsray . . . It's really hard to explain in simple terms.'

'I'm not stupid,' replied Drue, bristling with indignation.

Quinn smiled. 'No, of course not; what I mean is . . .

hmmm. There are different levels of reality. Of existence. The way we perceive things in the world and the way they really are. There's the life we live inside our skin and then there's the life we live outside it. And the Nsray are able to train their minds to cross that divide. To access . . . to influence the living energy that's all around us . . . hmmm.'

Drue's expression said she was none the wiser.

'OK, look,' said Quinn, reaching for the fork he'd eaten with. He tapped it on the side of the plate Drue still had in her lap.

'Sounds pretty solid, doesn't it?'

Drue nodded.

'Here take it. Have a go.'

It seemed silly, but Drue gingerly tapped the fork on the plate all the same.

'So there you have two solid objects, yes? The plate and the fork,' said Quinn.

'Uh-huh.'

'Only they're not.'

'Not what?' said Drue puzzled.

'Solid. That's the thing. It's just a matter of perception. That's how we think of them. Just like these seats,' said Quinn, becoming more animated, 'and this box and this van, and this hand.'

He held up his right hand and spread his fingers in front of Drue's eyes before getting to his feet.

'They're not solid at all. Even scientists eventually got around to figuring out that the atom, which for a long, long time was the smallest particle known to the greatest minds in physics . . .'

'Like Einstein,' Drue chipped in to indicate that she was keeping up.

'. . . the particle which is the building block for everything we see around us – you, me, the planet, that fork – isn't actually *solid*. Even the subatomic particles, the quarks and leptons, are just tiny pulsating nuggets of living energy. They're like . . . like . . . *ideas*. More like thoughts than things.'

'Thoughts?'

'Well, look how powerful the imagination can be. Every great adventure, every great invention, however crazy or impossible they seemed at the time, began as an idea in someone's mind.'

'I suppose.'

'Well, once you know that and . . . and can begin to look, to think, beyond the *surface* of things . . . then, and *only then*, can you truly *see*. And for the Nsray who found the key to that gift many centuries ago, it marked the beginning of a journey of discovery which continues to this day. It's not magic. It's not superpowers. It's simply harnessing the true potential of the human mind which, sadly, most people never get to do.'

'But if this fork isn't real . . .' said Drue.

'I didn't say it wasn't real.'

'OK . . . if it's not solid.'

'Better.'

'Then why does it hurt if I jab my hand with it?'

'Good question. What's it made of?'

'Metal.'

Quinn frowned, disappointed.

'Oh . . . Atoms . . . Quarks!'

'Right. And what are you made of?'

'Quarks.'

'And they are?'

'Energy!' said Drue brightly as if she suddenly grasped the concept. But then she realized that she hadn't at all.

'So when energy bumps into other energy . . . but . . . that doesn't make sense. Energy bumps into energy when I pick up the plate as well, or pull on my socks, or brush my teeth, but that doesn't hurt. I don't get it.'

'Good. You shouldn't. Not yet.'

'But . . . well, how come you never told me about any of this before?'

'It wasn't the time. You weren't ready.'

'But that's like a lie.'

'What is?'

'Keeping something as important as that a big secret.'

'Would you rather I'd told you our ancestors were feared and persecuted and burned at the stake by the weak-minded and superstitious, who believed them to be witches dabbling in black magic? Or that the inscription in our priest-hole wasn't carved by a renegade clergyman at all, but by a Nsray Adept who was eventually hunted down and shot through the heart by a terrified mob who believed him to be a werewolf? I planned to tell you everything, my darling, when you came of age.'

'Did . . . Mum know?'

'Yes. Yes, she knew.'

'And was she one of the . . . Cloud-Water People?'

'No. She wasn't.'

Drue tried to reel in her thoughts, which were swimming in a dozen different directions.

'This is mega-intense,' she said, sounding like a character from one of her comic books.

'In a way it couldn't be simpler, it's just . . . perception. Transforming wood into fire and smoke or water into ice must have seemed like magic to someone seeing it for the first time, but it wasn't. Anyway, that's enough for now. We have company.'

Drue's eyes flashed to the rear of the van and the band of daylight which framed the tarpaulin curtain. Outside, the snipe – the wading bird with the rapier-like bill almost half the length of its body – was wheeling back and forth.

Drue leapt to her feet and braced herself, the fork clutched in her tight fist like a dagger.

Quinn quickly moved over to her and gently cupped his hand round her wrist.

'It's OK, Angel. That's Gallinago. He's a friend.'

Drue looked on as her father strode to the back of the van, swept aside the tarp, stepped off the tailgate and in the blink of an eye . . . took to the air as the falcon once more.

Drue watched from the safety of the hideout as the snipe and the falcon circled one another, then settled on the roof of an adjacent lorry together.

This is way beyond weird, thought Drue. But, once she had got over the initial shock, her father's ability to shape-shift didn't seem all that surprising, the result perhaps of a childhood steeped in tales of magic and wonder: *Alice in Wonderland, The Lion, the Witch and the Wardrobe, Jonathan Livingston Seagull.*

Maybe that's why I was different from everyone else at school, she thought. *It wasn't just a vivid imagination like the teachers said; it was more than that. It was in my blood. In my genes.*

Drue studied the birds, and wondered what it felt like to have a real conversation with an animal. *What did their language sound like when you knew what they were saying? What would Will-C's voice sound like?*

Will-C. *Where was he? Why did he disappear when he did? Had he known what was going to happen, but didn't tell me?*

The thought played on Drue's mind.

Without Will-C, I'm all you've got, her dad had said. Without Will-C. It sounded as though her father knew something terrible had happened to him and, though part of her didn't want to know the truth, she planned to ask him about it the minute he returned.

Suddenly Drue felt vulnerable, foolish even, to still be dressed in her ragged pyjamas, and she was pleased to find that her dad had thought to throw a change of clothes in with the provisions.

CHAPTER FIFTEEN

Will-C and Yoshi emerged from the ancient yew forest, crossed Oakwood Lane and picked their way past the sawmill as they headed back to Kingley Burh village.

They still carried the scars of their ordeal and, once they were out in the open, they advanced with great caution. Each scanned the terrain left and right and above for Natterjack's minions and constantly checked the path ahead, along with their flanks, for signs of another ambush.

Sunlight bathed the sawmill's timber work sheds and the giant stacks of coppiced ash and beech in a golden hue; but, despite the hour, the place was as quiet as a grave. The fork-lift trucks stood idle in the yard. The bandsaws and chain-saws and machine tools that ordinarily filled the air with industrial song, as reliable and familiar to the cats as a dawn chorus, were eerily silent.

Remnants of denim and dyed cotton from clothes torn to shreds were snagged in the hedgerows and fluttered in the breeze. Leather gloves and work boots lay abandoned.

Skulls and bones, picked clean by scavengers, littered the dirt track that circled the sheds.

Will-C and Yoshi exchanged a look and quickly moved on.

As the road forked at the entrance to Callow's Farm, the feline friends knew it was time to part company. Both were desperate to learn the fate of their human companions, and neither wished to delay the moment any longer than they had to.

'You're sure you won't wait? Then I'll go with you,' said Will-C.

'No, it's OK,' replied Yoshi. Will-C felt guilty; Yoshi had endangered his own life to try to help him.

'Then I'll come with you first,' said Will-C. And, difficult as it was to say, he meant it.

'No, really. It's OK – you go and find Drue.'

'Are you sure?'

'Sure,' said Yoshi. Then quickly, 'I'm scared.'

'Me too,' admitted Will-C.

'But maybe it'll be all right.'

'Maybe so,' replied Will-C, doing his best to lace the words with a conviction he didn't feel.

'I'm sorry I wasn't more help.'

'You came after me; that took great courage.'

'It didn't feel that way.'

'You're much braver than you realize, Yow. And you're an example to us all.'

Will-C gently butted his friend's head with his own – a gesture that spoke volumes, of how their shared experience had deepened their bond – and then he turned and loped away to complete the journey home.

A few minutes later, Will-C was once again back on his own patch, negotiating the weathered flagstone path that led to the back door of the Beltanes' cottage. The sight of the curtains billowing through Drue's shattered bedroom window stopped him in his tracks. The ransacked interior of the cottage would do the same. But finding Drue's mobile phone beneath the apple tree was the point at which Will-C felt his worst fears had been confirmed.

He knew that whatever it was, Drue always carried the thing with her, and talked to it when it chirped, and treasured it. He remembered her nuzzling him, pressing her cheek against his as she turned its single glazed fish eye on them, and how she had laughed when it flashed and their faces had appeared inside it, like a reflection on a frozen lake.

Now it lay scuffed and broken, discarded on the ground beneath the very branch where they had first met all those years ago.

Remorse. An ache like a hunger that could never be fed. He had failed her. Lost her. And it seemed that life would never be the same again.

And of course it wouldn't. Once again Will-C could hear an echo of his late father's voice carried on the breeze that swept the Beltanes' garden:

Life is change.

CHAPTER SIXTEEN

Prior to the search for Will-C, it had been many years since Quinn Beltane had exercised his shape-shifting ability and it required his full concentration to be able to hold form and converse with the snipe, particularly as Gallinago's distinctive dialect was something akin to the sound of a broad Irish brogue to an English ear.

For the most part he was content to just listen as Gallinago shared what news he had gathered on the wing. It confirmed what Quinn had learned earlier from the Truckles imprisoned with Will-C, and it painted an even more vivid and distressing picture of the Earth Assembly's triumphant campaign.

Out of respect for his friend, Gallinago kept the gory details to an absolute minimum, and he was quick to share word of the burgeoning resistance movement: a disparate but bravely committed network of Truckles who had taken it upon themselves to provide safe havens for any humans who had survived the cull.

Quinn was cheered to learn that whether through circumstance, sheer good luck or dint of birth – the latter including the resourceful Ngadjonji Aborigines in Australia, the Kalahari Saasi and the Nicobarese in the Andaman Islands – there were a few other survivors. One thing was clear, however: industrialized Man's reign as the alpha species, the dominant force in world affairs, was over.

Quinn absorbed the news, good and bad, with the same measured response. Not because he was especially brave or lacked empathy – the weight of the loss of friends and neighbours, and the innocent millions who had perished along with the guilty, was almost too much to bear – but the truth is that the war hadn't entirely surprised him.

The timing and the scale of the tragedy, yes, but not the shift in the balance of power. That was woven into the fabric of Nsray lore: *All things are one and ever-changing.* Because of this, Quinn berated himself for not having prepared for the inevitable conflict sooner. He had let his guard slip, had spent too little time in the company of his own kind.

So vivid were the pictures in his mind that Quinn's concentration had momentarily drifted, but the first he knew of it was when Gallinago, his dumpy, long-billed companion, let out a fearful *kreech* and took to the sky.

Quinn's falcon-ness had begun to fade, resulting in a creature not quite human, not quite bird, perched alongside the snipe. Quickly resuming his feathered form, Quinn offered an apology and joined Gallinago on the wing, circling high above the breaker's yard.

From here on in Quinn knew he would have to be on his mettle. He would need to spend more time engaged with Animalians, and he suspected he would even need a little help from Mother Nature to see Drue through the journey they had been forced to embark upon.

'I can't thank you enough for all you've done, Gallinago, but I don't know how long we'll be safe here. You should go now. Before the next wave of patrols.'

'Ya saved me life once, remember,' said Gallinago, riding the thermals in a climbing spiral.

'A debt you more than repaid in helping me to escape the ravens and crows. Go home to your family,' said Quinn, mirroring the snipe's flight with a spiral ascent of his own, an aerial double helix reaching up into the heavens.

'Int got no family.'

'Your friends then.'

'I torht you was me friend.'

'Sure and true, which is why I'd rather you left now.'

'Jus' when tings are gittin' interestin'.'

'You're as stubborn as your bill is long.'

'Must be all dat time I spent in the oil slick. You managed to clean it off me fedders, but I think it's clogged me brain. No common sense.'

Quinn banked and wheeled a little closer before responding.

'It'll be dangerous.'

'Then ya have a plan?'

'More . . . an idea than a plan.'

'Which is what?'

'All in good time, my friend.'

'What about ya young'un?'

'She's stronger than she looks.'

'Ya sure about dat?'

Five hundred feet below, Drue poked her head out from the rear of the removal van in search of the birds.

Quinn spotted her in an instant, folded his wings and dived to join her. An exhilarating rush of pure static electricity buffeted his plumage as he picked up speed, a heady reminder of both the liberating power of transmutation and the presence – even in this grim backwater – of the primal elements that would ultimately shape their destiny.

CHAPTER SEVENTEEN

A Shape-shifter. The news reached Natterjack as he lay warming himself on a large slab of granite, at the edge of a grand ornamental pond, in the heart of an enormous glazed butterfly house.

Several panes in the glass roof had been shattered, as had the door of the main entrance, but still the temperature inside the Downs Nature Reserve glasshouse was considerably warmer than outside. Rare and exotic butterflies of all descriptions – glasswings, brimstones, buckeyes, lacewings, natives of all four continents – skittered between the tropical palms, the lavender bushes and the rhododendrons. Frogs, lizards and toads gorged themselves on abundant larvae and moth cocoons, but the pick of the crop, along with the captive living buffet flittering above, was reserved for Natterjack himself.

'Did you hear what I said, Natterjack?' said a brown rat – one of a large pack grouped so tightly that they appeared to form a single multi-headed, multi-tailed, ever-twitching entity. 'A *Shape-shifter*.'

'You're quite sure?' said Natterjack, snatching a beautiful blue morpho from the air with his tongue. He crushed its delicate body in his jaws, swallowed, then licked his bulbous lips, savouring every last morsel.

'No question,' replied the rat.

'At first he was a big dog . . .'

'Very big dog,' added a second rat.

'A bloodhound,' added a raven as he settled in the rafters.

'And then,' said the brown rat, 'when the human child was falling . . .'

'Like a chameleon changing his skin . . .'

'In the blink of an eye . . .'

'Quick as a grass snake . . .'

'Quicker.'

'He became a bird . . .'

'An eagle . . .'

'Wings as wide as this water . . .'

'Wider . . .'

'Talons thick as tree roots . . .'

'Thicker.'

'Snatched her right out of the air . . .'

'Right at the point of *death* . . .'

A carp surfaced in the pond close by, but then darted away as Faelken glided silently through the open door and swooped low over the water. The imposing bird settled in a tall potted lilac tree.

'A Shape-shifter,' mused Natterjack.

'It's true,' said Faelken. 'The crows and ravens have been talking about nothing else since. They gave chase, but lost it out at sea.'

'A pity you weren't there, Faelken,' grumbled Natterjack as he eyed a trembling chrysalis. A heath fritillary slowly emerged from a pupa, its distinctive dusky orange-and-black wings snapping briskly open and shut, as it adjusted to its new form, its new life.

The notion that Will-C's small human companion had escaped the cull aided and abetted by such a rare and exotic beast added an unexpected frisson to Natterjack's already bloated ambitions.

Enshrined in Animalian mythology, Shape-shifters were regarded as the Holy Grail to the predators of the animal kingdom: as elusive as the Himalayan yeti was to humans. They were the ultimate prey, imbued with extraordinary powers that, legend had it, could be acquired by any hunter skilled and courageous enough to capture the Shape-shifter and eat its heart.

'And you say this human, this young female that it saved, she lived with the three-legged Truckle?'

'The black cat without the . . . with the missing . . . aye,' said the brown rat.

'That's right,' added the raven.

The toad finally shifted his ample girth and waddled into the water.

'Shall we send out a hunting party?' asked the brown rat.

'For the Shape-shifter? No. You'll never find it. They're far too devious.'

'You're just going to let it get away?' said the brown rat scathingly.

'Who said anything about letting it get away?' said Natterjack.

'Then what do we do?' piped up another of the restless pack.

'Find the three-legged Truckle. If he's still alive, and his human companion is still alive, they'll be looking for one another. We find one, we'll find the other.'

'And then?' said the brown rat.

Oblivious to the danger, the heath fritillary lifted off for its maiden flight. Natterjack's whiplash tongue ensnared it in a flash.

'Then,' said Natterjack, finishing his snack, 'the Shapeshifter will come looking for us.'

CHAPTER EIGHTEEN

The microclimate of Sussex – odd weather, and weather often at odds with that forecast for the rest of the country – was an idiosyncrasy, a quirk that Quinn had always appreciated. Fine days suddenly awash with showers; storms whipping up out of blue skies in a matter of hours as they can do in the Mediterranean; hailstones falling in May. It kept one sharp. In touch with Mother Nature. But even so, never had he welcomed the promise of rain with such a sense of relief.

The sky above the breaker's yard was a stew of grey clouds rolling in off the Channel. The additional cover of the rising wind – which would help to diffuse and disperse scents – would work in the Beltanes' favour, but it was the promise of cleansing, the washing away of the physical scars of the carnage, that Quinn longed for. At some point his daughter would have to venture back out into that world – at least that's what he prayed for – and when she did so he wanted it to be a place of hope rather than despair; if not an entirely blank canvas, then at least one on which she would be able to paint her own future.

Not that the future was uppermost in Drue's mind. She was still clinging on to the past. As Quinn explained the events that had taken place at the Weoh Oak, Drue snapped.

'Swept away!' she cried, interrupting her father. 'Swept away doesn't mean that he drowned. Will-C could be out there right now waiting for me. He might be hurt. I have to go and look for him.'

'You're going nowhere,' said Quinn firmly.

'But how can we just leave him? After what you just said. He was a prisoner. He risked his life to help save us.'

'Drue, it's just too dangerous to go searching for . . . for . . .'

'A cat. Go on, say it: a cat!'

'I'm not going to argue with you.'

'Well, I'm going to argue with you!'

'Have you any idea what you're likely to find out there? Have you thought about that for one second? Even if it were safe for you to go, which it's not . . . No. What Will-C and the others did was an incredibly brave thing, and we should never forget the sacrifice they made. But, even if he were still alive, he wouldn't want you to risk your life. It's the very thing he was trying to save, don't you see?'

'And don't you see that's exactly why we have to go and look for him?'

Quinn read the determined look in Drue's eye. There was no doubt in his mind that his headstrong daughter would defy common sense and sneak off alone the first chance she got.

Gallinago had observed the entire exchange from a vantage point high inside the fugitives' hideaway and, though he hadn't understood a word, he could tell from Quinn's demeanour, from his body language, that a skirmish had been fought and lost. It came as no surprise to him when his old friend took to falcon form once more, and rejoined him in order to communicate the finer details.

Quinn had decided to fly back to Kingley Burh. It would be a useful exercise for a number of reasons. *One*: though he held out little hope of finding Will-C alive, the search would appease Drue – at least for the short term.

Two: he would get an opportunity to learn at first hand how the local Animalians had reacted to finding a Shape-shifter in their midst.

Three: he could check to see if there were people who had managed, against overwhelming odds, to survive the initial attacks and the merciless house-to-house searches that had followed. If there were, perhaps he could be of some help to them.

With these things in mind, and knowing that if he were captured he faced certain death, Quinn asked his friend to remain behind to keep a protective eye on Drue. Gallinago readily agreed, but, having seen how combative the young-ster was with her father, and how stubborn she could be, he voiced his concern that the task would be far from easy, particularly as the girl was unable to speak or understand Animalian.

Quinn conceded that his friend had a point, that there were risks involved, but, as that held true for whatever path they chose from here on in, he also felt that it was a risk worth taking.

Not that he intended to leave Drue entirely to her own

devices; that would be inviting trouble. Returning to human form, Quinn outlined his general plan. He delved into a packing case and retrieved a scuffed tan leather carrying case which contained a pair of vintage military-style 8 x 15 field glasses, half a dozen coloured pencils bound with a thick red elastic band, a new A4 sketchbook that had *Recycled Paper from Sustainable Forest* printed in bold letters on the cover and a shiny flip-top compass in a weatherproof nylon sock.

'What are these for?' asked Drue.

'I need you to keep watch. We need to build up a record, an exact record, of any birds that venture into the vicinity. Do the aerial patrols follow a particular pattern? What time do they pass over? Which direction do they travel in? Altitude? Number of birds? Which species?'

'What if I don't know the names of the species?' said Drue.

'Draw a picture. It doesn't have to be exact, but as much detail as you can. That way we can assess the level of danger. We need to know exactly what we're up against before we can expand our territory and move freely beyond the hideout.'

'I won't see much from in here,' said Drue.

'Agreed,' said Quinn, 'but there's the shell of a double-decker bus across the yard that'll provide good cover and a view of the horizon from the top deck. But you'll need to keep as still as you can when you're up there. Birds' eyes are similar to ours, but some of them can see just as far as you'll be able to with those field glasses. A hobby can detect the movement of a dragonfly two hundred yards away; a hovering kestrel can spot an insect the size of a pinhead forty feet below."

"Yards and feet. It's the modern age, Dad. We use metres now."

"Never mind that. Just be on your guard. Gallinago will help. He'll warn you when there's something coming so you'll be ready.'

'How will he do that?'

'Gallinago,' said Quinn, turning to the bird.

The snipe recognized his name – even Quinn's English equivalent – and he took that as a cue to demonstrate a few impressive aerial manoeuvres within the confines of the van.

'See how he tilts his wings from side to side like a see-saw.'

'Uh-huh,' answered Drue.

'That'll be the signal that there's something approaching in the sky.'

Gallinago climbed and flapped his wings in a clapping motion.

'Flapping means he's seen something on the ground.'

Gallinago performed a spiral dive and swooped so close that Drue had to duck to avoid being impaled on his bill.

'Hey!' cried Drue. 'Whose side are you on?'

'A spiral dive means hide,' said Quinn with a smile. 'You think you've got that?'

'Hrrmm,' replied Drue, fixing the snipe with a sour look.

Quinn reached for a backpack. He opened a flap and unzipped a deep pocket. Inside were three distress flares.

'And in an emergency, if you get into real trouble,' he said, proffering one of the flares, 'fire this in the air.'

Drue took the flare from her father. It was a dark orange tube roughly the length of a Pringles packet, and it had a red plastic cap on one end.

'It's a parachute rocket flare.' explained Quinn. 'To fire it, you grip the lower end with the cap facing the ground.'

Drue adjusted her grip, following instructions.

'That's it, good,' said Quinn. 'Now hold it away from you, parallel to your body. Unscrew the cap and you'll find there's an ignition ring inside. Pull hard on that and you'll fire the flare into the air . . . Careful, you don't want to set it off now,' he added quickly as Drue examined the device.

'It climbs to about a thousand feet before drifting back down to the ground on a parachute. It burns bright red and can be seen for about twenty-five miles, so only use it as a last resort; most animals will never have seen one, but they know about fireworks and they'll know it means one thing: humans.'

Drue nodded.

Quinn added a litre bottle of water, three green apples, a small bar of dark chocolate and a Swiss army knife to the kit and handed it to Drue.

'That ought to keep you out of mischief for a few hours.'

Drue carefully stowed the rocket flare in the front pocket of the pack alongside the others and snapped the clasps shut.

'Now, are you ready to catch that bus?' said Quinn with a smile.

'Yeah,' said Drue, a little apprehensively, 'I'm ready.'

CHAPTER NINETEEN

Gallinago, and her father in falcon form. They were Drue's first sightings as she raised the field glasses to her eyes. She watched them climb into the sky side by side, rising steadily as they passed her and banked towards the coast.

Drue had taken up a position on the padded bench seat at the rear of the red London bus. Few of the windows still had glass in them and the scorched internal paintwork suggested there had been a sizeable fire aboard at some point.

Maybe it was bombed like in one of them terrorist attacks, thought Drue. *All them wars. And for what?*

Referring to the chart she had drawn up on the first page of the sketchbook, Drue took a reading from the compass. South-south-east.

The falcon and the snipe were taking the same route out as Quinn had followed when he'd first carried Drue to the breaker's yard. Drue checked the time on her father's solar-powered perpetual-motion wristwatch. It was way too big and heavy to wear round her slender wrist so she wore it pushed halfway up her forearm like an arm-bracelet.

'A quarter to two,' said Drue. She selected a regular pencil and filled in the time alongside the other information on her chart:

Birds: 2
Species: 1 falcon 1 snipe
Time: 13:45
Direction: South-south-east
Altitude: ~~10~~ 15 metres . . . approx.
Duration:

Drue raised the field glasses again just in time to see Gallinago peel away from Quinn as he reached the far horizon. Drue wrote 3 minutes in the Duration column.

When she looked again, Gallinago had climbed even higher and was turning a wide circle over the yard. Drue considered beginning another column to add this information, but then thought better of it.

Snapping a bite from the chocolate bar her father had provided, Drue settled into a rhythm. She scanned the horizon in segments: north to due east, east to due south and so on around the compass for the length of time it took a square of dark organic chocolate to melt on her tongue.

Gallinago continued to circle, drifting effortlessly on the rising breeze. Drue envied him that freedom; she would have given anything to be able to fly off alongside her father in search of Will-C. Instead, the hours ticked slowly by, the chocolate slowly vanished and the vast grey sky filled with nothing more ominous or noteworthy than rainclouds.

Before long, the one question Drue had been reluctant to ask, afraid to ask, came swimming to the surface and made it almost impossible for her to concentrate on anything else. People had always said that although she looked more like her mother than her father her temperament, her character, was more like his. Well, if that were so . . . might she not have more of her father's blood in her veins than her mother's? And if that were the case . . .

Maybe I've inherited the gift, thought Drue.

Maybe I can learn to run like a cheetah, fly like a seagull, swim in the deepest ocean like a dolphin. It's not magic after all. It's not superpowers. It's just . . . seeing *things in a different way.*

She brought the field glasses up to her eyes again and adjusted the focus ring to sharpen the image.

From the shadows into the light.

Slowly but surely she was beginning to comprehend.

CHAPTER TWENTY

The point at which Will-C realized he was hungry was the point at which he realized he was starving. Literally. He hadn't eaten anything since he'd left home on the night of the Great Summit. And the moment at which this occurred to him was when he opened his eyes and, to his astonishment, found a live fish flapping and flopping about in front of him.

This was all the more startling as he was curled in a ball on Drue's dishevelled bed. He had settled there shortly after he'd found her mobile phone in the garden, and now it took a considerable effort just to lift his weary head from his crossed front paws. The fish – a carp – continued gasping for breath and snapping its silvery scaled body this way and that.

For a moment Will-C thought he must be hallucinating, like the time he chewed on some grass to aid his digestion and inadvertently swallowed some periwinkle leaves: the whole of the following day he'd been convinced that his tail was an eel chasing him.

Will-C blinked to see if the carp would disappear. But it remained, flipping and flopping. Beyond the fish, the foot of the bed and room itself were a vague blur of shapes and colours that lacked definition. Will-C thought about simply closing his tired eyes again and drifting off into a deep, final sleep, but then he heard the voice:

'Well, aren't you going to eat it?'

Will-C raised his head again and through the haze he saw movement.

'Truckles,' continued the disembodied voice with disdain.

Will-C sniffed the air, but his sense of smell was as dull as his vision. The carp performed one final desperate somersault, which launched it, in quite spectacular fashion, from the mattress on to the floor.

Will-C jerked his head back in alarm as a gyrfalcon swooped past him, retrieved the fish and, with a sweep of its broad wings, settled on the curved iron frame at the foot of Drue's bed. Faelken dropped the carp in front of Will-C once more. The fish was now still, lifeless.

'If you don't want it, I'll eat it. You looked hungry,' said Faelken.

Will-C's eyes moved from fish to bird and back to the fish. Hungry as he was, he still wasn't entirely convinced that either was real.

'Fine. Then I'll have it. Best while it's still fresh,' said Faelken as he hopped on to the crumpled bedsheet, sliced the carp in half with a single snap of his beak and swallowed the head.

Will-C tried to speak, but his throat was dry, his tongue heavy, his voice no more than a faint rasping sigh.

'Look, I was just trying to help, OK?' said Faelken.

'Why . . .' Will-C managed to whisper. 'Why would . . . you . . . help . . . me?'

'You don't trust me. That's smart. That's why they made you Clerk of the Feline Council, because you're clever. It saves us a lot of time. You see, I could have tried to trick you into believing I've had a change of heart, that I feel sorry for all you abandoned Truckles, but that wouldn't be the truth. And deep down in that super-smart feline brain of yours you'd have known it was a lie. So here's the truth, plain and simple: I need your help.'

'You need my help?' replied Will-C weakly.

'That's right. You see, my guess is that you're in here feeling sorry for yourself and starving to death because you're mourning the loss of your human companion; am I right?'

Faelken took another bite of carp.

'You're sure you don't want some of this? It's delicious. Anyway, the fact is she's still alive.'

Will-C felt a surge of emotion wash over him. The gyrfalcon now had his undivided attention.

'At least, we think so.'

'*We?*' said Will-C. 'You mean Natterjack?'

'That's right,' said Faelken. 'The toad sent me here in the hope of finding you because we all want the same thing. We want to reunite you with your human friend.'

'Of course you do,' said Will-C, unconvinced.

'The truth, remember. I won't try to fool you. Personally, I don't care if she lives or dies, but right now, as far as we know, she is alive and she's being held captive.'

'By who?' said Will-C.

'By a Shape-shifter. It snatched her from the apple tree right outside that window. So you see, it may just be that you know something we don't. Something that would lead us to the Shape-shifter's lair.'

'So you can kill them both,' said Will-C.

'Well, it's true that's what Natterjack has in mind, but I'm willing to strike a deal. You see, I want the Shape-shifter all for myself. So if you help me, I'll help you. The human child is of no interest to me. Lead me to her and, when the Shape-shifter is mine, the two of you walk free. I won't harm you, and I'll see to it that the toad doesn't trouble you either.'

'Why should I believe that?' said Will-C.

'You could go to Natterjack now and tell him of my treachery. How long do you think I would survive? He has every Animalian for miles around under his spell. You saw them at the Great Summit. Weak minds baying for blood. Mine will taste as good to them as any. I've taken a big risk here today. Think about it.'

'If he's as feared as you say ... then what makes you think you'll ever be able to protect me and Drue?' said Will-C, finding his voice.

'Drue. That's her name?'

Will-C silently chastised himself. *Knowledge is power*, his dad used to say. Guard it carefully.

'Once the Shape-shifter is mine, not even the Earth Assembly itself would dare to cross me,' said Faelken. He opened his wings, rose into the air and hovered by the broken window.

'And if I refuse to help you?' said Will-C.

'Natterjack will find the Shape-shifter eventually; he's

even sent for a tubenose petrel to help track it down. Those birds can sniff out anything. And, when he does, you'll all die. Give it some thought. I'll be back for your answer before nightfall.'

And, with that, Faelken was gone.

Will-C eyed the mutilated fish once more. Starving though he was, the fact that it lay on Drue's bed seemed wrong, so he nudged the remains of the carp off the crumpled bottom sheet with a paw and watched it fall to the floor. Then, mustering what little strength he had left, he picked himself up and followed it over the edge. Though his back leg held firm, his front legs buckled under him as he landed, his jaw striking the bare floorboards. The jarring impact was more shocking than painful; he was even weaker than he'd imagined.

And, with that jolt, any reservations that he might have had about accepting Faelken's butchered offering melted away. If Drue were alive, and he was to help her, he needed his strength. He desperately needed food, and he desperately needed water. Without wasting another moment, Will-C settled beside the dead fish, lapped at its still-moist flesh and began to eat.

CHAPTER TWENTY-ONE

By the time Quinn had turned a circle above the Weoh Oak, the surrounding forest glistened with a halo of fine, misty rain. He was no longer a falcon, but a swift, employing the enhanced speed and mobility of the species to complete his reconnaissance trip at a breakneck pace.

The shopping trolleys still lay abandoned in the adjacent river, and Quinn buzzed them low and fast in search of signs of life. There were none. He pressed on, weaving through overhanging branches and bulrushes as he followed the snaking river downstream. Having doubled back several times and swept both banks thoroughly, he was relieved not to find Will-C's body among the fallen Animalians that still lay in the woods.

As the rain began to fall harder, Quinn altered course and set out for home. Slicing through the air like a slick black arrow, he flew over the village of Kingley Burh. It was a grim task. The casualties of war – people, now little more than broken bones and bundles of rags, and fallen Truckles and wild animals – had transformed the entire area into a blood-soaked battlefield; a sprawling, tragic monument to a civilization that had lost its way and paid the price.

As Quinn swooped over the roof of the Callows' red-brick farmhouse, he detected a noise coming from the vast metal storage barn beyond the adjacent stable block. With the slightest flick of a wingtip, he circled back for a closer inspection. There it was again: a pounding that shook the towering galvanized-steel sliding doors of the barn. Something or someone was beating on the doors from inside.

Quinn ventured closer still. Though the doors were bolted shut, the heavy-duty padlock lay abandoned on the floor. Soaring to the corrugated roof, he quickly found an entry point beneath the guttering.

As he dropped from the shadows on to a steel roof support, Quinn became a barn owl to improve his vision in the gloomy, windowless space. Beneath him, a weary grey mare shook her head, drew a breath of dank air, bucked her hind legs and hammered the metal doors with her hooves. Tired as she was, the effort was now more of a protest than anything – the doors had held fast despite her best efforts – but each time the vast doors rattled in their running tracks, a hundred hopeful faces lifted from the dirty concrete floor in expectation.

The majority of the imprisoned Truckles were cats and dogs, but there were also goats, geese, a donkey, a rooster and a pair of peacocks. Quinn swooped down to the grey mare before she clattered the doors again.

'Wait. Stop. Save your strength. I'll open it.'

The mare looked at the owl with glazed eyes.

'You?' brayed the donkey. 'Why would you help us?'

'Who did this?'

'Who did this? You! Your kind. Animalians. The Earth Assembly. They're worse than the humans. We've no food, no water. They left us here to die.'

'Just because we're Truckles,' added a goat.

'They've always hated us,' said another.

'It's not the Earth Assembly,' argued one of the peacocks, 'it's the local Elders; they've seized control.'

'It's the toad. He's poisoned their minds,' hissed a goose.

'Aye, it's Natterjack,' said a Highland terrier. 'He'll be the death of us all.'

'My kittens?' said a frail, disoriented Manx cat to nobody in particular as she picked her way through the carpet of listless Truckles. 'Have you seen my kittens?'

As the barn owl disappeared back into the shadows beyond the highest rafters, the grey mare hung her head. She was now too weak even to protest.

Quinn shape-shifted from owl to swift to dart through the small hole beneath the metal roof, then, as he touched down on the ground outside the barn doors, he checked to ensure that he was alone, before adopting human form once more.

Quinn gripped the bolt with his hands; it slipped from the latch with ease, but, as he tried to slide the heavy doors open, he realized that the mare's pounding had buckled the tracks they ran on. A grinding of metal on metal and the doors stuck fast just a few centimetres apart.

Quinn pushed and pulled with all his strength, straining every muscle in his body, but to no avail. The doors remained jammed.

The grey mare caught sight of Quinn through the narrow channel.

'A human!' said the mare, aghast.

'A human? Is it possible?' said the donkey.

'It can't be,' said another Truckle prisoner.

'What's that?'

'Let me see.'

'I've seen him before . . . talking to Farmer Callow. He'll help us,' said the mare. And suddenly the whole storage barn was alive with movement, animals crawling over one another to reach the doors.

'Wait,' cried Quinn.

'Quiet!' brayed the mare. 'There may still be rats on the farm.'

Quinn moved off across the yard, shifting back into swift form as he did so. The grey mare, with one eye pressed to the gap in the doors, witnessed the metamorphosis.

'A Shape-shifter,' whispered the grey mare in astonishment.

'What's that?' said the donkey. 'What's going on?'

'Hush,' replied the grey mare.

'He'll get us out. You'll see. He'll get us out.'

A few moments later, the roar of a diesel engine was heard and a tractor rumbled across the yard with Quinn – back in human form – at the wheel. Black smoke belched from the exhaust as he worked the gears and swung it round on its huge tyres. Driving the vehicle as hard as he could, he began to reverse at speed towards the steel doors.

'Get back!' he yelled from the cab.

The grey mare didn't need to understand the words to comprehend their meaning.

'Get back! Get back!' she bellowed to the other Truckles.

As the tractor smashed into the steel doors, the entire building shook on its foundations. Quinn shifted gears again, pulled the tractor forward, adjusted the angle of attack and then reversed into the doors once more. At the third impact, one of the doors buckled and toppled from its fixings, clattering down on to the cobbled yard. Moans and sighs of relief rose from inside the storage barn.

Quinn instantly shifted from human form back to swift. He circled the yard as the frail Truckles slowly emerged from the shadowy storage shed and turned their faces skyward, mouths open to catch the life-restoring rain.

The grey mare tossed her mane and lapped at a puddle.

'Thank you,' she said softly, having quenched her thirst.

Quinn-Swift settled on an upturned pail beside her.

'Farmer Callow and his family?' he said.

The grey mare shook her head.

'There was nothing we could do.'

The Truckles began to fan out across the courtyard, fear and uncertainty in their eyes. None had the slightest notion of what to do or where to go.

'Where will they go?' asked Quinn-Swift.

'Where would you go?' asked the grey mare in return.

'You might be better off sticking together. Safety in numbers.'

'It didn't help us before,' said the grey mare, turning her head to survey the bodies of those Truckles who had not survived the imprisonment.

'I'm sorry,' said Quinn-Swift.

The grey mare supped some more rainwater.

'Will they come back for us?'

'Honestly, I don't know. I don't think so. But I don't know. It depends how long the Animalian coalition holds. There's a lot of history, a lot of bad blood between the species. With Man out of the way, the chances are that hostility will soon resurface. The predators will be at each other's throats in the battle for dominance.'

'Then the war against the humans has been won?'

'I don't even know that for sure. But they're no longer in control,' said Quinn-Swift.

'They never were. That was the problem,' said the grey mare.

'Well, that's in the past now,' said Quinn-Swift. It was the future that troubled him more. 'Winning the war with the human race was one thing. What emerges from that remains to be seen.'

'Time will tell, I suppose,' said the grey mare. 'And you? Will you stay with us?'

'I'm needed elsewhere.'

The grey mare nodded solemnly. 'I understand. Tell me . . . are you the future?'

'The future?' said Quinn-Swift.

'The Nsray,' said the grey mare. 'If the legends are true, your people were once a force to be reckoned with.'

'Well . . .' Quinn dipped his beak into the puddle of water on the upturned bucket and drank before completing the thought. 'Nature thrives on diversity. Always has. I see no reason to doubt that it always will.'

And, with that, Quinn spread his wings and took to the

air once more. The grey mare watched as the tiny bird climbed in a spiral towards the rooftops.

'I didn't get your name,' said the grey mare, calling after him.

'Quinn,' chirped Quinn-Swift.

'I'm Kipling,' said the mare. 'Should you ever need . . .' but Quinn-Swift was by now out of earshot, darting away at speed across the open sky.

CHAPTER TWENTY-TWO

As Quinn-Swift glided on the thermals and resumed his search for Will-C, the grey mare's words returned to him: *Are you the future?*

Gallinago had spoken about pockets of human survivors scattered around the world. The question then was whether a truce could be brokered with the Earth Assembly before those survivors were hunted down, and modern Man faced the same fate that befell the once all-powerful Neanderthals: extinction. As an emissary, who better than one who could walk between the two worlds?

Throughout the ages, the Nsray had been feared and revered in equal measure – and hunted by both humans and Animalians – but Quinn now saw a potential end to his people's persecution. From the ashes of one culture would sprout another to take its place – enlightened, evolved, transformed. A terrible price had been paid, but perhaps, one day, it might be said that the lives of millions had not been lost entirely in vain.

Quinn-Swift beat his wings a little faster and turned his

full attention back to the task in hand. The rain fell harder now, drumming on the rooftops, pooling in the gutters, washing down the quiet streets. Quinn-Swift pressed on across the grey sky, finally dropping from the clouds to take a tour of his own garage, workshop and gardens. He circled his old Defender, which still sat where he had abandoned it the night he'd rescued Drue. And then there was their former home. Memories etched in bricks and flint and wood and mortar; a snapshot of a family, a way of life, frozen in time.

Quinn-Swift settled on the sill of the kitchen window and listened for signs of life. All was still, quiet. Hopping through a broken pane, he changed form once more and, swapping speed for stealth, became a tiny wren.

That damage had been done came as no surprise, but it nonetheless took Quinn a few moments to come to terms with the extent of it, and the violence with which it had been perpetrated. All his life he had done what he could to protect indigenous wildlife and the environment, but still he and Drue had felt the full force of the Animalian backlash. Their good intentions – and those of the many thousands like them – had not been enough to protect them. And yet he felt no malice for the creatures responsible; with the survival of those you love as the prize, he knew that he too was capable of just about anything.

Quinn-Wren flew through the living room, perched briefly on the panel of the exposed priest-hole, then flitted across the room and settled on the newel post at the foot of the staircase.

The claw marks and splintered panels in Drue's bedroom door were testament to the ferocity of the attack that she had endured, and again Quinn said a silent prayer of thanks for his daughter's narrow escape.

Flying up the stairs, Quinn-Wren hopped through a jagged hole in Drue's door and glided across to the bed. Settling on the iron frame, he surveyed the room. He spotted fishbones on the floor. But still there was no sign of Will-C.

Quinn-Wren started for the window and, as he did so, he heard a noise, a movement, from inside the house. He settled by the broken panes for a moment. Rain danced on the interior sill, soaked the torn curtains, trickled off his plumage. Quinn was ready to take to the open sky; he'd been gone a while and was eager to return to Drue.

But there it was again. Something else was in the house. Quinn-Wren spread his tiny wings, soared across the room, hopped back through the gash in the bedroom door and landed at the top of the stairs. And his feet had barely touched the floor before he was smothered by a black projectile, a snarling, thrashing ball of fur and claws and sinew ...Will-C!

The impact carried both predator and prey tumbling down the stairs in a bundle of writhing feathers and fur.

Fortunately for Quinn, though he was trapped between Will-C's front paws and his lower jaw, given the flight of the fall, the snapping feline was unable to administer a death bite.

On they tumbled as Quinn shape-shifted from wren ... to cat ... to Dobermann pinscher. Too late. Landing heavily on a leg caught beneath him, he felt the bone crack. Instinctively, he reeled, his neck twisted and his head struck the stair rail, which knocked him out cold.

The mad flurry of movement was all over in seconds. And it took Will-C several more to realize what he'd done. For a brief few moments, with the Dobermann lying prone beside him, the fact that he had actually captured a Shapeshifter was both a shock and a thrill. And he couldn't quite believe how easy it had been. The most elusive creature on the planet overpowered by a mere Truckle. He thought of his father, how proud he would have been. It was the stuff of legend. Or might have been . . .

As the Dobermann form began to fade, and the unconscious Quinn metamorphosed back into his human form, it was then that Will-C realized exactly what he had done.

'Oh no,' he cried. 'No, no, no! You're . . . it's you! You're you! And I've killed you.'

Will-C didn't know much about human physiology, but he knew enough from time spent with Drue that humans had a heartbeat just like other mammals, and that you could feel their breath when they exhaled. He flung himself at the crumpled figure and pressed his face against Quinn's to check for signs of life.

'Breathe. Don't die. Breathe. Please.'

And then he felt a faint puff of breath against his nose and shrank back in relief. Quinn groaned, and his breathing became a little more pronounced, but he didn't recover consciousness.

Now it dawned on Will-C that he had a whole other crisis to worry about: the imminent return of Faelken. Will-C might not have killed Quinn, but given half a chance the gyrfalcon wouldn't hesitate to do so.

Will-C clamped his jaws on Quinn's trouser leg and pulled, hoping he could drag him to a less exposed spot. It was hopeless. Quinn's dead weight was far too much for him to move. Will-C sat beside the prone figure and caught his breath.

Wake up, thought Will-C. *You have to wake up*.

CHAPTER TWENTY-THREE

The first night that Drue spent alone in the junkyard hideaway, she followed the routine that her father had set to the letter, fully expecting him to return before she fell asleep in her hammock. When she awoke the next morning to discover that he still hadn't returned, she began to fear the worst. It felt like being back in the priest-hole. Should she simply wait or venture out to look for him?

Gallinago was perched on a crate by the door, wings folded at his side.

'My dad,' said Drue, clambering to her feet. 'Quinn. You have to go and look for him.'

Gallinago eyed her quizzically.

Drue's frustration at not being able to communicate in Animalian added a threatening edge to her voice.

'Don't you understand? You have to go look for him!'

Gallinago rose into the air in alarm as Drue stabbed a finger at him.

'You! Go! There!' said Drue, hauling back the tarp curtain and jabbing a finger at the sky. The falling rain trickled up the sleeve of her crumpled pyjama top.

Gallinago kept his distance, turning small circles above her. Drue's eyes scanned the van in search of a prop, something to help her cause. *A drawing!*

She found her notepad and made a crude sketch of three figures: a snipe. A girl. And a man with wings. She gestured for Gallinago to come closer and, though hesitant, he finally settled beside her. Drue ringed the sketch of the snipe and pointed at Gallinago.

'You,' she said firmly. 'Gallinago.'

She did the same with the illustration of the girl.

'Me. Drue.'

As Drue ringed the final figure, Gallinago said, 'Quinn,' but to Drue's ears it sounded like a sneeze.

'*Qqquuu-iiiii-nnnnn,*' said Drue with added emphasis. 'My dad. Do you understand? Nsray. Shape . . . shifter.'

Gallinago's head ducked and bobbed, but there was no indication at all that he got the gist of what Drue was saying.

She made the shape of a pair of wings with her hands and flapped her fingers, emulating the flight of a bird.

'Flying. We call this flying. What you do.'

Gallinago flapped his wings.

'Yes!' exclaimed Drue. 'Exactly. Flying. You. Fly.'

She rushed to the door and pulled back the tarp again.

'Fly. Find Quinn. Find my dad.'

Gallinago swept past Drue and rose into the sky. Then he banked and dropped back towards her. Drue raised an arm and pointed at the spot on the horizon where she had last seen her father.

'Go. Fly. Find my dad.'

With a loud *kreech*, the snipe wheeled away and took off in the direction that Drue had indicated.

She watched her feathered companion glide through the moist air. *Fly*, thought Drue. *Fly*. She looked down at her hands, her arms. *I wonder*, she thought. Eyes closed, lips puckered up in fierce concentration, she willed her limbs to turn into wings.

Fly!

Nothing happened. *Wings. Give me wings. Make my arms wings.*

Still nothing.

I'm a bird. I'm a seagull. I can FLY!

Drue opened her eyes. Her hands were still just hands. Her arms still just arms. She was still plain Drue Beltane: a gangly twelve-year-old girl in crumpled pyjamas. She tried again. Actually jumped a little to see if that would help.

It's not magic. I can FLLLLYYYY!

Still nothing. Drue tried again, and this time leapt from the rear of the van and landed in a heap on the ground, scuffing her right knee in the process. The taped dressing on her leg held firm, but the impact had clearly opened the wound beneath it, as blood began to soak through the white gauze.

Annoyed with herself, Drue brushed the dirt off her hands and got to her feet. As she raised her eyes skyward once more, she saw Gallinago circling the compound. Had he found Quinn so soon?

She scrambled back into the van, retrieved the field glasses and scanned the sky. No sign of any life but the snipe. Throwing caution to the wind, Drue ran through the rain, splashing barefoot through greasy puddles until she reached the lookout bus. She darted inside and raced up the stairs to the upper deck, the chrome handrail cold as ice to her touch. Again she raised the field glasses and completed a full three-sixty-degree sweep of the terrain.

Quinn was nowhere to be seen.

Drue trained the binoculars on Gallinago once more. He drifted in a wide circle, patrolling the perimeter as before. Drue fumed. *Had he not understood her? Or had he understood but defied her?*

Pushing her damp hair from her face, she slumped on a grubby seat. Her feet were wet and slimy with mud. Her pyjamas were sodden. Her right shin now sported a red rivulet of blood from her weeping knee. She wanted a warm bath, a boiled egg with buttered toasted soldiers, a steaming mug of milky hot chocolate. She wanted her dad to come back. She wanted to go home. She wanted to snuggle beneath her old quilt in her old bed in her old room. She wanted to see Will-C. She wanted to turn the clock back and make everything go back to the way it was before.

She watched Gallinago complete another circuit. The hurt and confusion and frustration boiled inside her until she could stand it no more. She lunged at the open window and *SCREAMED* for all she was worth. The piercing cry echoed through the rusty metal canyons. Startled, Gallinago abruptly changed course and flew back towards the bus, fully expecting to find Drue grappling with an assailant. Instead, he found her glaring up at him defiantly. Gallinago performed a spiral dive to indicate that it wasn't safe, that Drue should take cover.

'I don't care!' she spat in response.

The snipe climbed and fell in another spiral dive, this time coming closer.

'I don't care! I don't care if they find me!'

Gallinago could see that his actions were feeding Drue's frustration so he wheeled away, put a little distance between them and resumed a regular flight pattern. Leaving the worried snipe turning circles in the rain, Drue picked her way through the bus, splashed down into the puddles once more and brazenly marched back to the hideout.

CHAPTER TWENTY-FOUR

Will-C sat on Quinn's chest and lapped at his cheek. He'd been doing so for the best part of an hour, but still Quinn hadn't stirred. Finally, out of sheer frustration, Will-C bit the tip of Quinn's nose. It had the desired effect, as Quinn instantly let out a yelp and sat bolt upright, sending Will-C tumbling to the floor.

'Oww. Oww, that . . . owwwww.'

Will-C sprang back on to Quinn's lap, overjoyed to see him awake.

'You're OK! You're OK!'

'Will you . . .'

'I was so worried . . .'

'Will you . . .'

'I didn't know if you . . .'

'Will you get off me, you damned fleabag!'

Will-C didn't understand the words, but Quinn's tone said it all. He slunk away with his tail between his legs and settled beneath the kitchen table with a guilty look on his face.

It became apparent that the fall down the stairs had left Quinn with a badly fractured wrist. Quinn could see the matter weighed heavily on the cat, so he adopted feline form to reassure Will-C that he did not hold him responsible. Quinn blamed himself for having let his guard down.

Will-C was grateful, if a little unnerved – Quinn's injury didn't hamper his general ability to shape-shift, but it did impair his concentration and, as had happened in Gallinago's presence, Quinn's metamorphosis remained fluid rather than fixed, his physical presence slightly soft, blurred, as if seen through a heat haze.

A more immediate issue for Quinn was the fact that his injury also severely limited his choice of form: there was little point in shape-shifting into a winged species as he wouldn't be able to fly. This in turn meant that the journey back to Drue would now have to be completed on foot, a road trip of epic proportions.

Will-C was eager to join Quinn on that trip as soon as possible, but once he had outlined Faelken's devious proposal to betray Natterjack and claim Quinn's powers for himself, Quinn insisted that they had to stay. He was adamant that they needed to deal with Faelken and the toad before returning to Drue, or risk exposing the safe house and placing her in even greater danger.

Little did he know that for his daughter, danger and destiny would prove to be but two sides of the very same coin.

CHAPTER TWENTY-FIVE

Bats. Waking from a deep sleep, it took Drue a moment to realize that the air was alive with them. Then instinct took over, she tumbled out of her hammock and scrambled through the pitch-black darkness on hands and knees in a frantic bid to escape.

Drue felt bony fingers, thumb claws, fleshy wing membranes whipping round her head. She caught glimpses of small, mean, wrinkled muzzles, with razor fangs and blazing eyes. Arms flailing, she did her best to keep her assailants at bay.

Gallinago's *KRRREEEECH* echoed off the metal walls as he turned frantic circles, buffeted and bruised by the whirlwind of flying mammals.

Drue tripped on her rucksack. She tore it open; a rocket flare tumbled out and she grabbed it. With the bats tearing at her hair and her face, Drue ripped the safety cap off the flare and pulled the firing ring. The space erupted with light and noise as the distress flare careened into the metal roof of the van, exploded and ricocheted round the interior, enveloping everything in a cloud of red smoke.

Radars jammed, flesh singed, the bats panicked. They crashed into the walls, collided with one another and fled as best they could.

Drue dived for cover behind the packing crates as the furious firework burned bright. She scanned the hideout. No sign of the snipe.

'Gallinago! Gallinago!'

With one last show-stopping burst of sparks, the flare finally died. Still the air was choked with dense red smoke.

Glowing red-hot sparks rained down on the hammock, fell on Drue's sketchbook, settled on the boxes of supplies. A gust of wind and suddenly the place was ablaze. Tongues of flame sprang up between Drue and the exit so swiftly that she didn't have time to flee. She shrank back.

'Gallinago!'

Still no reply. The fire surged. There was no way out. Except . . . the hole punched in the rusted wheel arch where the grass had grown through. The blades, dry as tinder, vanished as curls of smoke, leaving a ragged cavity the size of a dinner plate. An escape route of sorts, but was it large enough for Drue to crawl through?

The packing crates caught fire.

The tarpaulin curtains flared.

Drue choked on the fumes. She dropped flat on the floor of the van and wriggled snake-like towards the wheel arch. The heat grew even more intense. Drue reached the hole and, realizing at once that she would never fit through it, she began to claw at the rusted edge with her bare hands. Flakes of corroded metal fell away, but still the hole was far too small.

The fire raged. Drue tore at the rust, but it was no use. Seconds from being lost to the smoke and the flames, she let out a piercing scream: HELP! and screwed her eyes shut to block out the terrifying reality. Then . . .

She felt the scorching heat inside her skin.

Inside her bones.

Inside her mind.

A searing electrochemical fire burning inside her skull that was every bit as wild and terrifying as the one blazing all around her. And when she opened her eyes again . . .

She was outside! Upside down, clinging to the hot metal of the removal van's chassis, which now seemed the size of an ocean liner.

Her hands had clawed toes!

Her short arms were grey-green and her scaly body was flecked with a band of white dots that reached to the tip of her long fleshy tail . . . She'd become a lizard!

Reeling from shock, Drue lost her grip and fell from the chassis. She hit the ground as a young girl once more. Petrified, but fuelled by adrenalin, Drue flipped on to her stomach and crawled away from the flames that were curling out of the wheel arch above her.

A pile of tyres offered a temporary haven a safe distance from the blazing vehicle. Drue climbed inside, curled into a ball and, shaking uncontrollably, hugged her muddy knees close and prayed that her narrow escape had passed unnoticed by the bats.

Across the yard, the fire continued to flicker, but, thanks to the incessant drizzle, it hadn't spread beyond the Beltanes' former hideout.

An hour passed before the last glowing ember died away, and Drue – though cold, damp and scared to death – drifted into a deep sleep.

CHAPTER TWENTY-SIX

In preparation for Faelken's return, Quinn had encouraged Will-C to return to the foot of Drue's bed, while he, in the guise of a lynx – to take advantage of the wild cat's nocturnal prowess – kept watch from beside the wardrobe; it was a vantage point from which he could monitor both the door and the window without being seen.

As dawn crept into the sky, Quinn stretched and yawned, and, leaving Will-C asleep, broke cover to limp down to the kitchen in search of sustenance.

Taking care to stay away from the windows, Quinn shape-shifted back into human form to fashion a makeshift sling from knotted tea towels: a means to relieve the pressure on his fractured wrist. He found arnica and painkillers in a cabinet in the downstairs cloakroom, and swallowed both with a glass of cool water. He then returned to the ransacked kitchen cupboards. As he'd expected, he discovered tinned foods that had been of no interest to the Animalian looters.

Following a hasty breakfast of mackerel fillets in brine

and some tinned tomatoes, Quinn opened a second can of fish for Will-C and set down some fresh water beside it.

Tentatively massaging his injured arm, Quinn's thoughts turned to Drue. Throughout the night he'd been plagued by a sense of unease. He felt sure he was needed back at the hideout, but was equally sure that danger was close to home. He could sense it, could feel it in the core of his being; dark intentions swimming towards him through the living energy of the atmosphere, as plain to a Nsray Elder as oil floating on water.

Quinn gazed out through the broken windows, across the garden where he'd watched Drue take her first steps – it seemed a lifetime ago now – and prayed that she was still safe. Still hidden. Still protected from the cruel realities of the new world order.

CHAPTER TWENTY-SEVEN

*W*ater. Cool. Clear. Deep as the Atlantic. Light breaking the surface, drilling down from above, shimmering stalactites of pure, bright energy slicing through viscous aquamarine. All around were walls of crystal: a vast jewel-encrusted underwater canyon of dazzling brilliance. Drue reached out a hand to touch the sparkling escarpment, but it slipped out of reach as she began to sink towards the point where the light faded; a tiny lone figure adrift in a liquid void. Below her lay darkness, black as charcoal, and something . . . a feeling. A presence. Beckoning. Then a sound. A familiar sound . . .

★ ★ ★

Kreech. Kreech.

The noise tugged at her, distracted her, drew her away from the depths and the mysterious shadows below that she felt compelled to explore.

There it was again, louder now.

Kreech! Kreech!

Drue opened her eyes and, from her nest of old tyres, she saw Gallinago silhouetted against the white morning sky.

He was circling high above the charred removal van. He was searching for her.

The events of the previous night came flooding back.

The bats.

The fire.

The lizard!

Drue held a hand in front of her face. Turned it this way and that as though seeing it for the very first time. She wiggled her fingers. Jabbed a thumb into her palm. She was relieved to find she had fingernails – even dirty fingernails – rather than claws. And yet . . . *hadn't she shape-shifted to escape the fire?*

'Gallin—' began Drue excitedly, and then caught herself. Maybe raising her voice was not such a good idea. She felt certain – and guilty – that her rash behaviour the day before had led the bats to the hideout, and now all her father's careful preparation had been undone and their supplies lost to the flames.

Drue got to her feet and studied her arms and legs as she had her hand. The body she inhabited suddenly seemed foreign, alien, familiar and yet totally unfamiliar at the same time. She caught sight of her reflection in a puddle and peered at her face. She brushed a tangle of hair from her forehead. A frown creased her brow. She pulled a face, bared her teeth, stuck out her tongue.

Seagull, she thought, hoping to trigger the magical transformation. Nothing happened. She screwed her eyes shut in an effort to help her concentration.

Seagull. She focused on the image again. Then opened one eye to peek at her reflection. Still the face of a grubby young girl stared back at her from the puddle. She tried to picture a specific species: a blue-grey herring gull with pink legs, black wingtips and a yellow-and-orange bill.

Herring gull . . .

Drue felt the breeze on her face. Lifted her arms as though they were wings and imagined soaring across the sky. Still her reflection stubbornly refused to play along. She stamped in the puddle in frustration.

Kreeeeeech!

Gallinago had spotted her and came swooping down.

Kreech, kreeeeech!

'Yes, OK. It's good to see you too,' mumbled Drue.

But the snipe's cry was no mere greeting – it was a warning. He beat his wings furiously. Flapped them right in Drue's face until she got the message.

'What? What? What?!' said Drue.

Gallinago flapped harder, exaggerating every beat.

'Oh . . . flapping,' said Drue. 'That means . . . what did Dad say that means? Flapping, that means . . . oh, you've . . . you've seen something . . . on the ground?'

She scanned her surroundings and spotted a tide of rats, hundreds of them, surging towards her through the canyons of rusty metal.

For a second Drue froze. Then, as Gallinago let out another *kreech*, she turned and ran. She slipped, fell, picked herself up, ran some more, pushing herself as fast as her feet could carry her.

Gallinago dive-bombed the rats, but they were far too numerous, far too intent on reaching their terrified prey.

Blood pumping in her temples, legs beginning to tire as

she scaled a stack of crushed cars, Drue tried once more to conjure flight.

To create it.

To become it.

It's not magic, she reminded herself.

It's not magic. I did it once: I can do it again!

As she reached the crest of the jagged hill of wrecks, and the rats surrounded the base, Drue spread her arms wide and, in a last-ditch leap of faith, threw herself from the tower of rusted garbage. Her tiny body sprang forward, seemed almost to be flying, but then gravity took hold and she began to fall like a stone, plummeting back towards Earth and the salivating vermin who awaited her. And just when it seemed she was doomed . . .

She began to climb, tracing an arc on broad, white-feathered wings!

Gallinago flew alongside, amazed at what he'd witnessed. 'Ya can shape-shift!'

'*Yaaahhhhhhhhhhh!*' cried Drue, thrilled and terrified in equal measure. She had *become* a herring gull.

'An' ya can un'erstand me!'

'What?!' yelled Drue-Gull as they began to pull away from the seething, snarling river of rats below. For a maiden flight, she was not doing too badly at all, but it was obvious to Gallinago from her clumsy, jerky movements that Drue did not have full control over her new-found abilities.

'Dat's it!' encouraged Gallinago. 'Ya doin' fine. Keep flappin'!'

Drue-Gull dipped and wove and skittered across the yard, almost collided with the lookout bus, spun helter-skelter through a gorge of scrap metal and finally settled into a steady rhythm, climbing ever higher.

'Easy now. Dat's it. Relax ... not too much! Steady. Watch out for dem termals. Dat's it. Dat's it!'

In truth, Drue could only make out every other word that Gallinago was saying – like flying itself, it would take time to master the Animalian language – but at that moment, with the feel of the sun on her face, buoyed by the wind streaming beneath her wings – wings! – it hardly mattered.

She had opened the door to a whole new world. Freedom. Potential beyond her wildest dreams. It was exhilarating, all-consuming.

Gaining confidence, she attempted a barrel roll, loops, spirals, and, as she saw the blue ribbon of the Channel stretching across the horizon, she beat her wings faster and sped towards the coast.

Giddy with excitement, the waves crashing on to the beach far below her, she dived headlong into the spray. Gallinago kept his distance until Drue-Gull began to fly out over the open sea. He then cut across her flight path and beckoned her to retreat.

'Da beach,' said the snipe. 'We need to talk.'

Taking the lead, Gallinago banked and glided to an elegant landing on a sturdy, weather-bleached timber breakwater. Drue-Gull aimed for the same perch, but overshot and crash-landed clumsily on the pebbles below. To add to her humiliation, before she could pick herself up, she was drenched by a wave of the onrushing tide. Gallinago shook his head like a long-suffering parent, but even the soaking didn't dampen Drue's spirit.

'Mental! It's . . . it's bonkers! I just want to fly right round the whole world!'

'Den we'd best learn to land, hadn't we? Dat's a helluva long trip to do widout ever settin' down ya webbed pinkies,' said Gallinago derisively.

'How high can we go? Past the clouds?'

'We'll come to dat . . .'

'And what's the fastest? What's the fastest bird ever? A swift, I'll bet?'

'No, no. A peregrine falcon . . .'

'A falcon.'

'Aye, in a huntin' dive it's da quickest Animalian on da planet, but . . .'

'How fast?'

'Well, we measure speed different to humans loike, but, oh, dey can plod along at 200 miles an hour or so . . .'

'Two hundred miles an hour! That's like a racing car!'

'But dat's during a stoop dive, mind. A plover or even a spur-winged goose will ruffle its tail feathers on a flat-out chase. An' you're not wrong, dem needle-tailed swifts are no slouches eider.'

'Will you teach me? Will you? I won't be any trouble and I'll pay attention and everything, I promise.'

'Well, first off I'm not a falcon,' said Gallinago, 'and second off ya forgettin' dat I made a promise to ya farder to keep ya safe. Now . . .'

'My dad, yes, we have to find him. I can't wait to see the look on his face.'

Gallinago spoke more slowly. Shaped his words with more care.

'Ya farder's instructions ... were ... to wait ... for his return.'

'Wait? But where can we wait? The hideout is all burned up ...'

'And ya tink he'll be pleased about dat?'

'Gallinago, we have to go find him.'

'It's far too dangerous.'

'If you're afraid, then I'll go on my own.'

'Afraid?!' squawked Gallinago.

'Don't worry, I won't tell him,' said Drue-Gull as she opened her wings and allowed a breeze to lift her into the air. 'Two hundred miles an hour!'

'Now don't be gettin' notions,' chastised the snipe.

The wind picked up and carried her a little higher.

'I can't hear you!' called Drue-Gull, though of course she could.

'Chicklets!' grumbled Gallinago as he set off after her. 'Dey tink dey know everyting!'

CHAPTER TWENTY-EIGHT

With an army of minions in tow, his considerable girth spread across the thick neck of his dejected bulldog steed, Natterjack had abandoned the rich pickings of the Nature Reserve to make his way through woodland, and across rain-soaked fields and flooded roads, to reach the Beltanes' former home.

Burdock, yarrow, fool's parsley and a host of other wildflowers grew in abundance beneath the hedgerows around the perimeter of the garden, a wildlife corridor that now acted as the perfect screen for the Animalians charged with keeping the cottage under surveillance. And the ground forces were matched in number by the birds hidden in the leafy canopy above.

Faelken noted the arrival of the warty District Proconsul, and swooped down to report.

'Well,' said Natterjack as the wheezing bulldog lowered its head to allow the toad to slide to the ground. 'What do you have for me? Has the Truckle taken the bait?'

The army of rats, mice and weasels fanned out to surround the property.

'The cat hasn't left the house since I spoke to him,' said Faelken.

'You're certain of that?'

'We've been on constant watch.'

Natterjack eyed the cottage. 'And I heard tell of a visitor?'

'A swift,' said one of the crows nestled in an adjacent beech tree.

Natterjack looked at Faelken, then at the crow, then back at Faelken.

'A swift?'

'Flew in through the top window yesterday. We haven't seen him since,' said Faelken, 'which is why I sent word to you.'

'I see,' said Natterjack.

'Could 'ave been eaten by the cat,' said a rat.

'Most likely eaten by the cat,' said another.

'Could be the swift and the Truckle are just friends,' said a hooded crow.

'Or it could be the swift is the Shape-shifter,' said Natterjack.

All eyes turned back to the cottage; the morning light glinted off the flint of the façade.

'We have numbers. If we attacked from all sides ...' began Faelken.

'No,' said Natterjack. 'Not yet. First we need to be certain that it is the Shape-shifter or we risk losing the element of surprise. We need eyes inside.'

'Could be a trap. Maybe they know we're out here. That's why they've stayed hidden,' said a rat.

All of those within earshot began to melt into the undergrowth; the scouting mission sounded dangerous, possibly deadly, and nobody wanted to be chosen as the sacrificial volunteer. Natterjack scanned the terrain and weighed up his options.

'I'll go back in,' said Faelken, spreading his wings and flexing his talons.

'No,' said Natterjack. 'For this we need stealth as much as cunning and speed. And we also need an Animalian who won't look out of place in the human's lair should he be discovered.'

As Natterjack's gaze washed over them, the Animalians lowered their eyes, each hoping to avoid being selected, like children in a classroom ducking the gaze of a teacher. Finally, the toad found what he was looking for . . . a dormouse.

'You!' snapped Natterjack.

'M . . . m . . . m . . . me?' replied the dormouse.

'You. You will be my eyes and ears. Find the three-legged Truckle and see what kind of company he's keeping.'

★   ★   ★

The dormouse knew a dozen different tried and tested routes to the Beltanes' kitchen, so gaining entry unseen was not a problem. The route he chose brought him out behind the scuffed kick plate of the unit that held the sink. It was familiar territory for sure, but, since the war had begun, all human dwellings had taken on an unsettling atmosphere: an eerie silence, devoid of the usual background hum of electrical appliances that the creatures who had lived alongside them had become accustomed to.

Though reluctant to proceed any further, the tiny fleet-footed spy made his way across the room, weaving a path through the broken crockery and debris that littered the floor.

There was no sign of cat or bird, and for a moment the relieved dormouse considered scurrying back to Natterjack to report as much; then, as if on cue . . .

Will-C leapt down to the floor from the kitchen table with a swift clamped in his jaws. Will-C's sudden appearance startled the mouse, but as far as he could tell he hadn't been seen. He watched with interest as Will-C moved across the room and released the bird from his mouth. It dropped limply to the flagstone floor beside his food bowl.

From where he was hidden, the dormouse's view was partly obscured by a toppled chair, so he made a dash across open terrain, scampered along a skirting and crept up behind the leg of the kitchen table for a clearer line of sight.

The cat appeared to be toying with the motionless swift: he nudged it with a paw, backed away, raised himself up, then pounced and began patting it again. The swift remained motionless, and it was clear from the angle of one of his wings that it was badly injured.

If it isn't dead already, thought the dormouse, *it soon will be.*

He had seen enough. Natterjack had been wise to delay storming the house. The elusive Shape-shifter was yet to appear. Lulled into a false sense of security, the dormouse retreated round the leg of the kitchen table and scurried back the way he came . . . across the open floor.

In a heartbeat, the swift shape-shifted into a lynx and leapt across the room. The dormouse was in its jaws before he even knew he was in danger. Quinn-Lynx's fangs held him tight – terrified though otherwise unscathed – until Will-C joined them, dragging a large wire colander across the floor. Quinn-Lynx set down the dormouse and held him fast with a paw until Will-C flipped the colander over to create a holding pen.

'I wasn't going to say anything. I promise I wasn't,' jabbered the dormouse.

'Say anything to who?' said Quinn-Lynx, circling the strainer.

'The Proconsul and the others.'

'Natterjack is here?' said Will-C.

'Right outside.'

'Good,' said Quinn-Lynx.

'Good?' replied Will-C.

'The place is completely surrounded,' said the dormouse.

'Clever,' said Quinn-Lynx.

'But let me go, and I'll tell them . . . I'll tell them you managed to sneak out and get away. I'll tell them you're dead. I'll tell them whatever you want me to tell them.'

'That's OK,' said Quinn-Lynx, his eyes narrowing. 'I'll tell them myself.'

'Are you mad?' said Will-C. 'Setting a trap for the falcon was one thing. We can't fight Natterjack's entire army. We don't stand a chance.'

'Who said anything about a fight?' said Quinn as he shape-shifted into a dormouse bearing a remarkable similarity to the captive.

'Just see to it that our new-found friend stays put.'

'What are you . . .? Wait, where are you going?'

'To deploy our most potent weapon.'

'Which is what?'

'Natterjack's thirst for power.' And with that Quinn scampered away, darted through the gap in the wall and disappeared.

*   *   *

As he reached the vegetable garden at the rear of the cottage, Quinn began to catch sight of the creatures hidden in the surrounding trees and hedgerows. His slender rodent snout searched the air for the scent of the toad.

He needn't have worried about locating him as a pack of rat scouts had tracked his progress since he emerged from the house. Thinking that he was the spy they'd sent in, they now fell in to form an escort to lead him back to the District Proconsul. One of their number – a wily senior member of the pack – continually sniffed and eyed the dormouse with suspicion, so Quinn picked up the pace and deliberately cut through a thick patch of wild mint in the hope of disguising his Nsray scent.

The giant toad had made his camp in the compost heap behind the potting shed at the end of the garden. A hill of live snails had been set before him, and he was enjoying feasting on them as each attempted a painfully slow escape. But, if his appetite knew no bounds, he was even hungrier for information. As Quinn-Dormouse approached, the rats retreated a respectful distance.

'Well?' said Natterjack as the small rodent stood before him.

For a moment Quinn toyed with the idea of shape-shifting into a fox and ending the toad's life with a snap of his jaws. He fought the impulse; there was no telling how the massed Animalians would respond – he might escape, but Will-C might not fare so well. Far better to defeat the enemy without a fight.

'Did you find the feline Truckle?'

'I did.'

'And the swift?'

'The bird has gone.'

'Gone?'

Faelken flew down and settled on a fallen tree.

'North.'

'What!' spat Natterjack, scattering the snails.

'That's impossible,' said Faelken. 'We've been on constant watch.'

'He was the Shape-shifter,' said the dormouse.

'I knew it,' said Natterjack.

'He shape-shifted into a pygmy shrew and sneaked out.'

'The rodent lies,' hissed Faelken.

'Then search the human's lair. There's only the Truckle,' said Quinn-Dormouse. 'The Shape-shifter fears you, Proconsul. He knew you had set a trap.'

'How?'

'I don't know. All I know is I heard them talking. He returned to reunite the cat with his human companion, but, when he learned of your presence, the Shape-shifter fled.'

'Where did he go? Where is the human child?'

'North, beyond the Downs. A big city. The place the humans call London.'

'The Truckle knows where?'

'No. The Truckle knows nothing. He was left behind as bait . . . to keep you here while the Shape-shifter returns to the child.'

'And you overheard all this?'

'Yes.'

'Then he has only just escaped! Get the crows in the sky!' cried Natterjack. 'Search the woods and the fields! Not a single creature passes beyond the Downs,' he yelled at the four-footed hordes.

In an instant, the sky was alive with birds, the ground crawling with Animalians breaking cover. Natterjack loped to his bulldog mount and leapt atop it. He twisted its ears to press for more speed, but the lumbering beast wasn't built for pace.

'FAELKEN!' cried Natterjack.

The gyrfalcon circled back and glided down alongside the dog, and Natterjack leapt on to its back. Though reluctant to carry the warty passenger, Faelken knew better than to protest. It took him a moment to adjust to the extra weight, but soon he was climbing skyward once more.

Quinn's plan seemed to be working perfectly; both he and Will-C were completely forgotten in the heat of the moment. He breathed a sigh of relief and looked on as the Animalian forces mobilized. But then . . .

A herring gull swept over the property, dived towards the garden and tumbled to a clumsy crash-landing, scattering cane stakes and netting in its wake, as it flipped head over tail into the vegetable patch. The Animalian hordes looked on, surprise turning to amazement as the gull slowly metamorphosed into a chuckling child. Drue!

'Look! There!' cried a crow.

Faelken checked his flight path, banked and turned. And, as Natterjack's face lit up with delight, so Quinn's filled with horror.

'Drue!' he cried. But his rodent voice was merely a thin squeal lost on the wind.

'Go!' barked Natterjack, anxious to claim his prize.

The falcon swept back its wings and plummeted from the sky.

Still quite unaware of the impending danger, Drue sat up and brushed the dirt and bark chips from her clothes.

In a flash, Quinn transformed from dormouse, to lynx, to cheetah as he bounded across the garden, sprang from the ground and snapped at the diving falcon, halting its attack on his daughter.

Faelken survived the cheetah attack with just the loss of a few tail feathers, but it gave Quinn a precious few seconds to shape-shift back into human form.

'Run, girl, run!' yelled Quinn at Drue. 'Get in the house!'

Above them Natterjack urged Faelken to make another attack. All around the Animalian forces were returning to the garden; the sky was suddenly black with birds, the ground alive with movement.

Quinn shape-shifted into an enormous grizzly bear and *ROARED* at the oncoming Animalians. The booming sound and sharp, gleaming fangs sent the less committed combatants scurrying for cover. Not so the rats, minks and weasels, who closed ranks and advanced as one, albeit more cautiously.

A cloud of cawing crows and ravens descended on the grizzly and, despite his fractured paw, Quinn twisted and swung, and swatted them away like flies. Blood, spittle, fur and feathers filled the air and, in the frenzy of the battle, it took Quinn-Grizzly a moment to realize that he had an ally: a snipe had joined the fray, putting his rapier-like bill to good use to fight alongside him.

'Gallinago!'

'Aye!'

'Get Drue away from here.'

'Where is she?'

Seemingly oblivious to the rats leaping on to his coat, Quinn-Grizzly scanned the combat zone for his daughter.

'DRUE!' he roared.

A harrier hawk swooped and began pecking and tearing at the rats clinging to the blood-spattered coat of the writhing grizzly.

'It's OK, Dad, I'm here,' said Drue-Hawk.

'No!' yelled Quinn-Grizzly. 'This is not for you! Go now. Go!'

With the bear's attention momentarily diverted, the ground forces attacked in even greater numbers, biting and slashing with razor tooth and claw. Quinn-Grizzly howled in pain, but still he kept swinging and working his powerful jaws, smashing bones and slicing flesh to defend himself and his daughter from the terrible onslaught.

'Kill them!' screamed Natterjack, still clinging to the back of the gyrfalcon. And then he saw his chance . . .

The grizzly was so thick with rats it appeared that he was wearing another fur coat atop his own; the snipe was locked in a deadly duel with a curlew, and Drue-Hawk had been driven to the ground by a clutch of ravens.

'There!' yelled Natterjack at Faelken as he jabbed a fleshy digit in Drue-Hawk's direction.

The falcon swooped and the toad sprang from his back . . . only to collide in mid-air with . . . a three-legged Truckle. Will-C had thrown himself between the Proconsul and Drue-Hawk. The two tumbled across the lawn, wrestling for superiority.

'Will-C!' cried Drue. Then realizing that the toad was getting the upper hand: 'No. Leave him alone!'

Natterjack clung to Will-C's back and tore at his whiskers.

Faelken climbed, set himself, wheeled about, splayed his talons and zeroed in for the kill.

But just when all hope and prayers seemed exhausted, the mean torbie cat named Lennox threw himself into the fray. A single blow from the torbie had Faelken spinning off course again, and Lennox's streetwise crew launched themselves into the thick of the battle, putting themselves between Drue-Hawk, Will-C and Natterjack's Animalian mercenaries.

Faelken lunged. The torbie parried. Faelken lunged again, and this time the contest was ended . . . by Natterjack's bulldog slave. The bulldog caught Faelken in its jaws, snatched him right out of the air and, with a jarring crack of bones, crushed the life from him.

Natterjack looked on, wide-eyed, as the bulldog tossed aside the bird of prey and turned to glare at his former tormentor. The big toad tried to flee, but the bulldog chased him down in a few short bounds and threw his whole weight on to Natterjack, pounding his body into the earth.

Natterjack's death had an instant impact. With their leader defeated, his Animalian followers fell back to regroup.

It was a skirmish won rather than a battle, and certainly not the war, as Quinn knew only too well. Taking full advantage of the momentary lull, however, he spat out the blood oozing from a wound in his mouth and barked orders at the ragtag platoon of Truckles.

'Fall back.'

'But we can take them,' growled Lennox.

'No. We're outnumbered. They'll fetch reinforcements and come again. Fall back.'

'To where?' said Will-C. 'The house?'

'No. Callow's Farm. There are others there. Friends.'

'You're coming too,' said Drue-Hawk anxiously.

'No. You and I must leave.'

'I'm not leaving Will-C again!'

'You'd rather see him killed? We are the ones they want. We need to draw them away. Get to the Land Rover and fire it up. The keys are still inside.'

'But we could just fly.'

'I can't. I'm hurt. Besides, they have our scent now. They'd track us.'

'But the car will be even easier for them to . . .'

'DO AS I SAY! GO! NOW!' roared Quinn-Grizzly.

Without another word, Drue-Hawk wheeled away. She met Will-C's frightened eyes, held his gaze for a split second and then flew away over the cottage roof.

Quinn-Grizzly shook his bristling coat; it was soaked in blood, still warm, still sticky. Much of it was Animalian, but some of it was his, and he could feel a hundred bites and gashes beneath his grizzly fur.

'Gallinago, you go with the Truckles. Wait for us at Callow's Farm. We'll join you by nightfall,' he said.

'An' if ya don't?'

'Then we won't be joining you at all.'

The rats and crows gathered round the Proconsul's broken body as the other wild Animalians looked on in eager anticipation; they were waiting for a sign, a signal. Was it over? Were they to disperse or re-engage the enemy?

Quinn retained his grizzly form as he slowly backed away from the scene, flanked by Will-C, the bulldog, Lennox and what remained of the torbie's lion-hearted crew.

The sign from the rats and crows was unequivocal: after a moment of deliberation, a silent motion was passed between them and, all at once, the carnivores tore at the dead toad's flesh and feasted on it.

A shiver of guilty excitement and expectation rippled through the onlookers; corrupt, ruthless sociopathic though he was, Natterjack had nonetheless been the officially appointed District Proconsul, the chief of the local Council of Elders, and it had been his office, rather than the force of his personality, that had caused the Animalians of the county to fall in behind him. But here they were picking over his bones.

In that small brutal act, the nature of the conflict was transformed. With the toad gone, and the other Elders absent, the mercenaries would fill the void. With adrenalin coursing through their veins and the smell of blood in the air, they intended to embark on a feast of slaughter, for which none would be held to account.

'Go,' said Quinn quietly to the Truckles as he shape-shifted from grizzly to cheetah. Will-C and the others took that as a cue and sprinted away across the garden.

Drue had reverted to human form to start the engine of the 4 x 4, and she slipped across to the passenger seat as she saw the cheetah bound up alongside. Quinn also became human again as he pulled open the passenger door.

'Get behind the wheel!'

'Me?!' cried Drue anxiously.

'You can do it. You've done it before.'

'Three-point turns in the driveway!'

'Drue . . .' said Quinn as a wave of pain swept through him like a tide.

'Dad!'

'Seat belt! Drive!'

Suddenly a buzzard landed on the windscreen; its hooked bill cracked against the glass.

'DRIVE!' yelled Quinn as he leaned across and flipped on the wipers. Drue gripped the steering wheel and slipped down, almost off the seat, to reach the accelerator pedal with her toes. Crows, rooks, ravens and seagulls began circling, pecking and clawing and slamming themselves against the windows.

'Hit the gas!' cried Quinn.

'What?! What gas?!'

'The accelerator!'

'I'm trying!' screamed Drue.

And with that the Defender roared into life. It burst forward, careened off the gravel drive, chewed up a flower bed and fishtailed, slamming into the open five-bar gate with a bone-shaking crunch as Drue swung it out on to the lane.

'Go! Go! Go!' yelled Quinn, craning his neck to catch sight of the Animalians in hot pursuit.

'Go? W-w-where do I go?' stammered Drue, her hands gripping the steering wheel so tightly her knuckles were white as bone.

'Just keep it on the road!'

The Defender sideswiped a parked car with a juddering clash of metal on metal.

'Sorry,' said Drue.

'More gas, move up a gear. More gas!'

As the Defender picked up speed and snaked away down the street, the Animalian ground forces thinned out.

But the aerial threat was another matter entirely, the sky thick with birds following in the 4 x 4's wake.

A raven managed to draw up right alongside Drue, causing her to jerk the steering wheel and clip another parked car. The impact ripped the nearside wing mirror off and sent it clattering on to the tarmac behind them.

'Steady,' said Quinn. 'Ease off the gas a bit. You're doing just fine.'

'But the birds . . . we'll never lose them!'

'We don't want to lose them.'

'But if they catch us they'll kill us.'

'The plan is they kill us before they catch us.'

'What?!'

Quinn snatched the wheel.

'Turn here, off the road; cut through that field. Brace yourself . . .'

All four wheels of the Defender left the ground as it flew across a drainage ditch, ploughed through a hedge and came crashing to the ground again in a vast field of horticultural greenhouses. Quinn tugged on the steering wheel and the vehicle smashed through a pair of glass doors.

As the 4 x 4 thundered on through the interior of a vast glasshouse, the birds kept abreast on the outside.

'There!' said Quinn, pointing at a gap between some saplings on the edge of the wood up ahead.

'How?!' cried Drue.

'Faster!' yelled Quinn.

The lead crows swooped low.

'Look at them,' said a crow contemptuously. 'They think they can outrun us. Once they get stuck in the forest, we'll move in for the kill.'

The Defender burst out of the far end of the industrial unit in an explosion of glass, and hurtled on through a barbed-wire fence, ripping fence posts from the ground as it did so. The wire stuck in the vehicle's grille and the wooden stakes were dragged beneath the chassis, bouncing dangerously close to the wheels.

'Dad,' cried Drue.

'Have faith, Angel. Just a little further.'

And then a stretch of water appeared up ahead.

'Dad!' screamed Drue. Unless they changed course, they had no option but to drive straight into the lake. And that is exactly what Quinn had in mind.

'Don't go too fast; we don't want to flip over when we hit the water. Roll down your window.'

'What?'

'Roll down your window!'

Drue struggled to do as instructed as the Land Rover thundered on through the undergrowth, splintering saplings and ripping low-hanging branches from the trees.

'Steady now.'

But, despite Drue's best efforts, the trailing barbed wire had wound round the front axle and, with a bone-shaking jolt, a fence post locked the front wheel on the driver's side. The 4 x 4 juddered, skidded in the soft earth, flipped on to its side, somersaulted through the air . . . and came crashing down into the water on its roof.

Dangling upside down in a cab rapidly filling with slimy green water, Quinn and Drue had been saved from serious injury by their seat belts.

'Drue. Are you hurt?'

She was in shock, tears streaming from her eyes.

'Drue. Reach down and release your belt. Take a deep breath!'

A beat. A groan of twisted metal. And then the 4 x 4 sank like a stone through the swirling algae soup. The chasing flock turned circles over the lake as air bubbles broke the surface.

In the murky depths, the water-filled vehicle continued to glide to the bottom of the deep lake.

Quinn had released his own seat belt, and he helped Drue slip free of hers. Her face was contorted with fear and the strain of holding her breath; tiny air bubbles escaped from her lips. Quinn indicated that Drue should follow him and, by way of a demonstration, he shape-shifted into an otter.

194

Drue didn't respond or acknowledge him in any way. Quinn reverted to human form again. He held his daughter's face in his hands, lifted it into a small air pocket trapped in the footwell above their heads. She gasped for air. Quinn took another breath himself and then shape-shifted once more into an otter.

Finally, Drue seemed to get the message and she too became an otter. They swam with ease from the wrecked car and fanned their webbed feet to push away through the dense silt cloud that had risen from the lake bed.

Up above, kittiwake gulls joined the crows and began to dive into the water in search of the Land Rover. But the depth of the lake, the quantity of algae and the silt kicked up by the impact of the crash made it impossible for the kittiwakes to reach the wreck, or even make out if the shape-shifting fugitives were still inside it.

'It's too deep,' said one of the kittiwakes, emerging from the water with a thin film of slime on her plumage.

'Hmmm,' said a crow. 'We need someone who can get down there. A water shrew or a vole maybe.'

'Keep watch. I'll go for help,' said another member of the flock.

And, while the birds settled in the surrounding trees and turned tight circles over the rippling lake, two otters finally emerged, gasping for air, in a thicket of bulrushes half a mile from the crash site. For the longest while they just lay on the riverbank, catching their breath. There was so much to say. So much to share. But at that moment they were content just to be.

Chapter Twenty-Nine

The journey back to Callow's Farm was a difficult one for Quinn Beltane. He had sustained a broken rib when the Defender crashed into the lake, and multiple wounds from the fighting, to add to his fractured wrist. Despite this, he did his best to mask the seriousness of his injuries from Drue.

They travelled as a pair of foxes to attract less attention. To avoid having to talk too much himself, Quinn asked Drue to tell him about her flight from the breaker's yard.

Drue didn't need to be asked twice, and Quinn could see she was filled with wonder and excitement at the discovery of her gift. By the time she had finished reliving the blow-by-blow details of how she had made good her escape from the bats and the rats (whose ranks had swelled to ten times the actual number during the telling), Quinn realized that it was time to inject a cautionary note.

Though Drue's intuitive if rudimentary grasp of the mechanics of shape-shifting pleased her father, he knew full well that, given her character and youthful exuberance, the finer details of becoming a true Nsray Adept might easily be neglected. It was time to spell out the golden rules and, as Quinn-Fox did so, he insisted that Drue-Fox repeat them back to him to make sure that she truly understood.

'Rule one,' said Drue-Fox in her soft vixen voice, 'a Shape-shifter cannot retain the form of another creature when asleep. He or she will revert back to human form.'

'Good. Golden rule number two?' said Quinn-Fox.

'Animals have more evolved senses than humans, and some of them are able to detect the scent of a Nsray Shape-shifter.'

'Even when we're in animal guise. Good. Three?'

'It takes time to master the nature of each creature; choose your species carefully.'

'With the greatest of care,' added Quinn. 'In some ways, the third rule is the most important of all: it's easy to forget the part that instinct plays in how we behave. Take the collective consciousness of predatory pack animals . . .'

'Like what?'

'Lions, wolves, even feral dogs. That pack mentality can be dangerously intoxicating – you can quickly lose sight of yourself. Be absolutely sure that you retain control when you adopt a form.

'To evolve from Novice to Adept is no easy thing: it takes a great deal of study, meditation and practice; whether that's your destiny, only time will tell. But never forget that it's a journey that begins and ends in the mind. These bodies we inhabit, skin and bones, they're incredibly useful, of course, but really they're just vessels, vehicles for the . . . well, the expression of the spirit.'

'What is the spirit?'

'That's a question Man has been struggling to answer since the beginning of time,' said Quinn.

'But that's where Mum is now, isn't it? In the spirit world?'

'Yes, she is.'

'In heaven.'

'Well, different cultures have different ideas about what that is.'

'Well, if Mum's there, it must be a nice place.'

'Yes, you're quite right, Angel. It must be.'

Shafts of sunlight lanced through the dense canopy of the woodland, and cabbage white butterflies fluttered across a vast carpet of early bluebells and wild garlic. For a moment, at one with the beautiful unspoilt landscape – a favourite haunt of his beloved soulmate Serah – Quinn was almost able to forget his pain, and the scale of the challenge that lay ahead.

They travelled several miles before the shady woodland opened out on to a vast undulating field of oilseed rape. The lemon-yellow crops burned so brightly after the dense canopy of the trees that it almost hurt the eyes, but it told Quinn that the journey back to the farmhouse was almost complete. While skirting the field, padding along a bramble-strewn public footpath, the Shape-shifters heard a noise that stopped them dead in their tracks . . .

A telephone rang.

A *telephone*. Rang!

And it continued to ring. A sound that was at once both familiar and, in the circumstances, truly startling. It took a second or two for Quinn to register that he really was hearing the sound rather than imagining it. Pricking his ears, Quinn-Fox took off at a sprint in search of the source. Drue-Fox stayed close, ducking through nettles and brambles and tall grass, exhilarated and puzzled and fearful all at the same time.

A steep bank led to an even steeper slope, which in turn ran down to a single-lane back road. A stone's throw from where the two panting foxes emerged from a thicket stood a red, graffiti-scarred phone box. The payphone inside continued to ring.

Drue was surprised to find that, having got so close, her father was now hesitant. She had expected him to race up, shape-shift, tear the door open, grab the phone and answer the call. Someone was out there! It didn't matter who it was. It didn't matter where they were. Someone else had survived! Someone else was on the other end of that line!

'Dad!' said Drue-Fox.

''Ush,' said Quinn-Fox.

'But Dad . . .'

''Ush, child,' said Quinn-Fox softly but firmly as he trawled the air with his muzzle.

Still the phone rang.

Finally, Drue-Fox could bear the suspense no more and, despite her father's caution, she broke free and ran.

Just as she reached the phone box . . .

A huge eagle owl landed on the roof. Drue-Fox froze, her vixen instinct attuned to the fact that the bird of prey – a formidable hunter with talons capable of crushing bone – was a serious threat. And, if a solitary eagle owl spelled trouble, the arrival of its mate, turning slow circles round the phone box, filled Drue-Fox with even greater dread.

Still the phone rang.

The menacing bird shifted its head this way and that, tall ear tufts twitching as it listened to the curious artificial chirping of the phone beneath it.

'A human call?' said the eagle owl, its blazing orange eyes appraising the cowering vixen.

'Do you see any?' barked Quinn-Fox, taking both Drue-Fox and the eagle owls by surprise. He loped up to the phone box, scanning the surroundings like a soldier on patrol.

'Humans. Do you see any?' said Quinn-Fox again. 'We heard the call and thought we might be needed. You see anything from up there?' he asked, engaging the eagle owl on the wing.

Neither bird responded. Quinn-Fox noted a thick flock of rooks and crows passing overhead, and a pack of wild boar crashing through the woodland across the lane. All were travelling in the direction of the lake from which the Beltanes had escaped.

Finally, the telephone fell silent.

'Well,' Quinn-Fox announced loudly, 'if there's nothing to be done here, we'll be on our way.' Then in a whisper to Drue-Fox, 'Do not run.'

The circling eagle owl settled beside the first, folded its great wings and watched with interest as the two foxes ambled away from the phone box and continued on down the open road.

'Slowly,' whispered Quinn-Fox, 'slowly. And do not look back.'

Quinn could sense Drue's tension, her desire to break into a sprint and flee into the woods, and, in an effort to dispel any suspicions their behaviour might have raised, Quinn paused in full view of the giant birds to nonchalantly scratch at his neck with a hind paw. The ploy seemed to work, and when he sneaked a glance he saw the eagle owls take to the sky once more.

As they sailed away in the opposite direction, Quinn caught up to Drue and ushered her back into the relative safety of the undergrowth.

'What were you thinking?' chastised Quinn-Fox.

'I'm sorry,' said Drue-Fox.

'Well, sorry isn't good enough,' grumbled Quinn-Fox, his paternal anxiety getting the better of him. 'I told you to pay attention to your animal instincts. I won't always be there to get you out of trouble.'

'But the phone call . . .' said Drue-Fox, fighting the tears welling in her eyes.

'I know.'

'Someone's out there.'

'I'm aware of that.'

'Well, maybe we could have helped them!'

'It was too dangerous.'

'But Dad . . .'

'Sometimes it's necessary to risk everything, but right now getting ourselves killed isn't going to help anyone.'

Drue-Vixen hung her head.

'Look, I'm sorry. I'm just . . . I'm tired . . . OK . . . I'm sorry, Angel. The good thing is, if there are survivors out there, then they're being helped by Truckles and the

Animalian resistance. When we get back to the farm, we'll see if anyone has heard anything. OK?'

Quinn lifted Drue-Fox's muzzle with his own.

'OK?' he said again.

Drue-Fox nodded.

'Then we'd best move on. Will-C and the others will be waiting.'

And so they resumed their journey, travelling in silence the rest of the way, each pondering who could have been on the other end of that line, and whether they might, one day, get to meet them.

CHAPTER THIRTY

In stark contrast to the peace and serenity of the bluebell wood, the eighteenth-century stone grain barn at Callow's Farm rang with the sound of heated argument. A large middle white pig held court as the assembled farm animals and Truckles – including Will-C, Yoshi, the bulldog and the remains of Lennox's gang – looked on.

'I say the Nsray Shape-shifters will only bring us more trouble. From what these Truckles have told us about the Proconsul and the Council of Elders, it's madness to align ourselves with them.'

'Natterjack's dead. A victim of his own doing,' said Yoshi.

'That's not the point. The toad was merely a puppet of the ruling authority. Do you think his actions went unnoticed by the other members of the Council? Or the Earth Assembly itself?'

Mention of the revered Earth Assembly triggered a series of worried looks and much disconsolate murmuring.

'That's right: I'm not afraid to say it. The fact is, with Man facing extinction, the world is no longer a safe place for peace-abiding Animalians. The kin of Japheth may have survived until now, but their days are numbered, and ours will be too if we consort with them.'

'Aren't ya forgettin' ya was bred to be eaten? Ya weren't so safe wid humans around,' said Gallinago, indignant.

'They provided food and shelter, and protection from the very threat we're faced with now,' argued the sow.

'And apple sauce to make you taste better,' quipped a mangy tomcat, regretting the comment the moment he caught Lennox's disapproving glare.

'So what would you have us do?' said the grey mare.

'Maybe what you say is true and we have to face facts: the world has changed. There's a new order to things now, but we're not alone. The felines, canines and other Truckles are our allies . . .'

'And the Shape-shifters are our best means of ensuring our safety and freedom,' said the middle white.

'Now you're contradicting yourself!' replied the grey mare, exasperated.

'Not at all. I don't like it any more than you, but the truth is, if we turned the Nsray over to the toad's attendants . . .'

'Bunch a rabble,' growled Lennox.

'. . . we might just secure our future in this new world you speak of,' said the middle white.

Gallinago, Will-C and other Truckles bristled at the suggestion.

'The Shape-shifter saved our lives. And now you'd have us betray him,' said the grey mare with contempt in her voice.

'The sow has a valid point,' came a voice from the top of a stack of hay bales.

'My bill has a sharper one! Would ya loike to deal wid dat?' snapped Gallinago, his patience finally at an end.

All eyes turned in search of the challenger and found two foxes eavesdropping on the proceedings.

'I'd rather not, old friend,' said Quinn-Fox. He leapt from the bales and shape-shifted in mid-flight, transforming into a formidable tan-and-white English shepherd, a breed of collie guaranteed to command respect from the farm dwellers.

'Quinn! Ya made it!' cried Gallinago.

The middle white tried hard to hide her blushes.

'I'm sorry,' said the mare. 'The pig doesn't speak for the majority.'

'No. It's OK,' said Quinn-Collie. 'As I said, she does have a point. We're being hunted and so, by harbouring us, you risk putting yourselves in danger.'

'That's all I meant,' said the sow apologetically.

'But,' continued Quinn-Collie, 'turning us over to the renegades will do nothing to increase your chances of survival. Once they're done with us, they'll turn on you. Do you honestly believe that you can negotiate with the rats, the crows, the minks or any of the others? They were ready to see you perish in the tractor shed.'

'Then what can we do?' asked a sheep.

'Who will take Natterjack's place as District Proconsul?' said Quinn, answering the question with one of his own.

'Usually, it would be put to the vote, but now, with the chaos of the war and everything, it's difficult to say,' said Yoshi.

'Rauthaz, the red stag Elder, is the most senior member of Council,' said the mare.

'The toad should never have been appointed to begin with,' said Yoshi.

'There was talk that Natterjack fixed the ballot, but we'll never know the truth.'

The comment triggered a torrent of claims and counter-claims about who had and hadn't voted for Natterjack's appointment to the post and, during the debate, Will-C scaled the bales of hay to join Drue.

Though finally face to face once more, something both had been desperate for, each now found that they were shy in the presence of the other. It didn't help that Drue was a fox, of course, and Will-C sampled the air, a little unsure of her, trying to read her scent.

'It is me,' said Drue. 'See?'

And with that she transformed back into her human form, scooped Will-C up into her arms and hugged him close. He in turn nuzzled and nudged her chin with his whiskered cheeks, and purred with delight. Drue set him down and, with a smile, became a black-and-white short-haired cat.

'Now we can actually talk,' she said, delighted.

Will-C struggled with the idea.

'We . . . can talk?'

'Isn't it just the freakiest thing?'

'We can talk,' repeated Will-C, amazed.

'I've always wondered what you'd sound like if I could talk to you, and now, well, here we are . . . talking.'

'But how do you do that?'

'Shape-shift?'

'Does it hurt when you change?'

'Hurt? No, it's . . . it's kind of . . . there's like this . . . this tingling . . . but it's . . . like pins and needles. But really quick. Do cats get pins and needles?'

'What's pins and needles?'

'It's . . . Hey, I'm purring! It's like . . . like smiling on the inside.'

Drue-Cat leapt on Will-C and the pair rolled playfully in the hay.

Beneath them, a more serious exchange unfolded.

'So is this Elder, the red stag, to be trusted?' asked Quinn.

The middle white was the first to respond. 'Trusted with what?'

'My life,' answered Quinn.

The statement met with a resounding silence. Quinn-Collie's brown eyes roved across the Truckles and farm animals. Though it was not apparent to them, he was tired, aching from head to foot and in desperate need of rest and recuperation. Drawing on his last reserves, he puffed out his chest and in a commanding voice said:

'Drue. Will-C. Pay attention! I do not want to repeat myself.'

The two cats broke off from their playful reunion.

'The time has come to make a choice,' said Quinn-Collie. 'There are many paths ahead, and if any of you wish to pursue a different course I won't stand in your way, save to protect my daughter. But, having listened to your arguments, having seen the bloodshed first-hand, I have a plan that'll give each and every creature here the best possible chance of survival. Drue and I could take our chances in the new world order as could each of you, but together . . . *together* I believe our chances of success are that much greater.'

The animals fell silent. Finally, the grey mare spoke.

'So what would you have us do?'

'We send an envoy with a message for Rauthaz and the Council of Elders. And the message is this: in return for a guarantee of safe passage and an amnesty for the Truckle escort, we will deliver Natterjack's killer – the Shape-shifter *you've* captured and have held in custody – to the Earth Assembly's Court of Judgement.'

'Dad?' interjected Drue-Cat anxiously.

Quinn-Collie silenced her with a look, then turned his attention back to the Truckles.

'That's right. You turn me in and buy your own freedom.'

The bulldog hung his head. Everyone knew that he had in fact delivered the death blow to the toad, but here was a Nsray Adept willing to assume responsibility.

Yoshi had been present at the death and he could see the bulldog struggling with his conscience.

'Why would you do this when the Earth Assembly are certain to order your execution? They hate your kind even more than ours,' said Yoshi.

'Let's just say I don't believe in hatred. And belief is a powerful weapon. I'm prepared to take my chances with that.'

The Animalians began to whisper among themselves.

'Talk. Think. Decide what you want to do,' said Quinn. 'Give me your answer in the morning. Gallinago . . .'

'Yes?'

'Drue and I will be in the farmhouse. Can I rely on you to keep watch?'

'Ya know ya can.'

The crowd parted as Quinn-Collie moved off across the cobbled yard.

'Drue.'

Drue-Cat shared a look with Will-C. 'Come on,' she said.

'Are you sure?' said Will-C.

'Drue!' Quinn's voice bristled with uncharacteristic impatience.

'I'll join you in a bit,' said Will-C, a little worried by the tone of Quinn's voice.

'His bark is worse than his bite, but you already know that,' said Drue. Then she bumped Will-C's head affectionately and, still in feline form, sprang down from the hay bales and bounded after her father.

CHAPTER THIRTY-ONE

Alongside the east wall of the Callows' farmhouse lay a substantial wooden gate, which opened on to a large parking area – empty now save for a vintage tangerine Citroën Deux Chevaux raised on breeze blocks. It was bordered by a complex of kennels large enough to house as many as a dozen dogs, though it now stood as empty and redundant as the yard itself.

The door leading to the boot room off the kitchen was ajar, and it was through this that Quinn-Collie gained access. Once inside, he shape-shifted back into his human form and slumped exhausted into the only chair still standing beside the oak dining table. Just like the Beltanes' kitchen, this one had been ransacked and pots, pans and cookery books spilled over the flagstone floor.

Drue also reverted back to her human form and closed the kitchen door behind her. For a moment she studied her father, his head now resting in his hands, elbows supported by the table.

'Dad, are you OK?'

Quinn turned, beckoned to her and opened his arms to receive his only child. Drue wrapped her arms round his broad back, his flannel shirt damp with sweat and blood. He hugged her close, his breathing shallow and laboured.

'My darling girl,' said Quinn. 'My darling girl.'

Pain, anguish, fear, frustration, hope, concern and parental pride were all manifest, all infused, in that precious moment. The relationship between father and daughter would never be the same again, yet it was more potent now, more profoundly charged, than it had ever been. And it was during the course of this simple, yet remarkable exchange that Drue felt the first blossoming of true responsibility. With his guard down, it was clear that her father was suffering; his multiple injuries had finally begun to take their toll.

'Dad, you're hurt.'

'I'll be fine.'

'You're bleeding.'

'I'm just tired.'

'You're more than that. We need to clean those cuts. I'll see if there's any medicine and stuff in the bathroom.'

'Boil up some water,' said Quinn weakly. 'The stove runs on propane gas.'

He reached down to pick up an iron saucepan from the floor. The effort was almost too much.

'Leave that, I'll get it,' said Drue. 'Just rest. Leave everything to me.'

★ ★ ★

Later, having dined on hot soup made from vegetables gathered from the kitchen garden, with his cuts and bruises cleaned and dressed, Quinn lay dozing on an old utility sofa in the living room. As a precaution against a surprise attack during the night, Drue barricaded the casement windows with whatever furniture she could lift, while Will-C did his best to stay out from under her feet.

There were perfectly good beds to be found on the floor above, but Drue had discovered – to her horror – that there were bloodstains dried black on the stair carpet and upstairs landing. As a result, she and her father had agreed (even though it was patently clear that the Callow family had perished and were never to return) that it would be improper, disrespectful, to occupy the abandoned bedrooms.

Will-C looked on as Drue sat beside her father and adjusted the heavy blanket covering him. Quinn seemed to sense her presence and stirred. He studied her pale young face, her fine hair, her pretty blue-green eyes. She in turn studied his features: tanned and lined, his salt-and-pepper stubble now a full-face beard. Lying there, he seemed less intimidating, frail almost.

Drue put a palm to his forehead; it was damp with perspiration.

'Do you feel hot?'

'I'm a little chilly if anything.'

'I could make a fire, maybe . . .'

'No! Never! Remember . . .'

'I know, I know, the smoke. It's just . . .'

Quinn studied his daughter's face.

'You look more like your mother every day,' he said, cupping his good hand to Drue's flushed cheek. The move, though tentative, put pressure on his broken rib and sent a wave of pain surging through his body. He withdrew his hand.

'What can I do? Do you need anything else?' asked Drue.

'Just to know that you're safe, Angel. Just to know that you're safe.'

'I think we're OK here tonight, don't you?'

'Yes. But check on Gallinago before you turn in. Be sure there's always more than one pair of eyes on watch. We don't want any more surprises.'

'I'll go and talk to him now.'

'Don't be too long. And don't spend all night yacking with that damn fleabag feline.'

Drue knew full well that, despite his gruff manner, in his heart her father had a soft spot for her beloved cat.

'Dad,' said Drue softly, 'did you mean what you said?'

'About that mangy cat?'

'About giving yourself up to the Animalians?'

Will-C's ears pricked up, though he had no idea what was being discussed. Quinn's words came more slowly now: a combination of fever and exhaustion beginning to dull his sharp mind.

'Don't worry. I've no intention of offering myself up as Sunday lunch. But the truth is we can't just keep running and hiding. The chances of us being hunted down and caught increase every day. And if there are other survivors out there . . . and it seems that there might be, well, they have even less chance of finding a safe haven than the Nsray do.'

'So you plan to do what . . . to talk with the . . . what is it? The Earth Assembly? Who are they anyway?'

'They're kind of like the government or the United Nations; they set the rules by which the animal kingdom live their lives.'

'Is there like one Prime Minister or a President in charge?'

'Something like that.'

'So they're the ones who started the war?'

'The decision to fight would have been made by them, yes.'

'What will you say to them? And what makes you think they'll listen?'

'Well, we need to demonstrate that they have more to lose than to gain by not listening to us.'

'How?'

'I was hoping you might come up with something.'

'Me?' The worry was etched in Drue's face.

Quinn's jaw softened and he smiled gently.

'I'm just teasing, Angel. Faith. Faith will play a part, so I need you to stay strong. Your journey will be every bit as challenging as mine.'

'What do you mean? What journey?'

'There was a trip I'd planned to make, but the way things have turned out . . . well, now it's up to you.'

'You don't fool me. You're just saying that to keep me out of the way.'

'No . . . I wish that were true. What I'm going to ask of you will be extremely dangerous. You'll need your wits about you, and every bit of Nsray courage you possess. With luck, the Truckles' negotiations with the Council of Elders will act as a distraction, so that you can slip away unnoticed.'

'To where?'

'The Lonetal. The Valley of the Lone. It's in Germany.'

'What's there?'

'The Lionman.'

'The Lionman?' said Drue, more than a hint of trepidation in her voice.

'You didn't think we were the only two Shape-shifters on the whole planet, did you?'

'No. That is, I didn't . . . I hadn't . . .'

'Well, we're not.'

'Can Will-C come too?'

'Across the Channel? No. It's not a journey to be taken on foot or I'd go myself even in this condition. Gallinago will fly with you. Besides, we need someone here who we can trust implicitly to carry word of my capture to Rauthaz. As envoys go, I don't suppose we could do much better than that mangy three-legged moggy of yours.'

Drue's eyes moved to Will-C. He was desperate to know exactly what was going on, but could tell from Drue's expression that he would have to wait a little longer.

'Are you sure this is the only way? I don't want to leave you.'

'I wish there were another way, my darling, but don't worry: the road will rise to meet us. You'll see. Just stay true to your gift and always follow your heart. And here.' Quinn took a smooth, flat white pebble out of his pocket and handed it to his daughter. 'If you ever get lost, really lost, and don't know which way to go, hold this in your hand and concentrate hard and it'll point the way.'

'How will it do that?'

'I hope you never need to find out.'

Quinn sighed and groaned and shifted to make himself more comfortable.

'I'll go and check on Gallinago,' said Drue.

'Then get plenty of rest. We'll talk some more in the morning,' said Quinn, shutting his eyes.

Drue kissed her dad's forehead.

'Night, Dad.'

'Night, Angel.'

Drue secured the white pebble in a pocket and started for the door.

'Drue.'

'Uh-huh.'

'Not a word about the Lionman to Will-C, OK? It's not that he can't be trusted; it's just . . . it'll be safer for him, for the Truckles, for all of us . . . if we keep it between you and me.'

Drue considered the request for a moment . 'OK.'

'Promise?'

'Promise.'

'I love you, Angel.'

'I love you too, Dad.'

With that, Quinn drew in a deep breath, shivered from the chill he could feel in his bones and settled once again beneath his blanket.

Drue slipped quietly out of the room with Will-C at her heels.

In the dark boot room, she opened the door to the yard before shape-shifting back into cat form once more. Though she and Will-C were exhausted, neither would find it easy to sleep. Their lives, the whole world, were in flux all around them, and they didn't want to miss a precious second of whatever time they had left together.

The cobbled yard was a maze of moon-shadows and, as Drue-Cat picked her way across it, she found herself drawn to the star-filled sky. The distant beacons of light seemed more numerous, seemed to burn brighter than ever before, and she wondered whether that was due to the lack of light pollution emanating from the Earth or her newly acquired Animalian instincts heightening her awareness.

'What is it?' said Will-C, staying close to her side.

'Do the stars look brighter to you?'

'Not really,' replied Will-C.

'Do animals ever wonder about what's up there?'

'Up there?'

'In space, beyond the clouds, up there in the stars.'

'The same thing as down here.'

'How do you mean?'

'Well, I don't really understand it exactly, but my dad used to say that it's all one thing. All connected. There is no up there and down here. It's all the same.'

'How would he know?'

'Animalians were the first ones from Earth to explore it.'

'Outer space?'

'Sure. Working with the humans and their rocket machines. Mice, dogs, monkeys. All sorts. Many of them died before they could share what they'd learned, but there was one, a squirrel monkey from Peru: she came back from the stars with all sorts of stories.

'The humans must have been impressed too, maybe even

a little worried that they were getting left behind, as shortly after her trip they stopped working with Animalians and started to travel in the rocket machines themselves. My dad said the humans should have sent a cat if they really wanted to learn something, but they seemed to prefer the species who were more . . . well . . . not stupid, but easier to manipulate, I suppose.'

'I heard that,' said the bulldog, giving Will-C a sour look as they ambled past his lookout post.

'Not that dogs are dumb or anything . . .' added Will-C quickly. 'But,' he added in a conspiratorial whisper, 'they never really grow up, if you know what I mean.'

Drue-Cat smiled and surveyed the yard. There were geese perched on the roof of the hay barn and the tractor shed. Gallinago had done a sound job of organizing a rota of sentries and he had elected to take first watch on the weathervane attached to the farmhouse.

'Everything OK?' Drue called up to the snipe.

'Fine,' said Gallinago. 'How's de old man?'

'Sleeping.'

'Ya should get some rest yaself.'

'I will,' said Drue, 'but let me know if you need any help.'

'We got it covered. Dem geese make better guard dogs dan guard dogs.'

'I heard that too,' said the bulldog from the shadows.

Drue-Cat and Will-C worked their way full circle back to the kitchen door. All was quiet and still, and Drue glanced up at the stars one last time before heading back inside.

Padding across the room on soft feline paws, Drue leapt up on to the makeshift bed – blankets atop cushions straddling the seats of two wing-back armchairs – that stood adjacent to the sofa where her father slept. Will-C joined her, and, as they circled and settled, two cats in a cradle, Drue noticed that Quinn was groaning and mumbling in his sleep. The fingers of his good hand twitched, even curled into a fist, as he battled with some internal struggle.

'A bad dream,' whispered Will-C.

'What?' said Drue, distracted.

'I said it looks like he's having a bad dream.'

'Yeah, I guess,' replied Drue.

Part of her, a faint whisper in the back of her mind, feared that it was something worse than that, but it wasn't a voice she was ready to acknowledge. As Quinn settled into a regular breathing pattern, Drue-Cat turned her attention back to Will-C and the bizarre reality of her own adopted feline form. She toyed with her whiskers with a paw.

'It's so weird having these things sticking out of your face,' she said softly. 'And a tail. How funny is that?'

'It's not just for show, you know.'

'Oh, I know; it twitches when you're cross.'

'That comes in useful for communicating with species who don't speak Animalian, but the tail does a lot more than that.'

'Like what?'

'Like helping with balance. And we use them to sense changes in temperature. Even to tell which way the wind is blowing when we're hunting, so we know if our scent will be detected.'

Will-C could see that Drue was itching to ask a question, but couldn't quite bring herself to do so.

'What?' he said.

'Well ... I've always wanted to know ... I mean, you don't have to say, but ... it doesn't make any difference ... you know that I love you anyway ... but ...'

'How come I've got three legs instead of four?'

'Was it an accident? Did you get hit by a car or something?'

'I had a brother. A twin. In every other way, we were just like any other cats, but we were born joined together. We both had two front legs, but ...'

'You were joined together?'

'Yes. And the human family my mother was living with ... well, I suppose they didn't take to us.'

'What happened?'

'We weren't more than a few weeks old when they put us in a little box. It was dark. We didn't know where they were taking us. We could hear our mother calling and then we couldn't hear her voice any more ... just this roaring sound. And suddenly we were moving really fast, being bounced around ...'

'You were in a car, I bet.'

'And the next thing we knew we were falling. It was still black as night inside the box and we were huddled together ... and then we hit something hard. Water started gushing in the lid of the box and we realized we were in a river. We would have drowned for sure, but, as the box sank, the water made the walls soft, and we kicked and scratched and clawed a hole in it.'

'What happened then?'

'Somehow, we must have made our way to the bank, I'm

220

not sure how because I passed out. Eventually, we were found by a Truckle . . . a canine called Poppy, and she went off and brought back her adopted human.'

'I'm amazed you ever trusted a human again.'

'We did think she might throw us back into the river . . . but instead she took us to this place where they take sick Animalians . . .'

'A vet.'

'A vet?'

'Yeah. A vet. Veterinarian. A doctor for animals.'

'What's a doctor?'

'A . . . vet . . . for sick people.'

'OK, well, they took us there and they looked after us for a bit, and then they did this thing that separated us.'

'An operation.'

'There were other Truckles around the place who had heard that it would be dangerous, that maybe we wouldn't survive after the humans cut us.'

'And the woman who found you?'

'Didn't see her again, nor the dog Poppy.'

'So what happened to your twin?'

'We knew when the cut day came as they didn't feed us like they normally did. Water, that was all. And then they gave us something that made us sleepy . . .'

'Anaesthetic.'

'Anis—?'

'Anaesthetic.'

'Anyway, it made us sleepy and my brother Te, he thought that maybe if we put in all of our concentration, all of our shared energy . . . maybe one of us had a chance to survive, but not both. So we did. And then I guess he just . . . let go of life. That was the last time I ever saw him. On that table under the bright lights.

'I still miss him every day. Sometimes when I wake up, just for a moment, it's like I can feel him there again. Like he's still a part of me.'

'He is . . . in a way I mean.'

'Hmm, that's what my dad used to say too. Anyway, I still miss him.'

'I know that feeling.'

For a moment they sat in silence, each just content to be in each other's company.

'You talk about your dad; what about your mum?'

'I don't know what happened to her. I don't even know if she's still alive. The humans she lived with moved away to a different country somewhere. My father, he was . . . he was pretty wild, independent, a loner I suppose. Nothing against humans, but he preferred to live off the land. He was Feline Proxy for the area at the time, and he'd been searching for me and my brother ever since we were taken away from home. When he heard what had happened with the cut . . .'

'Operation.'

'Op . . . er . . . ation. All these strange new words. Anyway, Dad came and found me. I'd been sent to live on a farm not too far away. They were OK, the humans, but the other Truckles that lived with them . . . because I didn't have four legs . . . they could be pretty cruel. Right from the off they let me know that I wasn't accepted, I didn't fit, I wasn't one of them. They kept it from the humans, of course, but they'd steal my food, gang up on me when I was asleep, scratching and biting. They even put fleas and lice in my fur. Everyone called me Freak.'

'Is that why you ran away?'

'I used to think that. But now I'm not so sure that I ran away at all. I got out . . . but I wasn't running from something, I was running towards something. Do you know what I mean? I just knew somehow that there was another life, a different life I could be living, if I just . . . if I just never stopped believing in it. But that probably sounds crazy . . .'

'As crazy as a twelve-year-old girl from Kingley Burh sprouting whiskers and a tail and speaking Animalian!' she giggled.

Drue-Cat and Will-C shared a look. It was a look of mutual affection and admiration, of friendship and of love, the impossible made possible through the power of the mind.

Drue's feline eyelids began to feel heavy and she shape-shifted back into human form. She adjusted the blankets to make the bed more comfortable, draped a protective arm round her feline friend and drifted quickly into a deep and peaceful sleep, the first she had enjoyed in a very long time.

CHAPTER THIRTY-TWO

Rat-bite fever. That's what Quinn's symptoms suggested to Will-C. He'd seen a cairn terrier succumb to it after a particularly violent scrap once, so he knew that in some circumstances it was potentially fatal. Which made it all the more surprising when Drue, unable to rouse her father from a deep, coma-like sleep, announced that she was leaving.

'But your dad . . . You can't leave him like this,' said Will-C as the two cats sat facing one another like bookends on the kitchen window sill.

'I have to,' replied Drue. 'There's nothing else I can do. I have to go for help.'

'Where?'

'I can't say.'

'Then I'm coming with you,' said Will-C.

'I wish you could,' said Drue, 'but I have to cross the sea and . . . we'd attract too much attention if I carried you. Besides, we need you here; I need you here to look out for my dad.'

'What about Rauthaz and the Council of Elders? Your dad's plan?'

'He can't do that now. We have to get him well again first.'

'But what about the others?'

'Stall them. Buy me some time. I'll be back with help as quick as I can. Gallinago can be trusted; he'll help,' said Drue as she shape-shifted once more into the familiar herring gull form she'd adopted to flee the rats at the breaker's yard.

'Maybe Gallinago should go with you?'

'No. It's better I go alone,' said Drue.

'How long will you be gone?'

'I'm not sure. A day. Two maybe. Not too long.'

Will-C looked less than convinced by the whole idea.

'Look, my dad said there was a Li— another Shape-shifter. I have to find him, that's all. He'll know what to do. We just ... we just have to have faith, that's all; I can't explain it any other way. You know I wouldn't leave you again if I had any choice.'

'I know,' said Will-C.

Drue-Gull flew to her father's side once more. She hovered beside him, registered his shallow breathing. Though he didn't open his eyes, his eyelids flickered with movement. Drue sensed that he was fighting another battle now, one just as testing as that which had laid him low: a battle to ward off whatever virus or infection was attacking his immune system. Reverting back to human form, she took his good hand between hers.

'Dad, if you can hear me ... I'm going now; I'm going to find the Lionman just like you said. And I won't let you down again, I promise. I'll get help. And I'll be back soon. I love you.'

She kissed her father's forehead. Still his eyes didn't open, and his lips didn't move, but Drue was certain that she felt him communicate. A wave of warm, comforting, uplifting energy washed over her, through her, bathing her senses in radiant white light; *I love you too, Angel*, it seemed to say.

Drue shape-shifted back into a herring gull, flew to the kitchen and circled Will-C.

'Be careful,' said Drue-Gull.

'You too,' said Will-C, 'and don't worry. Worry gives a small thing a big shadow.'

'You know your brother would have been proud of you,' said Drue-Gull, hovering by the broken kitchen window.

'You think so?'

'I know so.'

'I wish he could have met you,' replied Will-C.

'Well, maybe one day he will,' said Drue-Gull.

'Is that possible?'

'Anything's possible.'

And, with that, Drue-Gull slipped behind the boxes she had piled up against the kitchen window and ducked through a broken pane.

'Wait,' said Will-C. 'What exactly am I going to say to Gallinago?'

'Tell him . . . tell him I'll try to keep below 200 miles an hour.'

Drue-Gull stretched out her broad wings and soared away up into the sky. Will-C looked on through the broken window as she banked and climbed and flew due east, her grey-and-white plumage quickly becoming little more than a fine, dark line silhouetted against the salmon-pink dawn.

'Anything is possible,' said Will-C to himself.

PART III
INTO THE VALLEY
OF THE LONE

CHAPTER THIRTY-THREE

As Drue-Gull glided east, glad of a 25-knot tailwind, she scanned the landscape below. It was familiar of course – she had been born and raised in West Sussex – but seeing it from the air was really like seeing it all for the very first time.

She flew over the woodland and the lake where she and her father had crashed in the Defender, soared above the grounds of her old school, pressed on over the still and silent racetracks of Goodwood, where sheep, cattle, pigs and even llama now grazed on the verges of the famous motor circuit. Finally, she spotted the spire of Chichester Cathedral. As it came into view, Drue-Gull began her descent, all the while running her last conversation with her father through her mind, sifting it for clues:

Have faith . . . stay true to your gift . . . danger . . . the Lionman . . . The Valley of the Lone.

'The Valley of the Lone,' Drue muttered to herself as she swooped down Tower Street in search of the Chichester public library.

The automated doors to the library – a circular, two-storey glass and timber building – were sealed shut, as they had been since the night the Animalians cut the electricity supplies to the town. Drue pondered the best means of gaining access, and flew up on to the roof to see if the ventilation system might offer a solution.

Though frustrated by the delay, Drue realized that in some respects the difficulty in entering the building boded well, as it meant that it was unlikely that she would encounter any animals inside.

Taking care to shape-shift where she wouldn't be seen by passing birds, Drue became a dormouse to work her way inside. Then, in need of a little more strength and, crucially, fingers for turning pages – but not daring to risk being spotted as human – she adopted the form of a red squirrel.

Moving quickly and quietly, the only sound that of her own light footfalls on the polished parquet floor, Drue-Squirrel skirted the Enquiries desk, slipped round the isle of redundant computer terminals and scaled the tall magazine rack. A short leap and she was soon scrambling across the shelves of the travel section like a freestyle rock climber.

Homing in on a row of publications about Germany, Drue selected a paperback hiking guide, nudged it from the shelf and let it fall to the floor. The book landed with a sharp slap, and Drue-Squirrel froze, senses alert. Satisfied that she was quite alone, she scurried to the ground, opened the book and flipped to the index in the back.

She found what she was looking for: a reference to the Lonetal, the Valley of the Lone. The guide stated that the Lonetal was located beyond the Black Forest in the

Swabian Alps mountain range in the state of Baden-Württemberg in south-west Germany.

Drue-Squirrel consulted a map to get a clear visual reference. She traced a line with her paw across the Channel. A direct route would see her reach the French coastline somewhere around the town of Berck, take her across country and over the commune of Charleville-Mézières, then to a place called Metz and on into Germany, crossing the border at Saarbrücken.

Drue wished she had paid more attention to her geography lessons at school; none of the landmarks were names she had encountered before, and she feared that getting lost could add considerably to what was already over a thousand-mile round trip. On the plus side, at least she now knew exactly where her final destination lay, even if she wasn't quite sure how she was going to locate the mysterious Lionman when she finally got there.

CHAPTER THIRTY-FOUR

The English Channel. Given that crossing it was the first leg of her journey, Drue opted for the familiar form of a herring gull. Though she was aware from her conversations with Gallinago that the gull was not the fastest bird in the air, it proved to be an inspired choice. As the white cliffs of the Sussex coast receded, and Drue found herself flying over a vast blue-green liquid landscape that stretched out as far as her eyes could see, the seabird's innate ability to navigate over water kept her on a steady course.

Apart from the occasional flocks of birds silhouetted against the pale blue sky above, and the dorsal fin of a basking shark breaking the surface of the choppy sea as it circled the wreckage of an upturned fishing boat, Drue's journey passed without incident.

At least until a gigantic 4000-tonne, steel-hulled passenger ferry appeared on the horizon about ten nautical miles from the French coast. The ferry was listing badly to the starboard side, sitting very low in the water, yet appeared to have stabilized; if it was sinking, it was doing so very slowly.

Drue's first thought was to give the vessel a wide berth, but a movement on the main aft deck caught her eye. Something scrambled from the bone-white guard rail to the open steps that led to the deck above. Drue was still too far from the vessel to identify what she had seen, but she felt a surge of excitement . . . could it be a person? A survivor?

Without a moment's hesitation, Drue-Gull banked, increased her speed and buzzed the crippled ferry for a closer inspection. There it was again, a flash of movement. And yes, it was a child! A young boy – propelled by sheer terror – broke cover to scramble up the exposed metal staircase to the second deck.

Drue-Gull wheeled about, but, as she did so, the lad bolted through a double-leaf door and disappeared from sight.

'Wait!' she cried, but then remembered that she was speaking Animalian; to the boy it would just have sounded like the caw of a seagull.

Gliding down to a row of windows on the second deck, Drue-Gull searched for signs of life inside. She found none. The ship was enormous – a floating village really – easily large enough to carry 1500 or so passengers, and it occurred to Drue that it could take some time to track down the boy if he had gone into hiding and didn't want to be found. Still, a fellow survivor: it was nothing short of a miracle.

Turning a broad circle round the gargantuan red funnels on the top deck, Drue weighed up her options. She noted that all but one of the lifeboat stations stood empty, and the remaining lifeboat, still attached by chains to its winch, hung precariously over the port side. Because of the shift in the vessel's centre of gravity, and the way the ferry now sat in the water, it would actually have been possible to walk down the side and climb into the dangling lifeboat as it rested against the hull above the waterline.

Drue imagined the panic and chaos that must have ensued when the ship was attacked: birds leading an assault from the air; sharks, whales, giant squid – who knows what – rising up from the deep to cripple the ship and scuttle the lifeboats as they touched down on the waves. The boy would have been terrified, just as she had been when hiding in the priest-hole. How distant that moment seemed now, given all that had followed, but the memory was still vivid, still frightening.

Swooping back down to the double-leaf door that the boy had entered, Drue-Gull landed on the white metal staircase and reverted to human form.

As she stepped inside, Drue let the heavy door swing shut behind her. The listing ship groaned from somewhere deep down in its bowels, but otherwise the interior was eerily quiet.

'Hello. Hey! Hello, can you hear me?' shouted Drue.

No response.

All around there were abandoned rucksacks, suitcases, jackets, shopping bags, even a toppled pushchair. And there was dried blood. It was on the shattered windows, spattered on the seats and tables and video-game machines. Seagull feathers littered the floor.

'Hello?!' bellowed Drue once more.

Ahead of her a wide flight of stairs spiralled down to the

level below. Either side of it were doors with porthole windows that led to long passageways lined with cabins, and yet more doors and steps leading to different decks: an impossible maze of options.

'Hey, I just want to help. You don't have to be scared!'

A tapping ... metal on metal ... coming from the deck below. Drue moved to the top of the stairs and peered down into the dark stairwell.

'Hello?'

Still no response.

Though she sensed danger, Drue crept down the narrow treads one cautious step at a time. A movement above. She spun round. Too late. A fishing net dropped over her and the weight of it knocked her off her feet. Drue tumbled with a yelp of alarm. Three figures dashed out from the shadows below, and two more clambered down the stairs behind her.

A cry rang out: 'Got her!'

'*Cállate!*' snapped another in Castilian.

Drue squirmed beneath the tangled net as her assailants closed ranks around her. They were boys. A motley crew, sharing but one common attribute: a wild look in the eyes that blazed with fear and adrenalin. The youngest looked about seven, the eldest – twice his height – maybe fourteen or so.

Dishevelled and dressed in crumpled clothes, they were armed with an assortment of makeshift weapons: broken chair legs, a cosh of knotted rope, a stainless-steel soup ladle and a single spear, fashioned from a broken broom handle and a carving knife that was bound to the handle with strips of rag.

The boy with the spear was the next to speak. Slight of frame, with a mess of unkempt hair sticking up from a face that wasn't nearly as menacing as he thought it to be, it was nonetheless apparent that – although he was neither the tallest nor the eldest – he was in charge. His name was Adan and the others hung on his every word, which even in English sounded as though they'd been dipped in Spanish.

'Jack. Go check on the gull-bird. Dobs, also you.'

Jack, it transpired, was the boy whose presence had lured Drue to the wrecked ferry in the first place. As he and Dobs – a chubby pre-teen with a shaved head – darted away up the stairs, Drue struggled to free herself from the net.

'Wait,' she said.

'Shhhh,' hissed Adan, and the razor-sharp blade of the spear glinted with reflected light.

The other boys took up positions on the stairs and crouched down in the shadows. All eyes were fixed on the top of the stairwell, everyone anxiously awaiting the scouting party's return.

'Look, if you'd get this off me . . .' began Drue, trying to sit up.

'I said for quiet,' hissed Adan again. 'And no move. I no tell you again.'

Drue fell silent and stopped wriggling. The entire gang was a cord of nervous energy, fear and fatigue etched into their innocent young faces. One wrong move and Drue feared she might provoke them further; risk getting hurt. Best to bide her time.

Before too long, Jack and Dobs reappeared at the top of the stairwell and scurried back to join the others.

'No sign of the seagull, Ads,' said Dobs.

'Maybe he saw us?' said Jack anxiously.

'You see no others?' asked Adan, leaning against the shaft of his spear.

'Nothing in the sky,' said Dobs. 'No sharks or nothing in the water neither.'

'This may be trick,' said Adan after a moment. 'Best to keep a look in case.'

Jack and Dobs nodded in agreement, but neither moved. They, like the others, were intrigued to learn more about their captive.

'*Vale* . . . we go,' ordered Adan.

And suddenly Drue felt four pairs of hands lift her from the ground. She was still bound in the net as they bundled her down a pitch-black corridor.

'Hey!' yelled Drue as she began kicking and wriggling. But it was more a reflex than a genuine attempt to free herself and, before she knew it, they had hauled her through the doors of a small auditorium.

Battery-powered hurricane lamps glowed like beacons in the darkness. The shadows of maybe a dozen more children – prepubescent girls and a couple of even younger boys – were cast against the huge, pale, empty cinema screen.

They sat quietly, blankets draped round their shoulders, discarded bags of crisps and sweets scattered about them; the trauma of the events they'd witnessed – and thus far survived – visible on their faces. A few of the younger ones lay sprawled out on the floor, absorbed with board games and colouring in old newspaper articles with wax crayons.

The scouting party carried Drue down the centre aisle

and set her down on the stage where finally she wriggled free of the net – a decorative prop from one of the ferry's restaurants.

'It's all right now, you're safe,' said Dobs.

'Safe!' exclaimed Drue, indignant.

'Yeah, Ads'll look after you, you'll see. He's got us organized. You're lucky we found you when we did. You'll be safe here. You'll see, the grown-ups'll send a rescue helicopter and we'll all be in the papers and on the telly and everything.'

'*Vale* . . . is enough,' said Adan as he set aside his spear. 'You give the fright to her.'

Dobs backed off a little and Adan swung himself up on to the stage beside Drue.

'You are thirsty?'

'Not especially,' she snapped.

'Jack, *dámela*,' said Adan, pointing to a case of mineral water. Jack tore open the plastic binding, tugged a bottle free and handed it to Adan. Adan unscrewed the top and proffered the bottle to Drue.

'Is OK,' he said reassuringly.

Drue ignored the offer and straightened her clothes.

'Where you was hiding? I thinked . . . I think . . .' said Adan in an attempt to correct his English, '. . . we find everyone who is on ship.'

Drue met the eyes of the children who were staring at her. They looked exactly like what they were: a ragtaggle bunch of fearful, unwashed, homeless refugees.

'What is you name?' asked Adan after a pause.

'Drue. Drue Beltane,' said Drue, shrugging off the last folds of the net and tossing it in Adan's direction.

'You are still the afraid. Is OK. But don't to worry, you are the safe now . . .'

'Look, I'm not afraid, and I don't need your help. I came to help *you*.'

'. . . not even the seabirds can get to here. No windows,' continued Adan.

'I wouldn't be so sure about that,' sniffed Drue.

'Is OK to be a scared . . .'

'Look, I told you I'm not scared. And I don't need you to tell me what to do.'

'Somebody has to be in charge,' chipped in Dobs who sat on the stage, his stocky legs dangling over the side. 'Otherwise, otherwise . . . well, for the littluns. You know. Ain't that right, Ads?'

'Is right, yes,' said Adan, sliding a little closer to Drue. 'My name is Adan. Adan López de Haro, from Muleta, Mallorca.'

Despite her best efforts to stay angry, Drue felt herself warming to the boy and his quiet authority. Again he proffered the water, and this time she took the bottle.

'Are there any grown-ups still on board?' she asked.

'Just as you see,' answered Adan.

'They'll be back though, won't they, Ads? Someone'll come an' rescue us before too long,' said Dobs, punctuating his words by drumming the heels of his grubby trainers against the stage. 'They got transponder tracers and radar an' GPS an' all sorts on these big ships.'

'What if nobody is coming?' asked Drue, prompting several of the little ones to raise their eyes from their drawings.

'Don't be a dingbat,' said Dobs. 'Course they will.'

Adan got to his feet and patted Dobs on the shoulder reassuringly.

'*Hablas Español?*' said Adan to Drue.

Her blank look told him no. He scooped up some discarded crisp packets and sweet wrappings and stuffed them into a bulging plastic rubbish sack. Adan deftly tied the garbage sack and handed it to Dobs along with his spear; an honour bestowed.

'How come he gets the spear?' protested Jack.

'Because he gave it to me,' said Dobs defensively, handing Jack the bag of rubbish.

'But it's not my turn,' moaned Jack.

Adan leaned towards him and whispered: 'You don't want the girl to think you have afraid, do you?'

Jack glanced at Drue, huffed, swung the sack over his shoulder and started for the exit. Dobs followed, proudly brandishing the spear.

'Take care with this,' said Adan, 'and keep a look. We want no surprise.'

Having successfully distracted the two boys, Adan climbed the centre aisle of the small screening room to move out of earshot of the rest of the group. He flopped into a seat and hooked his legs over the one in front.

One of the smaller boys was lost in a game of shadow puppets, using the light from a glowing lantern to cast great shadows on the cinema screen with his hands: a huge bird-like beak chased two running fingers, then it lunged, caught the fleeing figure and lifted it from the ground in its massive jaws. A second lad added more running fingers to the scene – they too fell victim to the giant beak; a pattern of repeated violence played out again and again against a muted chorus of growls and grunts and yelps.

The other children watched the re-enactment or stared vacantly into the middle distance.

Drue clambered off the stage. A little girl, maybe four or five, followed her with her eyes as she moved away from the huddle. Drue met the child's stare and gave her a smile, and the little girl did her best to smile back.

Drue climbed the steps to join Adan, settling in a seat two along from him. For a moment they just sat observing the shadow play on the big screen.

'I like very much the movies,' said Adan.

'*Alice in Wonderland*,' replied Drue.

'*Spider-Man*.'

'*Avatar*.'

'*Hunger Games*!'

'*Spirited Away*!'

'Why no person is come to rescue?' said Adan, suddenly changing the tone.

Drue shifted in her seat. An awkward silence.

'We have the food and water for many month if the ship she does not sink more, but the little ones . . . they have afraid. They want to go home. I tell them OK. Soon. But first we must wait. The birds don't come at night, so in the day we stay inside. We still have one little boat . . ."

'A lifeboat.'

'*Sí*, but all is afraid of the sharks.'

'What happened to the crew? The Captain? The grown-ups?' asked Drue.

'You really don't know?'

'I was ... hiding ... the whole time,' she said. It seemed much simpler to tell a white lie than to try to explain the truth.

Adan suspected there was more to Drue's story than that, but for the moment he too played along.

'There were whales. The blue ones. Three of them. First we see them swim alongside. They was giants, fifty, sixty metres big! Everybody they run to look. It was amazing. Beautiful. Then the whales they disappear. They dive deep. Very much deep.

And then *Boom!* They strike. *Boom!* again. Like the earthquake, yes. The ship she rocks. Peoples is thrown to the water. The sharks they come. Everywheres. Many, many of them. The sea is red with the blood now. The engine no work and the ship she is sinking.

'The Captain say everybody to the little boats. We don't want because of the sharks, but we go. Then *Boom!* again more. All is crying, screaming. Then the seabirds attack. Hundreds of them. Attack. Attack. The grown-ups they try to fight. We run. We hide for many hours. And then ... is over. Is quiet ...'

He paused. 'Is just as you see.' Adan waved a hand at the children huddled beneath the screen. 'No more the grown-ups. Is but this. Just this.'

Drue studied Adan for a moment in the warm light of the lanterns: a ragged rebel with tousled hair and bright eyes. But it was his honesty, his vulnerability, the boy beneath the street-tough exterior that touched Drue. Still she didn't know how to explain what she knew of the war with the Animalians. Her fingers found her dad's white stone in her pocket, and the touch of its smooth surface reassured her.

'Maybe we take a chance now. Maybe we try again with the little boat,' said Adan, turning his head to meet Drue's gaze.

'I think . . . I think it's safer to stay here. Safer than . . . on land,' she replied.

Adan took his feet from the seat and leaned closer.

'You was not hiding on this ship, Drue Beltane. I don't know how you came to here, but, as you did, is possible others will follow, no?'

'I . . . don't know,' said Drue tentatively.

'But you know more than you say.'

'I want to tell you . . . I do . . .'

'Then tell.'

'OK,' said Drue, gathering her thoughts. But still she tried to temper the truth, to soften the blow. 'First . . . well, there's . . .'

'Come on. Just to tell.'

And finally Drue just blurted it out.

'The attack on the ferry was not a freak thing. The animals . . . everywhere . . . birds, weasels, toads, rats . . . like the whales and the sharks . . . There's a . . . a war . . . a war, you know . . .! Them against us.'

'Us?'

'People. Humans. Humankind. We . . . I don't know, the way we were destroying the planet and cutting down forests and poisoning rivers and everything . . . The animals decided it was . . . too much. They decided . . . it was us or them.'

'But this is crazy.'

'Maybe, but . . . but it's . . . that's what happened.'

'But how is this possible? How could they do this?'

'They did, that's all.'

Adan thought for a moment. 'And the armies? Europe, America, Russia . . . with the bombs and planes and war-ships and . . . and . . . missiles?'

'Gone.'

'Gone?!'

'All gone.'

'So war is over?'

'Pretty much.'

'We no win?'

'No. And now you know why I didn't want to say any-thing in front of the others.'

Adan fell silent for a moment. 'Then . . . we will be pris-oners?'

'No. There are no prisoners. No prisons. Just . . . animals.'

'But there is us peoples,' said Adan, with a nod to the band of survivors.

'And if the animals know that you're still alive they'll come after you. Which is why you have to stay with the ship a bit longer. Has it sunk any more since the attack?'

'No. No much.'

'Then you need to just . . . just . . . do what you've been doing. Hide and wait and maybe . . .'

'What?'

'I . . . there's someone I have to find who might be able to help. I don't know; my dad thinks . . .'

'*Tu padre?* Where he is?'

'In a safe place.'

'Then we go there.'

'You can't . . . not yet . . . not with the little ones . . . You're too many to travel without being seen. It wouldn't be safe.'

'Then I come with you.'

'You can't.'

'Is OK for you, but no for me?'

'Yes.'

'How is it so?'

Drue thought for a moment about how to explain. 'You know . . . it's er . . . it's . . . like . . . well . . . like magic.'

'Magic?'

'Uh-huh. Like a superpower. Like the X-Men or something.'

Adan didn't look convinced.

'And my superpower is . . . I can . . . I can become any animal I want.'

'*Estúpido.*'

'It's true.'

'Come on. You put the lie to me.'

'No. No lie.'

'An animal?'

'Any animal.'

'Like Wolverine?' said Adan sceptically.

'Yes . . . well, no . . . not exactly because . . .'

'But is not real, Drue. Is just stories. Made-up things,' said Adan.

'But it is real. Oh, I can't explain it properly, because even I don't really understand it.'

Adan paused for thought.

'And what if I say no? I don't let you to go. Is too dangerous.'

'You . . . you just have to trust me, Adan.'

'You don't think I can stop you?'

The question hung in the air as they eyed one another. The doors behind them creaked open and Dobs and Jack reappeared. Drue got to her feet and backed away towards the exit.

'I'll come back. I promise,' she said.

'We talk some more,' replied Adan.

'There isn't time. Not for any of us.'

Drue kept moving to the exit. Adan was slow to follow. He puzzled over his attraction to this strange girl and what he interpreted as her disregard for his authority. As Drue reached Dobs, Adan gave a nod and the boy brandished the spear to block her path to the exit. Jack stood shoulder to shoulder with his mate and gave Drue a look that said you're not going anywhere.

Drue eyed them both for a moment. They were bigger than her, stronger without a doubt. But when it came to cunning she easily outmatched them.

'Adan. Please tell them.'

Adan glared. He wasn't quite ready to relinquish control.

'OK then,' said Drue.

She turned her back on the boys as if to rejoin Adan. Then, in a flash, she jabbed an elbow into Jack's midriff, dropped to her knees, spun, ducked beneath the spear and scrambled for the exit.

She burst through the doors with Dobs and Adan in hot

pursuit and sprinted through the darkened hallways of the lower deck. She ran blindly, turning this way and that in search of a staircase. Finally, she stumbled upon one and raced up the stairs two at a time.

By the time Drue burst into a restaurant on the main deck, two more lads had joined the chase. For a split second they slowed, convinced that they had her cornered.

Drue caught her breath, dropped to the floor, rolled beneath a table and bolted through a door out on to an open sun deck. Though the boys were hesitant to follow her out-side, they didn't want to lose face in front of Adan. As he took the lead in the chase once more, they closed ranks behind him.

Out on deck, Drue had stopped short of the guard rail. Adan gestured for the others to stay back as he moved towards her. Because of the way the ship sat in the water, the steep rake of the deck was difficult to negotiate even when it was calm, but now, with a swell beginning to roll the vessel, even the shortest distance was hard to cover without stumbling.

'Drue. Please. Come, we go inside,' said Adan.

The other boys were content to hang back by the door. They scanned the wide, cloudless sky for birds and studied the foamy peaks of the waves for dorsal fins.

'I have to go now,' said Drue.

'Go where? There's no place for to go,' said Adan.

'Someday I'll explain properly.'

Drue moved to the guard rail; a swirling wind raced across the white-crested waves and whipped the hair from her face. Adan edged closer. He crouched low for balance. Held out a hand.

'Drue. Come back.'

'I will come back, Adan. I promise,' said Drue. And then, to the astonishment of the boys, she climbed up on to the top of the guard rail and sprang from the ferry in a perfect swallow dive.

Adan scrambled to the rail, but, by the time he reached it, Drue had vanished.

Buffeted by the wind and briny spray, Adan clung to the rail as he searched the water. There was no sign of Drue. Then one of the boys shouted: 'Gull!'

Adan looked back at the boy, then followed the line of his outstretched arm to a point in the middle distance. For a moment he couldn't see anything, then finally he spotted a herring gull moving swiftly, just above the rolling peaks and valleys of the ocean, off towards the far horizon. As Adan watched the bird soar away into the distance, his scowl melted away to be replaced by a look of wonder and amazement.

'*Bona sort*, Drue Beltane,' he mumbled to himself. '*Bona sort.*'

CHAPTER THIRTY-FIVE

By the time Drue-Gull reached the French coastline, she had begun to regret not taking full advantage of all that the ferry had to offer. She was tired, from the physical exertion of flying such a distance, but also from the mental concentration required to simultaneously retain gull form and navigate. And it wasn't until her energy levels began to dip quite seriously that she realized she should have eaten something while she had had the chance.

Still she pressed on, over farmland, vineyards, rivers, forests, scattered villages and silent motorways threaded with abandoned vehicles. Every once in a while she would glide over the wreckage of a crashed aircraft, an abandoned train or an overturned juggernaut that had been forced from the highway, and each time the sight of animal scavengers drove her to gain a little more altitude, a little more distance from the fallout of the terrible events that had shaken the world.

Focusing inward, Drue-Gull gave herself over to the innate Animalian navigation system that was as vital a part of her adopted form as the mercifully wind-resistant plumage or the broad wings that carried her aloft. Not for a moment did she understand it, but she knew enough about her new-found gift to trust it, to keep the faith; for without that she felt certain she would be lost.

The further east Drue travelled, the colder it became, until finally she found herself flying over a landscape of mountains with forests of evergreen firs. Here and there were scattered hamlets – seemingly devoid of life – buried beneath a shroud of deep spring snow.

Finally, unable to ignore her hunger and fatigue any longer, Drue-Gull descended through the clouds. Giant green pylons with redundant power lines cut a swathe through the dense forest of the Swabian Alps, and sheep, deer and hares grazed side by side on the frozen scrub of the surrounding heaths and rolling grasslands. In the distance, a clutch of magpies swirled above a stand of wild sandthorn shrubs that were still heavy with winter fruit.

Mindful of the rattling cries of the winged scavengers, and well aware that they often possessed a mean streak, Drue-Gull set down in a leafless beech tree and shapeshifted into a squirrel. As she was now some distance from the nearest ocean, a gull was liable to attract unwanted attention, and the notion of attempting to eat with a beak seemed . . . well, just too weird. In squirrel form, she would have the use of nimble fingers and teeth.

Triggering a mini-avalanche of powdery snow from the beech as she scrambled to the ground, Drue-Squirrel approached the sandthorn bush with caution, and clambered in among the dense silvery-green leaves of the barbed branches. Several magpies immediately swooped over to investigate, and for a moment Drue feared she might have to defend herself from attack. Following a cursory inspection, however, the birds quickly left her to her own devices. Given the abundance of soft orange berries, it seemed there was sufficient harvest for all.

Food at last. Drue-Squirrel plucked one of the plump berries with her spindly fingers. So soft was its flesh that the skin split as she picked it and its sticky juice ran down her forepaw. As she raised it to her mouth, she heard a voice . . .

'I wouldn't eat that if I were you.'

Drue-Squirrel's tail bristled and her head darted nervously this way and that. Had a magpie taken offence after all? But no: the voice came from a fellow grey squirrel perched on a low branch of an adjacent fir.

'I said, I wouldn't eat that if I were you,' said the grey squirrel again in what sounded like an Animalian equivalent of a thick eastern European brogue.

'Well, you're not me,' said Drue as she weighed up the situation. A territorial squirrel was hardly a threat when she could shape-shift into a wolf or a bear if she wanted to.

'That's true,' replied the grey squirrel, 'but I wouldn't eat that if I was.'

Drue had raised the juicy fruit to her open mouth once more, but still she hesitated.

'It's a sandthorn berry. They're perfectly nice. And packed with vitamins,' she said defensively.

'Not only vitamins,' said the grey squirrel.

'What do you mean? I've eaten lots of them before and they've never done me no harm.'

'Then truly you have journeyed a long way.'

'Why do you say that?'

'You're not from here.'

'Yes I am,' answered Drue-Squirrel cautiously; she didn't want to have to explain herself and perhaps let slip anything that might jeopardize her mission.

'No you're not.'

'How would you know? And anyway the magpies don't seem too bothered. They're eating the berries.'

'Yes. Only they're not magpies. Look more closely,' said the grey squirrel.

Drue studied the wheeling, shrieking birds. It took a moment, but she realized that the squirrel was right. The birds were black with patches of white, and their feathers shimmered with a blue-green sheen, similar to a magpie's, but their tails were much shorter, and their bills longer, more pronounced.

'They're rooks,' said the grey squirrel.

'But . . . aren't rooks meant to be all black?' replied Drue-Squirrel.

'Yes, and now you see why I wouldn't eat those berries if I were you,' said the grey squirrel, scurrying a little closer. 'Much of the place is OK now, but in some of these higher peaks . . . still it's not so good.'

'What's not good?' asked Drue-Squirrel, baffled.

'The radiation,' explained the grey squirrel. 'It was carried here on the wind all the way from the Ukraine. A place the humans called Chernobyl. You've heard of it perhaps?'

Drue said nothing.

'Well, there was a big disaster there. A big explosion. It

sent a giant cloud of poisonous dust halfway round the world.'

'But there are towns near . . .' She caught herself. 'There are human settlements; didn't it poison the people who lived here?'

'In Chernobyl, yes; here, no, the contamination was not so bad for humans. But for Animalians . . . well, you can see what it did to the rooks. And many other creatures have suffered even more.'

Some of the birds began to take exception to being stared at, and they demonstrated the fact by swooping closer and closer to the squirrels, cawing and shrieking as they did so.

'I think we've outstayed our welcome. We'd better go. Follow me,' said the grey squirrel. 'Oh . . . my name is Csaba.'

'Cha . . .' said Drue-Squirrel, struggling with the accent.

'Csaba,' repeated Csaba.

'CHAW-baw,' said Drue-Squirrel, finally getting a grasp of the sound.

'I knew you weren't from around here,' shot back Csaba as he hopped away through the snow. With every leap, he disappeared into a new hollow, popped up his head and beckoned for Drue-Squirrel to follow. She did so, despite a nagging sense of trepidation and a clutch of noisy, very persistent genetically altered rooks flapping overhead.

By the time the pair finally set paw on the icy cobbled streets of the nearest town, Drue would have been prepared to eat anything that even resembled food. Csaba led her to a bridge across a fast-flowing river, down a narrow terrace of medieval half-timbered houses – nestled cheek by jowl with towering stone warehouses and incongruous brick and steel apartment blocks – over a high wall into a scruffy paved backyard and finally through a cat flap, into the rear of a bakery.

The aroma of freshly baked bread hung in the air like a ghost, even though the place had been abandoned since the first wave of attacks. The mouldy remains of rotted pastries and rolls were stacked in large trays beside the ovens, along with stale, rock-solid pretzels the size of dinner plates.

Drue-Squirrel was ready to scavenge what she could, until Csaba ushered her to a cool, dark storeroom where bulging sacks of corn, wheat flour, poppy and sesame seeds stood in bins raised from the ground on rough wooden pallets. Csaba dipped a paw into a sack and pulled out a mitt full of sunflower hearts.

'Sunflower seeds. Packed with energy. Nothing better.'

As Csaba wolfed down the seeds, Drue nimbly climbed up beside him on the rim of the bin and dipped into the open sack. Food. At last. Truly, nothing had ever tasted better.

The meal of grain and seeds made her thirsty and she hopped over to the sink in the bakery kitchen, where she attempted to turn on the cold water tap. Csaba watched her for a moment, seemingly puzzled by the purpose of her struggle.

'You could help,' said Drue-Squirrel, straining every sinew to turn the tap. Then, as Csaba added his weight to the effort, the two of them finally managed to release a trickling column of clear, cool water.

'How did you know how to do that?' asked Csaba, using the stream to wash the dust of the grain sacks from his paws.

'Oh, I . . . my . . . mother . . . showed me,' answered Drue-Squirrel honestly, without adding that her mother had been human. As she dipped her head to take a drink from the flow, Csaba eyed her with suspicion.

'How did *she* know?'

'Where is this place?' said Drue-Squirrel, changing the subject.

'This place?'

'The town . . . the human settlement?'

'We call it Danu . . . after the big river.'

'And what did the humans call it?'

'Ulm,' said Csaba.

'Is that in Germany?'

'Of course.'

'Then I made it!' said Drue, thinking out loud.

'What?' said Csaba, giving her a quizzical look.

Drue thought for a moment. Csaba had saved her from the poisonous berries. He had led her to food and water. And he knew the local terrain well enough to be a real ally. She felt she must confide in him . . . if only a little.

'Have you ever heard of . . . the Lionman?' she said, watching Csaba carefully to gauge his reaction.

'The Lionman,' replied Csaba, his eyes darting to the window, through which a pack of wild boar could be seen foraging in the snow drifts outside.

'Is that why you're here?' he continued in a whisper.

'Then you have heard of him?' replied Drue-Squirrel as she wedged herself against the wall and used her body as a lever to turn off the tap.

'Of course. Everyone has. He's a legend,' said Csaba.

'Do you know how to find him?'

'Why?'

'Do you?'

'It might be dangerous.'

'Well . . . I'd have you with me,' said Drue-Squirrel.

'I'll tell you if you tell me first why it is you want to find him.'

'I can't . . . I'm sorry . . . You wouldn't . . .'

'I wouldn't what?'

'You wouldn't understand.'

'How do you know?'

'Trust me, Csaba, please. I have to find the Lionman. You were right. I'm not from around here. I've travelled a long, long way across the sea from . . . a place the *humans* call England,' she added swiftly, 'and it's a matter of life and death. I must find him.'

Csaba studied her for a moment.

'And if I don't take you?'

'Then I'll just have to find him myself. But please, I've lost so much time already.'

'Very well,' said Csaba.

'Is that a yes? You'll take me?' said Drue.

'Yes.'

Drue-Squirrel's eyes lit up with hope and her broad bushy tail twitched with nervous anticipation.

As Csaba led them deeper into the heart of the city, it seemed to Drue that there was a surprise on every corner: a sculpture of a sparrow clutching a twig in its beak – clearly a local mascot – appeared again and again in dozens of brightly painted variations, frozen in flight above shopfronts and bridges and office buildings. A bizarre bronze bust of the scientist Albert Einstein – with his tongue poking out – peeked out from behind a rocket-shaped fountain.

An enormous glass pyramid, which had housed a civic centre of some sort, stood in the main square and, on street after street, the fresh blanket of snow was criss-crossed with trails of paw marks: some were tiny, like those that she and Csaba left behind them, some as broad as dinner plates. Could they perhaps have been made by the legendary Lionman she had come in search of?

With every step they took, so the creature's myth grew larger and more frightening in Drue's mind. It suddenly dawned on her that she didn't even know what it was she was supposed to ask of him. How could she have come so far without a plan? Had she missed something her father had said? She began to think that perhaps she should delay, take time to gather her thoughts, find somewhere to rest and collect herself.

Just then she caught sight of the Gothic spire of the Ulm Minster, its fantastically ornate steeple stretching high above the rooftops, halfway to heaven. It made Drue think of her mother. She felt the urge to go and say a prayer and light a candle. Instead, she stayed on Csaba's heels, pressing on through the shadows of a narrow lane of medieval houses which seemed to lean towards one another as if huddling together for warmth and security.

Booooom!

Drue-Squirrel snapped out of her reverie as the earth trembled beneath her.

Booooom!

Boooooooooom!!
Booooooooooooom!!!

So great was the shuddering impact that spears of frozen stalactites and even a shower of terracotta roof tiles rained down and shattered on the cobbles where the squirrels stood. Fearing it was an earthquake, Drue-Squirrel instinctively bolted for the open tree-lined square up ahead. Just as she was about to reach it, however, Csaba shrieked, caught her by the tail and pulled her back.

'Watch out!'

A gigantic grey pillar pummelled the ground a whisker away from Drue-Squirrel's nose. She tumbled backwards as the broad leathery pillar lifted off the ground and another swung past. It took her a moment to realize that these were not pillars at all: they were legs!

'An elephant!' squealed Drue-Squirrel. 'What's it doing here?'

'Liberated from Stuttgart Zoo. I should have warned you.'

The two squirrels gingerly poked their heads round the corner as the great beast lumbered on across the snowbound square. An abandoned car lay in the elephant's path and, with a single stride, it crushed the roof right down on to the chassis.

The screech of tearing metal and splintered glass triggered a gibbering chorus of approval from a troop of baboons in the nearby trees. Across the wide square, a giraffe chewed on a house plant in a third-storey window, zebras lapped nervously at meltwater in a gutter, and a lynx and a jackal engaged in a vicious squabble over the bloody carcass of some small mammal.

Drue-Squirrel looked on, amazed.

'We must take care,' said Csaba. 'Thousands of refugee predators are drifting in from the forests in search of food. They've gained their freedom, but without humans to provide for them, they're having to learn to hunt again and adapt to a completely new environment. There are even alligators in the Danube. One slip and you could end up as dinner.'

'I thought there was a truce between all Animalians?' said Drue-Squirrel.

'With humans as the common enemy, the leadership of Earth Assembly was unquestioned. Now that the Sixth Wave has been repelled, and the most dangerous predator on the planet has been hunted to extinction, the other carnivores have less to fear. More blood will be spilled as they battle for dominance and new territory. Make no mistake, the world is still a very dangerous place for the likes of us.'

Drue-Squirrel was quietly impressed; how lucky she'd been to happen upon such a wise and knowledgeable companion.

As they turned on to a smaller square paved with cobbles, Csaba stopped in his tracks.

'Well . . . here we are. The home of the Lionman.'

A line of snow-encrusted bicycles stood chained to a rack, and beyond them stood an unprepossessing three-storey townhouse. Buff-coloured walls and formal rows of Georgian-style windows were framed by dark wooden shutters; all in all, it suggested a grand family home rather than a cave of wonders, with only the barred steel-and-glass front entrance hinting at something different.

'Come,' said Csaba, 'this way'

Drue-Squirrel followed as Csaba scrambled up a drain-pipe and disappeared into a space between the roof tiles and the guttering.

Behind the traditional pitched, tiled roof was a modernist extension with huge horizontal windows that created a well of natural light inside the building. As they padded across the roof lights, Drue-Squirrel peered down at the deep marble staircase below.

A few moments later, they were inside. A ventilation shaft carried the pair into a hall of glass, concrete and graphite steel beams. Shadowy galleries led off the central stairwell, and Drue surmised that the Lionman must be an art collector or an archaeologist of some kind as there were all manner of ancient artefacts on display in glass cases: prehistoric flint tools and Bronze Age swords, even a human skull.

Again Csaba took the lead, directing them through a maze of exhibition spaces. Drue-Squirrel was alert to danger, but the only sound she could hear was the soft fall of their paws on the parquet floor. Racks of redundant spotlights lined the low ceilings, and white blinds masked all the windows to the gallery spaces, creating pockets of deep shadow beyond the pools of diffused natural light.

A faux-chalk cliff face curved away into a corner and Csaba stopped just short of it.

'Are you certain that you still want to meet the Lionman?' he said.

Drue-Squirrel squinted into the shadows ahead. 'Yes . . .' she whispered nervously. 'Is he . . .? Are we . . .?'

'Yes,' said Csaba.

Drue heard what she thought was a low growl, the deep

sonorous rumble of a big cat. Something was moving in the shadows just beyond the faux-chalk partition.

'Well . . .' said Csaba, gesturing for Drue-Squirrel to continue alone.

Drue took a breath to steady herself. *Dad wouldn't have sent me if it wasn't safe*, she thought.

'OK,' she said, trying to sound as confident as possible. Bounding forward, she turned into the corner gallery and took a second to adjust her vision. The few rays of natural light that penetrated the space seemed drawn inexorably to one particular spot . . . and that's when she saw him . . . or rather *it* . . .

A piece of carved ivory supported by a slender wire cradle stood atop a tall granite-grey plinth. The whole thing was encased in a protective glass box that reached all the way to the floor, lending the primitive sculpture a noble, mysterious, almost sacred air.

'The Lionman,' announced Csaba triumphantly.

Drue-Squirrel moved closer. The yellowing ivory figure appeared to be half man half beast – standing upright on two legs. The noble head with its prominent jaw and broad nose resembled a mountain lion rather than the African variety Drue had been expecting.

'That's him? I mean, that's it? It's just an old carving,' exclaimed Drue-Squirrel.

'It's more than that,' replied Csaba. 'It's over 40,000 years old. The oldest known sculpture in the world. Hand-carved with flint knives from the tusk of a mammoth.'

'But . . .'

'You expected something else?' said Csaba, circling the

glass display case as two rats, one black, one white, emerged from the shadows.

Drue sensed danger, and in the blink of an eye shape-shifted into a wolf. She bared her fangs and braced herself, waiting for the rodents to attack ...

To Drue's amazement, the two rats also shape-shifted into snarling wolves. And then into human form: a handsome boy with tight Afro curls and skin as dark as night, and a fair-haired girl a little older than Drue, whose cheeks were a mask of freckles.

'It's OK! You're with friends,' said Csaba quickly, afraid that Drue-Wolf might lunge.

'You came to find the Lionman just like we did; this is the meeting place for the Nsray,' said Csaba in Animalian as he too shape-shifted into a gangly teenage boy with a kind face that was pockmarked with acne.

As the girl began to speak, Drue shape-shifted into her human self again so that she could understand.

'I'm Piera,' said the girl, with a heavy Parisian accent.

'Piera's French,' said Csaba. 'I'm from Hollókő in Hungary. And this is Yaya ... He's from Cape Verde, you know, near Senegal.'

'Hello,' said Drue with a smile. 'I'm Drue.'

Yaya grinned, but had trouble looking Drue in the eye.

'Yaya's a bit shy,' explained Csaba. 'He speaks three languages: Portuguese, *Crioulo* and one I cannot even say the name of ... but not English ... so you'll just have to talk to each other in Animalian.'

Drue smiled at Yaya again to indicate that Csaba had explained. Yaya smiled and ducked his head.

'So you see . . . you're not the only one who's far from home.'

'Why didn't you say something before?'

'I had to be sure of you. The Animalian spies are hunting us. They're cunning.'

'Are we . . . the only ones?'

'Don't be stupid,' said Piera contemptuously.

'There are many. The clan is gathering. That's why we were on lookout. You'll see,' said Csaba.

Drue considered the Lionman sculpture once more.

'I still don't understand . . . Why this? Why here?'

The walls of the gallery were papered with huge photographs of archaeological digs – black-and-white images of caves, excavations and ancient treasures recovered from the sands of another time. Csaba waved a hand at the text printed alongside the photographs. It was written in German, which he translated.

'The Lionman sculpture was discovered in a cave . . . the Hohlenstein-Stadel in Lonetal, in 1939. The archaeologists and all the history experts seemed to think that it was a symbolic thing . . .'

'Hah. Idiots,' added Piera dismissively.

'. . . a gift to the gods maybe,' continued Csaba, 'to make sure that a hunt would be successful. Or maybe a way for Neanderthal man to pass on information from one generation to the next. You know: which animals are good to hunt, which are dangerous. Some scholars even said it was used as part of an early religious ritual . . . but none of them discovered the truth.'

'Which is what?' said Drue, turning her attention back to

263

the intricately carved statue. On closer inspection, she could see that it had been pieced together from hundreds of small fragments, and parts of the figure were still missing. The more Drue looked at it, the more potent its allure became; it felt strangely familiar.

'Is it not obvious?' said Piera.

'No,' said Drue.

Piera gave her a withering look.

'He was one of us. A Nsray shaman. A Shape-shifter,' said Csaba.

'You mean . . . he was real?' replied Drue.

Piera huffed as if it was the most stupid remark she had ever heard.

'Of course,' said Csaba patiently.

The carving seemed to glow, to breathe with light. Drue studied it with wide-eyed fascination.

'Come,' said Csaba, 'let's take you to meet the others. It'll all begin to make sense. You'll see.'

And with that Csaba, Piera and Yaya became sparrows, flew tight circles round the Lionman display case and darted off towards the main staircase. It took a moment for Drue to get over the shock that there were others who shared her gift, but, fearing she'd lose track of them, Drue shape-shifted into a sparrow herself and joined the Nsray flock.

CHAPTER THIRTY-SIX

Will-C and Yoshi were asleep on the sill of the kitchen window in the Callows' farmhouse when they heard the cry.

'Will-C!' called Gallinago. 'Look!'

Will-C's mind raced. Was it Drue? Had she returned? He peered through a broken pane and located Gallinago on top of the barn across the yard. Gallinago gestured with his bill, and Will-C craned his neck to get a better view of the paddock beyond the driveway.

All hopes of an early reunion with Drue were dashed when he realized that the snipe had raised the alarm over the arrival of someone else entirely: a large white seabird with prominent nostrils on its upper bill.

'A tubenose,' said Yoshi. 'He'll be able to sniff out the Shape-shifter.'

The petrel turned a slow circle, glided down to the fence that bordered the field and perched on the top rail. As it began to sample the air, a pack of rats and weasels emerged from a hedge. At the head of the pack was a creature whom

Will-C recognized only too well: the mink who had held him and the other Truckles captive at the river. The Chief of Natterjack's Guards: Mustela.

Will-C jumped down from the sill and ran into the living room to check on Quinn. The blanket Drue had covered him with lay on the sofa, but there was no sign of the man himself. Yoshi appeared behind Will-C.

'Where is he?' said Yoshi.

'I don't know,' replied Will-C as he jumped up on to the sofa and felt the blanket with his nose. 'It's cold. He's been gone a while.'

He darted out into the hall with Yoshi on his heels, and they both slipped out through a cat flap into the yard.

Lennox and crew had already taken up positions around the cobbled yard, ready to spring a surprise attack should the tubenose lead Mustela's forces into the farm. Will-C and Yoshi worked their way over to Lennox using a tractor as cover.

'Mustela must have taken over from the toad,' whispered Yoshi anxiously.

'Seems like it,' replied Will-C.

'Maggot, keep ya tail down!' growled Lennox at Yoshi. 'You too, Freak,' he said as Will-C scurried up alongside him. 'De element a surprise can make all the difference when you're ahtnumbered.'

'How many are there?'

''Ard to say. Could be four or five against one.'

'Then we can't win.'

'Dat's da spirit,' said Lennox sarcastically.

'No. I mean ... maybe, maybe there's another way. Instead of fighting.'

'Just keep ya tail down and ya meathole shut. All I want is a clear run at that mink.'

'Look,' called Gallinago from above. 'Mustela is talkin' to da tubenose.'

All eyes turned to the mink and the seabird. An exchange of words, and then Mustela clambered up on to the top rail of the fence and rose up on his hind legs to survey the farmhouse and yard. He studied the house for quite some time before he finally gestured to the pack, and they began to fall back and fan out across the field.

'What's happening?' asked Will-C.

'Hard to say,' said Gallinago.

'Dey comin'?' growled Lennox.

'No,' replied Gallinago, 'looks loike dey're diggin' in.'

'Damn,' said Lennox.

'Maybe they're afraid,' said Will-C hopefully.

'Maybe dey know we're waitin' for 'em,' said Gallinago.

'Maybe dey're da ones who are waitin',' said Lennox.

'What do you mean?' said Will-C. 'Waiting for what?'

'Reinforcements,' replied Lennox.

Will-C turned his attention back to Mustela, who remained on the fence, studying the farmhouse. Will-C felt his tail twitch with anxiety and quickly drew it back into the shadows in which he was hiding. Mustela's beady eyes flashed to Will-C's position. The mink couldn't see him, but Will-C still silently chastised himself. Lennox didn't need to add anything except a look of disdain.

Finally, as the tubenose took to the sky and wheeled away, Mustela clambered down from the fence.

'He's gone,' said Will-C.

'Who's gone?' said Lennox.

'Quinn Beltane. The Shape-shifter.'

'Gone? I thought 'e was sick? Near death. Rat-bite fever you said?'

'I know what I said, and he was, but now he's . . . gone.'

'When?' growled Lennox.

'I . . . I don't know, I only just . . .'

'Oh,' said Gallinago up on his lofty perch.

'What?' said Lennox.

'Eh . . . eh . . . uh-oh . . .' stuttered Gallinago.

'What?' repeated Lennox.

'I tink we're gonna need a better plan.'

'*What?*' snarled Lennox.

Gallinago flew from his hiding place to the apex of the barn roof. From his elevated position he could see the surrounding fields and lanes crawling with hundreds of Animalians, and they were all headed in the same direction: Callow's Farm.

'A . . . much . . . better . . . plan.'

CHAPTER THIRTY-SEVEN

The Ulm Minster was no less impressive from the air than it had been from the ground, its ornate pillars, finials and buttresses dusted with a coat of virgin snow. Csaba-Sparrow led the small flock in a slow spiral round the pyramid atop the west tower and Drue-Sparrow marvelled at the spectacular view. Bengal tigers supped at the banks of the Danube, African elephants and wildebeest drifted across the far Swabian Alps. Impala swept across the plains of Bavaria to the south.

'Come on. Keep up. Pay attention,' snapped Piera as she ushered Drue down towards the lofty bell tower. A dozen eagle owls were perched upon it, looking as fearsome in their way as some of the stone gargoyles that manned the parapets. As the four sparrows continued to circle, one of the eagle owls spread its wings and approached them.

'I haven't eaten since dawn; you sparrows would do well to play elsewhere,' said the eagle owl, orange eyes and razor talons glinting in the sun.

'The Lionman is hungry too,' replied Piera cryptically.

'Where does he hunt?' said the eagle owl.

'The Mountains of Ararat,' replied Piera, completing the coded password.

'You may pass, friend,' said the eagle owl.

Swooping on down to the bell tower, the sparrows glided past the eagle owl sentries, past the great bells and on down the internal winding stairwell to the next level. There they were confronted by a tetchy Asiatic black bear – and a second checkpoint.

Secure within the walls of the church, and therefore masked from the prying eyes of any passing Animalians, they were each required to shape-shift back into their human form under the watchful gaze of the burly guard: a measure designed to ensure that no Animalian spies gained entry by passing themselves off as Nsray.

Satisfied that they were genuine Nsray and fit to enter, the black bear opened a heavy oak door that revealed a dark stone spiral staircase that would lead them all the way down to ground level. As they began their descent, Drue took her cue from her new-found companions and pressed her palms against the smooth stone of the ancient walls to check her balance. They felt cold and damp, and for a moment she was transported back to the priest-hole at the Beltanes' cottage in Kingley Burh.

Ex umbra in solem ... From the shadows into the light.

But was it so? wondered Drue. All she had seen on her journey so far was darkness.

No sooner had the doubt entered her mind than Drue stumbled. She lost her footing on the polished stone steps and inadvertently nudged Piera, who was a few paces below her.

'Hey!' the French girl reprimanded her. 'Are you trying to kill us all? Do you know how far down these steps go? It's the tallest steeple in the world, so watch it!'

'Sorry. I'm sorry,' said Drue.

By the time they reached ground level twenty minutes later, Drue was in no doubt at all that the steeple was indeed the tallest in the entire world.

'It's not just the tallest,' said Csaba, 'it's also the coldest.' And to illustrate his point he blew a small cloud of breath into the air.

An oak door at the foot of the stairwell opened on to a small wood-panelled reception area. Beside the abandoned ticket kiosk and information booth stood display racks laden with postcards and booklets about the history of the place: a solemn memorial to a different time, a different world, for it was hard to imagine that tourists would ever again queue to enter its portals.

A second door led directly into the south aisle of the church proper and, as Csaba lifted the latch and swung it open on its iron hinges, Drue's eyes widened at the sheer scale of the vaulted interior.

'Wow,' was all she could think of to say as she craned her neck to take it all in.

'It was designed to accommodate as many as 15,000 worshippers at any one time,' explained Piera haughtily. 'That's why most people think of it as a cathedral even though it's actually a church. It dates back to the fourteenth century. The architects intended it to be like a waiting room at the gates of the Kingdom of Heaven. Because of its size and magnificence, all who entered would be humbled, intimidated, reminded of just how small we are was in the bigger plan of the universe.'

She gave Drue a look of disdain. 'But I suppose *wow* will have to do.'

Piera drifted away down the central aisle, linking arms with Csaba and tugging him along with her. Csaba offered Drue a helpless, apologetic smile. It was clear that Piera felt threatened in some way by her presence, though quite why, Drue couldn't imagine.

To Drue's amazement, the pale wooden pews were filled to bursting with all manner of creatures, of every race and creed: men, women, children, sloths, lions, monkeys, doves, even a few species that Drue had never seen before. All were Nsray Shape-shifters, of course, but many still adopted Animalian forms in order to communicate freely with one another.

Part surreal Sunday service, part shelter for the homeless, part casting call for some epic Hollywood fantasy – the bizarre throng was completely hidden from the outside world thanks to the design of the structure: the only windows in the towering walls were fitted with stained glass, and none was less than four metres from the ground.

With surprise and wonder etched on her face, Drue drifted down the nave after her companions. Though in her regular human guise she couldn't understand the animated chatter and excited banter ringing out all around her, it was clear that the general mood was one of optimism, camaraderie.

'Don't worry,' said Csaba over his shoulder, 'some of them may look strange, but they're all the same as us.'

Drue craned her neck to study the relief sculptures on the walls and the intricate frescoes painted on the magnificent vaulted ceiling high above her.

A makeshift soup kitchen had been set up in the north aisle and Csaba nudged Drue's arm and suggested she join the food queue.

'I have to go back out with Piera, in case there are more late arrivals. You'll be safe now. Get something to eat. We'll meet up again later. Yaya will stay behind and see that you're OK.'

'He doesn't have to. I'll be fine.'

'I think he wants to stay. I think he likes you,' said Piera conspiratorially.

Drue smiled and Yaya smiled shyly in return; then he quickly shape-shifted into a pied wagtail and turned excited circles above their heads.

'We'll be back before dark,' said Csaba. 'Liliuk plans to speak to everyone tonight.'

'Liliuk?' said Drue.

'She's in charge,' replied Csaba.

'She's amazing,' added Picra.

'She can read minds,' said Csaba.

'Not minds, dreams.'

'Same thing.'

'I must see her,' said Drue. 'It's important. I need to talk to her.'

'You will meet her. Later. She and the other Adepts are in private session in the chapel – an emissary has just returned from talks with the Elders of the Earth Assembly.'

'Who . . . what . . . what did they say? Maybe the war is over and we can all go home.'

'Maybe. We'll be told when the time is right. You'll see. Rest now,' said Csaba as he and Piera headed back to the main entrance.

Steaming cauldrons of soup sat on propane-fuelled camping stoves on the bench tables of the kitchen area. As Drue shuffled forward in the orderly queue, the smell took her back to her father cooking in the hideaway in the breaker's yard. It seemed so long ago. She longed to know that he was OK, and Will-C too, and found herself saying a silent prayer; a simple wish that somehow, someday soon, they would all be together again.

As Drue reached the head of the queue, she helped herself to cutlery from a tray and an earthenware dish from a large stack. One of the volunteers – a large woman with spiky red hair bound in a bright floral scarf – ladled vegetable broth and flour dumplings into Drue's bowl until it was almost overflowing. She said something in German to a fellow volunteer behind the food table, and he in turn helped Drue to a large portion of sauerkraut, spooning it on top of the broth.

Drue smiled by way of a thank you and slowly shuffled off with her bowl, taking care not to spill it. As she settled down in a pew to eat, Yaya appeared in human form, clutching a folded blanket. Drue set down her bowl, draped the blanket round her shoulders and then resumed eating.

'Thanks, Yaya.'

Yaya smiled.

With the hot food in her belly, and comforted by the warmth of the blanket, as soon as Drue had finished eating, she began to feel sleepy and lay down to rest. She studied the fresco on the ceiling high up above. An angel accompanied by a bull, a lion and an eagle. The eagle clutched a scroll in its talons, which began to move, as if caught by a gentle breeze. The angel's halo seemed to glow more intensely. The figures became more vivid, animated, alive. Was it a trick of the light?

Drue closed her eyes and then opened them again. The scroll was still once more, the painting restored to pale flat pastels. She closed her eyes again and drifted off to sleep.

Water. Cool. Clear. Deep as the Atlantic. Light drilled down through the surface, causing starbursts of pure energy to flare off the crystal walls and bejewelled, shimmering stalactites. Drue dived, pushed herself down into the depths to where the light faded. She was eager to feel the presence. But was this an ocean? Was she really breathing underwater?

A pinpoint of light appeared below her now, just as the darkness seemed to fold in above. The light grew brighter. And, as Drue drifted deeper into the void, closer to the source, she realized that it was a ball of fire. A fiery globe, like a miniature sun, burning white-hot, tongues of golden flame shimmering and flickering over its surface as it remained suspended; a lone star in a vast liquid cosmos.

Drue felt the warmth of the fire on her cheeks, on her arms. The burning orb turned on its axis and slowly began to trace an orbit around her. As it did so, it left a trail of flame in its wake, like the tail of a blazing comet. Around and around it spun, creating a glowing spiral in the dark ocean until Drue was entirely enclosed by a radiant whirl-

pool of soft golden light. But it was more than light. The warmth it generated enveloped her with a sense of serenity and well-being.

Then, as quickly as it had appeared, the spiral of light faded, and Drue was confronted by a wave of giant sea turtles, hundreds of them, paddling slowly through the water. They seemed oblivious to Drue's presence and, as the nearest slipped by her, she ran a hand over its domed back.

To her surprise and delight, the scutes, the bony plates that made up its shell, were etched with faint symbols, a strange alphabet of some kind, and each individual plate glowed a different colour: violet, indigo, blue, green, yellow, orange, red. It looked for all the world like a stained-glass window bathed in moonlight . . .

*   *   *

Moonlight. As Drue awoke from her dream and wiped the sleep from her eyes, she saw that the church was bathed in its soft glow. Her fellow Nsray were quiet, subdued, and she realized she must have been asleep for quite a while. A familiar wagtail perched on the back of the pew beside her, and Drue shape-shifted into sparrow form to see if it was Yaya.

'Yaya?'

'I'm sorry if I woke you,' said Yaya.

'How long was I asleep? What's going on?'

'The Adepts are still in private session.'

'What can they have been talking about for so long?'

'It can take a lot of words to build a future.'

'Well, I want to see,' said Drue-Sparrow as she lifted off and flew down the central aisle.

'Wait,' said Yaya-Wagtail, darting after her. 'It's not permitted to go there.'

'Well, don't you want to know what they're talking about?' said Drue-Sparrow as they flew tight circles in front of an ornate carved stone pyramid located at the far end of the central nave.

'I already know,' replied Yaya-Wagtail.

'You do?'

'Of course.'

'Well, what then?'

'Noah.'

'Noah? Who's Noah?'

'You know . . . Noah . . . like in the Bible story . . . Noah's Ark.'

'What's that got to do with anything?'

'You don't know?'

'What?'

'Come. I'll show you.'

Yaya-Wagtail climbed in a spiral up towards the vaulted roof of the nave. Drue-Sparrow followed, and Yaya led her directly to the fresco that had caught her attention when she had first entered the church: the ancient painting that she had been drawn to just before she fell asleep.

Up close, Drue could see that it was rendered in pale pigments and that each of the four characters – the animals as well as the angel – had a golden halo above it. A large gilt ring lay between them, with four bars, like the spokes of a wheel radiating out from the perimeter, dividing the work into four sections: the first contained the bearded angel clad in pale robes; he had youthful human features framed by dark, flowing, shoulder-length curls. In the second was a brooding, powerful winged bull; in the third a giant eagle, its razor-sharp talons clutching a snaking scroll; and in the fourth and final segment was a lion – even larger in scale than the bull – with broad white wings sprouting from its muscular shoulders.

'Nobody knows exactly the story of the painting, but some say that the angel is Japheth himself, one of the sons of Noah,' said Yaya. 'The great father of our people.'

'Noah?' said Drue.

'Why do you think he was chosen to lead the Animalians into the Ark?'

'I don't know,' said Drue.

'Think about it. He was no ordinary man . . . even in the Bible stories it says he lived to nearly 1000 years old. Does that sound like an ordinary man to you?'

'I never thought about it.'

'And do you think it's just by chance that this church was built and this painting made hundreds of years before the ancient Lionman sculpture was discovered buried in the very same valley? You can see the caves where it was found from the bell tower.'

'I still don't follow,' said Drue-Sparrow, flying closer to the winged lion.

'No. That's just it. You do. We all do. We are the followers. This site was chosen as our meeting place many thousands of years ago . . .'

'Before the church was even built?'

'Long before there was even a settlement here, when our ancestors occupied the caves of the Lonetal. It was always the destiny of our people to return here when the Sixth Wave came to flood the world.'

'But what does this old painting have to do with that?'

'What do you see?'

Drue-Sparrow studied the fresco closely.

'A gold ring and four . . . angels.'

'Why do you say they're all angels?'

'Because all four have halos, and wings.'

'All four or . . . one wise man in four different guises.'

Suddenly Drue began to see the link.

'You mean . . . this . . .?'

'Is a painting of the Lionman himself. A Nsray Shape-shifter. Japheth was one of us. And the story the picture tells in the scrolls is our story. That is why the figures are placed around a ring: it's the cycle of Life; and the four spokes leading from it represent the paths to the four corners of the Earth. But this time it's not the water we need to fear, and it's not the animals who will need to be saved from the wrath of the Creator of all things . . . it is us.'

Drue studied the fresco. The faded lettering on the scrolls was written in the same strange alphabet she had seen in her dream, the symbols etched on the shells of the turtles. She was about to ask Yaya if he knew what they meant when a flurry of activity below announced that Liliuk's private session with the Adepts had come to an end.

The doors to the Neithart Chapel opened and the Nsray Adepts filed out into the nave, shape-shifting back into human form as they took their places in the reserved front pews. Drue and Yaya flew back down to ground level just as Csaba and Piera – still in their sparrow forms – returned.

The crowd fell silent, all eyes on the open doors of the chapel.

Finally, Liliuk emerged, first as a black swan and then as a beautiful woman with a mane of ash-white dreadlocks that fell loose around her face. Her fine features and dark skin were etched with the lines of a long life lived to the full. Her piercing brown eyes swept over the assembled Nsray, and then she shape-shifted back into her swan form once more. Unfurling her powerful ebony wings, she beat them slowly and rose above the heads of the crowd.

'Nsray. Forgive me for keeping you for so long. I have listened at length to the wise words of the Adepts, and to the voice of our courageous scout – one of the two Nsray who dared to brave the Animalians' inner sanctum to carry our message of peace and hopes of reconciliation to the Guardians of the Earth Assembly. I know that you are anxious to hear word of their journey.

'First, though, let me say that the response to our plea exceeded my expectations. It seems that there is real hope, the possibility of a negotiated truce. But only if each and every one of us surrenders to the representatives of the local Animalian Council.'

Liliuk's words caused a rumble of discontent.

'What guarantee do we have that we can trust them?' came a cry.

'How do we know they'll not just cut us down or enslave us?' said another.

'Why should we believe them?'

'Reasonable questions all,' said Liliuk, 'and perhaps it is best if I now let our envoy recount the detail of the Animalians' proposal himself. He has, after all, risked life and limb to carry this olive branch back to us. First I would ask you all to return to your human incarnations.'

There was a moment of hesitation. If they all returned to their native human forms, then language barriers would become a problem once more.

'Please trust me,' said Liliuk. 'I ask this for good reason.'

Every creature in the place – wolves, monkeys, birds, otters, bears – shape-shifted back into their natural form, until there wasn't a single animal of any kind, only people of every race, creed and colour.

'Now,' said Liliuk, 'let us ask our special envoy to share the message he carried back from the Earth Assembly.'

Heads bobbed this way and that as everyone searched for the envoy in question.

'Please,' continued Liliuk, her gaze drifting over the crowd, 'August Beyer, come . . . address the people . . . tell them how our message of peace was received. Share with your Nsray brethren all that you have shared with me.'

All eyes were trained on the Adepts in the front pews, and finally Liliuk stared directly at one of them. The eyes of the crowd followed her. The Adept scratched nervously at his beard; he seemed surprised to have been singled out.

'August? Have you forgotten your own name? Have you nothing to say?' asked Liliuk, knowing full well that the man would be unable to answer.

August Beyer rose to his feet and backed away from the other Adepts as he tried to speak. He worked his jaws and finally words began to form, but he had little control over them, like a child speaking for the first time.

'I ... Ba ... Bea ... eay ... er ...' Stuttering badly, and panicked by Liliuk's accusing stare and the attention of the surrounding crowd, Beyer began to cut a path through the nave.

'Guard the doors!' bellowed Liliuk.

Beyer suddenly shape-shifted into a jackal and tore away through the crush of bodies, snarling and snapping. Several young Shape-shifters transformed into panthers, blocking the jackal's dash for the exit. In desperation, the jackal sprang at the door. He was quickly overpowered and pinned to the ground, his throat clamped in the jaws of one of the big cats. He shape-shifted once more back into August Beyer, but this time he was fooling no one.

'Make no mistake,' cried Liliuk, 'that is not August Beyer. August is dead. He allowed himself to be captured by the Animalians in order to carry our message to their leadership. This was their answer. August Beyer was killed by the jackal so that the Animalians could infiltrate our ranks; they sent a spy to carry word of our plans back to the War Council of the Earth Assembly. Their lust for blood is far from sated!'

Beyer's face was contorted with fear as the panther tightened its grip on his throat, its deadly fangs just stopping short of drawing blood.

'Can we be sure August has been taken?' came a cry from the crowd.

'Trust me, brother,' said Liliuk. 'By eating his heart, the jackal was able to steal his gift, take on his physical appearance, but no animal has yet mastered human speech. Not even with Nsray blood in its veins.'

The mood of the crowd shifted from alarm to anger. The jackal returned to its true form once more.

'Finish it!' came a cry from the assembly.

'No!' snapped Liliuk. 'Remember what we are. Who we are. We fight only to defend ourselves. To take a life in anger, for revenge, is not the way of the Nsray. We will keep the jackal captive until we have left this place. Take him to the catacombs. Guard him with your lives.'

As the jackal was led away, Liliuk wove her magic on the crowd once more.

'Forgive me, fellow Nsray. I did not mean to offer false hope, but I needed to be sure that my suspicions were correct. In our private session, the jackal painted a picture too good to be true: a world in which we would once again live alongside the Animalians as equals. Perhaps one day that dream will come true; but it will not be achieved without a struggle.

'The decision to wage war against humankind was not taken lightly, and the road to salvation will be twice as hard. Much blood has been shed, much pain endured, too many lives lost. So we owe it to the spirits of the fallen to embark on the next stage of our journey with heavy hearts but clear minds.

'I know that there are some among you who would still gladly take the fight to the Animalians. But that is not, *has never been*, the way of the Nsray. Anger, hatred, revenge . . . these are not the words to make our spirits soar, and they are not the tools to equip us for the future, to build the road to peace.'

'Where will we find that road?' came a voice from the crowd.

'First we must set our feet on safer ground,' continued Liliuk.

'But we're safe here, aren't we?' muttered Drue.

'The church has offered a safe haven, for which we must be grateful; but the jackal was not operating alone. We must expect others like him to follow. An attack, if not imminent, is inevitable.

'Our future lies beyond these walls. We need time and space. We need land to plant seeds and provide shelter. We need to be able to raise our children beyond the shadow of fear, beyond the reach of all those in Animalia who would drive us from the Earth forever.'

'Surely there's no place in the world that can provide such a guarantee?' said another restless soul from the pews.

'There is but one . . . the Mountains of Ararat. It is there, between the Turkish, Iranian and Armenian borders, beneath the cradle of the great volcano, that we will begin a new life. Only there, on the fertile plains of Iğdir, can we guarantee the safety and security of our people.'

'How can we be certain the Animalians won't hunt us there?'

'Because even the most radical and bloodthirsty of their kind respects the hallowed ground on which Noah's Ark finally came to rest.'

'Mount Ararat is over a thousand miles from here,' said an anxious polecat. 'For geese or some of the other larger birds it may be possible to cover that distance in a few days, but many here are carrying injuries and are unable to fly. How do you propose we reach this new promised land?'

'Mother Nature thrives on diversity. So shall we. We'll

form flocks of migrating birds, yes, but others will travel by paw in small packs. Those who are not strong enough to walk will be carried. And don't forget we also have the former Truckles on our side; the resistance movement has promised to provide security and temporary shelter along the route wherever they can.'

'But still, on foot it could take weeks, maybe more, to reach safety.'

There were rumblings of discontent.

'Look,' said Liliuk, 'our journey will not be easy. More blood will be spilled before this war is over and some of us may not make it to our destination at all. But the Adepts still believe it offers the best hope for the survival of our race.'

'What about the survivors who aren't Nsray? What about all the other *people*?' Drue's voice, though small and thin, resounded in the air with the weight of a cathedral bell.

Liliuk scanned the crowd in search of her.

'I mean, couldn't we try to . . . there must be some way to stop all the fighting and killing. Some way to just *end* the war?' said Drue.

Csaba, Yaya and Piera all eyed her nervously.

'What is your name, child?' asked Liliuk.

'Drue . . . Drue Beltane.'

Liliuk studied her long and hard.

'Our young friend speaks bravely of continued negotiations with the Animalians.'

The notion elicited some jeers and derisive laughter.

'No. Please. Despite August's fate, reconciliation remains foremost in our hearts and minds. And he would want it no other way. But for now we must move forward; we must secure our future before we rake over the ashes of the past. Now rest, take nourishment. Gather your strength. Throughout the night the Adepts will speak with each of you regarding your needs and the group you are to travel with. The journey to Mount Ararat will begin before first light tomorrow.'

Having appeased the crowd, Liliuk now turned her attention to Drue and adopted a more gentle, maternal tone.

'So, Drue Beltane. These human survivors you speak of, have you seen them with your own eyes?'

'I have,' replied Drue, her words tumbling out, 'on a ship . . . a ferry . . . It was attacked out at sea, but it didn't sink. There are boys and girls. Twenty of them, maybe more. We have to help them too, don't we?'

'Just like your father. Always trying to save the world. Well, now he has his work cut out for him, does he not?'

'You know . . . my dad?' said Drue, surprised.

'Quinn Beltane. Only too well.'

'He needs your help too. He's hurt . . . I didn't know what else to do . . . He told me to find the Lionman . . .'

'Of course. So you could join us.'

'But he sent me for help . . .'

'Take heart, child. I've been expecting you. Your father will join us in good time.'

'Then he's OK? How . . . how do you know?'

'There's a great deal more you have to learn about the Nsray, Drue Beltane. Trust me. Right now, your father just needs to know that you're safe. Now come, share some herbal tea with me. It'll keep the chill from your bones. And I want to hear all about your journey from England.'

Liliuk turned and drifted away past the choir stalls to a private room – the Besserer Chapel – a place for private prayer and meditation that had been sequestered as a make-shift headquarters. Drue stood spellbound as Liliuk beckoned to her.

'Come, child, don't be afraid.'

'I'm not afraid,' replied Drue, though for once even she wasn't sure that she meant it.

CHAPTER THIRTY-EIGHT

The Besserer Chapel, a well of natural light, contained little inside its rough-hewn stone walls besides an oak refectory table, a matching oak curule seat and several rickety chairs. The table was laden with maps of antiquity, and the faded papyrus and vellum parchment swam with exotic names and places that Drue had never before set eyes on: Ancient Vindelicia and Illyricum; Asia Minor after the Treaty of Apamea, 188 BC; the Kingdom of Pergamum.

Liliuk settled in the oak curule and gestured for Drue to join her at the table. As she did so, one of the Adepts entered bearing a tray. Liliuk cleared a space before her so that he could set the tray down. She thanked him with a nod, and the Adept retreated without a word.

On the tray was a glass pot of steaming tea, two tall glass tumblers with stainless-steel handles, a wedge of fresh lemon on a saucer and some dark chocolate. Liliuk lifted the glass pot, and with a deft flick of her wrist had the loose leaves and herbs inside dancing in a spiral in the bubbling water.

As Liliuk poured the tea, Drue's attention wandered to the light playing on the ornate stained-glass windows above them, which glowed with dramatic scenes from the Old Testament. The Fall and Expulsion; Abraham's Feast; the Sacrifice of Isaac and . . . Noah's Ark, adrift on flood waters: a lone dove was pictured above the vessel. It clutched a green sprig in its beak, as Noah – with the tumbling locks and full white beard of the Adepts – reached up to the bird, hands clasped in prayer.

Liliuk noted Drue's interest and, as she squeezed the wedge of lemon into a tumbler of tea and set it in front of Drue, she said: 'A symbol of hope in a world of despair.'

'Is it true that he was . . . that his son . . . had the gift?'

'As I'm sure your father will have told you, the gift is not magic . . .'

'Just a different way of seeing,' said Drue.

'Precisely that. The gift is merely a way of tapping into the living energy fields that surround us.'

'But that doesn't answer my question,' said Drue.

'Hmmm, the directness of your mother too: you really are your parents' daughter.'

'But is it true?' pressed Drue.

Liliuk took a sip of herbal tea before she continued.

'Truth. Hmmm. A concept as slippery as a fish at the best of times.'

'That doesn't sound like a yes,' said Drue, reaching for the chocolate.

'Well, the story of a Great Flood that swamped the Earth is one that appears in many guises in many different ancient cultures and philosophies, but, as the events happened a very long time ago, it's difficult to say with absolute certainty what is fact, what is fiction and what is a heady brew of both.

'What we can be sure of, though, is the intention of the tale passed down through the ages: guardians were chosen to survive the disaster to prepare for a new world. Just as the Nsray have been chosen now. It's a story that symbolizes hope: one that shows the value of true faith in the face of despair.'

'But, if you're not sure that the story is really true, how do you know the Mountains of Ararat will really be safe?'

'Because the Animalians believe it to be true. And belief is a very powerful tool.'

Drue sipped her tea, lost in thought. Liliuk studied her face.

'You have your mother's eyes, you know.'

Drue lowered her head.

'She was a very special soul too. I'm sorry her passing had to cause you such pain.'

'You knew her?' asked Drue tentatively.

'Yes.'

'You were friends?'

'Not friends exactly. I knew your father before they met. We were . . . close.'

This piqued Drue's curiosity, but, though she searched Liliuk's face for a clue, she did not ask the question that was on the tip of her tongue.

'The truth is that your father loved your mother more than life itself. When I finally met her . . . well, let's just say that I . . . I *understood*. Their union was meant to be. You ask about truth – it's right there in your heart, in your eyes, in your genes.'

'She didn't have the gift,' replied Drue, probing.

'No, not the gift we share, but she had another just as powerful, just as potent: she was of the light. That's what drew your father to her to begin with, and it's also why she was taken from us so early. I'm sure of it.

'It won't heal the hurt you carry inside to know this, Drue, at least not yet, but, though you and your father loved her, and she loved you too with all her heart, the cradle of her light was needed elsewhere. That need was even greater than yours, if you can imagine such a thing. Her spirit lives on, and she is engaged in an even greater struggle than we are. The purest, the most enlightened, are needed to guard the Gates of Shambhala.'

'Shambhala?'

'It goes by many names, and means different things to different cultures. Some call it heaven, others *Tian*, *Loka*, *Giizhigong* . . . The conflict at the Akashic Gates is still the same.'

'Gates? Like the gates of a garden, you mean?' said Drue.

'Not exactly, no. Think of them as a . . . a portal, a door to another world. A world that exists alongside our material realm. The Akashic Gates are the electromagnetic barriers that separate one from the other. Did your father ever talk to you of the BlackLight?'

'No,' said Drue.

'*Ex umbra in solem.*'

'From the shadows into the light.'

'Very good,' said Liliuk, impressed.

'I don't really know Latin, only that; it was something . . . from home.'

'But still.' Liliuk read Drue's expression, her body language, her aura. 'Tell me about your dream.'

'What dream?'

'I think you know, Drue. Recurring dreams leave an aura about a person. And the more they occur, the more potent the aura.'

'What does an aura look like?'

'Did you ever draw round your hand at school? You know, with a pencil, leaving an outline of your fingers on the page. To those who can read them, an aura appears much like that, like an outline.'

'But a dream is just a dream, isn't it?'

'That really depends on who is doing the dreaming. What's your dream about?'

'Water.'

'Water?'

'Deep. Like an ocean. And I'm swimming in it . . . no, not really swimming – sort of floating, but floating downwards instead of up. And I'm not holding my breath or anything, I'm breathing just like normal. And there are crystals, a whole underwater mountain of them, and a light. Like a ball of fire. And it moves around me . . .'

'How does it move?'

'In circles. Around and around.'

'Like a spiral?'

'Yeah, like a spiral, like a whirlpool, only made of light.'

'Mmmm. And how does it make you feel?'

'It's not scary. It's . . . it feels . . . it feels like home.'

'And then?'

'That's usually where it stops.'

'Usually?'

'Today I . . . there was . . . this will sound weird . . . there were these . . .'

'Turtles?'

'Turtles! Yes! How did you know? Is that from the aura thing?' Drue studied the air above her head in search of some evidence of it.

'Tell me more about the turtles. Were they swimming? What kind were they?'

'They were . . . they were turtles, I don't know.'

'Brown, green, large, small?'

'Reddish brown, with . . . kinda yellowy skin.'

'Loggerhead sea turtles.'

'Well, anyway, one of them had the most amazing shell. Like it was painted, only the paint glowed, like those glow-in-the-dark stars you can stick on your ceiling. I used to have some in my old bedroom . . .'

'What colour was the turtle painted?'

'All different colours.'

'Such as? Red, yellow, indigo?'

'What's indigo?'

'Blue-violet.'

'Oh yeah, all those, and green and purple and orange. How did you know?'

'They're the colours of the chakras. The energy centres. Was any one of the colours stronger, brighter than the others?'

'Hmmm. I dunno. Maybe the indigo one. That or the green.'

'The Third Eye and the Heart.'

'Uh?'

'Indigo denotes the area concerned with perception, understanding. Green is related to the Heart chakra. It signifies independence. Did you touch the shell?'

'I . . . yes. Is that bad?'

'No, no, it's not bad.'

'As well as the colours, there were some funny symbols, letters: I don't know, a bit like Latin or something. Like the ones in the painting of the angels.'

Liliuk's dark eyes blazed with interest.

'Can you remember exactly what they were? Could you draw them for me?'

'No.' Drue shook her head, 'I didn't see them all that well. They was just, I don't know, squiggles and stuff.'

Liliuk drew a braided hemp chain from inside the folds of her dress. At its end was a small, round, antique locket made of shimmering, dyed, pearl ray shagreen. Liliuk's nimble fingers loosened a hidden clasp, the pendant sprang open like a clam and a tiny piece of translucent shell fell out into her open palm. Enveloped by the steam from the tea, the shell began to glow.

'Like these perhaps?' said Liliuk, proffering the shell between thumb and forefinger.

Drue studied the shell and saw the tiny mysterious symbols that Liliuk referred to: fine and white as fishbones, the lines and dots and sweeping curves seemed to be embedded within the very fabric of the thing.

'I dunno really,' said Drue, studying the symbols. 'It was the colours I noticed mostly. What is this anyway?'

'A piece of carapace: the domed upper shell of a loggerhead sea turtle.'

'What do the squiggles mean?'

'Language existed in a spoken form long before it was written down, so the first alphabets used symbols to create meaning.'

'Like the cave drawings on the walls where the Lionman was found?'

'Something like that, yes. And this particular script is similar to Ancient Aramaic. That was the language spoken in the time of Noah.'

'I guess it must be very important then. What does the writing say?' asked Drue.

'A question that has occupied the finest minds of our most learned scholars throughout the ages. It's only a fragment, you see. And, though similar to Aramaic, there are some characters that we simply don't recognize. Some say it was written by Mother Nature herself, a message delivered to the creatures of the ocean . . . They did not fear the Great Flood; after all, they had no need of an Ark.'

'Huh, so it's kind of like the missing link of joined-up writing?'

Liliuk seemed disappointed, lost in her thoughts. She palmed the shell like a magician, snapped the locket shut and tucked the hemp chain beneath the folds of her dress once more.

'Next time you have the dream, see if you can remember what the symbols are, OK? Will you do that for me?'

'I'll try. But how did you know they were turtles, in my dream I mean?'

'A lucky guess.'

'But you could have guessed anything.'

'Well, it was a little more than that perhaps: modern-day psychology grew out of dream interpretation, and some of the elements you described have come to be associated with specific qualities or meanings. Water is generally the Fountain of Life, for example. And we are, after all, made mostly of water. Swimming denotes change.

'Fire, well, it depends on the context; it can represent transformation, enlightenment, but it can also mean danger, anger, pain. The light: purity, divinity. And the spiral . . . the spiral is the most powerful conduit of energy in the universe. You'll find it everywhere from the tiniest nautilus shell to tornadoes, right up to the vast spiral galaxy which makes up our known universe.'

Drue was captivated.

'And what about the turtles?'

'The turtles mean you are well protected. But because they were swimming slowly, and you were able to touch them, it also portends that whatever is to befall you, good or bad, it's to happen soon.'

Drue wished she hadn't asked.

'And many ancients believed that turtle shells were a window into the future.'

'So is everyone having this same dream about the water and the turtles and everything? I mean, why would it just be me? I don't know anything about telling the future. I don't want to know . . .' Drue's voice tailed off.

'It's difficult enough living with the past, isn't it? You still miss her greatly every day, don't you? Of course you do. I'm sorry; you don't have to talk about it.'

Drue hadn't any intention of sharing her innermost thoughts with a total stranger, but something about Liliuk's essence, her straight talking, her directness, opened the floodgates.

'I miss my dad. And Will-C – he's my cat and my best friend – I miss him. I miss just . . . going to school. My mates. The teachers. Texting. I miss having my phone and my iPod. I don't know, stupid stuff. Just going into town . . . boring stuff . . . but most of all, most of all I miss my mum, because I know she's not ever coming back.'

Liliuk extended a hand and rested it gently on Drue's.

'Sometimes . . . sometimes the things we're forced to endure are the things that truly make us who we are.'

'But why? Why do bad things have to happen?'

'Just as you said . . . *Ex umbra in solem. Shadows into light.* Perhaps we need the one to recognize the other.'

'Well, I wish we didn't.'

'Maybe one day, if we keep the faith, that wish will come true.'

Drue now felt uncomfortable, vulnerable, awkward in Liliuk's presence.

'Faith seems to do as much bad in the world as it does good,' said Drue. She looked up at the ceiling.

'Sorry, maybe I shouldn't say that in a church and everything.'

Liliuk held on to Drue's hand as she tried to slip it away.

'True faith hurts no one, Drue. Never forget that. People's interpretation of faith to serve their own ends . . . intolerance, the quest for external power, control over one's neighbours, over other nations, through brutality and indoctrination, now that's a different thing altogether. That has nothing to do with true faith. As for the Creator, well, I'm pretty sure that your frustration is understood.

'Beautiful as the church is, if you smashed every pane of these stained-glass windows, tore down the altar and the walls, melted down the bells, crushed every last stone to powder . . . you'd still be left with faith. True faith. For it doesn't reside in any one place. You can find it just as easily in the forests and the mountains and the streams that carry rainwater back to the sea. And, above all, it's to be found in your own heart.'

Drue slumped in her seat, chin resting on her chest. Despite Liliuk's words of comfort, she still felt the pain of having lost her mother. As Liliuk cleared away the tea things, Drue seized the opportunity to change the subject.

'Are these maps of real places? I've never heard of them.'

'Real places, long ago,' replied Liliuk, gathering the maps together.

'Then if they don't exist any more what are you doing with them?'

'Perception, remember? The whole world changes, but at the same time everything remains the same. The places are still there; it's just the names that have changed.'

'Will they help get us to the safe place in the mountains?'

'The Mountains of Ararat? I hope so. But you see this vellum parchment the map is drawn on? This was once the hide of a living creature – a young calf perhaps. I wonder, will they ever let us walk freely among them again. What do you think?'

'I dunno. But what about the children . . . on the ferry?'

'If their destiny is linked to ours, then perhaps they too will be spared.'

'But we can't just wait and see what happens. We have to go back for them. They need our help.'

'Why don't we let fate decide?' replied Liliuk.

'Because if . . . if everything is all joined up, if everything is all really one thing like my dad said . . . if everything is *energy* . . . then, well, fate must be energy too, and so we . . . we are also fate. Don't you see? So we can decide that fate should help.'

Liliuk let out a chuckle of admiration.

'My, you do have a sharp mind! Very well, Drue Beltane. I will ask for two volunteers to retrace your path over the Channel and see what they can find.'

'I'll go with them.'

'No. You must stay with us. You've done your part. As we saw with the jackal, our battle with the Animalians has reached a critical phase. It's more dangerous now than ever. A rescue stands more chance of success if we send those with . . .'

'With what?'

'With a little more experience.'

Liliuk leafed through the ancient maps and selected one of Western Europe.

'Here, this shows the English Channel. Now, where did you encounter the ferry?'

Drue studied the map and pointed to a stretch of water off the coast of France.

As if summoned by telepathy, the Adept who had delivered the tea returned along with another.

'Leave us now, Drue. Return to your friends . . .'

'I don't have any friends here.'

'On the contrary, you have only friends here; it just takes time to settle. Trust me. Rest. Sleep. We all have a long journey ahead of us tomorrow.'

'But what about my dad and Will-C?'

'If your feline friend is so important to you, I'm certain your father will have taken measures to ensure his well-being. You'll meet them again in Ararat.'

Drue was still not entirely convinced.

'Well, if you won't help me, I'll go back for them myself. You can't keep me here if I don't want to stay. I promised to get help and go back . . .'

'There's nothing to go back to, child!' For a split second Liliuk lost her composure. 'Drue, I'm sorry, I tried to protect you from this, but . . . I said before that there were two emissaries sent to negotiate with the Earth Assembly. August Beyer was one. The other was your father.'

Drue sat in stunned silence.

'He hasn't been heard from since. We don't even know if he's still . . . alive.'

Drue leapt from her seat, knocking the ladder-back chair to the ground, and ran from the chapel. Several Adepts were about to enter as Drue burst through the door and barged into them. They exchanged looks with Liliuk – shall we stop her? Liliuk shook her head. And, as Drue ran off into the shadows of the nave, and the last rays of the setting sun drained from the stained-glass windows, the Adepts joined Liliuk once more and pored over the maps of antiquity.

CHAPTER THIRTY-NINE

D rue kept to herself for the rest of the night, even withdrawing from Yaya. Beneath her sorrow, she felt belittled and betrayed by her father and by Liliuk. Deep down inside she knew that they had both been trying to protect her, but in so doing they had deprived her of her sense of self. As far as she was concerned, she was no longer an innocent who had to be shielded from the harsh realities of life and she felt she had done enough to prove that.

And so it was with a simmering sense of injustice and a badly bruised ego that Drue sat thin-lipped through Liliuk's final address to the assembly.

The mass exodus was planned in fine detail. Each member of the clan was assigned to a group, and each group allocated a time for departure along with a specific route to follow and an animal guise to adopt. Drue and two other late arrivals were assigned to join Csaba, Yaya and Piera, and they were to travel as a flock of ospreys.

Diversity was seen as key to ensuring that all would reach the safety of Mount Ararat, and the instructions were repeated until it was clear that each and every person knew exactly where they were supposed to be and at what time their particular party would slip away from Ulm.

A secret passageway – accessed from beneath the choir stalls – connected to the city's sewer system and a tunnel that led directly to the banks of the Danube in the Fishermen's and Tanners' Quarters; this was to be used for the majority of the mass evacuation, to avoid drawing undue attention to the church itself.

It was not until the early hours of the following morning that the seemingly foolproof evacuation plans were dealt a shattering blow.

*   *   *

When it seemed that all had settled for the night, Drue became a mouse and crept quietly down to the catacombs.

The jackal was being held in a dank, cell-like storeroom beside the escape tunnel. Two of the Nsray guards were sleeping – and therefore appeared in their natural human guise – but the third had taken the form of an owl and was perched atop a huge barrel opposite the cell. At least, he was an owl when Drue first turned a corner in the underground passageway and caught sight of him.

Fortunately for her, he was absorbed with shape-shifting, seeing how swiftly he could change from one form of bird to another: owl, parrot, eagle, crow, owl again.

Drue took full advantage and, while his attention was diverted, she scurried beneath the door of the cell.

As soon as she was inside, Drue took the form of a hawk. It took her a while to locate the jackal in the darkness, but as she was able to hover in an almost stationary position at

303

ceiling height in the middle of the room, she felt reasonably safe.

'Who's there?' said the jackal in a rasping growl.

'Keep your voice down,' replied Drue-Hawk.

'Ah, there you are,' said the jackal, following Drue's voice. 'And why should I do that?'

'Because I'm not supposed to be here.'

'Oh? Then why are you?'

'I have a question.'

'I've already told the Adepts . . .'

'The other Shape-shifter. The other Shape-shifter who carried the message to the Earth Assembly. Is he . . .? When you . . . when you took . . .?'

'Ah, I detect a little apprehension. You Nsray are so weak. If you had any spine, you'd have taken my life already. A kill for a kill. I could respect that.'

The jackal shape-shifted into August Beyer and then returned to beast.

'Why we waited so long to reclaim the Earth I do not know,' he said.

'That doesn't answer my question,' said Drue-Hawk.

'Why should I tell you anything?'

'If you help me, maybe, maybe I can help you.'

'I'm listening.'

'First I need to know if my fath— if the other Shape-shifter is still alive.'

'Why is he so important to you?'

'Is he alive?'

'A blood connection perhaps?'

'Is he alive?'

304

'If I tell you what I know, you'll help me?'

'Is he alive?'

Silence.

'Is he?'

'Yes, the Nsray called Quinn is alive,' said the jackal.

Drue lost her balance for a moment, then resumed hovering.

'You know this for a fact?'

'He's being held prisoner. The War Council are smart. They knew that a captive Nsray was of value. We have much to learn about the ways of the Shape-shifters. If he has a weakness, they'll prise it from him.'

The jackal flipped back and forth between beast and man.

'Please. Don't. Please don't do that.'

'So,' said the jackal, 'I have helped you. Now, how will you help me?'

'Where is he being held?'

'Somewhere from which escape is impossible.'

'Where?'

'The ancient caves of Chal-Nakhjir in Markazi. But they are many and well guarded; you will never find him without my help.'

'You could . . . lead me to him?'

The jackal hesitated a moment. And then he said: 'You're just a pup; the Nsray Adepts would never allow it.'

Drue-Hawk hovered above the jackal a moment longer, then swooped down to the door and shape-shifted back into a mouse.

By the time Drue-Mouse peeked back beneath the door

of the cell, even the third guard was dozing. She took a chance and shape-shifted back into human form. She watched the guards for a moment, then, with her back to the cell door, she very carefully turned the key in the lock behind her. It opened with an audible *clack!*

On a reflex, Drue shape-shifted into a mouse again. It was a wise move, because one of the guards stirred, opened his eyes, glanced at the door, then the passageway, and seeing nothing untoward drifted back to sleep.

Drue waited a few more moments before taking on human form again in order to turn the handle and open the cell door. The jackal crept out and started down the tunnel at a lope. Drue became a border collie and followed.

They had only travelled a few hundred metres when a thunderous *CRASH!* reverberated through the walls of the passageway. The source of the noise was clearly above them.

Drue stopped in her tracks as a second *CRASH!* shook the ground they were standing on, an impact so powerful, it dislodged mortar from the arched brick walls. She looked back in the direction of the cell. She heard a human voice cry out. Had they discovered the jackal's escape so soon?

And, in the split second that Drue took her eyes off the jackal, he vanished into the shadows.

The tunnel up ahead forked. Which way had he gone? If she became a swift, she could catch up to him, but a third *CRASHHHHHH!* and Drue shape-shifted back into human form. She could hear muffled cries, screams ... It wasn't the jackal's escape that had shaken the Nsray from their slumber. The church was under attack!

CHAPTER FORTY

Drue reached the central nave just in time to witness the main doors burst open in an explosion of splintered wood and buckled hinges. Three white rhinos – the Animalians' battering ram – were the first through the door, and they charged at the terrified Nsray, who scattered in panic. Liliuk moved quickly to rally a defence.

'Engage!' she cried. 'Remember your stations!'

Her words were lost in a torrent of noise and movement as hundreds of Nsray shape-shifted into Animalian predators capable of defending themselves against the murderous flood of screeching, howling, roaring beasts that poured by their hundreds through the shattered doors.

Lions clashed with grizzly bears. Elephants with rhinos. Wolves with tigers. A frenzy of fangs and claws and tusks and hide and spittle and blood.

Forced back into the escape tunnel by one of the Adepts, Drue found herself in a tide of fearful youths being swept away along a dank, dark passage.

The sound of a hundred pairs of feet splashing through

puddles of muddy seep-water echoed off the arched tunnel walls. Here and there, tributaries, smaller passageways, branched off from the escape tunnel linking it to the main sewer system.

A young girl tripped and fell at the head of the group. Csaba pulled her to her feet and they were once again swept along with the other children. The further the group ran, the louder the sound of rushing water.

Somebody yelled: 'Listen. It's the river!'

'Quiet!' called out somebody else. 'The animals may hear us.'

Drue caught sight of a beacon of light up ahead. The tunnel snaked and finally came to an abrupt halt at a rusty-grilled hatch. Beyond the hatch lay the River Danube, the swirling water running high and fast between the channel of tall stone warehouses that flanked it.

Yaya and another boy set to work on the hatch and forced it open. Csaba shape-shifted into an osprey to hold back the tide of Nsray novices with his outstretched wings. Many of the younger children were terrified, wild-eyed, but they followed his example and shape-shifted into their allocated forms. As Drue was to travel with Csaba, she too adopted the guise of an osprey.

'OK, everyone. You all know the plan. Remember what Liliuk told us and we'll all be OK,' said Csaba-Osprey.

Yaya's hands were stained with rust from the hatch and he squatted down to wash them in the river.

'OK then,' continued Csaba-Osprey, trying to raise everyone's spirits, 'good luck. See you in Ararat.'

As Yaya shook the water from his hands, he spotted the

danger . . . As the only one still in human form, it was futile to shout, so in an instant he shape-shifted into an osprey to warn the others.

Too late. In an explosion of movement, a huge crocodile burst from the rushing water, plucked Yaya-Osprey from the air and locked its jaws shut as its momentum sent it crashing back down into the river. One second Yaya-Osprey was there. The next he was gone.

'No!' cried Csaba-Osprey.

Driven back into the tunnel by fear, the young Nsray began to panic. Several took the form of swifts and made an aerial dash for the open gate. But again the monstrous crocodile launched itself from the river and plucked them from the air with its powerful jaws.

As it crashed back into the water once more, Csaba-Osprey screamed: 'Now!'

A wave of birds bolted from the dank tunnel and took to the open sky.

'Wait!' cried Drue-Osprey, blocking the passage with her outstretched wings. Her instinct proved correct as the crocodile sprang from the river again, and this time hurled itself right into the mouth of the tunnel. The bony slates of its olive-green armoured skin shuddered with the impact. It lashed its tail and worked its terrifying jaws to block the Nsrays' escape route.

Some began to retreat the way they had come. Others took a chance on the connecting sewers, only to find an army of rats advancing through them.

'We're trapped!' cried Drue-Osprey.

'No: everyone, this way!' screamed Csaba-Osprey as he

shape-shifted into a crocodile himself and hurled himself at the onrushing beast.

'Csaba!' screamed Piera-Osprey. But it was too late . . .

A terrible clash of deadly jaws and Csaba's momentum drove the pair out of the mouth of the tunnel and plunging into the river.

The Nsray poured forward and fled on the wing, leaving only the two ospreys, Drue and Piera, turning tight circles above the spuming water.

Locked in deadly combat, the crocodiles thrashed and writhed and kicked up so much mud and silt from the riverbed, it was impossible to follow the fight from above the surface.

As the rats poured through the escape tunnel and gathered at the open gate hatch, they began, in frustration, to call for aerial reinforcements to attack the Nsray-Ospreys.

'Where are the others who are meant to be with us?' asked Drue.

'I don't know!' cried Piera.

'We have to find them!'

'There's no time!'

Drue realized that Piera was right; they had little time left to make good their own escape. Piera climbed a little higher, but Drue held her position over the river, hoping beyond hope that Csaba would resurface. As the river began to run red with blood, however, she feared the worst.

Fight or flight. With the rats continuing to rally support, Drue-Osprey made a split-second decision and plunged into the murky water.

Down she travelled, through the chill current, in search

of a glimpse of the battling crocodiles. And then she saw one. Blood streaming from its slashed throat as it floated lifeless, bound in a rusted chain. But which was it, and where was the other?

The thought had barely registered in her mind when the second crocodile sped up towards her from the riverbed. Drue-Osprey broke the surface of the water like a bullet, the crocodile just a beat behind her, and as its deadly snout pierced the air . . . the creature shape-shifted into Csaba-Osprey.

'Csaba!' cried Piera-Osprey.

'Go!' he yelled in reply.

With rats tumbling from the escape tunnel like maggots from a rotted carcass, and the battle raging on in the snow-bound square around the great church, the three ospreys soared away above the rooftops of the warehouses and headed east as fast as their wings would carry them.

CHAPTER FORTY-ONE

It took several miles of hard flying before the Nsray-Ospreys felt they had put sufficient distance between themselves and the battleground of Ulm to slow their pace. If there had been an avian posse on their tails, they had lost it, and Piera – who had been trailing behind the others – took the opportunity to land and catch her breath. Drue and Csaba circled back, but, although Csaba also settled in a high branch of the stand of fir trees, Drue-Osprey kept on circling.

'I'm not sure we should stop just yet,' cautioned Drue.

'I only stopped because you were straying off course,' complained Piera.

'What? No, we're heading south-south-east. That's right.'

'You were drifting too far east.'

'I don't think so.'

A potholed two-lane highway snaked through the landscape below. At a junction was a road sign.

'What language is that?' asked Piera.

'German?' said Drue.

'You see, what do you know? We've passed over Austria and Croatia . . . so that is Slovakia, no?'

'That's what I meant. Slovakian,' said Drue.

'Hah! You see. South-east is Bosnia, not Slovakia.'

'So what?' snapped Drue, exasperated.

'So you're taking us off course and that will add miles to the journey and use up valuable time.'

'OK. Then stop lagging behind. You take the lead and show us the way,' said Drue, tired of Piera's attitude.

'I was only holding back to see if the others who were meant to travel with us had managed to catch up.'

'That was good thinking,' said Csaba-Osprey timidly.

'Oh rubbish,' said Drue. 'She's just making excuses.'

'Well?' said Piera-Osprey as if anyone could possibly dare to question her sincerity. 'If putting others before myself is a crime, I suppose I am guilty.'

'I'm sure Drue didn't mean anything bad by what she said. She just misunderstood.'

'Misunderstood!' snapped Drue-Osprey.

'There, you see,' said Csaba, appeasing Piera.

Before Drue could muster a response . . . a piercing scream rang out.

A human voice!

A shrill cry of terror.

Drue was the first to react and set off at speed to investigate.

Beyond the stand of fir trees lay a hillside that had been the target of extensive deforestation: vast swathes of the landscape were now a graveyard of sawn tree stumps and abandoned logging vehicles, one of which, a dropside flatbed transporter, was still laden with giant trunks piled high and strung with chains.

Drue scanned the terrain for signs of life. There were none. She drifted on the breeze and widened her search. A potholed road snaked away from the razed forest, and beyond it, a little further down the valley, lay a small hamlet: a mill and a cluster of small houses nestled round a narrow stream. Drue-Osprey drifted closer to the village.

A large pack of timber wolves patrolled the narrow streets and were conducting a thorough house-to-house search. As none were gathered round a kill, and silence had descended, Drue surmised that the scream must have come from someone who was now in hiding.

Csaba and Piera flew up alongside and turned circles round Drue's position.

'What is it?' said Csaba.

'Wolves. See – they're searching the village. Someone must be hiding there.'

'Nsray?' said Piera.

'Maybe,' said Drue, 'but that scream didn't come from an animal; why would they have risked exposing themselves?'

'Well, if they're not Nsray, they have no chance,' said Csaba.

'Unless we can distract the wolves somehow,' said Drue.

'That's crazy,' said Piera.

'How?' said Csaba.

'Draw them away or something – I don't know,' replied Drue.

'Maybe we could join the pack,' said Csaba.

'And get ourselves killed? It's too dangerous,' said Piera.

'Piera's right,' agreed Drue. 'The golden rules, remember?'

'What?' said Csaba.

'You know ... wolves. Pack animals. My dad said it's really dangerous to take the shape of predators who hunt in packs. You can lose yourself to the ...'

But Csaba-Osprey wasn't listening. He swooped down towards the hamlet, touched down in a garden behind a house that the pack were about to reach and transformed himself into a timber wolf.

Drue and Piera watched from above as three wolves from the pack turned a corner, sloped through an open gate and ran into Csaba-Wolf. Taking him as one of their own, they immediately broke ranks, split up and began to search through the outbuildings that flanked the property.

'You stay here as lookout,' said Drue.

'Wait,' said Piera.

But Drue followed the route that Csaba had taken, and shape-shifted into a timber wolf as she too touched down in the Bosnian village.

Drue-Wolf loped across a street and into the courtyard garden where Csaba had landed. Neither he nor the other wolves were in sight. The chemical trail of the pack hung heavy in the air, a potent musk of raw power laced with adrenalin.

Try as she might, Drue was unable to distinguish Csaba's scent from that of the real timber wolves, and she persuaded herself that that was a good thing: if she couldn't do so, perhaps the wolf pack couldn't either, and that made her feel a little more secure in her own disguise too.

The hamlet, a ramshackle collection of simple dwellings,

seemed larger than it actually was because of the haphazard layout, and presented more of a challenge to the hunt, as the connecting lanes and pathways doubled back and criss-crossed like a maze.

Drue leapt through an open window into the kitchen of a cottage and came face to face with a timber wolf twice her size. Ears pricked forward, tail bent, fangs bared – its stance was intended to strike fear into an opponent or a lower-ranking member of the pack and, fortunately for Drue, it did just that. Her ears flattened against her head, her tail curled between her hind legs and she broke eye contact as she adopted a crouch. The alpha female immediately real-ized that Drue posed no threat and she relaxed.

'You startled me,' growled the timber wolf. 'Any sign of the human cubs?'

'Er . . . no, none,' said Drue-Wolf weakly.

'Well, they can't have gone far.'

A second wolf trotted down the stairs from the first floor and stopped at the kitchen door.

'Anything?' said the alpha female to the new arrival, though all the time keeping her eyes trained on Drue.

'Nothing,' said the other wolf.

'Well, keep looking. They're here somewhere.'

As the second wolf moved away to an adjoining room, the alpha female raised her muzzle in Drue's direction and flared her nostrils. Drue knew at once that the wolf was reading her scent, and her eyes flicked round the room looking for an edge, an advantage should her humanness be detected. She spotted a rack of bottled condiments – oil and vinegar – up on the worktop by the window.

'I'm not sure I know you,' said the timber wolf.

'I . . . did you hear that?' Drue-Wolf said as she sat bolt upright and pricked up her ears.

'What?'

'That . . . I'm sure I heard . . .' Drue-Wolf leapt up on to the worktop and, doing her best to make it look like an accident, toppled the oil and vinegar bottles with her tail. Just as she hoped, the bottles rolled from the worktop and smashed on impact with the stone floor. The timber wolf reeled as the acrid smell of vinegar assaulted her nostrils.

'Careful, you idiot!' she barked.

'Sorry,' said Drue-Wolf disingenuously. 'I thought I heard a cry.'

As if on cue, a blood-chilling howl reverberated through the village. To Drue's great relief, the female timber wolf lost interest in her and leapt through the window she had entered.

Drue followed a moment later, crossed the yard and headed for the open gate. Before she reached it, however, she was confronted by another lone wolf. Drue braced herself, expecting more trouble, then sighed with relief when the animal spoke.

'Drue?'

'Csaba?'

'Yes, it's me.'

'You scared me half to death.'

'We must be careful; the pack is everywhere.'

'I know.'

'Did you hear that howl?'

'The leader. A signal to the others. He's picked up a human scent.'

'Are we too late?'

'I don't know.'

'Where is he?'

'Across the street. Come, look.'

Drue and Csaba trotted out of the gate and along to the end of the wooden fence that surrounded the property. A few hundred metres away was a crossroads where the pack had gathered in front of a two-storey stone cottage. The leaders – the alpha male and the alpha female who had confronted Drue – stood at the middle of a pack twenty strong.

The alpha male deferred to his partner, and the female zigzagged along the path that led to the cottage, with her nose held low to the ground, eyes wide, ears erect, tail extended flat behind her.

'They're close,' said Csaba-Wolf.

'How do you know?' said Drue-Wolf.

'I've seen them at home. Hunting in the mountains in Hungary. When they close in on their prey, it's like this.'

'Then we have to do something. I'll lead them away. You check the cottage.'

'What!' exclaimed Csaba.

Before she had time to lose her nerve, Drue shape-shifted back into her true self once more and ran out into the street where she was sure to be seen by the pack. She locked eyes with the alpha male. Feigning surprise, Drue screamed, turned on her heels and fled. The ruse worked and, bristling with murderous intent, the pack gave chase.

Drue led the pack down the hill away from the cottage and scrambled over a garden fence. She tore through a yard, ducked beneath washing on a line, burst through a tall gate and sprinted down a narrow path. She was determined to retain her human form as long as possible, to present the best visible target for the wolves to follow. Not that shape-shifting would throw them off her scent; now that they had identified it, their highly sensitive noses would be able to pick it up instantly whatever form she chose to adopt.

As the pack gained ground and closed in for the kill, Drue cut away from the village and into the woods. As soon as she was quite sure she was masked by the undergrowth, she transformed into a sparrow and soared straight up into the canopy of the tall trees.

Panting, exhausted, but still charged with adrenalin, Drue-Sparrow watched the wolf pack crash through the woodland in search of their prey. Knowing that every second counted, and that they wouldn't be fooled for long, she took to the air and flew back to the spot where she'd left Csaba.

Csaba, still in wolf guise, had already gained entry to the cottage that the pack had been about to storm, and Drue found him searching a ground-floor bedroom. A large ham-ster cage – its wire door open wide – stood on a small dresser papered with flowers cut from magazines, and the walls were covered in colourful drawings of mice and rabbits and smiling faces. It was a picture of childhood innocence that struck a chord with Drue, even though she was eager for news.

'They'll be back in no time; we have to hurry. Find anyone?' she asked in a breathless rush.

Csaba-Wolf fixed Drue with a steely glare: head low, ears pricked forward, tail bent – it was the same stance the alpha female had adopted, and Drue knew it meant trouble.

'Csaba. Csaba, it's me, Drue.' Drue shape-shifted back into a young girl again.

Csaba-Wolf's lips curled back to bare his fangs. His eyes blazed with hatred.

'Csaba! Wait! You're—'

Too late. Spellbound by an irresistible force that had melded his spirit with that of the pack, Csaba-Wolf launched an attack and sprang across the room with a blood-curdling snarl.

If not for her Nsray reflexes, Drue would have been finished. In a heartbeat, she became a sparrow and Csaba-Wolf's massive frame sailed beneath her and slammed into the bedroom wall with a sickening crunch of bone and cartilage.

Drue-Sparrow lingered just long enough to see that Csaba wasn't critically injured, then she darted out of the room, shape-shifted back into herself once more and slammed the bedroom door shut. She listened at it for a moment, then jerked away with a start as Csaba-Wolf threw himself against it from the other side and the flimsy wooden door rattled in its iron hinges.

'Csaba! Csaba, please!' cried Drue in desperation.

As the door shuddered from impact once more, she turned her attention back to the mission that had led them there.

'Hello! Hey! Is anyone there?!'

Scurrying from room to room, Drue called out again and again. Her eyes flashed to the windows. One or two wolves were already retracing their steps on the street out front. She could still hear Csaba-Wolf slamming his weight against the bedroom door. Time was fast running out.

'Hey! Hello!'

Drue's mind raced as she tried to plot a course of action: the wolf pack had identified the house as the refuge of their prey, yet Csaba had surely had time to search the whole cottage, every room, and hadn't found a soul. And if he hadn't done so, with the aid of highly attuned wolf senses, then how could they be there?

Unless . . .

Drue dashed into the small living room: a sparsely furnished, wholly unremarkable space except, if one knew where to look, for one feature: a panelled wall beside the open fireplace.

Drue dropped to her knees and began to search the panelling, tapping on it with her knuckles. *Tap, tap, tap . . . clack.* A change in the sound suggested a change in density. There was a large cavity in what was otherwise a solid stone wall. And to Drue that meant one thing . . . a secret compartment like a priest-hole!

She knocked louder, more urgently, and pressed her ear against the wood panel. Was that a stifled sob she heard?

'Hey. Open up. Quickly. It's OK. You're safe. Hello. Hello. Please answer.'

If she had ever heard a sweeter sound than that of the bolt being drawn inside the hideaway, Drue couldn't imagine what it was. As the hinged panel swung open, she caught sight of two scrawny, barefoot urchins, a little girl and a little boy, maybe six or seven years old, huddled in the cramped space. Their faces were filthy and their clothes hung from their frail bodies like rags, but otherwise they seemed unharmed. Drue reached out a hand.

'Come. Quickly.'

The children were hesitant. They didn't understand English; it was the sound of a human voice that had drawn them from their hiding place. The girl looked to her brother, and he in turn looked to a bundle that he had snuggled in his shirt. It was a black-and-white hooded rat. The boy said something to the rat in Bosnian, and then something more to his sister that Drue didn't understand, but to her relief the pair then clambered out into her arms.

A terrifying howl pierced the silence. Csaba-Wolf was still trapped and now summoning help from the pack. The children clung in terror to Drue's legs. What to do?! The surest means of escape was to shape-shift into a bird, but Drue knew that, even as an eagle, or a condor, she would never have the strength to carry both children at the same time.

As the ravenous wolf pack sprinted towards the front of the house, Drue grabbed hold of the children's hands and wrapped her fingers tight round theirs.

'Don't you let go, OK? Do you hear me? Hold on tight and don't you ever let go!'

She had no idea whether the children understood, but she hauled them to the back door and down a flight of wooden steps to a dirt yard. On three sides were high fences. The fourth consisted of a dilapidated lean-to and stable block.

Drue and the children flinched as they heard the front windows of the cottage shatter. The wolves had hurled themselves right through the glass in their desperation to reach their prey.

Which way to turn? What now? She heard her father's

voice: *Stay true to your gift ... always follow your heart ... have faith.*

Faith! What good was it now?

Drue prayed for an answer. Inspiration. Help.

Then, as everything appeared to unfold in slow motion, a sudden breeze whipped round the fugitives and lifted a loose spray of feeding hay from the ground. As the grass and debris spiralled through the air, caught in a miniature tornado, it lured Drue's eye to the threadbare bridle hanging on the broken stable door.

Of course, she thought.

She dropped to her knees and pulled the children close. She prised their fingers from her hands, swung the little girl on to her back and encouraged her to grab hold of a hank of her long hair. The little boy looked on wide-eyed with terror, his pet rat scurrying nervously from shoulder to shoulder.

'Now you!' yelled Drue. 'Quickly!'

The little girl didn't need to understand English to grasp Drue's intention and she held out her free hand to encourage her brother. As Drue dropped on to all fours, he too climbed aboard and lashed a length of her hair round his hands.

Glass exploded on to the yard as Csaba-Wolf burst through the bedroom window in pursuit. The children screamed and buried their faces in Drue's hair. A blur of movement and Drue shape-shifted into a powerful Arabian light horse. Though terrified, the children instinctively clung fast to her thick mane as Drue's sleek chestnut roan reared up on her hind legs and drove the snarling Csaba-Wolf back with her hooves.

323

A second wolf attacked from behind, and this time Drue-Roan dipped her head and kicked the animal with her hind legs, sending him flying across the yard, squealing in pain. She raced for the high fence surrounding the yard and leapt over it – and the startled wolves approaching from outside – like a champion hurdler.

The children clung fast as their mount hit the ground hard and galloped away at full stretch. On Drue-Roan ran, dodging potholes, desperate to pick up speed as she fled through the village.

The wolf pack gave chase.

Suddenly an osprey dropped from the sky.

'Piera!' cried Drue-Roan.

'The hill,' called out Piera-Osprey. 'Head for the woods at the top of the hill!'

Drue-Roan threw a sharp turn to the left, veered from the main street, jumped a drainage ditch and began to climb the hill of tree stumps. Still the wolf pack gave chase. And, given the steep incline of the hill, they were gaining ground. Had Piera driven her into a trap?

Piera-Osprey beat her wings furiously and raced to the abandoned transporter. As Piera shape-shifted back into human form, Drue-Roan recognized just what it was her Nsray companion had in mind. Redoubling her efforts, pounding the soft earth with her hooves, Drue thundered on.

'Piera, wait! Csaba is . . .!' But Drue's Animalian cry fell on deaf ears.

Piera pulled the bolts from the dropside flatbed and, as it fell open with a screech of its metal hinges, she clambered on to the cargo of stacked, unsawn tree trunks and set about unfastening the chain-link restraints.

Gravity did the rest.

A fraction too soon as it turned out, and Drue-Roan was forced to leap the first of the huge trunks as it crashed from the bed of the transporter and plunged towards her.

The leaders of the chasing wolf pack were not so fortunate: caught by surprise, they could do little to avoid being crushed beneath several tonnes of rolling deadwood. Those in the pack that were lucky enough to dive clear, quickly turned on their heels and scattered, as one after another the massive tree trunks tumbled from the flatbed truck and careened on down the hillside, pulverizing everything in their path.

At the peak of the hill, at the edge of the fir forest, Drue-Roan paused to catch her breath. She could feel the grip of the urchins' fingers bound tightly round her mane; for now, though frightened, they were safe. Piera shape-shifted back into an osprey once more and flew to Drue-Roan's side.

'Where's Csaba?'

'With the pack. You weren't to know,' said Drue.

Realizing the implications of what she had done, Piera-Osprey climbed and turned a wide circle, surveying the fallen wolves on the hill below. Three, four, five broken victims lay scattered across the hill of tree stumps, but Csaba was not among them.

'These two stand no chance out here,' said Drue-Roan. 'I have to try to get them to safety.'

'To Ararat?'

Drue-Roan nodded.

'But it's hundreds of miles just to reach the Turkish border.'

'I have to try. It's their only hope.'

'And Csaba?'

'I . . . don't know.'

'I'll stay. Try to find him. He won't be safe with the pack for long,' said Piera-Osprey after a moment.

'I wish I could help.'

'You tried to warn him. I'm sorry.'

'For what?' replied Drue-Roan. 'You saved us.'

'For everything I said before. It wasn't fair. I was . . . I don't know, jealous.'

Jealous, thought Drue. Of her? Because of the attention Csaba had paid her. These were new feelings, complex emotions that she was only just beginning to grow aware of. Strangely, reflecting on Piera's bond with Csaba brought another face altogether swimming into her consciousness: the Spanish boy from the ferry.

What was his name? Adan. Adan López de Haro.

Drue chased the thought away: there was no room for distraction, no room for error.

'You'll find Csaba,' said Drue-Roan. 'I can feel it. And don't worry, because, well, worry gives a small thing a big shadow.'

'What?' said Piera-Osprey.

'Nothing. Just something a friend told me.'

Drue-Roan turned a circle. At the foot of the hill, as the last of the tree trunks had rolled to a standstill, a few wolves were tentatively exploring the terrain once more. It wouldn't be long before they plucked up the courage to launch another assault.

'South-south-east,' said Drue-Roan with a nod.

'South-south-east,' agreed Piera-Osprey, acknowledging that Drue had been right all along.

'You'll have to cross Serbia and Bulgaria. If you make it that far, head to Istanbul.'

'How will I know it?'

'The cradle of great civilizations? Symbol of the Ottoman Empire? The eastern capital of Ancient Rome?' said Piera-Osprey, incredulous.

'Just tell me how I'll know,' said Drue-Roan, slightly embarrassed that she didn't share Piera's encyclopaedic knowledge.

'When the ground beneath your feet turns red, you're there. But that's the easy part. Then you need to cross the Bosphorus River. Its currents are fast and dangerous.'

'Isn't there a bridge?'

'Sure. It joins one part of Turkey with the other . . . if it's still standing.'

'Why wouldn't it be?'

'It's built on a fault line.'

'A what?'

'You know – earthquakes.'

'How do you know all this stuff?'

'My father. He's . . . he *was* a geologist.'

Drue nodded.

Dad, she thought. *And the jackal. How could I have been so stupid?*

It dawned on her that the jackal could now report back to the Earth Assembly. He would identify Liliuk as their leader. Thanks to her, her dad and the Nsray were in even greater danger.

'Drue?' said Piera. 'Drue, are you OK?'

Drue-Roan reared up on her hind legs to encourage the children to cling fast. Then, as she took off at a gallop through the woods, she called out: 'See you in Ararat!'

PART IV
WHITE STONE - BLACK SEA

CHAPTER FORTY-TWO

Gallinago, Yoshi and Will-C gathered in the Callows' hay barn for a conference while Lennox, his crew and the farm Truckles kept watch. Mustela's forces had not advanced any further than the post-and-rail fence at the paddock, though quite why, none of the Truckles could fathom.

'With Drue's father gone,' said Will-C, 'there's no reason for me to stay. I'm going to search for Drue.'

'The other Truckles need you,' said Yoshi.

'They have Lennox,' said Will-C. 'Now we're at war, he's better suited to be a leader than I am.'

'But you don't even know where Drue is. How will you find her?'

'I don't know, but I have to try. I have to do that much,' replied Will-C.

'But she could be anywhere in the world!' protested Yoshi.

'Then I'll search the whole world!'

'It's impossible. Tell him, Gallinago. Talk some sense into him.'

'Der is someting . . .' said the snipe.

'What?' said Yoshi.

'News travels quick as a needle-tail on da wing. I have heard tell of a meetin' place. A place dat da Shape-shifters tink of as sacred.'

'Where?' said Will-C, anxious for details.

'It may be . . . it may be nothin' . . .' added Gallinago.

'Nothing is all I have to go on anyway. Where is it?' said Will-C.

'Da birthplace of da Nsray clan . . .'

'Gallinago?!' pleaded Will-C impatiently.

'Da home of da Lionman.'

'The Lionman?'

'Dat's roight.'

'Do you know how to find it?'

'I could try.'

'Then what are we waiting for?'

''Tis a good many days' hard march. And we would have to cross da great ocean.'

'The ocean,' said Will-C, his heart sinking at the thought of more water.

'Humans crossed the ocean without getting wet. Burrowed like moles right underneath it. I knew someone who had a friend who went . . .' began Yoshi.

'Will you show me?' said Will-C to Gallinago. 'Will you lead the way?'

'I owe Quinn Beltane me life,' replied Gallinago.

'OK then,' said Will-C.

'I'm coming too,' said Yoshi.

'You might be safer here.'

'I'm the one who knows where the human burrow is, remember,' said Yoshi.

'You're forgettin' one ting though,' said Gallinago.

'What's that?' asked Will-C.

'Mustela's army. Dey're not about to let ya trot roight by.'

Will-C thought for a moment.

'We'll need a diversion. Something . . . something to draw them away.'

'Like what?' said Yoshi.

'I don't know,' admitted Will-C. 'But I know who will: Lennox.'

The three shared a look, and then started out of the hay barn in search of the streetwise torbie.

CHAPTER FORTY-THREE

By the time the battle at Ulm was over, both sides had sustained heavy losses and the main square was littered with the aftermath: fallen combatants, splintered trees, shattered shop windows and blood-spattered snow.

The local Animalian Council of Elders – led by Ibex, their District Proconsul, a scrawny goat-antelope with huge recurved horns – and a clutch of attendants picked their way through the debris, past the Animalian guards and into the church itself, as they assessed the extent of their losses.

'Not a single Nsray captured alive?' said Ibex.

'None,' replied a wild pig attendant.

The Proconsul stopped to consider the body of an African lion that had been cut down in the nave.

'And the jackal-Nsray?'

'Missing.'

The Proconsul found himself drawn to the fresco on the high ceiling: the angel, the bull, the eagle and the lion.

'But we already know the Nsray will try to reach Japheth's Land,' said an elk Elder.

'Well,' said Ibex, 'good luck to them. It's no longer any concern of ours.'

'What makes you think that?'

The voice came from above. A ragged shadow washed over the huddle of Elders as four vultures swept into the church. They turned lazy circles over the fallen Nsray and lifeless Animalians scattered among the pews.

'And do I detect a note of sympathy for the Nsray, District Proconsul?' continued the vulture, settling on the back of a pew and stretching its unfeathered neck.

Unsettled by the tone of the scavenger, the Proconsul hit back.

'This is a private meeting of the Council. By whose authority . . .?'

'Hshukha. My brothers and I have travelled directly from the Sanctum of the Earth Assembly. The Guardians are not pleased with the way you let the Nsray slip away. It is our duty to ensure they don't do so again. All Animalians are ordered to join the drive to push them south and prevent any retreat.'

'There's too much work to do here. With the influx of refugees from the zoos and surrounding farms, the local situation is already under great strain. There's a danger that the whole system will collapse if . . .'

'All Animalians! That's a direct order. Our legions will be lying in wait for the Nsray at the City on the Seven Hills. It is there that they will draw their last breath. Not one is to cross the Bosphorus. Not one is to set foot on Japheth's Land,' snapped Hshukha.

The Council of Elders exchanged nervous looks.

'Go. Now. Spread the word. Rally your charges. There is nothing more to be done here,' said Hshukha as he spread his wings again.

As the vultures retreated and the Elders and their attendants filed back out on to the square, one of their number – a red squirrel – discreetly slipped away from the entourage and doubled back.

Scuttling swiftly through the church pews, the red squirrel made directly for one of the fallen Nsray – a beautiful black woman with a mane of white dreadlocks: Liliuk.

The squirrel checked to ensure that he was quite alone before he lifted a fold of Liliuk's cloak to reveal the braided hemp chain still secure around her neck. The shagreen locket rippled with inner light as the squirrel weighed it in its paw. Slicing through the hemp chain with its incisors, the red squirrel tugged the pendant free, leapt on a pew, shape-shifted into a raven and flew directly to a shattered stained-glass window with the looted treasure secure in its claws.

Outside, the air was alive with movement and the ground trembled with the Animalians' evacuation. As the vultures circled the bell tower, overseeing the deployment of the ground forces, the raven quickly took to the air and was instantly lost among the multitude of feathered squadrons heading for the City on the Seven Hills . . . Istanbul.

CHAPTER FORTY-FOUR

Mile after arduous mile, Drue-Roan pressed on with her terrified young charges clinging fast to her mane. The further south they travelled, the greener the landscape and the firmer, the easier the ground beneath her restless pounding hooves. Forests, farmland, rolling fields and rivers slipped by them as day turned to night, and night back into day.

With every long stride she took, Drue focused harder, melded more fully with the muscle and sinew and nature of the beast whose form she inhabited. And the deeper she delved, the more fluid her movements became. Settling into a fast but comfortable rhythm, she found that by maintaining a steady pace she could expend less energy over a greater distance.

Though Drue-Roan chose to give the towns and villages they passed along the way a wide berth – for fear of running into further hunting parties – she was nonetheless surprised that their bid for freedom had met with so little resistance. True, a lone brown bear had given chase at one point, as

Drue shape-shifted to forage for dandelion leaves, haw-thorn berries and purslane stems to feed the children, and she had galloped unwittingly right through a pack of sleeping wild boar, but otherwise the journey had been rel-atively trouble-free.

It was not until she reached the outskirts of a vast shanty town, a sprawling landscape choked with makeshift breeze-block and scrap-metal squats, linked by a seemingly random web of rubbish-strewn dirt tracks, that her Nsray sixth sense warned her of unseen danger.

Reluctant as she was to pass through the narrow, aban-doned streets, so large was the settlement – Drue calculated it would take her an extra two days to avoid it, and she simply didn't have sufficient reserves of energy for that – she decided she had little choice. Sweating heavily, partly as a result of the endurance test she had completed, but also due to the uncomfortable change in humidity, Drue-Roan assessed the terrain.

Which way to go? Which of the pathways ahead offered the least cover for an Animalian ambush? She pawed the ground and kicked up the damp russet earth: Piera's words immediately sprang to mind: *When the ground beneath your feet turns red, you're there.*

We made it! thought Drue, and that gave her the impetus she needed to press on into the slums. Taking it all in at a walking pace, she caught her breath. Her mouth was dry. She was thirsty and she realized that the children must be too. Frustratingly, though there were mud-caked plastic water butts the size of oil drums outside every other building, most had been toppled, and those that did stand upright had debris – dead flies, spiders, even the bodies of rodents – floating in them.

Drue-Roan scoured the surroundings for an alternative source. She found it amid the patchwork architecture: a plastic tarpaulin had been used to create a sheltered extension to a single-storey home and its folds glistened with early-morning dew. She stopped to lap at the refreshing moisture and encouraged her charges to do the same.

The children needed little encouragement and, though reluctant to let go of Drue-Roan's mane, they were soon rubbing their faces in the dew and lapping at the plastic with eager tongues.

Drue peered into one of the empty hovels as the children slaked their thirst. The walls were caked with more red earth, and the floor covered with a threadbare rush mat. Though there were signs that it had once been inhabited – a stack of clay bowls, some simple wooden furniture and even a satellite TV dish that had been used as a brazier – it was still little more than a shelter from the elements: more a cave than a house.

This is Istanbul, thought Drue. *Pride of the Ottoman Empire, eastern capital of Ancient Rome?*

It looked more like the breaker's yard where she had holed up with Gallinago and her dad.

Drue's mind wandered. How she longed to see them again, and to be reunited with Will-C. With her father a prisoner of the Animalians, she feared for Will-C's safety. How would he and the other Truckles fare in Kingley Burh without them?

A yelp of concern from the children pulled Drue back

into the moment. As her concentration had drifted, so Drue's Arabian roan form had begun to lose definition. Before she could collect herself, Drue lost control completely, automatically shape-shifted back into her human self and all three tumbled to the ground. Drue cursed and checked to see that the children were unharmed by the fall.

A movement in the shadows; sunlight glinted on a dozen pairs of yellow eyes. There were creatures moving through in the interlocking shacks all around them. Quick as a flash, Drue shape-shifted into a lioness and stood over the children, ready to ward off any attack.

'Welcome to Gecekondu,' said a scrawny, dirty white Van Kedi cat as he stepped out into the morning light. Cocking his head, he conducted a swift surveillance of the street and the sky above, then turned his penetrating gaze – which had a slightly peculiar cast, given that one eye was auburn and the other blue – back to Drue-Lion and her human cubs.

'Though unless you are try to be attracting the attentions, you might want to rethink the Queen-of-the-Jungle get-up. Not too many lions in this neck of the woodlands.'

'Who are you?' said Drue-Lion, wary of the gang of scraggy alley cats emerging from the shadows left and right.

'Oddeye. Your mostest humble of servants, O mighty Nsray warrior.'

Oddeye's eccentric patois did little to mask the sarcastic subtext.

'And this rabble are what pass in these parts for the Domesticated Animal Resistance.'

They didn't look very domesticated to Drue, but she

wasn't about to quibble. She shape-shifted into a cinnamon-coloured Van Kedi cat to fit in with the crowd.

'I'm Drue and . . .'

'*Iyi*. Well, now we've got the introducings out from the way, shall we get these two mangy human cubs off from the street? They're starting to attract the flies, and maybe also some even more unwelcome visitors.'

Drue-Kedi's eyes darted to the sky and she caught sight of a massive flock of birds sweeping towards the slums. Leading the line was the vulture Hshukha.

Shape-shifting back into human form, Drue grabbed the children and hauled them off the dirt track just in time to take shelter before the feathered squadrons swept overhead. Drue kept her hands clamped over the mouths of the children as she scoured the terrain for Oddeye and his gang. The cats had melted back into the shadows as quickly as they had appeared.

'*Merhaba*. Let's to be going . . .' said Oddeye, appearing once more from behind a corrugated tin partition wall. 'I'll take you to the others.'

Though every bit as odd as his name, Oddeye and his gang of feral Van cats knew every twist and turn of the ramshackle shanty town, and they led Drue-Kedi and the children through it without once needing to break cover.

Along the way, Oddeye explained that Gecekondu was not Istanbul proper; it was a settlement of squats that had sprouted like weeds around the outskirts of the great city. In the local vernacular, the name literally meant *built overnight* and that is exactly how the slum had formed, cobbled together under cover of darkness, from dusk to dawn, with whatever materials the homeless human refugees could find to hand.

Its poor construction – and lack of proper sanitation and infrastructure – had led to many accidents, even fatalities in the past, but now its weakness was its inherent strength. There had been numerous tremors in the last few weeks, each a little stronger than the one before, precursors to what the Animalian forces believed would be a formidable earth-quake that was very likely to raze the slum to the ground.

As a result, though they had the City on the Seven Hills entirely surrounded, they were loath to begin a full-scale, house-to-house search of the sprawling man-made warren for fear of being buried alive when the quake struck. This meant that the Nsray were, for the time being at least, secure in the safe house that Oddeye and the local Truckles had set up for them in the heart of the grim sanctuary.

CHAPTER FORTY-FIVE

Thirteen. That was the number of fellow Nsray who had taken shelter in Gecekondu the day that Drue arrived with the two children, whose names she had finally learned from Kemal – a local Nsray – were Sanja and Ezal. By day three of the siege, their ranks had swelled to twenty-eight. But by the time they'd been dug in for a full week, it seemed clear that no others would be joining them.

Twenty-eight. Maybe that's all that's left, thought Drue. All that was left of the multitude who had gathered in Ulm.

It cast a pall over their own good fortune and, to keep their spirits up, Drue reminded her companions that the majority of their kind had been able to travel on the wing. Surely they would have made good their escape in greater numbers and would be in Ararat already? Yes, that was it; they would be counting the days, waiting to celebrate with them once they too had set foot on the hallowed land.

Kemal – a scrawny lad with a flame tattoo on his right forearm, and a mop of hair as dark and wild as his eyes – had grown up on the streets of nearby Güngören. He knew the city every bit as well as his Animalian counterpart Oddeye and, in the absence of any Adepts, he had taken on the mantle of leadership. Rations were meagre, but a full night of rain had topped up the fresh water supply, and apart from some moans about how difficult it was to sleep in the hot, sticky night air, the Nsray endured their forced captivity with relatively little complaint.

A rota was drawn up to ensure that there were always two pairs on watch in the main camp, and scouting parties comprising one Truckle and two Nsray conducted regular sorties into the surrounding area to build up a picture of the Animalians' movements. Each report was shared among the whole group at the end of each day, with enemy numbers and no-go areas added to a map of the territory that had been scored into an earth wall.

It didn't take Drue long to realize that her greatest test lay ahead. Legions of wild animals had completely surrounded the city, and others had set up impenetrable guard details across the two steel suspension bridges that spanned the vast Bosphorus, thereby cutting off the Nsrays' one overland route to the Turkish heartland.

Vultures, eagles and falcons flew daily reconnaissance flights over the city and the surrounding slums and, though they stood little chance of pinpointing the Shape-shifters' hideaway, it did act as a show of force: a strategy designed to demoralize rather than defeat the enemy.

The Earth Assembly's ultimate battle plan was clear: time was on their side. They could afford to wait until the Nsray made a mistake and revealed their position, or they ran out of food and were forced to surrender, or Mother

Nature finished the job for them and sent an earthquake to bury the fugitives alive beneath the walls of the shanty town.

All talk now centred around means of escape. The forces waged against them meant that fighting their way out was doomed to failure, but Drue also knew that they could not hold out indefinitely in the slum under siege. When she wasn't tending to the needs of the children – who, though still shy of their shape-shifting rescuer, were happily distracted teasing and petting the Truckles – she found herself a quiet corner to think and studied the white pebble her father had given to her, turning it over and over in her palm.

If you're truly lost, isn't that what he'd said? If you ever get really lost, it'll point the way.

Drue concentrated hard, day after day, but if there was magic in the stone – a directive, some profound wisdom – it escaped her. The only thing that was clear, and she didn't need the stone to tell her as much, was that to realize their dream of reaching Mount Ararat, the Nsray would first need to negotiate a safe passage across the dangerous waters of the Bosphorus.

The only city in the world to span two continents – a metropolis which stretched from the Sea of Marmara to the Black Sea in the north – Istanbul's eclectic brew of Byzantine palaces, spice bazaars, eight-lane highways and domed Ottoman mosques was more exotic, even as a ghost town, than anything Drue had ever seen. And viewed from the top of the *Christea Turris* – a fourteenth-century fortified tower the locals called Galata, which dominated the skyline above the Golden Horn bay – the contrast between the city itself and the slums of Gecekondu could not have been more striking.

Here, where the ancient civilisations of Europe and Asia had once met, the very spot where Drue's own Nsray ancestors would, thousands of years earlier, have begun their migration north, stood a sad monument to what those rich ancient cultures had evolved into: a lavish testament to squandered opportunities, misplaced hopes and forgotten dreams.

'It is strange, is it not?' said Kemal-Kedi to Oddeye and Drue-Kedi as they scanned the city from the broken windows of the lookout tower.

'A city that was once bursting with life, home to many millions of people, now belongs to the wind and the rain, the sun and the weeds.'

'It always did,' replied Oddeye. 'That was the mistake you humans made.'

Kemal eyed his feline companion and an awkward silence descended.

'I'm sorry, but this is the truth,' said Oddeye. 'From deer tick to Bengal tiger, we are all just passing through, no? Humans too. Even a flea-brain alley cat like me knows that much.'

Drue-Kedi moved to a window with a better view of the bay and the vast suspension bridge that spanned it. An industrious spider was busy shortening and tightening a large web it had strung across a broken pane. Drue observed it for a moment and knew only too well the significance of its behaviour: a storm was on the way.

'You said you had something to show us?' she said.

Kemal-Kedi joined her at the window.

'There,' he said, pointing a paw in the direction of the

346

river. 'You see, on the stretch of beach there? That's a caïque.'

'A *kai-eek*?' said Drue.

'A what do you call it . . . a rowing boat.'

Drue craned her neck to try to get a better view. She could just make out the silhouette of a long, upturned skiff lying on a patch of shingle.

'I can't really see. We need to get closer.'

'Dangerous,' said Oddeye. 'The riverbank she is teeming with hostiles.'

'Maybe after dark we could send someone to take a look,' said Kemal-Kedi.

Unlike Kemal and the other Nsray, Drue was not carrying an injury that obliged her to travel on foot, so in an instant she shape-shifted into a herring gull and – leaving her anxious companions in her wake – set off to investigate the boat.

Taking care to mask the purpose of her mission, Drue-Gull joined the vast array of birdlife drifting on the breeze above the Bosphorus. The ominous sight of dorsal fins, of porbeagle, mako and great white sharks, patrolling the choppy waters below gave her pause for thought, but still she pressed on.

Allowing the thermals to carry her a little closer to the shoreline, Drue-Gull managed a couple of low, surreptitious passes over the boat. A simple wooden construction, the vessel was no more than a metre wide and around six metres from bow to stern. Crucially, the smooth hull was sound, and a pair of long oars was stowed with a hefty coil of rope and a tangled fishing net on the boardwalk above it.

Drue considered the stretch of shingle beach. It wouldn't prove a problem to launch the craft from there. And then it struck her: the shingle, the pebbles – they were just like the one her dad had given her. Maybe it had played a part in pointing the way after all; she was convinced it was a good omen.

Drue-Gull climbed high in the sky – keeping half an eye on the sentinel vultures perched on the steel struts of the giant suspension bridge – to reconnoitre the bank on the far side of the river. The banks and jetties and roads on the Asian side were relatively clear in comparison to the European quarter where the Animalians had the Nsray penned in.

Freedom. Safety. So near and yet, it seemed, so far. The boat offered hope, but how could they make the crossing and go unnoticed by so many watchful eyes?

Drue-Gull circled a little longer in the cloudless sky. A light wind buffeted her feathers as she rode the thermals and communed with the elements.

Maybe there is a way, she thought. *Maybe there is a way*.

★   ★   ★

By the time Drue, Kemal and Oddeye returned to the other Nsray in the heart of Gecekondu, they had the makings of a plan.

'The Animalians have the two bridges that cross the river heavily guarded,' said Drue, having shape-shifted into a Van Kedi, 'and they have complete control of the city on this side of the water as well. From what I could see, though, the banks on the other shore aren't nearly so well patrolled. They're obviously not expecting us to get that far, so if we can make it across the water I think we have a pretty good chance of escape.'

'But this boat you're talking about,' said a Nsray-Tomcat, 'it sounds pretty small.'

'And we'd have to revert to our normal human selves in order to row it,' said another.

'That's true,' replied Drue. 'At least two of us will have to handle the oars; Sanja and Ezal are too small to row as the currents are so strong.'

'I'll row,' said Kemal.

'Me too,' said another Nsray-Cat.

'Right then,' said Drue, 'and if the rest of us went as cats or mice then we'd all fit in easily.'

'I'd rather take my chances in the water,' said another.

'With all the sharks?' replied Kemal. 'You'd be torn to pieces.'

'Word is that their orders are to attack any creatures they don't recognize,' said Oddeye.

'Well, even if we could all fit in the boat, how are we going to sneak past the guards? Even at night there are bats that will be able to spot the children,' said the Nsray-Tomcat.

'Fog,' said Drue, eyes brightening.

'Fog?' said a cat.

'Fog,' said Drue again. 'My dad used to go on about how to read the signs that the weather was changing. Well, you know how horrid and sticky the air has been at night? That's called humidity.'

'So?' said the Nsray-Tomcat.

'So, there are no clouds in the sky, there's almost no wind and a lot of dew collects on everything by the time we wake up. Well, those are the perfect conditions for fog.'

Drue's grasp of the elements impressed even Oddeye.

'We do get a lot of it here,' agreed Kemal. 'They were always having to shut the shipping lanes because of it causing accidents on the water.'

'So what's the plan?' said a Nsray-Kedi, feeling encouraged.

'Simple,' said Drue.

'Oddeye has found us another hideout, much nearer to the river,' said Kemal. 'We'll move to that. Better not to spend too long in one place anyway. Next time we have rain during the night . . .'

'We'll watch for fog on the water in the morning,' said Drue. 'Soon as there's cover, we'll sneak down to the river and launch the boat.'

'What if the fog doesn't come?' said another Nsray-Kedi.

'It'll come. You'll see,' said Drue, 'and we can help it along too. All of us. We just have to all want it the same. You know, really wish for it to happen.'

'You mean . . . we'll just imagine it and . . . and it'll happen?' came another doubtful voice.

'Why not?' said Drue. 'That's how we take on different forms, isn't it?'

The crowd fell quiet; they were not quite convinced.

'Well, we've nothing to lose,' added Kemal. 'I'm with Drue.'

It was, as Drue had said, a simple plan, but a plan nonetheless. And so it was, with a sense of urgency, even a little excitement, that the Nsray and the Truckles called the meeting to an end and – to the delight of the fidgety Sanja and Ezal – began preparations to break camp.

CHAPTER FORTY-SIX

Lennox was just beginning to brief his crew – with details of a plan that would enable Will-C, Yoshi and Gallinago to escape Callow's Farm – when word came back from a lookout that Mustela's Animalian army had retreated.

While Gallinago took to the air with a pair of geese, all their four-legged companions who were able scrambled up through the hay bales to the roof of the barn to see for themselves. Sure enough, the paddock and the fields beyond, where just hours before the massed ranks of Animalians had been dug in, were now quiet and clear.

'Maybe it's a trap?' said Yoshi.

Will-C called out to the birds above.

'Gallinago. You see anything from up there?'

'I'll take a closer look,' called back Gallinago.

'Be careful,' said Will-C as the snipe banked and soared away over the paddock.

It took just a few minutes for Gallinago and the geese to complete a full aerial inspection of the immediate surroundings and, even after they widened the search to include the edge of the forest at Kingley Burh, the verdict was the same: Mustela's forces had vanished.

'Why?' said Yoshi. 'Where do you suppose they've gone?'

'I don't know,' said Will-C, 'but I'm not going to hang around to find out.'

'Wait,' cried Yoshi as Will-C worked his way back to the ground at a sprint. 'I'm coming too, remember.'

And, as Will-C and Yoshi set off down the track that led back to Kingley Burh and beyond, Gallinago turned circles overhead.

'Hey, Will-C, look,' said Gallinago.

'What?' replied Will-C. And then he traced Gallinago's flight path, which carried him over Lennox, who was following at a distance.

'Good to have you along, Lennox,' said Gallinago as he swooped low over the head of the torbie.

'Nothin' ta do with da freak show,' growled Lennox. 'Just like to get me a look at dis Lionman is all.'

Gallinago climbed up into the sky once more and pushed out ahead of Will-C to act as scout for the path ahead. And, as far as he could see, that path was clear and trouble-free.

CHAPTER FORTY-SEVEN

Liliuk's shagreen locket shone like a tiny star in the talons of the Nsray-Raven as he flew through the night sky. He soared high above fields and woodlands, over empty motorways and countless deserted villages, and paid no heed to anything save his need to press on as fast as possible. And, as the land far below turned to broiling ocean, and the prevailing wind turned against him, so he shape-shifted into a sea eagle, a creature better suited to the conditions, and one better able to protect his precious cargo.

His final destination lay several hundred miles east, and though he had not been given more than the briefest details regarding his mission – in case of capture by the enemy – he knew enough to understand that he had to guard the locket and its secrets with his life; that the very future of the Nsray was bound to the tiny piece of carapace shell now in his possession.

Whether it was the moonlight catching the locket that gave away his position, or a pre-planned ambush, the Nsray-Sea Eagle did not live long enough to find out. A huge Andean condor dropped from the sky and collided with the Nsray-Sea Eagle with such force that for a moment, in shock, the young Nsray reverted to human form and began to freefall from the sky. Still he held on tight to the locket.

The condor swooped and tried to tear the prize from his grasp. Still the Nsray held fast and shape-shifted back into a sea eagle. Down they fell, a spiralling blur of feathers and talons until . . . they hit the freezing water.

Both were stunned by the impact, which broke the sea eagle's neck. The lifeless Nsray shape-shifted back into human form and floated dead in the water. The condor also shape-shifted back into human form and began treading water. Within seconds, he had mutated once more – this time into a great white shark – but those few seconds were all it took for the locket to sink down into the deep, dark ocean. The Nsray-Shark dived in search of the prize.

Before he could reach it, however, the glowing locket suddenly burst with light as bright and powerful as an exploding star. Spokes of pure white light lanced through the ocean, a shock wave of energy that vaporized the Nsray-Shark and triggered multiple tsunamis that sped from the core of the blast in every direction.

★   ★   ★

Many miles inland, in Ulm Minster, Liliuk's prone body suddenly twitched with life. Her eyelids flickered and opened. She instinctively reached for her locket. Her fingers found the severed hemp braid. Bruised and bloody, she shape-shifted into a nightjar. She took a moment to check that her long, dark wings were free of injury, then she soared up into the air and turned a wide circle.

Below her the bodies of Nsray and Animalians lay where they had fallen. Liliuk-Nightjar surveyed the carnage in search of any fellow survivors, in search of her locket. But deep inside she knew that the hemp braid had not been broken in battle. And she knew just who was responsible for stealing the locket. She circled for a moment longer beneath the vaulted roof of the nave, beneath the mysterious ancient fresco; then she glided silently away, out through the splintered doors and up into the night sky.

CHAPTER FORTY-EIGHT

Fog. Dense and clammy, more like thick smoke than white cloud, crept down the Bosphorus from the Black Sea and settled over the Golden Horn bay, until even the vast bridge that spanned the river was entirely swallowed up and obscured from view.

Word spread quickly among the Nsray and Truckles. It seemed their prayers had been answered, and a scouting party was quickly dispatched from the safe house to ensure that the route to the banks of the river and the awaiting boat was clear. Oddeye himself broke the news everyone was waiting to hear: the passage was safe, the conditions perfect.

Drue – who had been spending as much time as she could in her human guise in order to provide the children with a reassuring presence – kissed the white pebble when Kemal confirmed that her plan was unfolding just as she had said it would.

★   ★   ★

Not ten minutes later, Drue, Kemal, Sanja, Ezal and a chain of Truckles and Nsray-Kedi felt the crunch of shingle beneath them and heard the water lapping at the shore. The fog was so dense on the banks of the Bosphorus that it took a moment to locate the rowing boat, even though they were standing right beside it.

A good omen, thought Drue as she, Kemal and several others struggled to turn the boat right side up. *If we can't see it, then neither can the Animalians.*

A second group stole up to the boardwalk to gather the oars and the coil of rope as the others carried the caique to the water's edge, making as little noise as they possibly could.

All was well. Those that were to travel as cats shape-shifted and hopped lightly up into the boat. Kemal waded into the river to steady the bow, which slid easily into the black water. The oars and rope were quickly loaded and Drue felt the chill of the river lapping round her ankles as she lifted Sanja into the boat. And, just as it seemed they were home free, disaster struck. As Sanja moved aside to make room for her brother, her foot broke through the wooden hull.

Drue heard Sanja's yelp, and she set down Ezal on the bank. Drue gestured for the other Nsray and Truckles to hold their positions. She then picked up an oar and carefully prodded the hull. Even with minimal force behind it, the oar also punched a hole right through the boat. Drue tossed the oar aside.

'What are we waiting for?' came a whispered voice in the fog.

'It's no good,' said Drue as she lifted Sanja back on to the bank.

'What?'

'We have to go back.'

'What? We can't,' said Kemal.

'We have to. It's rotten through.'

'Rotten?'

'The wood. The boat. It's not . . . It'll sink like a stone.'

Like a stone, thought Drue. *That damn pebble.* It hadn't shown them the way at all.

'Come on,' she said, 'we'd better get back.'

'No, Drue, look!' said Kemal as he pointed back at the city.

And, as Drue turned, she saw the reason for the alarm in his voice. The fog had lifted over the city. It had already thinned on the boardwalk and was slowly receding from the riverbanks. Any retreat now would leave them all completely exposed and at the mercy of the Animalians. Yet to stay put meant that they would also soon be trapped, pinned back beside the shark-infested waters, easy prey for the predators on the shoreline.

Sanja and Ezal gripped Drue's legs. They were too terrified even to cry. The Nsray and Truckles cast about for a hiding place. There was nothing. Nothing but the fog that continued to melt away.

One after another the Nsray adopted Animalian forms, predator warriors ready to do battle in what would surely be their one last stand.

Drue felt the pebble in her palm and silently cursed it. She had placed her faith in it, had risked everything, and it had failed her, just as she had failed the children and the Nsray and the Truckles who had given so much and come so far.

As she struggled to focus, to suppress the terrible feelings of guilt and fear and remorse that were clouding her ability to think, Drue hurled the pebble into the Bosphorus. And in that flash of anger lay a lifeline. It took her a moment to realize it: the pebble had not hit the water with a splash. It had hit something . . . solid.

Something solid floating on top of the dark, fog-shrouded water. Drue picked up a stone from the beach and tossed it into the river. Again it bounced with a solid *crack*. She threw another pebble. And another. None hit water.

Drue beckoned to Kemal and he helped to prise the children from her. He held them tight as Drue took a step closer to the lapping Bosphorus. She peered through the fog; it was difficult to see anything. She took another step. And another. She waded into the river until it reached her knees. And then she saw them . . . hundreds of them . . . Giant loggerhead turtles, their domed shells shimmering in the diffused moonlight; a floating bridge of stepping stones that reached out across the river.

The pebble, thought Drue, *it really did show the way.*

The roar of a grizzly bear cut through her reverie. The Animalians were beginning to patrol once more. And some were so close the Nsray could almost touch them.

'Drue,' said Kemal in a whisper, 'whatever it is we're going to do, we need to do it now.'

'This way,' said Drue as she climbed on top of a turtle.

'What?' said Kemal. 'Which way?'

'This way, everyone, quickly: follow me.'

'Where?' exclaimed Kemal.

Drue knelt and placed a hand on the domed shell of the

turtle beneath her. The carapace beneath her palm radiated a golden glow as if lit from within.

'Trust me,' she said. 'It's OK.'

'How do you know it's not a trap?' said Kemal.

'I just . . . know. Come, quickly.'

With the fog now dispersing as rapidly as it had settled, Kemal lifted Sanja and Ezal on to the floating turtles and beckoned to the others. Once everyone had safely left the shore, Drue led the line and pressed on across the Bosphorus, a chain of Nsray and Truckles dwarfed by the vast suspension bridge above. Progress was slow, and every step had to be carefully measured, as just metres away, slicing back and forth through the dark waters, were the dorsal fins of the patrolling sharks; a reminder that certain death was but a slip away.

'Where did they come from?' asked Kemal as he clambered from one bobbing shell to another.

'I don't know,' answered Drue.

'And how do you know they reach all the way to the other side of the river?'

'I don't.'

'I wish I hadn't asked,' said Kamal.

'Me too,' said Drue, as she helped Sanja and Ezal clamber from one bobbing stepping stone to another.

CHAPTER FORTY-NINE

Will-C and Yoshi stood in the mouth of the Channel Tunnel and peered into the dark interior as Gallinago flapped around above them, gliding in and out of the entrance.

'Well,' said Yoshi, 'this is it. Didn't I tell you? Some burrow, isn't it?'

'Dark as noight in dere,' said Gallinago.

'Bound to be,' said Yoshi. 'It stretches for miles under the sea.'

'Under the sea,' repeated Will-C gloomily.

'It's OK,' said Yoshi, 'the humans used it for years and years; it's safe enough.'

'How far under the sea exactly?' said Will-C.

'I don't know, but . . .'

'But it's da only way to get to da lair of da Lionman,' said Lennox as he ambled up alongside. 'C'mon, Freak, you an' Maggot 'ave come this far, and there can't be anythin' in dere dat's any more scary dan you two fleabags.'

Lennox nonchalantly strolled on and disappeared into the shadows inside the tunnel.

'Drue would understand if you wanted to turn back,' said Yoshi.

''Tis your decision,' added Gallinago.

'The humans used it for years, you said?' said Will-C. 'And it never flooded?'

'Flooded?' said Yoshi. 'No, this friend of a friend whose human friend used to take them through it all the time, he said it was fine. It would take an earthquake . . . a tidal wave as big as . . . as big as the biggest ever tidal wave in the history of tidal waves.'

'Waddaya tink?' said Gallinago to Will-C.

'RUN!' bellowed Lennox as he came hurtling towards them out of the tunnel. 'It's coming!'

Will-C and Yoshi froze in terror.

'What?!' cried Gallinago.

'The flood!'

And with that Lennox stopped in his tracks, lifted a hind leg and peed in Will-C's direction.

'Dat's disgustin',' said Gallinago.

'That's not funny,' said Yoshi.

'Oh, c'mon,' said Lennox, enjoying himself, 'be a feline!'

Will-C gave Lennox a wide berth and started into the tunnel. Gallinago and Yoshi exchanged a look and followed.

'Truckles,' grumbled Lennox to himself. 'Jus' like humans, no sense a humour.'

He shook his coat, stretched, scratched behind an ear and finally trotted after the others as they were swallowed up by the shadows inside the tunnel.

CHAPTER FIFTY

As Drue and the ragtaggle band of Nsray and Truckles inched closer to the Asian banks of the Bosphorus, so the tension mounted. None had slipped, which was little short of a miracle, and the loggerhead turtles – as though thinking as one – had held fast their positions despite the swirling currents and the ever-increasing number of sharks, electric eels and saltwater crocodiles patrolling the waters around and below them.

It was not until the river itself began to recede that Drue sensed a danger even greater than that posed by the Animalian predators. She urged her companions to quicken their pace and clamber ashore. And, as the last of the fog lifted, Drue caught sight of the threat that she had sensed: a gigantic tidal wave – taller than the Bosphorus Bridge itself – sweeping towards them from across the Sea of Marmara.

'Run!' she cried, before she shape-shifted into an eagle and cried out again in Animalian . . .

'Run! Fly! Now!'

Drue shape-shifted back into herself, clasped the hands of

the children and all three leapt to the relative safety of the far bank as the river, and all the Animalian life within it, was siphoned from the Bosphorus as if a giant celestial hand had suddenly pulled the plug. Drue held fast to the children, transformed once more into an Arabian light horse and scaled the steep, slippery bank with Sanja and Ezal on her back.

The moment she felt firmer ground beneath her, Drue-Roan broke into a gallop and, with her young charges clinging to her mane and each other, she fought with every fibre of her being – just like all the other fleeing Nsray, Truckles and Animalians – to put as much distance as she could between herself and the advancing tidal wave.

She felt the ocean falling as rain. She heard the Bosphorus Bridge disintegrate beneath the cresting wave. A roar like thunder. The ground shook. And suddenly it was not just water falling from the sky: fish, rocks, splintered boats, buckled girders and even vehicles rained down all around them.

Still Drue-Roan galloped on, pushing herself to the limit, weaving this way and that, praying hard that she could outrun the tempest and carry her young charges to safety.

For a moment time seemed to speed up, and then, as the wave finally engulfed them and they were plunged into a churning sea of surf, it felt to Drue as if time had slowed to the point of stopping altogether. The last thing she saw, as she tumbled and twisted and shape-shifted back into her human form, was a fiery globe, like a miniature sun, tongues of flame shimmering and flickering over its surface; a lone star radiating soft, golden light in a vast black liquid cosmos.

BlackLight. The word flashed through Drue's mind, and then she lost consciousness.

CHAPTER FIFTY-ONE

Just as the tidal wave had swept away all before it as it tore across the Mediterranean, so its force had been felt on the north coast of Africa, the east coast of America and even on the southern shores of Greenland.

For Will-C and his travelling companions, the impact on the Channel Tunnel could not have been more terrifying. The entire length of the structure groaned and quivered, and as Gallinago and the Truckles froze in the darkness, a network of fissures appeared in the internal walls, rivets popped like bullets from the ventilation ducts above and the train tracks beneath them hummed like a vast tuning fork.

'RUN!' cried Gallinago as he turned circles above Will-C.

The three cats remained rooted to the spot. They had ventured much too far to turn back, yet the coast of France was still many miles away. Which way should they go?

A crack! A fearful roar! A rush of water! And then the Truckles and the snipe were swept away, flushed along the length of the tunnel like fallen leaves through a gutter.

Chapter Fifty-Two

Kemal found Drue lying on a rough patch of ground. Her breathing was shallow, her face as pale as the wide sky above.

'Drue? Can you hear me? Drue?'

Drue's eyes flickered and finally opened. It took her a moment to adjust to the light.

'You had me worried.'

Drue recognized Kemal's voice before she saw his face looming over her.

'What happened? Where are we?'

'Almost home,' replied Kemal brightly.

'Home?' said Drue.

And then, as Kemal took her hand and helped her to sit up, Drue saw that Sanja and Ezal were at her side, and they were surrounded by the bedraggled band of Nsray and Truckles from Gecekondu, who were scattered across a landscape of uprooted trees, debris and dead sea creatures that floated in a patchwork of shallow seawater lakes.

Beyond them, to the east, the peaks of an imposing

mountain range formed a jagged horizon. And, in the middle distance, a sight both familiar and yet strangely exotic: smoke. Woodsmoke. It curled into the sky from a cluster of fires. Kemal helped Drue to her feet and she gazed in wonder at her surroundings.

'Nsray?' said Drue, indicating the distant fires and a huddle of figures who were making their way towards them.

'Yes,' said Kemal.

'Then this place . . .' began Drue.

'Those mountains you can see,' said Kemal. 'It's still a day's march, but that's Japheth's Land.'

'Impossible,' said Drue as Sanja and Ezal snuggled close, and the little boy's hooded rat – looking sorry for itself, but still very much alive – emerged from his shirt.

'Yet here we are,' said Kemal.

'Then we made it.'

'Thanks to you.'

'Thanks to the turtles,' said Drue as she scanned the lakes in search of them. 'Where are they?'

'I don't know,' said Kemal. 'There are fish of all kinds scattered for miles . . . dead sharks, squid, saltwater crocs, but I haven't seen one loggerhead. Seems like they just disappeared. Weird, huh?'

'Weird,' agreed Drue.

Sanja began to sob: a combination of shock and fear and relief.

'It's OK,' said Drue as she lifted the girl into her arms. 'It'll be OK.'

And, although Sanja didn't understand the words, Drue's tone and her warm smile were enough to quiet her sniffles.

CHAPTER FIFTY-THREE

By nightfall, Drue and her travelling companions had completed the last leg of their long march, and the makeshift Nsray settlement seemed a paradise compared to what they had left behind.

Once they had bathed and been allocated sleeping shelters – temporary communal dwellings constructed with drystone walls of local volcanic rock – they gathered round the blazing fire pits to share stories and feast on steaming turmeric rice and sweet ginger tea: the first hot meal many had eaten since the outbreak of the war.

A thunderstorm swept across the plains that first night in the mountains and, as Drue did her best to allay Sanja's fears, and sat with the little girl until she drifted off to sleep alongside her brother, Drue was reminded of her own early childhood in Kingley Burh, scampering down the hall to her parents' bed to escape the twin terrors of thunder and lightning.

How long ago it seemed. A different life. A different world.

Drue ached to learn the truth about her father, longed to be reunited with Will-C and felt more keenly than ever the enduring presence of her mother Serah, who she was now – thanks to the emotional bond she had formed with her two young charges – beginning to understand in ways, and in depths, that she could never have imagined.

Once Drue was certain that Sanja was asleep, she draped a blanket over her shoulders and stepped outside to clear her head in the cool night air. Kemal was waiting for her.

'How are the little ones?'

'Sleeping,' said Drue as she gazed at the spectacular electric storm dancing across the distant foothills.

'They were lucky you found them,' said Kemal.

'You think so?' said Drue.

'What do you mean? Of course,' replied Kemal.

'I think,' said Drue, 'that I was the lucky one.'

'You?'

'If it hadn't been for Sanja and Ezal, I don't know, I don't know if I'd have . . . if I'd have made it this far that's all. I had to keep going for them.'

A log shifted in a fire pit and spat a shower of burning embers into the night air. Drue studied the flames. Kemal studied her.

'Well, we're here anyway. We're safe. What's gone is gone. It's the future we need to think about now.'

'Is it?' replied Drue.

'Of course it is,' said Kemal. 'That's all we have now. A chance to start over. We're safe from the Animalians. We have all we need right here. It's time for the Nsray to step out of the shadows.'

'I . . . no . . . yes, yes, of course, you're right. I'm just, I'm just really . . . tired,' said Drue, wanting time to think alone.

'Tomorrow there's a group of us going to look for a base that's better protected from the elements, somewhere higher up in the mountains. A place where we can build a . . . a village maybe. You'd be . . . it'd be . . . with your help . . . you should come along.'

'We'll see,' said Drue, an echo of her mother.

'OK then. See you in the morning,' said Kemal.

'Night,' said Drue.

'Goodnight,' said Kemal as he reluctantly drifted away.

Drue pulled the blanket tighter round her shoulders and looked up at the bright crescent moon. A million distant stars twinkled in the vast black sky. Drue let her mind wander. They were safe, it was true, but never had she felt quite so small. Never had she felt quite so lost or alone.

CHAPTER FIFTY-FOUR

Your father could name every constellation.

The words drifted into Drue's consciousness. They filtered into her dream and roused her from it. The voice was familiar. But had she really heard it?

She opened her eyes. The sun had not quite risen on the horizon and the pale crescent moon was still visible in the sky.

'At a glance, anywhere in the world, he could read the sky.'

'Liliuk!'

Liliuk surveyed the stars from a nearby outcrop of rock. She was clearly in some pain, her movements slow and deliberate, and with each one she winced a little.

'I'm pleased to find you in one piece, child.'

'We thought you were . . . that you'd been . . .'

'I thought so too.'

'But you're hurt. Let me . . . I'll get the others . . .'

'No. Not . . . not just yet. There's time enough. I didn't dare hope that I'd find you, but it seems that fate has granted us this moment at least.'

'What do you mean?'

'I must speak to you about your father.'

'Why did you lie to me? The jackal said my dad was being held prisoner.'

'I was trying to protect you. It's what Quinn wanted. He knew the risk he was taking. It's why he sent you to join us. It's why . . .'

'I'm not staying here. You can say what you like, but I'm not . . .'

'Drue . . .'

'I can't . . .'

'Drue . . .'

'Not with Dad out there somewhere . . .'

'I know.'

'And Will-C and Csaba and Adan and all those children on the ferry . . .'

'I know.'

'I don't care what you . . . You know?'

'Yes. It's why I needed to talk to you alone. Your dream. It's more than just a dream, Drue. You have a special gift.'

'No . . . no more than . . . than the others.'

'Wisdom beyond your years, and a gift that may yet save our people.'

'No.'

'It's true you're young to shoulder such great responsibility . . .'

'No, no, I'm just a . . . it was me, it was my fault . . . at the church. The jackal. I helped him escape.'

'I know.'

'That's why the animals attacked when they did. It was my fault. It was all my fault.'

'That's not true.'

'It was! It was! It was all my fault!'

'No. The Animalians knew we were there. The attack was planned long before the jackal escaped.'

'What? How?'

'We face a new danger. Dark forces have been unleashed that pose an even greater threat than that of the Animalians.'

'What do you mean?'

'I had prayed it wasn't so, but now that he's emerged from hiding, now that his mark has been made . . .'

'Who?'

'A . . . a fallen Nsray.'

'One of us?'

'A former Adept. One of the brightest. One of the strongest. One who had such promise until he strayed from the path. It was he who betrayed your father and August Beyer to the Animalian War Council. It was he who sent the jackal spy. And it was he who sent a thief to steal my locket.'

'A Nsray. But how can that be?'

'All the while he draws breath there can be no peace. He has bent the will of the Earth Assembly in order to defeat Mankind and gain power for himself. The Animalians might never have waged the war if it weren't for him. He has blood on his hands, Drue, and he will not stop until he reigns supreme over every creature in creation.'

'Who . . . is he?'

'A child with poison in his heart. A lost soul trapped forever in a living hell, neither Man, nor beast, nor Nsray.'

'Then . . . what is he?'

'He is Cernunnos. He's my son.'

LOOK OUT FOR BOOK TWO
IN THE ANIMALIAN SERIES
COMING SPRING 2015

ACKNOWLEDGEMENTS

Heartfelt thanks to my literary agent Zoe King and all the wonderful team at The Blair Partnership for making the dream a reality; to Ingrid Selberg of Simon & Schuster for taking a leap of faith; and to Jane Griffiths, editor *extraordinaire*, whose diligence enhanced the telling of the tale.

Special thanks also to my wonderful in-laws Jeanette and Keith Michell, Jeannie Brooke Barnett, Isabel Tamarit and Sarah Roses Lambourne.

I must also declare a huge debt of gratitude to all the animals – both wild and domesticated – who have chosen to spend time with me over the years. They have taught me a great deal, and it's their characters that have helped to shape the heart of this story. To name but a few: Whiskey, Yogi, Rusty, Zeeta, Jacob, Kipling, Poppy, Dribbler and the baby kestrel – Tatterdemalion – who appeared out of a howling wind storm and took shelter on my window sill as I typed the final page of the manuscript. Hope you made it home OK.

Finally, a special mention for Bagheera, a devoted feline friend and muse, who was the inspiration for Will-C and part of our family for fifteen years. Writing will never be quite the same without him snoozing between me and the keyboard.

ABOUT THE AUTHOR

Simon David Eden is a graduate of the Royal College of Art who has written screenplays for film and award-winning television drama. He has also worked as a lyricist and playwright, and his abstract fine art – which has been exhibited in London, Nassau and Beijing – can be found in private collections all over the world. He lives in rural West Sussex, England, with his wife Helena, their trusty, feline companions Bea and Mosey and a whole host of wild animals. *The Savage Kingdom* is his first novel.

Further information can be found at:
www.SimonDavidEden.com

For more background on the Animalian Series go wild at:
www.TheSavageKingdom.com